KINGDOM KEEPERS

SHELL GAME

BOOK FIVE

ALSO BY RIDLEY PEARSON

Kingdom Keepers—Disney After Dark
Kingdom Keepers II—Disney at Dawn
Kingdom Keepers III—Disney in Shadow
Kingdom Keepers IV—Power Play

Steel Trapp—The Challenge
Steel Trapp—The Academy

WRITING WITH DAVE BARRY

Peter and the Starcatchers
Peter and the Shadow Thieves
Peter and the Secret of Rundoon
Peter and the Sword of Mercy
The Bridge to Never Land

Escape from the Carnivale
Cave of the Dark Wind
Blood Tide

Science Fair

RIDLEY PEARSON

KINGDOM KEEPERS

SHELL GAME

BOOK FIVE

Disney • HYPERION BOOKS

New York

The following are some of the trademarks, registered marks, and service marks owned by Disney Enterprises, Inc.: Adventureland® Area, Audio-Animatronics® Figure, Big Thunder Mountain® Railroad, Disney®, Disneyland®, Disney's Hollywood Studios, Disney's Animal Kingdom® Theme Park, Epcot®, Fantasyland® Area, FASTPASS® Service, Fort Wilderness, Frontierland® Area, Imagineering, Imagineers, it's a small world, Magic Kingdom® Park, Main Street, U.S.A., Area, Mickey's Toontown®, monorail, New Orleans Square, Space Mountain® Attraction, Splash Mountain® Attraction, Tomorrowland® Area, Toontown®, Walt Disney World® Resort.

Buzz Lightyear Astro Blasters © Disney Enterprises, Inc./Pixar Animation Studios

Toy Story characters © Disney Enterprises, Inc./Pixar Animation Studios

Winnie the Pooh characters based on the "Winnie the Pooh" works by A. A. Milne and E. H. Shepard

For information address Disney • Hyperion Books, 114 Fifth Avenue, New York, New York 10011-5690.

Printed in the United States of America

First Edition
10 9 8 7 6 5 4 3 2 1
G475-5664-5-12046

Library of Congress Cataloging-in-Publication Data
Pearson, Ridley.
Shell game / Ridley Pearson.
p. cm. -- (The Kingdom Keepers; 5)
Summary: The Kingdom Keepers have their hands full when, during a cruise of the *Disney Dream* to exotic locations, they discover that the Overtakers have infiltrated the cast, stolen a journal that belonged to Walt Disney himself, and plan to unleash a powerful evil, the Chernabog.
ISBN 978-1-4231-5336-8 (hardback)
[1. Cruise ships—Fiction. 2. Cartoon characters—Fiction. 3. Holography—Fiction. 4. Good and evil—Fiction. 5. Walt Disney World (Fla.)—Fiction.] I. Title.
PZ7.P323314She 2012
[Fic]—dc23
2011038531

Reinforced binding

visit www.disneyhyperionbooks.com
www.thekingdomkeepers.com
www.ridleypearson.com

SUSTAINABLE FORESTRY INITIATIVE
Certified Fiber Sourcing
www.sfiprogram.org

THIS LABEL APPLIES TO TEXT STOCK

They say the Devil's water, it ain't so sweet

You don't have to drink right now

But you can dip your feet

Every once in a little while

—The Killers, "When You Were Young"

KINGDOM
KEEPERS

SHELL GAME

BOOK FIVE

1

Finn Whitman held up three fingers, indicating he'd identified the enemy. One wore a full-length black robe with purple piping: Maleficent; the woman next to her, a high, starched white collar—like a nun's habit—her hair perfect, not a strand out of place: the Evil Queen; and the last wrapped in ermine and stoat: Cruella De Vil. He could just make out the backs of their heads and shoulders given his position on all fours and the location of a wooden card index island ahead. The three were huddled together in the darkened library stacks just beyond the central card index. But these were not any ordinary stacks. This was a private library deep within the Imagineers' offices, backstage at Disney's Hollywood Studios in Walt Disney World.

Finn and Willa, the girl to whom he held up his fingers, were not ordinary teenagers either: they were holograms. Projections of light—"flaming photons," as one of their fellow Kingdom Keepers called them—an invention of Disney Imagineers and technicians with too much time on their hands. By day, their holograms served as guides in the four Walt Disney World parks—the Magic Kingdom, Animal Kingdom, Epcot, and Disney's Hollywood Studios. By night, it was a different story.

The Kingdom Keepers were full of stories. What had started out as a middle school thrill—being models for Disney World hologram guides and the ensuing celebrity it caused—had matured into something more formidable. Finn and the four others, high schoolers now, found themselves as the last line of defense between the darker forces of Walt Disney's impressive imagination—the villains and witches and fairies now called the Overtakers—and the joy and magic of the Walt Disney World experience.

Willa's dark, confident eyes signaled her understanding. She pointed to herself and gestured to her right, down the library shelving that currently hid her and Finn from the others. Then she waved him forward and around; they would come at the three from either end of the stacks. Like Finn, she'd dressed in all black before she'd gone to sleep, when the crossover of kid to hologram happened. Like Finn, she'd awakened as her hologram wearing the same clothes in which she slept. She blended well with the shadows. One of the three women held a flashlight—the only real light in the room.

Finn nodded. It was incredibly dangerous for him

and Willa to challenge these particular three Overtakers by themselves. The Kingdom Keepers were sworn enemies of the Overtakers—but the women before them were like generals, commanders. He and Willa wouldn't be taking on common soldiers. But Finn saw no choice: at the very least he and Willa had to know what the three were up to. They'd been searching the stacks for the past forty-five minutes. If the Overtakers were stealing something, the Kingdom Keepers would get back whatever it was, keeping the Overtakers from expanding their powers.

The three were scary enough as it was. Maleficent had in the past nearly killed Finn and the others with her ability to throw fire; the Evil Queen could conjure spells that crippled and transfigured her foes. Cruella was, well, an annoying nuisance.

Finn reached for a three-ring notebook on the metal shelf and indicated for Willa to do the same. He held the notebook with two hands in front of his chest like a shield. Willa nodded, understanding: defense. With one final nod, they separated.

Finn moved through the carpeted, museumlike space beneath a ceiling of dormant tube lights. A few hours each day the private library was opened to scholars and researchers. Within these walls were records of the early beginnings of Walt Disney World, the creative ideas behind some major Disney characters, and creative templates for films. The Disney Imagineering archives were among the most sought-after records in the Disney empire. The planning. The stages of development. The secrets. Some of the material had recently been digitized and made available on the D23 Web site. But not all. Not by a long shot.

The Overtakers' presence here, the breach of security, seemed unthinkable. The possible results of their gaining insider secrets and knowledge could be devastating, Finn thought: unallowable. Whatever they sought, it was to be used against the Kingdom. That was not going to happen.

He crept up to the island containing the index cards, screening himself. He counted silently, giving Willa time to get into place. The DHI—Disney Host Interactive—2.0 upgrade was still in beta. He worried that if he allowed fear to get the better of him, his DHI might erode, losing its pure state, resulting in some percentage of him becoming solid—material and therefore mortal. Vulnerable to curses and attacks. He could be wounded or even killed. So a big part of his staying safe relied upon his ability to keep fear from his thoughts— not easy when Maleficent or the Evil Queen directed her powers at him. He focused now, pushing away the fear as if leaning against a strong wind.

Time!

He came around the card case, the notebook extended in front of him. Willa had just turned up the narrow aisle between the stacks. Two of the three witches spun to face her: Cruella and the Evil Queen. Maleficent—technically a fairy rather than a witch—started in that direction, but rocked her head over her shoulder to see Finn charging. It was always like that—a disturbing connection existed between the two. She'd sensed him.

Back went her hand, like a baseball pitcher, and a fireball erupted in her palm. Two years earlier, this would have filled Finn with terror—his fear degrading his Disney Host Interactive projection—exposing him to violence. But not this time. Not with 2.0.

He lifted the binder to cover his face and continued forward.

Behind Maleficent, the Evil Queen raised both hands as Willa charged.

Finn suddenly heard a deep growling, and though the fireball did not scare him all that much, he felt himself react primordially to the animal sounds. Fingers of flame burst around him, the ball disintegrating as it impacted the binder. Maleficent wound up for another pitch.

Willa's DHI passed through Cruella, who'd jumped

into her path to block her. Willa dropped her shield and snatched a notebook from the Evil Queen. She almost made it past Maleficent, but the evil fairy caught hold of her solid hand holding the binder and yanked her off her feet. Willa let go of the library volume and it skidded across the floor.

Finn deflected another fireball, his skin prickling with the grisly sound of the—dogs? He wasn't sure what kind of animals they were, but they had fast feet and a disturbing growl.

"Finn!" It was Willa, already on her feet. She was looking beyond Finn as she ran toward him and grabbed for his arm, the flames of the broken fireball bursting around them.

She spun Finn around. Hyenas! From *The Lion King*. Vicious, hungry-looking things. Drooling maniacally. Charging down an aisle between stacks, heads low to the floor, eyes wild and savage.

"Run!" she cried out. Finn needed no encouragement. There were times to stay and fight; this was not one of them.

Willa was a step or two ahead of him as they took off for the door. As a DHI he could, in theory, pass through a library stack or even a wall to put something solid between him and the hyenas, but he wasn't about to chance it. Wasn't about to end up a hyena snack.

Willa, however, reached the door and stepped through it like a ghost as a fireball cascaded over Finn's shoulder and exploded against the wall. The ricocheting flames passed through his hologram. He grinned, loving the new 2.0 upgrade, but he still did not fully trust it. Yanking the door open, he turned and looked back. Something weird was going on. The door was no longer a rectangle, but a square. The walls were covered in a glossy gray paint. There was heavy hardware on the door—hinges and levers. The hyenas raced through the door after him.

Finn continued running, sensing the hyenas at his heels. But if they were at his heels, then what had happened to Willa? He took in his surroundings: not a library. Instead he found himself on a clattery, grated metal catwalk surrounded on both sides by heavy machinery. Some kind of factory, he thought. He faced an oval door, elevated a good foot off the floor. He leaped through.

A hyena snapped at him, caught a piece of his pant leg, and tore his black jeans as if they were made of paper towels.

"Willa!" he cried out, spotting a steep metal staircase on the left. He stretched and grabbed hold of the handrail, nearly dislocating his shoulder in the process. The hyenas scratched at the metal flooring, but couldn't make the turn. They rolled and tumbled in a snarling mass as Finn got the jump on them, bounding up the staircase. He reached the first landing and turned.

The lead hyena had scrambled his way back to the stairs and began climbing.

Finn went faster, pulling himself up using the handrail. He looked through a window in a closed door and saw only a drab hallway. He continued up the stairs. Arriving at the next landing, he peered through the door's window.

This time he saw color and light. Marble. Rich carpeting. Like an expensive office or a fancy movie theater. He tugged open the heavy door and turned to heave it shut, but it was too late—a hyena thrust its head through the gap. He kept the pressure on: maybe he could choke the thing . . . but he couldn't bring himself to do it. He released the handle and took off toward a pair of big doors. These doors had bigger windows through which shone the flinty blue aura of moonlight on water.

Finn burst through the door into the night air, slipped, and crashed into a metal railing capped with polished wood. It was warm out. The fresh air smelled wonderful.

He heard the loud snap of a jaw. Finn lost his balance and fell, then struggled to his feet and sprinted off, the sound of claws on metal only inches behind him.

The Return. Similar in size and looks to a car's keychain remote, the small device served to end the DHI hologram projection and restore the kids to their sleeping bodies back home. But using the Return had to be coordinated. If he pressed the Return without Willa nearby, she would remain asleep in bed, her hologram locked on this side until a manual return could be arranged—precious time the Overtakers might take advantage of.

As if reading his thoughts Willa appeared, coming through a set of doors to his right and joining him stride for stride.

The hyenas were nearly upon them—jaws snapping inches behind.

"Get . . . us . . . out . . . of . . . here!" she cried.

The railing arced to the right up ahead. Beyond it, Finn saw only black sky and the twinkling of stars. We're on the roof of some building, he thought.

"We're going to jump!" he announced.

He reached out and took her hand with his right hand, the Return gripped firmly in his left.

"Please . . . no!" she shouted.

"Hang on to me. One . . . two . . ." They ran at full speed toward the rail. On "three!" they left their feet in a dive, flying through the air into nothingness.

As Finn crossed the rail, he pressed the button on the Return and released the device, leaving it behind on the roof.

Finn held to Willa's outstretched hand, not letting go.

2

FINN SAT UPRIGHT IN BED, sweating, his arm at his side, clutching a pillow. It took a minute for him to collect himself, as it often did. Being transported as a DHI was like traveling in a deep dream. Even when waking from such a dream it was difficult to separate fantasy from reality, the dream state from the living state. The first time Finn remembered having been transported into his hologram state he'd met an old man, a retired Disney Imagineer by the name of Wayne. They'd met on the Goofy bench outside of Tony's Town Square Restaurant. Finn suspected it hadn't been the first time he'd been transported, only the first time he'd realized what was happening to him. The experiences of dreaming and DHI were too closely correlated; learning the difference between them had taken practice. Even now, Finn couldn't be sure what he'd just been through.

He reached for his phone—he wasn't supposed to keep it by his bed, but he did—and texted Willa.

u there?

He waited. The screen timed out, returning to wallpaper and the time: 2:33 a.m. He hoped she was all right. Hoped she'd ended up in her bed. But, he reminded himself, they'd been holding hands when he'd punched the Return. There was little to no chance she could have been left behind, trapped in the Sleeping Beauty Syndrome of no return in which her mortal body would remain asleep like an unkissed princess.

Finn wasn't about to get back to sleep. He tiptoed into the kitchen and made himself a strong cup of tea to help him stay awake. Tiptoed because he didn't want to wake his supportive mother or his doubting father; didn't want to hear them bicker about how to deal with their oddball son who claimed to travel into other worlds at night. His mother knew the truth. A scientist by training, she'd put together enough empirical evidence to convince herself. Finn's father was the exact opposite. He believed his son hormonally imbalanced, "poisoned by puberty," he called it. He wanted Finn to see a counselor—a shrink—to exorcise whatever demons possessed his son into convincing himself he could wake as a hologram in another world where evil witches vied for control of an amusement park. Finn and his dad barely spoke anymore. They avoided each other, living with the dismissive silence that hung between them, where things left unsaid were louder than any argument. There were times Finn wished they'd just take the gloves off and get into it. To fight it out until they could talk again; to get his father back. But not his father, he of the soft voice and button-down shirts—the guy who rarely showed much emotion beyond the occasional simmering anger.

Finn checked his phone a second time. Nothing.

He was halfway through the cup of tea in his room when he reconsidered his situation. The theft of the library volume—the notebook—had to be significant if Maleficent, the Evil Queen, and Cruella had teamed up to find it. What if the timing of the theft made a difference? At this point, he wasn't going to sleep anyway, so he got to work.

He texted Philby, knowing that despite the hour the message would be received. Philby was a cyber-freak, a tech genius, and computer nerd. For nearly two years now he had possessed the ability to control the DHI server remotely, to direct Finn, or any of the DHIs, into one park or another. Finn had left the Return behind on the warehouse roof—or wherever he and Willa had just jumped from—but such limitations could be overcome; Philby could return a DHI manually if need be. Finn included this request in his text.

snd me to MK plez
wll cll for RTRN
confirm

He grimaced as a text returned almost immediately.

just spoke to Wyn. he's waiting in MK 4 u.

Why was Philby talking to Wayne at this time of night? He checked his phone, assuming Wayne tried to call him first.

Nothing.

A troubled Finn climbed back into bed and closed his eyes. He pictured a train tunnel, pitch-black, and then, faintly, way at the end, a pinprick of light piercing the dark. Ever so slowly the size of the tiny speck of light increased, first to a dot, then a dime-size circle, and finally a dish of white light speeding toward him. Weighed down by a long day and a short night, he fell back to sleep.

3

WHEN HE OPENED HIS EYES, Finn found himself sitting on the pavers of the Hub—the central square—in front of Cinderella Castle. He looked up at the statue of Walt Disney and Mickey Mouse holding hands and heard the incredibly faint hum, like the sound of an irritated insect, that confirmed he wasn't dreaming. He'd crossed over as a hologram.

He studied his hands and looked down at his legs, admiring the radical improvements of DHI 2.0. It was like going from standard television to high-def. In its first iteration, the hologram-projecting software had created a blue outline around the edges. Now his full hologram barely even glowed in the dark, and there was no blue line whatsoever. Despite a few bugs that had yet to be worked out, he could see all the advantages the upgrade gave him and the others when battling the Overtakers.

He pulled himself to his feet, feeling the effect of his fatigue, wondering how he would make it through the day of school that would start in a matter of hours. With the ongoing battle at the Base, sleep had been an afterthought the past few weeks.

He kept in a crouch, wary of prying eyes, like a spy sneaking behind enemy lines. While many of the park characters sided with the Keepers, a significant number had joined the Overtakers in wanting to seize control of the parks and install black magic. Inconveniently, those characters aligning with the OTs typically possessed powers bestowed upon them by their creator, Walt Disney: magic, the ability to cast spells or to transfigure themselves. Some possessed a raw physical power that far exceeded that of humans—especially humans in the form of holograms. Disney had created not just memorable villains, but dangerous ones. It wasn't only Finn's hologram at risk, but his sleeping self back in his bed. He remained alert.

He had no desire to enter into what he and the Keepers called the Siege. It wasn't his night for defending the Engineering Base at Disney's Hollywood Studios—the ongoing siege by the OTs that had been in place for two weeks. More important, no arrangements had been made for backup. He'd notified none of the other Keepers—except for Philby, whom he needed to return—that he was coming here.

He had no idea where any characters that supported the Keepers might be: Minnie, Pluto, Goofy, or Ariel, among others. There was no time to seek them out. If they found him, they found him. The parks at night were a kind of no-man's-land, filled with risk. At any location, at any attraction, at any time, an Overtaker could appear. He moved ahead cautiously, well aware that as a leader of the Keepers he would be a big prize if captured.

He didn't love the idea of walking down Main Street, U.S.A., but it was the only way to reach the Engine Co. 71 firehouse. He started out at a cautious walk, but once onto the sidewalk, took off at a run. He hated to admit it, but sometimes not seeing or hearing anyone at all in a park at night was worse than being chased.

At the corner by the Emporium, he crouched and carefully studied every view in every direction, not wanting to lead any OTs to the apartment over the firehouse. Never mind that the old man who lived there, and had done so for decades without Finn's help, had not been seen there in well over a year. Finn did not want to be the one who accidentally sabotaged him. Finn had no idea how the man would contact him, only that he would—the way he'd secretly contacted him several times in the past few months.

The man had taught Finn everything there was to know about being a Kingdom Keeper, about being a leader. Finn wasn't about to question him now. He had faith that the man somehow knew Finn had crossed over, that the man would find him when it was safe to do so.

A few minutes later, when he heard the hiss from the Walt Disney World Railroad locomotive, he knew. The train had no business running in the wee hours of the night. Or if it did, it was Finn's business. Keepers' business. He took off at a run.

As Finn reached the top of the stairs at the station platform, the train was already moving. Finn jumped aboard and looked forward and back: empty. The only person was the engineer, seen from the back on the front side of the coal-car—the tender that carried wood or coal for the steam engine. After traveling a hundred yards or so, the train was up to speed, moving at a good pace. When Finn looked next, the engineer was gone, the locomotive driverless. Then a head popped up out of the coal-car, and the engineer struggled to throw a leg over the wall and climb down into the passenger cars. He moved through the first two cars and was wearing a smile by the time he faced Finn.

Wayne Kresky had reached that age where he no longer seemed to grow older. He looked perfect in the train engineer's garb: the overalls suited him, as did the dungaree cap that held down his wispy white hair. His translucent blue eyes twinkled with mischief. Finn and the other Keepers had recently discussed the man's invincibility (he was at the top of the Overtakers' most-wanted list), his longevity (he had to be ancient), how without him the Keepers would not exist in the first place, and how, if they ever lost him, maybe they would be lost, too.

Wayne was not one for small talk. He could be difficult to understand at times, but that was because he talked in circles or made Finn work to understand a point he was trying to make. It seemed he was always testing Finn, always pushing him and all the Keepers as if time were running out—not just to defeat the Overtakers, but because of something bigger. What that was, or could be, the Keepers had yet to figure out.

"You're not on duty tonight," Wayne said, referencing the Keepers' service in defending the Engineering Base from the Siege.

"Maybeck and Charlene. Why, have you heard something?" Finn asked anxiously.

"No. It's the same. They attack at random, seemingly trying to draw us out in order to isolate us and pick us off. To reduce our numbers."

The Engineering Base was the electronic nerve center for all the parks. To control the Base was to control the parks: the electricity, pavilion temperatures, security video. The Overtakers were smart to go after it. Wayne had enlisted Cast Members, had called upon characters, and had recruited volunteers to act in its defense. He served as the general in charge.

The battles had been raging. The Keepers served in pairs, from midnight to four, when a dark blue seeped into the black horizon, signaling the impending sunrise and the Overtakers' retreat. The skirmishes could be exhausting and, occasionally, life-threatening. School had become a roller coaster of exhaustion and alertness, depending on the day. If the Siege kept up much longer it was going to affect all the Keepers' grades.

Finn raised his voice to be heard over the din of the train. "You might want to tell your friends about a possible bug in 2.0. I did a location jump."

"Explain that, please."

"I moved from the library to . . . I don't know, a factory rooftop. But it was a time shift. A bug. The two places weren't connected. It was a jump of some kind."

Wayne had a pen out and was taking notes. "A jump."

"I don't know how else to explain it."

"I'll tell them."

Finn waited a moment, enjoying the *clackety-clack* of the train, and then said apologetically, "They got whatever they were after at the library. Willa and I tried . . . bad luck is all."

"We know a little bit about what they got," Wayne

said. It was weird: he didn't seem to be speaking any louder than usual, yet Finn had no trouble hearing him. He attributed this to 2.0 and the software's enhanced visual, audio, and tactile functions. "It was an Imagineering journal from 1940."

Disney Imagineers—who combined skills of imagination and engineering—were something like magicians: they took Walt's dreams and turned them into attractions and rides, parks and experiences. They had invented Disneyland. Disney World.

"I thought the Imagineers weren't formed until the 1950s."

"You've been studying."

Finn shrugged.

"Correct. Officially formed in 1952. But ahead of that, in the early, early planning stages to make Walt's dream a reality, he had his trusted advisers. They all kept notebooks and journals. Sometimes documenting meetings, sometimes Walt's visions, or just to sketch out ideas and concepts. The journals are among the most treasured documents, most important documents, in the Disney archives."

"Why would Maleficent go after that particular journal?" Finn asked.

"We don't know. We're checking how much we have. All the journals are in the process of being scanned and stored in case of damage. We're not sure about the one they got. Maybe we'll figure it out, maybe we won't. Each journal can be specific to a project or cover dozens of ideas, some that came to fruition, some that did not. We may never know exactly what's in that particular journal."

"Until it's too late, you mean," Finn said. The Overtakers were led by Maleficent, a highly intelligent and well organized fairy. If they'd stolen a particular Disney journal from seventy years earlier, there was a good reason for it, and Finn and Wayne both knew it.

"We believe the journal contained preliminary story ideas for both *Pinocchio* and *Fantasia*."

"Meaning?"

"As you know, the film *Pinocchio* tells a story about a boy who must prove himself brave, truthful, and unselfish."

"And his nose."

"The book is a little more complicated than that. Like the movie, it has the Blue Fairy, but Pinocchio's journey is more difficult and his fate far darker. It could be said of you—the Keepers—that you are not unlike the wooden boy. You, too, are proving yourselves brave, truthful, and unselfish. You also exist in two worlds— Pinocchio's wooden world is like your electronic world."

"But why would Pinocchio's story matter to the OTs?" Finn asked.

"If they are searching for a way to be rid of you, the early stories could be of great value."

"You mean like research?"

"Exactly."

The train continued on its track, circling the Magic Kingdom. Wayne paid the train no attention whatsoever, though Finn continually looked in the direction of the locomotive, feeling ill at ease with no one at the controls.

"When you said Pinocchio had a darker fate, what did you mean?" Finn asked.

"You're capable of reading, last time I checked," Wayne said. "So read the story. You'll see. We don't need to waste our time with that."

Finn hated it when Wayne treated him like a kid. He stifled his rising anger. Why should he go to the bother to read an entire book when Wayne could answer a couple of key questions? "Give me the 411," he felt like saying.

Why's he lost interest in me? Finn wondered. Because Philby is picking up the enhancements in 2.0 faster than me? Give me a chance!

"So what about *Fantasia*?"

"As to that—" Wayne said. But he was immediately cut off as two animals leaped onto the moving train. They were just blurs, but Finn reacted instantly by jumping to his feet and putting himself between Wayne and whatever now occupied the car behind them.

"You saw that, yeah?"

"Yes," Wayne said, also standing. He reached out to stabilize himself against the train's movements.

A fox poked its head up over a bench. The thing was so cute it was hard to take it as any kind of threat. But Finn had learned to trust nothing.

Next, a cat appeared, bounding from one seat to the next, its fur tousled by the wind as it moved toward them.

The fox's eyes flashed golden.

"I must warn you," Wayne said, "as adorable as these creatures may be—"

"I know," Finn said.

"The fox could do some real harm."

"To you," Finn said. "Not to me. With me, he only gets a bite of light."

"Unless he challenges your fear level."

"Version 2.0 changes all that," Finn said confidently.

The fox bared its teeth and hopped up over the bench seat, now a bench closer to the two.

The cat continued toward them along the far edge of the train car.

"How do you want to handle this?" Finn asked.

"You're the leader."

"Not with you around."

"Yes you are, Finn. Now and always."

"What about Philby?" he blurted out. He caught sight of the older man's troubled eyes, as if Finn knew something he shouldn't. *That's what I thought.* The moment passed.

"Do you know these animals?" Finn asked.

"Well, no. Not by name. But seeing as how we were discussing Pinocchio . . ."

"Yeah?"

"It is a fox and a cat that lead the wooden boy astray."

"Seriously? Oh, perfect. So they're after me?"

"I would doubt they'll discriminate."

"Okay, you take the cat," Finn said, finally having a plan. He liked cats; he couldn't see trying to hurt one.

"And the fox?"

"Is all mine," Finn said.

"He'll go for me," Wayne said. "The elderly have many more complications with rabies treatment. The fox can bite as strongly as a dog and is probably twice as quick."

"This is not cheering me up," Finn said.

"Nor is it intended to. His instincts will dictate he go for either the throat or the Achilles."

"Yeah, well, I won't let him get that close to you."

"I'm not talking about *my* throat, Finn."

Finn swallowed hard; 2.0, he reminded himself, knowing it hadn't been put to this kind of test. So, he thought, we have a fox, a cat, and a guinea pig.

The cat stretched and looked in the direction of the fox. It seemed just for a moment as if they'd communicated. Wayne was a good five feet from the path of the cat. Finn wanted to remind him about their assignments, but he kept quiet.

The fox launched himself at Finn. Wayne lunged for the cat.

Finn extended both arms and almost knocked the flying fox off the train. The animal squealed—a sound that cut Finn to his core—then rolled and slammed onto the floor.

Wayne miscalculated. By moving to intercept the cat, the feral creature put the move on him, feinting to the inside and slipping easily between Finn and Wayne. Finn caught this out of the corner of his eye, but his concentration remained on the fox. It came to all fours, reared back, and bared its teeth. Its eyes filled with golden light and it growled viciously, raising the hair on Finn's arms.

It pounced.

Finn caught it just beneath its front legs as the force pushed him back onto the bench. The fox snapped for

Finn's throat, spraying drool. The guttural sounds it emitted turned Finn's stomach—it meant to kill him. Another snap for his throat. And yet another. This time, it bit through the hologram. Without 2.0 it would have torn through Finn's flesh.

Wayne backed away, afraid of both animals. Finn had never seen him like this.

Finn hollered, "The cat!"

He threw the fox hard and high. It flew through the air and landed in the next car back. The moment it landed it charged again, coming at Finn like an airborne missile.

In that briefest of instants, Finn had gotten a look forward: the cat was streaking toward the locomotive. "The cat!" he said again, sensing the trouble before it happened.

Wayne climbed awkwardly over the seat, slow and uncoordinated. The fox landed on Finn, its glaring teeth leading the way. The creature was small in his hands, but unruly, strong, and slippery as a snake. It scratched with its feet and snapped its jaws. Finn reacted instinctively to avoid the teeth, hoisting it high overhead. He smashed it onto the floor of the train car. It let out a sickening cry. Finn felt consumed with guilt; he never hurt animals! But he thought back to the monkeys and ravens in Animal Kingdom, the orangutans bearing down on him—sometimes there was no choice but to fight back.

The fox whimpered and skittered off under the bench. Finn's guilt got the better of him, freezing him. Then the creature tried to lock its jaws onto his heel, snapping nothing but light. Finn screamed, thinking he'd been bitten, then kicked out and connected with the fox.

A shudder passed through his legs. Had the fox managed to bite him? No; the sensation was flooding up both legs—the train was gaining speed. One glance confirmed this: a pair of cat ears stuck up from the locomotive's controls. The cat was running the train.

Wayne had crawled into the coal-car.

The train roared ahead faster.

Working as a team, the fox had been a distraction. The real threat was the cat at the controls. The train cars rocked side to side; the speed increased.

Finn snatched the fox by the neck, whirled around, and let go. It flew off into the woods as the train sped ahead.

Finn grinned. But then: a brown blur between the jungle and the last train car. The fox had jumped back on.

It raised its tiny head, eyes glowing, and, leaping from one bench to the next, raced forward.

The train was moving at top speed, making it hard to stand. Each time Wayne attempted to get to his feet he was thrown to the opposite side of the coal-car and fell again.

The train's wheels lifted off the track. As it passed Space Mountain, it leaned to the outside. Metal twisted and cried out. Finn felt weightless as the inside wheels lifted off the rail and the train car briefly balanced on its outside wheels. It held there—suspended halfway between rolling over and derailing or returning to the track.

Finn turned toward Wayne, offering his back to the approaching fox. Wayne was planted against the coal-car's wall, his eyes bugged out, frozen in terror. Finn clambered over the benches, taking them like a hurdler.

As he reached the coal-car, he looked down and knew what had to be done.

He slipped between the coal-car and the first passenger car, the train still balanced precariously on only its outside wheels. The fox, teeth dripping drool, deftly jumped from one bench to the next.

Finn reached down and worked the heavy iron clamp that joined the two train cars together. With one look he understood how the mechanism worked. He pulled a piece of the clamp with all his strength. The tilting train shrieked.

The wide-eyed fox was a single car back. He could taste Finn's blood.

The car connector released. Finn unhooked a safety chain and the cars separated. One foot . . . three . . . eight . . .

The fox arrived at the end of the car and never hesitated. He sprang . . . but fell short, missing the coal-car and falling onto the railroad ties. He bounced, tumbled, and then rolled into a ditch. He came to his feet and tried to chase down the train, but he was too slow, no match for a runaway train.

Finn vaulted over the back of the coal-car, lost his balance, fell, and crawled toward Wayne.

* * *

With the release of the passenger cars, the locomotive and coal-car fell back onto the tracks. Finn, still crawling, reached Wayne. "You okay?"

Wayne nodded vigorously. "The throttle!" he hollered. "We're going to crash."

The train no longer felt anchored to the tracks. It rocked back and forth, first on the wheels to the left, then the right. It sounded like girls screaming at a rock concert.

Finn struggled to reach the front of the coal-car, where it connected to the locomotive. The cat was nowhere to be seen. The engineer's seat was vacant, a number of levers and hand grips to either side.

The throttle, Finn thought, seeing one lever pushed well forward. The train's unpredictable movements made it impossible to judge his vault into the locomotive. He threw a knee up onto the wall of the coal-car. The train's movement dumped him. After two more failed tries, he took a running start and vaulted atop the coal-car's pile of stacked wood and then into the locomotive. He lunged for the throttle to slow the train, but unintentionally shoved the throttle forward.

"Too fast!" Wayne hollered, reduced to playing spectator.

The locomotive was a stone skipping on lake water, a few tons of iron rising and falling, floating off of and then crashing back down onto the rails.

Finn grabbed for the throttle and pulled it back. In doing so, he discovered what he thought must be another feature of 2.0—enhanced strength when under pressure. He pulled so hard the lever broke off in his hand.

The locomotive screamed and gained more speed.

Finn stood there with a useless piece of metal in his hand.

"The brake!" Wayne hollered.

Finn climbed into the empty seat and tugged hard

on the only other lever. The wheels cried as sparks flew. The trained slowed slightly—enough that it settled onto the track. He spotted a massive red button marked EMERGENCY ONLY. He stretched to reach it. If this didn't qualify as an emergency, nothing did. Holding the brake required both hands and the strength of both arms. If he eased up even slightly, the train charged ahead, threatening to derail. He tried to reach the red button with his shoulder, but it was no use—too far away. The smell of melting metal and sparks filled the air. He repositioned himself—hands between his legs, his feet aimed above his head.

He kicked the red button with his heel. Instantly the groaning ceased—the motor had been disconnected or shut off. The sparks continued to fly, but now the locomotive actually slowed. A hundred yards later it ground to a complete stop. Finn spun around to see Wayne, his face in a total sweat, sitting on the floor of the coal-car.

"Let's get out of here," Wayne said.

* * *

"No more rides," Finn said as Wayne led him into Tomorrowland.

"Agreed," Wayne said.

He brought them backstage at the Monsters, Inc. Laugh Floor, under the faint glare of an exit sign. They leaned against the cool wall and rested a moment.

"So they know I'm here," Finn said.

"Apparently. Yes."

"You know what bothers me about that?"

"What?" Wayne asked, though his tone of voice said he didn't want to hear.

"With the battle going at Base, how can the Overtakers possibly focus over here at the same time?"

Wayne said, "Because they've increased their numbers dramatically. The Green Eyes, for instance."

Finn and the Keepers had discovered that some of their schoolmates had joined forces with the Overtakers. They wore green contact lenses in order to tell each other apart from the other students. It was one of many recent developments that suggested the ranks of the Overtakers had grown. Meanwhile, the Keepers remained at seven—the five original DHI models and two sisters, Jess and Amanda, both with intriguing powers. There was talk of six volunteer DHIs having been added, the result of an educational quest inside the Magic Kingdom. Finn had yet to meet them.

"Still outnumbered, and overtired," Finn said. "Great!"

Wayne glared at him.

"Before we get into the whole *Fantasia* thing," he said, "what about the maiden voyage?"

"That can wait," Wayne said. "We have more pressing matters."

"It's a week away."

"If we—you five—don't defeat the Overtakers at the Base, a week might as well be a year. DHI 2.0 lives on a server inside the Base. You think it's a coincidence the Overtakers want in there? Not to mention the Base offers every kind of physical control of the parks."

"Not to mention," a frustrated Finn said. "A siege is a siege. It's not like they're accomplishing anything."

"They're building toward a major offensive," Wayne said. "It's standard field warfare. They make incursions to test our readiness, our defenses. They test our strategy. Then, determining our weaknesses, they strike with everything they have."

"Way to cheer me up. It's not like we can defeat what we can't see. But if we just wait . . . that can't be good either." He wondered what had happened to Wayne the optimist.

"No," Wayne said. "We need to be proactive—to take the offensive. Especially in light of the upcoming cruise. Once you're gone . . ." He didn't need to finish that. If the Keepers abandoned the battle for the Base it would fall to the Overtakers. If the Base fell, the entire Kingdom—all the parks—might fall with it.

"*Fantasia*," Finn reminded him yet again.

"The film has an interesting history that goes way back. It was the only film that Chernabog appeared in. Walt Disney referred to Chernabog as Satan himself. He's been described as part Minotaur, part Mayan bat god. He can summon fire and control ghosts and harpies. He's a creature of confusion and chaos. He is considered the most powerful villain Walt Disney ever created."

"Then why haven't we seen any of that?" Finn wondered aloud. When Maleficent had animated the Yeti, he'd transfigured into Chernabog. And why do you sound so scared? Finn thought to himself.

"That falls under 'Be careful what you wish for.' Do you know what torpor is?"

"No."

"A hummingbird's resting state. Typically adopted during overnight hibernation."

Philby would have known that, Finn thought.

"Our assumption is that Chernabog has been, and is still in, torpor. We've expected more trouble from him than we've had. So where's he been? In point of fact, the only times we can confirm Chernabog's involvement is when Maleficent moves him. Maybe his transfiguration into and back from the Yeti rendered him powerless. Maybe they don't want us to know. Or maybe the missing journal has something in it that will help him regain his power."

"Now you're freaking me out."

"The Minotaur part of him is itself a combination of man and bull. It has no natural source of sustenance. In mythology, the Minotaur devoured humans. He lived in a labyrinth, a maze only he understood.

"Camazotz," Wayne continued, "is a Mayan bat god—the other half of Chernabog. Camazotz was also nourished by human sacrifice. At one time he bit the head off a young boy and offered it as a ball for a game."

"And you're saying Chernabog is a combination of the two?"

"Yes. Walt's darkest creation ever."

"And the journal is like an owner's manual?"

"Could be. We won't know until you get it back."

"We . . . ?"

"If you don't like Maleficent, think of Chernabog as ten times worse. Maleficent plots and schemes. She teases her prey. Chernabog bites your head off and makes a game out of it. He's fearsome."

"So we don't want them giving him a reboot."

"If that's what they're trying to do, then no. Definitely not."

"Does the battle at the Base have anything to do with the contents of the journal?" Finn asked.

"We won't know until—"

"We get it back for you."

"Now you're catching on."

Finn's throat tasted strange. Even more upsetting was that he couldn't recall having the sensation of taste before as a DHI. Version 2.0 was dealing him all sorts of surprises. Next, his chest tightened, like a clamp on his heart. He began shaking. He was going into seizure.

His body buckled as he fell first to his knees and then to the tile. He began twitching uncontrollably.

"A bug," he choked out. A failure of 2.0—it was all he could come up with. Wayne reached to help, but his hands passed through Finn's hologram.

"Finn?"

Finn fought as his eyes rolled back in his head. "Re . . . turn," he gasped. "Phil . . . by . . ." His body was out of control, like he was being electrocuted. "Call . . . Phil—" His throat gurgled, like he was gargling.

"No need!" Wayne pulled a small black fob from his pocket, smaller and more compact than the v1.6 Return.

"Godspeed!" Wayne said. He hit the button.

* * *

Finn opened his eyes.

His bedroom was dark. A shape loomed to his right—someone holding him down. A paramedic? His parents?

Another person moved to his left. In the steady

glare of his computer screen Finn caught sight of Greg Luowski, the resident bully of Finn's middle school and now his high school freshman class. A round-faced, wet-lipped, mean-spirited boy, Luowski took pleasure in dishing out pain.

The bedroom window was open, the curtains waving. In recent months, his parents had gotten lazy about activating the home security system that included sensors on his window; he'd been glad they had since it was easier to sneak out. But now someone had sneaked in!

Unless Luowski had four arms, he wasn't holding Finn down. That job belonged to someone else, the person to Finn's right. Finn couldn't see well enough to identify who it was.

Luowski was instead busy trying to keep a hose in Finn's mouth and down his throat. The hose connected to the end of a rubber funnel. Awake now, Finn bucked and threw his legs up. Luowski climbed onto the bed using his considerable weight—he was a chunk of muscle and bone—to pin Finn's legs as well. The whole time the boy worked to push the tube into Finn's mouth.

"Hold him still!" Luowski whispered to whoever was holding Finn. He got a plastic jug—it looked like apple juice from Costco—up to the funnel and began to pour.

Finn never tasted booze, but he'd smelled it on his

parents' breath plenty of times—and this was booze. Bitter and sharper tasting than he'd imagined. Nasty stuff. He spit as much out as possible, but gagged down some of it as Luowski drowned him in it. He quickly understood the plan: they'd wanted him drunk and unconscious while he'd been crossed over in his DHI state. If they'd managed it, he wouldn't have been able to return. He'd have been stuck in Sleeping Beauty Syndrome. SBS. The Syndrome.

The light pulsed again: there were half-dissolved pills dancing at the bottom of the jug. Finn guessed that Luowski had spiked the booze with drugs.

He coughed and spit. Luowski managed to get his sweating, disgusting mitt pressed onto Finn's forehead and held him down. He worked the mouth of the open jug to the funnel and poured. The disgusting concoction flooded through the hose and into Finn's mouth as he sucked for air.

If Finn didn't get out of this, his parents at the very least would find him drunk and drugged and would ground him for the rest of his life. He would lose the last family connection he had left—his mother's support of his being a Keeper.

Finn had an idea. He wrapped his lips around the tube and blew, like into a snorkel. The booze concoction blasted out of the funnel and into Luowski's face.

Luowski jerked back, giving Finn an opening to fight back.

Finn sat up, breaking the grip on his shoulders. He smashed his bedside lamp into Luowski's face and threw an elbow into the other person.

Here was the thing: his parents were constantly violating his privacy, coming into his room without knocking despite peace treaties to the contrary. Interrupting him, telling him to do things, bossing him around. So why was it that now, the one time he needed them, they were sleeping soundly down the hall while a pair of lunatics were trying to dispatch him? Didn't they have any kind of parental intuition that something was wrong? Wasn't his mom supposed to pop wide awake terrified something bad was happening? Weren't parents supposed to rescue you when someone was trying to poison you?

Finn drove his heel between Luowski's legs, causing the boy's face to pucker and his eyes to bulge in the strobe light. Finn then did a back somersault, knowing this was the last move the other kid would see coming. Indeed, the other kid's head ended up between Finn's knees. Finn clamped his knees tightly, balled his fist, and was about to punch the kid's lights out when he saw it was a girl. Sally Ringwald! Their faces were nearly touching. He knew he should, but he couldn't bring himself to punch a girl.

Instead, he stuck his fingers up her nose, released

her from the headlock, and drove her back with only a small amount of pressure to her nostrils. Spinning, he came off the bed and caught her again, then grabbed her arm and twisted it behind her back like he'd seen done in the movies. It worked surprisingly well.

He drove her forward and bent her over the bed from behind. That was when his mother opened the door.

"Lawrence Finnegan Whitman!" she said, seeing him alone with a girl in the dark. (Luowski was still rolling on the floor on the far side of the bed.)

She switched on the light.

Luowski stood and dove out the window. The coward didn't stay to help his partner.

"Oh!" his mother said. "Is that alcohol I smell? What are the three of you up to?"

"Overtakers, Mom. OTKs, we call them: Overtaker Kids. That was Greg Luowski. This is Sally Ringwald. Sally," he said, shoving her arm up higher, "say hello to my mother."

"Hell . . . o . . . Mrs. . . . Whitman," the girl choked out behind the pain Finn inflicted.

"They were trying to poison me," Finn said. "Trying to trap me in SBS using a new tactic."

Finn and his mother often strategized together. Given that his mother was a legitimate rocket scientist (retired), he valued her input. She was the smartest person he knew, and that included Philby.

His mother stepped inside the bedroom and eased the door shut gently so as not to wake Finn's father. If he became aware of all that went on under his roof he'd likely have both his wife and Finn committed to an institution.

"What is the meaning of this?" Mrs. Whitman asked harshly. She was well aware of the "meaning of this," but obviously couldn't think of what exactly to say given that Finn was leaning against a girl who was splayed across his bed.

"Should I call the police?" she whispered.

"No!" Sally and Finn said in chorus.

"Sally is going to behave," Finn said. "She's going to explain the meaning of this. Aren't you, Sally?" He wrenched her arm again, enjoying it just a little too much. "Lock the door, Mom. Then lock the window. If she tries to get out, I'll tackle her."

His mother followed his instructions, which was not a common practice. Finn released Sally's arm and spun her around so that she sat on the bed facing him and his mother.

"Who sent you?" Finn asked.

Sally wanted a way out, but realized her options were limited. She said nothing.

"My mother will call the police," Finn warned.

"You wouldn't dare. That would mean the newspapers and stuff, and the Disney Hosts Interactive would be canceled."

So she'd thought it through that far, Finn realized. He tried to pretend she was wrong.

"You think every arrest gets written about? Not by a long shot."

He won a few points. Sally looked deeply troubled.

"Greg," she said.

"He didn't dream this up on his own," Finn said.

"Maybe not. I wouldn't know."

"I don't believe you."

"Believe what you want."

"Whose pills were those?" Finn asked. His mother looked ready to scream.

Sally turned a pasty white. "My mother's. She has trouble sleeping."

That explained why he felt thickheaded: he'd swallowed some of what Luowski had been trying to force-feed him. But thankfully, not much.

"How does Luowski get his orders?" Finn asked.

"Text? Email? How should I know?" She looked at them both and said, "He texts me. Seriously! That's all I've got!"

"And how did you join up? The green contacts and all that?"

"This YouTube video. Greg sent me the link. I had to Friend him in order to watch it."

"Show me!" Finn said, pointing to his computer.

Sally hesitated.

"Now!" Finn's mother ordered.

Both Sally and Finn jumped. Sally crossed the room, logged in to YouTube on Finn's laptop, and played the video.

Images of all four Disney World parks played as a slideshow. A pair of teenage voices, sometimes female, sometimes male, spoke passionately.

"Are you tired of the Disney Hosts? Had enough of all the sweet smiles and plastic expressions inside the Kingdom? It's about time the Kingdom moved into the twenty-first century. Wouldn't you say? Darkened up a bit. Became more interesting. Think about it: the same people have been in charge for over fifty years. What's with that? Did you know that some of your favorite characters are rebelling? If you'd like to see things differently, you and your friends can join us. You won't be sorry. Enrollment is free and the benefits instantaneous. You will be trained. Assigned missions, inside and outside the Kingdom. See things you've only dreamed of—if your dreams are anything like mine. Click the link below to submit your application."

For a moment, Finn and his mother said nothing,

44

staring at the small screen within a screen. The video's final images had been of Cinderella Castle at night as it changed colors. In the final image it was a penetrating green.

"That's lame," Finn said.

"Unless that comes with a dose of hypnotism," his mother said, "I doubt its effectiveness." She spun the desk chair around so that Sally faced her.

"You broke into my home," she said. "You tried to poison my son. How many pills did you put in there?"

Sally began crying.

Mrs. Whitman turned to Finn. "How much of that did you drink?"

Finn shrugged. "Not much." His head felt even heavier now. He fought to keep his eyes open. But it was a good kind of fatigue, not a toxic one. "Hardly any," he said, honestly. "I'm fine." He said to Sally, "We don't poison people. We don't sabotage rides or kidnap kids. We try to keep that stuff from happening. You know, I love dark stuff. Vampires? Not so much. But I'll take *The Dark Knight* over *Superman Returns* any day. But do I want it to turn into the Tragic Kingdom? No, I don't. I happen to like it the way it is. If Maleficent wants a dark park, then she can go build one. But leave this one the way it is, thank you very much."

Finn had never articulated exactly how he felt about

what he and the Keepers did. It didn't come out exactly right, but it felt incredibly good. He wondered how the other Keepers would put it.

"We have an offer to make you," Mrs. Whitman said.

Finn looked at his mother curiously. He wanted to say, "We do?"

Sally raised her head. Her face was tear-streaked, her grim expression disturbing. When Finn's mother cried her contacts got messed up. But Sally's hadn't. In fact, being so close, getting such a good look, he wondered if they were contacts at all.

Sally shied away from Finn's stare. "What's with you?"

"Your eyes," Finn said. "They're contacts, right?" But the weird thing was, they weren't contacts: her pupils were changing size as he stared at her. The color of her eyes had actually changed. How could such a thing be possible? Unless . . .

She averted her head completely. "Leave me alone."

"Finn?" His mother said.

"You used to have blue eyes, Sally. So what happened? How's that even possible?"

"Finn, girls do these things," his mother said.

"Maleficent . . ." he muttered. Some kind of spell had been placed on her and the other OTKs. The spell had physically changed their eye color so they could identify each other. Maybe they had pigmented contact lenses or something to fool their families, but this OTK stuff was getting serious.

"To heck with her eyes! I will only offer this once," his mother told Sally.

"Mom . . . ?"

An upset Mrs. Whitman ignored her son. Addressing Sally, she said, "First, you're going to tell Greg Luowski that you escaped right behind him. Do you understand?"

Sally nodded her head.

"You mess this up, young lady, and your parents and the police will hear about what you tried to do here tonight."

Sally nodded shamefully.

"Next, you will spy for us," Mrs. Whitman said. "Anything you're asked to do, anything you're told. Any missions. Any rumors. Any *anything* that has to do with the parks or with the Kingdom Keepers is reported to Finn. You will text him the moment you hear about it. The first moment you possibly can. If we hear the same thing from someone else before we hear it from you then I'll make the call to your parents and to the police. Is that understood?"

Finn swelled with pride. Genius! His mother sounded on the verge of slapping Sally across the face.

In fact, he knew she couldn't even hurt a spider—not even a super-ugly spider: she trapped them and set them free outside. A real terror, his mother.

Sally nodded. "I don't hear all that much," she choked out.

"You will now. Don't think you're the only spy we have," Mrs. Whitman warned. Finn marveled at her ability to lie so effortlessly. He looked at his mother completely differently. "Don't think you can play with me. You'll regret that."

Sally nodded again. "I understand. I'm sorry, Mrs. Whitman." She looked up at Finn. "I'm sorry for what I . . . what we tried to do to you."

Finn felt his hands tighten. He should have punched her while he'd had the excuse. "Do as we ask," he said. "My mother means it."

Sally looked into his mother's face and recoiled. There was no mistaking Mrs. Whitman's intensity.

"Okay," she said. "I'll do it."

4

TECHNICALLY SPEAKING, a siege is when an attacking army surrounds another, often in a castle or fort. Usually the attacking army surrounds the castle or fortress and waits for the people inside—the besieged—to begin starving. The besieged then surrender. Sometimes a siege backfires: the attacking army runs out of food or disease diminishes its ranks.

A common tactic used by the attackers is to build an earthen wall to keep supplies from entering the castle. The besieged would often dig trenches to slow down the attackers.

Technically speaking, the Overtakers' threat to the Engineering Base located backstage of Disney's Hollywood Studios was not a siege. During the day, business was conducted as usual: employees came and went; the Disney villains assumed their characters in the various parks in which they lived. No trenches were dug. No one starved.

But at night things were different. Considerably different. Cast Members inside the Base dared not leave for fear of attack. Anyone outside dared not approach for the same reason. Those inside the Base were isolated and expected an assault. Fireballs were thrown at security guards and Cast Members who dared enter the area. Laser light cages appeared, trapping the innocent. Perfectly healthy people grew dizzy and fainted—the result of spells, no doubt. A young person was made to look old. An old person was transfigured into an animal. Storm clouds formed over the Base, dumping rain on it or lashing it with lightning. Definitely a siege.

How Disney had managed to keep it out of the press was anybody's guess. Finn attributed the privacy to both the stringent contracts Cast Members signed and the loyalty of Disney employees.

Terry "Donnie" Maybeck and Charlene Turner patrolled the area outside the Base and staged sorties into the shadows. Maybeck, a high school freshman like the other Keepers, was easily mistaken for a senior. He didn't mind that so much. What he did mind was that because he was African American and fit, nearly everyone assumed he was an athlete. He was in fact an artist. Charlene, on the other hand, was dainty and blond and blue-eyed, easily mistaken for a glam girl, yet she was an incredible athlete. As a freshman she had already been asked to try out for the varsity gymnastics team; she was currently on the football cheerleading squad. She was a climber, a runner, an anything-goes girl.

Courageous and confident in action, while often quiet and unopinionated in the company of her fellow Keepers, she was a good balance to Maybeck's arrogance and self-proclaimed superiority. He thought he was God's gift to everything—especially girls, who indeed threw themselves at him, though Charlene could not understand why. She could see in the mirror why boys liked her, but Maybeck's popularity with the girls baffled her. Philby had teamed the two as partners. They served Monday and Thursday nights together.

DHI 2.0 gave them the advantage over the Overtakers, but wouldn't help much if they faced Overtaker holograms. The ability of the OTs to cross over had made strategizing against them trickier.

Maybeck and Charlene were currently squatting on the far side of a Pargo—a Disney golf cart used to move Cast Members around backstage. The Pargo was parked next to the bland, boxy building that housed the Base on the second floor. The hour was closing in on 2:30, a time of night both kids, even as holograms, grew overly tired.

"Quiet tonight," Charlene said.

"Yeah. Bothers me."

"I know what you mean."

"It's like they're planning something," Charlene said.

"Count on it."

"Or they're busy somewhere else."

Maybeck shifted uneasily. "That's a disturbing thought."

"I'm just saying."

"I kinda wish you wouldn't," he said.

"Going on two weeks," she reminded. "So what if the plan is to tire us out? What if the purpose of the Siege is not to conquer the Base but to wear us down trying to protect it?"

"See what I mean? You're thinking too much."

"Or you aren't thinking enough. What makes more sense, them trying to get control of the mechanical side of the parks, or to defeat us?"

"Or both, you mean?"

"That's exactly what I mean! Yes. Wear us down with this siege. Spring some kind of attack or trap—on us, not the Base. And then, with us out of the way, take the Base, and the parks with it."

"You know the problem with you? You get really negative when you're tired. Thanks for the chill pill, Charlie. Just what the doctor ordered."

"I'm just being pragmatic."

"Don't do that. Don't use words like that. Don't be like Philby and start showing off how smart you are."

"Philby doesn't do that. Philby is just Philby."

"Well, you're not Philby. Am I right? You're Charlie. So don't go doing that."

"Okay," she said. "I'm just being . . . realistic. How's that?"

"Don't patronize me," Maybeck said.

"Don't use words like that," she complained, imitating his voice.

They both laughed.

The movement came from their right. A pair of blurs, definitely coming toward the building.

"I counted two," Maybeck said.

"Yes," Charlene said.

"Could be decoys," he said.

"Absolutely."

"I'll take this way. You take that."

"Way ahead of you." Charlene rotated to her left, ready to circle the building counterclockwise.

"Watch for a counterattack."

"You think?" she asked sarcastically. "Meet you on the other side. I'll be the girl in all black."

"Eyes open," he cautioned.

"On three," she said, and began counting.

* * *

Charlene appreciated that DHI 2.0 had significantly reduced the glow of her hologram. There had been a time when walking around in the dark was like wearing Day-Glo. But with the upgrade, she could sneak along the building's exterior wall like a shadow.

As she came around the opposite side, she saw them: two brooms-and-buckets climbing a drainpipe. There had been a time—years ago now—when such a sight would have stopped her cold. But she did not question what she saw for even a millisecond. Brooms, pirates, witches, fairies—there was nothing unexpected anymore. The Overtakers had recruited from nearly every group of Disney characters. All presented an equal threat, though each with specific skills.

The brooms could swing their handles like baseball bats. They were agile and quick. Their buckets were known to contain toxic fluids that could chemically burn. They could sweep up a hurricane-force wind in seconds.

None of which could harm her as long as she maintained her hologram state, as long as she kept fear at bay. But despite her courage under fire, Charlene considered herself the biggest chicken of all the Keepers. True or not, she didn't look forward to testing her resolve. Not now. Not ever.

But the two brooms were climbing—their limbs stuck through the buckets' wire handles—toward the Base's second-story windows.

Maybeck rounded the far corner and spotted the brooms. He and Charlene met at the drainpipe.

"We've got to warn them!" Charlene said.

"We got to get up there and stop them!" Maybeck countered. He bent down and found a pebble and hurled it at the glass. He missed. "You're the climber!" he said.

She'd sensed that coming. The problem was . . . well, there were several problems. First, in nearly any battle the person with the high ground won, and she'd be coming at them from below; second, she wasn't exactly sure what she was supposed to do. Pull them off the drainpipe? Third, there was the matter of fear and testing the full capabilities of 2.0: she would be climbing, therefore not fully a hologram—would that leave her vulnerable to injury and attack?

"Go!" Maybeck said.

Charlene took hold of the pipe and climbed, amazed at how easy 2.0 made everything.

"I'm going to sound the alarm!" Maybeck called to her—for she was climbing quickly. He took off around to the other side, where a warning device had been installed.

Charlene was instantly in her element: doing something physical. She wasn't going to worry about upgrades or fear or strategy. She was going to climb up to the first broom and pull it off the side of the building. Hand over hand, she ascended.

The broom bristles were divided into two "feet" that pressed to the pipe. Their limbs (they weren't really arms but more like tree limbs) held the buckets, leaving their twiglike hands free to climb. But possibly because of the weight of the buckets, or just plain inexperience with climbing, they were slow. She gained on them. Reaching the bristles of the lower broom, she grabbed and tugged, hoping to pull the creature free of the drainpipe. Instead, it slipped and sank toward her. One of the buckets beaned her. The broom was a warrior. He— it!—swung a bucket at her awkwardly, but with enough authority to smash her in the face. The next attempt hit her hand and she screamed out and let go, hanging by just her left hand. She blocked the next attempt, hooked the bucket, and leaned her weight on it. The broom tilted to that side. She intentionally allowed herself to slide down a few feet, pulling the bucket and the broom with her. It let go of the pipe and fell, crashing to the ground.

Both buckets spilled out a foul neon green goo. The broom scampered to get away from it, but too late. Its bristles made contact and melted away immediately. The melting spread like fire up the fuel of the bristles and the wood, dissolving it. A moment later, two wooden buckets sat on the asphalt. The green slime re-collected into two separate globs and oozed back into the tipped buckets.

She looked up and saw the handle of the broom above her bent down as if looking at her. She felt a chill. Recognizing it as fear, she tried to push it away. Fear could compromise her hologram, making her more "mortal." Had the upgrade to 2.0 eliminated that effect? The broom climbed quickly. Some of the goo sloshed out of a bucket. Reacting to an impulse of fear, Charlene spun on the drainpipe to avoid being hit—but wondered if that was necessary. Wouldn't the goo just pass right through her? Was she willing to trust that? Was she *able* to trust that? It slopped down onto the asphalt.

Unseen by her, the goo moved like an undulating starfish and then, finding no fuel, affixed itself to the wall and began oozing up the drainpipe, coming at Charlene's feet like an alien blob. It was trying to return to its bucket.

Charlene saw none of this. She reached out and took hold of the broom's bristles only to have it kick her away. The broom scampered higher and tipped a bucket toward her. Charlene let go of the drainpipe and hung from the broom's bristles. The spilled goo missed her, but the lower blob was now only a few feet away.

A security alarm sounded inside and out.

The broom stiffened in panic and then struggled to climb as Charlene now held to its stem. Reaching the window, the broom tipped the bucket toward the wall.

Charlene could not allow the goo to disintigrate the wood of the windowsill or the broom would be inside. With two hands she made herself perpendicular to the pole then swung her legs up and kicked the bucket, sending it flying. The goo spilled out, landing on the broom, dissolving it as Charlene completed her back flip, heading toward the ground.

Maybeck came around the side of the building at that exact moment. He spotted her falling and sprinted to catch her, but wasn't going to make it. He arrived a step short, his outstretched arms missing her.

Charlene stuck the landing, automatically lifting her hands overhead as she did in competitions.

A stunned Maybeck lay there, his eyes brimming with tears.

"You're crying!" she said. "I'm touched."

"Am not," he said, wiping his eyes. "I ran so hard my eyes blurred, is all. I . . . was almost . . . how in the world did you do that?"

"Practice, practice, practice," she said.

Maybeck looked up. "When I saw you headed for the asphalt, I thought . . ."

"I'm touched. Seriously. I really am."

"I . . . ah . . ." Maybeck knew there was no use trying to deny it. "Whatever," he said. Looking down at the buckets, he added, "Nice move."

"Thank you." She moved closer to the nearest bucket. "We need a glass jar to collect some of this stuff. The Imagineers should analyze it. It's like liquid fire or something. It eats through wood. Maybe flesh, for all I know."

"Sweet!" Maybeck said, always excited to see the next great horror in person.

"I think it uses itself up as it does whatever it does," she said. "There was definitely less of it after it chewed up each of the brooms."

Maybeck produced an empty soda can from a trash bin.

"No," she said. "There can't be any chance of spilling it."

"What if we just gave them the buckets?" he asked.

"Duh! Of course!"

On inspection, the buckets proved to be plastic looking like wood, possibly explaining why the goo hadn't destroyed them as well.

Maybeck carefully picked up two; Charlene, the two others. They carried them around to the front door of the Base, and Maybeck rang the exterior intercom. He explained to the person who answered what they were leaving on the doorstep and advised an extra dose of caution in handling it.

The intercom's welcome screen displayed the time as 3:13.

"There won't be any more action tonight," he said. Historically, very little happened after 3:00 a.m.

"Agreed," she said.

"What do you suppose they were trying to do?" he asked.

"Get inside," she said.

"Like the Rangers," Maybeck said.

"Excuse me?"

"The Rangers are an elite team of commandos that leads the way into battle. *Black Ops.* You know."

"They were supposed to burn a hole in the wall for others to follow through."

"Maybe you prevented that."

"We," she said.

"You," he said.

That was the thing about Maybeck: just when she thought he was the biggest egomaniac of all time he'd come out with something caring and thoughtful. Completely unpredictable. Somewhere behind all his bold and brash statements was someone with a real heart, and it endeared him to her. Maybe it was the artist in him. Maybe all the blowhard stuff was just a shell he hid behind.

"We'll stay until four," she said.

"Of course!"

Philby would manually return them at the appointed

time. To leave any earlier would require a phone call, as the Return device wasn't currently in Hollywood Studios.

"Let's patrol," she said, "in case you're right and there's some kind of backup team in place."

"Together," he said. "We'll patrol together."

She thought her near-suicidal fall had affected him. In any case, he was that different Maybeck she liked better. They roamed the area, alert for anything out of place, the slightest movement of a shadow, the tiniest of sounds. Somewhere near the art shop Maybeck took her hand and Charlene let him. It wasn't possessive or romantic. It was brotherly.

But it felt good.

To both of them.

5

SECOND PERIOD, Willa and Philby found themselves together in History. Both wanted to discuss Finn's bedroom attack, having been texted about it, but Mr. E. didn't appreciate "background noise."

Mr. Eisenower consistently won Edgewater High's annual "Best Teacher Award," which at least made the class tolerable. Today's class had been on the origins of mythological creatures, inspired in part by Rick Riordan's Percy Jackson series, which had swept through middle school like wildfire a few years before.

Mr. E. narrated a Keynote slide show of all sorts of weird and twisted creatures created in mythologies ranging from Indonesia to the Greeks and Africans. It was one of those blocks where no one fell asleep. Nearing the end of the period he showed a picture of Camazotz, the Mayan bat god. Both Willa and Philby gasped from opposite sides of the room.

Mr. E., who could put up with all sorts of distractions, did not appreciate being interrupted. Ever.

"Mr. Philby? Miss Angelo? Something you'd like to share with us?"

"No, sir!" Philby answered.

"Let me have both your phones, please."

The class *oohed* and stirred. A teacher reading through one's texts promised nuclear devastation. Ridicule. Social-life disaster. Romantic embarrassment. Detention.

"But—"

"Now!" Mr. E. extended his hand.

"I wasn't texting *him!*" complained Willa, hoping to take the pressure off him. The girls in the class giggled.

Philby turned to face Willa and clearly mouthed, *I don't need your help!*

"I don't want to hear it! And if I see your hand anywhere near that keyboard, Mr. Philby, it's automatic detention." Another collective gasp from the class. Detention had been moved to Saturdays several months earlier and was a curse of epic proportions.

Philby dragged himself to the front of class, understanding why some kids deleted their messages each night (to hide them from spying adults). He had never had any reason to do that. His only texts were with Finn and the other Keepers. But now, a few steps from handing over his phone, he was paralyzed by the idea that Mr. E. might intercept those particular texts. They suddenly struck him as top secret. Adding to his paranoia was that Willa's texts would, in many instances, reference or reply to Philby's. The existence of a group of teenagers battling the evil forces inside Walt Disney World was rumor compounded by speculation. Newspapers had written about it. A few blogs and Internet radio shows had reported it as if fact. To some, Finn, Philby, Maybeck, Willa, and Charlene were cult heroes. But there had never been any proof. They were stories, and that's all.

But Philby's phone contained a good deal of circumstantial evidence, and he was seriously reluctant to turn it over to Mr. E.

"I give you my word, Mr. E.: I wasn't texting anyone. I promise! I was just . . . scared," he lied. "That's all. Camazotz looks way creepy."

The class guffawed.

"Me too," Willa said from her desk.

Philby's phone hovered over Mr. E.'s open palm. He eyed each of his students warily. Perhaps he'd heard the rumors or read the newspaper articles. Perhaps he didn't want to twist the lid off this particular can of worms.

"I'm willing to stay after class and discuss it," Philby said, sensing the man's reluctance.

"Me too!" Willa repeated. She won some unappreciated giggles from the others.

Mr. E. accepted the phone from Philby.

The class reacted and he shushed them. He placed

Philby's phone on his desk without looking at it.

Philby breathed for what felt like the first time in the past several minutes.

Mr. E. continued the class. Philby returned to his seat and waited out the longest twenty minutes in recent memory.

Once the bell had rung and the students had left, leaving Philby and Willa at the front of the class with their teacher, Mr. E. said, "Don't you have to be somewhere?"

"Study hall," the two said, nearly in unison.

"If you're expecting your phone back, Mr. Philby, you can apply for it at the end of school today."

"Actually, Mr. E., I was wondering if I could mess with your PowerPoint for a minute."

"It's Keynote. What do you mean by 'mess with'?"

"I'd like to combine—"

"Two of the images," Willa said, knowing exactly where Philby was going with this.

Mr. E. smelled a conspiracy. He looked distrustfully between the two.

"Be my guest," he said, motioning to his laptop.

"It's why we . . . what caused . . . I'm sorry I interrupted," Willa said.

A straight-A student, Willa wasn't one Mr. E. could get too upset with. He said nothing.

"It's actually something the class may find interesting," Philby said, sounding like a teacher himself. No stranger to computers, he took over Mr. E.'s laptop, his fingers dancing across the keyboard. Less than a minute later two images appeared on the projected screen.

"On the left, the Minotaur. On the right, Camazotz. And now . . ."

On the screen, the images of the creatures—one, half bull, half man; the other half man, half bat—centered, overlapped, and dissolved into a single image. For a moment, the level of transparency was off, the Minotaur dominating. But Philby quickly adjusted the images to blend together. The face became a Venn diagram, and yet was unmistakable.

"O . . . M . . . G . . ." Willa said.

"What is it?" Mr. E. said.

"Not what, but who," Philby said.

"Okay. I'll play along. Who is it?"

Philby looked to Willa, who couldn't take her eyes off the screen.

"Who is it?" Philby asked Willa.

"It's Chernabog," she whispered.

6

MAYBECK LIVED WITH HIS AUNT above Crazy Glaze, her paint-your-own-pottery shop. It was old, in need of some repair, and located on a busy street with a fair amount of traffic. As he arrived, he could see through the front windows that business was booming, as was nearly always the case after school got out. He headed around back and bounded up the stairs and into the kitchen, which was just behind a storage room that held two small kilns and steel shelves of fired and unfired pottery. He yanked open the refrigerator and found the remnants of a cooked chicken that he devoured in minutes. He drank milk directly from the carton because his aunt wasn't there to scold him and made a peanut butter and banana sandwich—with honey—then strapped on his Crazy Glaze denim apron and prepared to help out front.

He wouldn't think about homework until after the shop closed and they cleaned up; after they cooked and ate dinner together. He and Jelly—his aunt's nickname—were quite the team. While he struggled through geometry, she would watch *Jeopardy!* in her recliner, beating most contestants to the answers in a loud and enthusiastic voice.

The storage room had a lot of freshly painted work on the shelves. Before he went any further, he took several minutes to stack the left kiln to the limit, close it, and set its timer. It was going to be a busy night. There were bigger items that would require the outside kiln. Maybeck began making a mental list of all that had to be done, trying to fit his homework into it. He was dog-tired from the Base patrol the night before—when the Keepers crossed over to their holograms, their sleep was so disrupted it barely counted.

"Bathroom?" he heard a boy's voice say from the main shop. He experienced a brain fart and forgot what he was doing. The voice had triggered this. A familiar voice, he thought. But familiar in the same way a rattle-snake's rattle tells you to jump.

Maybeck didn't hear Jelly tell the boy that the bathroom was off the storage room because his mind was already engaged—defensively. The small room was wall-to-wall steel shelves, with a big worktable in its center like a kitchen island that left extremely narrow aisles between it and the shelves. Every square inch was stacked with breakable pottery. Maybeck was stuck at the horseshoe end with the kilns. Past the table and to the right was the store. Past the table and to the left was the kitchen, and next to it a door to the small customer bathroom. A primitive instinct surged through him the moment he heard the voice: fight or flight. He knew it was no normal customer. Whoever belonged to the voice was after him.

Greg Luowski stepped through the curtain, spotted Maybeck, and smiled grimly.

Maybeck had gotten Finn's text. This was the same creep that had tried to poison his friend.

"Hey," Luowski said. "Bathroom?"

Every nerve in Maybeck's body was tingling as a second boy came through behind Luowski—another boy with green eyes, just like Luowski. They meant trouble. He was outnumbered.

"Right there," Maybeck said, indicating the door, but never taking his eyes off Luowski.

Luowski in turn did not take his eyes off Maybeck as he reached out and spun the somewhat smaller boy around in order to access the boy's backpack. The kid was unfamiliar to Maybeck—small but sturdy with narrow, deep-set eyes. From the backpack, Luowski withdrew what looked like two water guns. He handed one to the other kid.

"What's with the water guns?" Maybeck said, thinking he'd misread the situation and that Luowski simply wanted to fill a water pistol in the bathroom. "I don't think my aunt would appreciate—" He caught himself as Luowski raised the pistol.

Not a water gun after all.

* * *

Maybeck had already taken several steps toward the kitchen door after picking up on the familiar voice. As Luowski reached for the backpack, Maybeck reached for an unfired platter—some kid's attempt at becoming the next Picasso—and raised it like a shield when the water pistols (that weren't water pistols) were aimed at him.

Luowski pulled the trigger and fired.

Not a normal gun. No sound to speak of. No bullets. A vapor trail flickered, like animation.

No, not a vapor trail, he realized, but wires.

The platter broke into colorful pieces that rained down onto the floor along with the projectile: two shiny metal points like the ends of knitting needles. A stun gun, he realized. Luowski had tried to Taser him.

"Wait!" Luowski shouted at his pal, who was taking aim.

This, because Maybeck vanished through the kitchen door seemingly at the speed of light.

At the sound of breaking pottery, Maybeck's aunt pushed through to the back room.

"Terry?"

Luowski's sidekick turned in that direction a fraction of a second before the door came open. The door hit his arm as Jelly stepped through, and reflexively he pulled the trigger.

Maybeck's aunt sank to the floor like a sack of rocks.

Luowski said a string of words that didn't bear repeating. The sidekick dropped the Taser like it had just burned his hand.

Maybeck, two steps into the kitchen, heard his name and felt the floor shake, and he knew Jelly was down. He came back through the door, his engine running on pure adrenaline. He went through Luowski like a weed whacker through tall grass, a blaze of arms and fists and legs. Pottery fell off the shelves, striking the floor percussively. Luowski never knew what hit him: one moment he was standing there freaking out that Robbie Barry had dropped the old lady; the next, he felt like he'd been hit and run over by a truck. He found himself lying on the floor fending off plates and mugs that were raining down from the sky.

Robbie Barry, on the other hand, knew what it was like to be a soda can that someone crushed with their heel before recycling. Maybeck slammed him into the doorjamb, slammed him like he was a housefly.

Jelly mumbled.

Maybeck turned to help her. He was pushed from

behind and had to dive over his aunt and into the shop to avoid falling onto her.

Robbie Barry struggled to his knees and stood up. Luowski helped him through the back door. Maybeck rose to chase them, but his aunt mumbled something. She was semiconscious, muttering like someone in a nightmare. Her customers rushed to her side.

"It's a heart attack!" "She fainted!" "I hope it's not a stroke!"

Maybeck did not object when someone called 911. He wasn't about to tell anyone she'd been shot by a Taser by two kids under the control of a Disney fairy with green skin; if he did that, it wouldn't be Jelly taken to a hospital, it would be him!

He waited by her side. Just before the ambulance arrived she came around. Jelly knew a lot about her nephew's involvement with the Kingdom Keepers. Not all, by any means, but more than most parents or guardians, because her nephew had been the first to be trapped in the Syndrome—held asleep like he was in a coma. So when he leaned in, he whispered, "Please, Jelly, tell them you fainted. They'll run some tests. That's all."

She looked up at Maybeck with fire in her eyes. When his aunt got angry it was like a storm. Typically, Maybeck ran for cover. But not now. He held his own, staring right back at her, challenging her. It would help no one to bring the police into this, and they both knew it.

But deep within Maybeck another storm was brewing: these idiots had brought the fight into his home, had hurt the person closest to him. It aroused a primitive urge in him, one he hadn't felt to this degree before. An urge for revenge: *you have crossed a line you will never cross again.*

With or without his fellow Keepers, Maybeck intended to deliver that message.

7

MANY OF THE KEEPERS were now busier on the weekends than during the school week, trying to balance athletics and social commitments with their Keeper time.

Charlene—she was at cheerleading practice—missed the meeting in the Magic Kingdom's Columbia Harbour House. But the rest of the Kingdom Keepers made it, as did six recent recruits to their cause—four boys and two girls. The meeting was held upstairs where the crowds rarely ventured, in a small room that bridged the boundary between Fantasyland and Liberty Square.

The six newcomers were all Cast Members from the various parks, employees who supported the Kingdom Keepers' cause and had an allegiance to Disney and were sworn to secrecy by the nature of their employment agreements. It made for a tight group, where trust was never questioned.

Finn perched on the edge of a table looking at their faces. He felt a sense of pride and encouragement from there being twelve people where only a short time ago there had been seven. The oldest of the group was in her mid-twenties, a looker by the name of Megan Fuchs, a woman who had once helped the Keepers at DisneyQuest. Two boys were interns for an Imagineer named Alex Wright; because of this, they knew more about the Kingdom Keepers and their current activities than most.

"All of us," Finn began, "are part of the battle for Base." Heads nodded. "Some more than others. Some more in support. We all know it's getting worse there. The other night there was a direct assault. A pair of DHIs turned them back, but the OTs are getting more and more aggressive."

"If there was an enemy to fight, we could fight them," one of the newcomers said.

"Exactly!" Finn said. "The big problem is we don't know where they are and we don't know what they'll do next. Hard to fight an enemy you can't see."

"We see them by day," Megan said. She meant the witches and fairies, Audio-Animatronics and Cast Members, who were Overtakers by night. There was a growing sentiment among legitimate Cast Members to take the battle into the day, when the Overtakers were, in some ways, more vulnerable and more easily identified. But the reality was that it was difficult, if not impossible, to distinguish between a Cast Member playing a villain and the actual villain. Attacking Cast Members was frowned upon.

"If we can't launch our own attacks, then we're always on the defensive," said Bart, one of the two interns. He looked like a surfer. Willa couldn't stop herself from staring at him.

"That's how this goes," Finn said. "We all know the drill. We all know it's bogus."

"If we're always on the defensive, how can we ever win?" said Megan.

"We can win . . ." Finn began. But this was a legitimate issue and one he couldn't easily answer. He offered the short version: ". . . by recapturing Maleficent and Chernabog. By taking Cruella and the Evil Queen prisoner." He thought back to the theft at the library; that had been a missed opportunity. To have seized the three—all the principals but Chernabog—would have set the Overtakers back considerably.

A restaurant worker in uniform and hat went about wiping down some tables in the far corner. Finn motioned for the others to lower their voices. He did so as well.

"What about the home invasions?" Maybeck asked in a whisper. "I say we take out the OTKs right now."

"I agree. It's time," Finn said.

Eyes bulged. Finn had been the voice of calm and

reason for so long no one could believe he would advocate an attack on other kids.

"Finn?" Amanda asked, as if he had to be an impostor.

She and her sister, Jess, changed their looks all the time: hair color, length, makeup, the way they dressed; some believed they were just trying to be cool, but Finn knew that back in Maryland, the girls had been part of a group called the Fairlies—kids with "unusual or paranormal skills." Maybe part of their constant switching of looks had something to do with that.

"I was attacked in bed and nearly poisoned having just returned from crossing over," Finn said. "Maybeck was attacked at home. By Tasers! His aunt was injured." The group muttered among themselves. "It's become too dangerous for us. All of us! Enough is enough."

The murmur grew to a low roar.

"So what do we do?" Amanda asked. Any mention in the press of kids attacking kids might leave a trail to follow to her and her sister. Fairlies were often at the heart of such stories because of their unusual powers.

"I don't know. I'm open to suggestions," Finn said. "But since they're willing to send OTKs after us in our homes, we know how badly the OTs must want us out of the picture. And that must mean that we're doing something right."

"Maybe they're getting close to the end of the Siege," Maybeck suggested.

"Either through withdrawal or a full-scale attack on Base," said Willa.

"I wouldn't be too hasty." It was a man's low, gravelly voice. It belonged to the worker in the corner.

Finn was immediately alarmed that a Cast Member had overheard them. Worse, the old guy—ancient, by the look and sound of him—dared to butt his way into their discussion.

"Wayne?" Willa had a musician's ear. She'd picked out the man's voice instantly.

The Cast Member's tam lifted slightly, and translucent blue eyes appeared beneath a shock of white hair. It was a weathered face from years in sunny Florida, creased with worry lines. Etched with experience.

A sly grin swept over the man's face.

"Present and accounted for," Wayne said.

A collective gasp filled the room as the Keepers and volunteers identified the stranger. Being in a room with Wayne Kresky was like having a meeting with Bob Iger, the CEO of Disney—rare air.

Finn rushed over and hugged the man, experiencing a sense of guilt about his feelings the night before. Suddenly feeling very awkward, he let go of Wayne and returned to his perch facing the others. Wayne smiled at him, but the usual twinkle in the man's eyes was not there. Finn felt the pit return to his stomach.

"Haste makes waste," Wayne said. He introduced himself to the newcomers as "a friend of the parks." But they all knew who he was, if not by recognition, then by reputation.

"These are difficult times, no question. But if I heard right, for you to act against those you refer to as OTKs would be a mistake. This will only incite and inflame and allow your enemies to raise even more volunteers. That is something to avoid at all costs."

"But my aunt!" Maybeck said. "That's not happening again."

"Tasers!" Finn said.

"Yes. Problematic, and worthy of redress. But we must be wise. The smarter the army, the fewer the battles."

"So we just wait for the next attack?" Willa said.

"No. Not hardly," Wayne answered. "We must not be moved off our primary objective: undoing the Overtakers. Reducing their power base. Eliminating them as a viable threat to the Kingdom. I won't, for a moment, pretend we don't all have our individual grudges and causes. But for the moment, we must put these aside in favor of a higher calling."

"And that is?" someone said.

"First, defending the Base. You realize any effort, any energy you put into these OTK attacks is energy drained from the more critical battle."

"That's the point of them, isn't it?" Willa said.

"Of course," he answered. "Distraction is critical to any success in battle. That is why we must meet them head-on. We mount an offensive. It is unexpected. The timing is perfect."

"Tonight?" Finn asked.

"Haste . . ." Wayne said. "Need I remind you? We will act just as soon as we can organize an effective strategy. These things are not to be entered into lightly. There is much at stake."

"How 'bout our survival?" Maybeck asked. "I'm telling you, I am not putting my aunt through that again. I'd rather break some heads than sit around waiting for some dumb plan. No offense."

"The question we must ask ourselves is not how we defeat a particular enemy, but evil itself. Yes? For that's the real battle at hand. Don't be blinded by the powers of someone like Maleficent. Believe me, she is but a puppet. There are far higher powers at work here. Chernabog, for one."

That silenced Wayne's small audience. As far as the Keepers were concerned, things didn't get much scarier and dangerous than Maleficent. The idea she was someone's puppet did not bode well. Wayne had warned about the powers of Chernabog before, but they'd witnessed none of the beast's powers. Like the Yeti he'd once inhabited, he seemed more the puppet— a big, furry nothing. Only once, in a performance of Fantasmic! when Chernabog had transfigured into a dragon, had he presented a real threat. And that had seemed like Maleficent's doing, not his own.

Finn spoke first. "What are you saying?"

"I'm saying we need to present a unified strategy and realize the worst is yet to come."

"Worse than having your aunt Tasered?" Maybeck said.

"Worse," Wayne answered. "I believe an attempt will be made to kill one or more of you."

"You mean the Syndrome, don't you?" Willa said. "To put us in the Syndrome?"

"No. I mean what I said." Wayne settled in, sitting next to Finn on the windowsill. He looked ridiculous in the costume. "For months our technicians have been attempting to pin down the location of the Overtakers' DHI server. This is nothing terribly new, unfortunately. We've been through this before."

Philby nodded. He and Wayne had once entered the parks' Virtual Maintenance Network as gaming avatars in an attempt to defeat the Overtakers. He liked the man and Wayne liked him. He cradled his phone in the pocket of his shorts, happy to have gotten it back after Mr. E.'s imposed study hall; he hated being without it.

"We possess highly sophisticated equipment for such efforts," Wayne continued, "and yet the Overtakers continue to elude us. The Internet protocol address continues to move from place to place. We send in a strike team: no server. We've repeated this pattern, well . . . repeatedly. The only consistency in the pattern is that the IP address holds to coastal cities like Boca and Miami. That brings us to the more urgent topic at hand." He surveyed the faces gazing up at him. So young, he thought, recalling his own youth and the heady days leading up to his career with Disney. "The upcoming cruise has been well publicized, as has your participation in it."

The Keepers had connected a comment Maleficent had recently made to one of Jess's drawings of a uniformed officer. At the time, it had seemed as if Maleficent intended to steal the *Magic*—a Disney cruise ship. Now, the reminder of the upcoming cruise made Finn wonder if they'd gotten the ship wrong. Was it the *Dream*? Was it the cruise they were all about to take?

Finn interrupted. "But you told me the cruise was no big deal!"

"Things change, Finn."

Finn shuddered. Wayne had said it so condescendingly. Like he wanted to humiliate Finn in front of the others.

"Security on the *Dream*, as with all our cruise ships, is the best in the business," Wayne continued. "Better than any other line. But I put nothing past the Overtakers. Disappearance is the most convenient form of murder."

Amanda whispered to Jess, and they both looked over at Wayne.

"I don't love the sound of that," Maybeck said.

"A man overboard is a body never found," Wayne said. "It has never happened on a Disney cruise ship, but it has on others."

"That guy who threw his wife over the rail," Jess said.

"Among several others," Wayne said. "Yes. Should the Overtakers find a way to get aboard, or send their agents . . ."

"OTKs," Philby said.

"It would make for an easy way for them to do away with at least a few of you."

"Lousy Luowski is not a murderer," Finn said. "A tool, yes. But not a murderer."

"But if under a spell?" Wayne asked. "Can we be so certain these kids are acting of their own accord when they are attempting such heinous acts as poisoning and Tasering?"

"They're under spells?" Finn said.

"Do you have a more suitable explanation?" Wayne asked. "Finn, you watched that silly recruitment video. You think that explains how Maleficent has been able to enlist so many students so quickly? By some counts they have dozens."

A unison gasp filled the room. This was new information to all, including the Keepers.

"Then what?" Finn said.

"I have no proof," Wayne said.

"But you suspect something."

"I suspect it's not a video, but a spell. I suspect she 'owns' them."

For a moment only the joyful sounds of the park could be heard.

"I have no proof," Wayne repeated quickly.

"The green eyes are proof," Finn said. "They aren't contact lenses. I got close enough to one of them to see."

Another group gasp.

"Wait a second! Are you saying any kid aboard the *Dream* could be a potential murderer?" Willa asked.

"The desire to reduce your numbers, your effectiveness, cannot be ignored," Wayne said. "We are considering all options."

"DHIs," Philby said. "Version 2.0. If they throw our DHIs overboard, all we have to do is return. No harm. No foul."

Looking squarely at Finn, as if warning him, Wayne spoke. "There's always one in every crowd." For years that "one" had been Finn; he'd nearly always been the first to understand a given situation. Was Wayne cautioning him that his standing as the leader of the Keepers was not to be taken for granted? Philby always had the jump on technical stuff. His jumping to such a conclusion was to be expected! Wasn't it?

"With 2.0," Philby continued, "there's no way to tell the difference. No more blue line. We can allow ourselves to touch, or be touched. What if we just go aboard as DHIs?"

"A nice solution if your DHIs weren't already part of the plan, part of the canal inaugural."

"What inaugural? What's going on?" a volunteer asked.

"A fair question," Wayne said. "A new, larger set of locks on the Panama Canal is to be opened to commercial traffic. Many companies bid for the right to be the first ship through the locks—a terrific publicity opportunity, and one for the history books. Disney was awarded the prize, most likely because of our representing family and family values. And," he winked, "because we bid more than the others." Everyone laughed. "The *Dream*, the first of a new class of Disney Cruise Line ships, is to make the inaugural voyage, Cape Canaveral to Los Angeles. At the same time, the DHI next-generation entertainment is to be rolled out on all the cruise ships. The company has combined the two events: the debut of Disney Hosts Interactive on the cruise line with the first ship to pass through the new locks. More bang for the buck."

"Let's hope not," Willa said.

A nervous chuckle rippled through the room.

"Wanda is working on Taser-proof undergarments." Another rush of snickering. Wanda Alcott, Wayne's daughter, had come to their aid before. "Kind of like a space age chain mail. A grounding device that dissipates the electrical charge. Necessary for you because your DHIs will be on board the ship at the same time you are."

"But if at night we could find safe places to sleep . . . when our DHIs were thought to be down," Philby said, unwilling to take no for an answer. "We could be out there and relatively safe from attack."

"No question," Wayne said. "The protection is critical, however. While you are asleep you will be at your most vulnerable."

"I can work on that," Philby said.

"Can I ask a question?" A volunteer had his hand raised. Kenny Carlson, a freckled redhead who, at six feet one, could have used twenty pounds. Ninth grade was an unfair time of life.

Wayne nodded.

"Exactly where do we fit into all this?" Kenny asked. He indicated the other volunteers.

"I'm glad you asked that, Mr. Carlson," Wayne said.

Kenny looked like he'd been slapped. Wayne knew his name. Wayne had done his homework. Clearly, a volunteer wasn't allowed into the Keepers without a background check.

"First, we need a team at the Base. We cannot simply abandon that battle. While a possible diversion, the Base's role in the parks is too critical to be ignored. We are in the process of moving significant equipment during daylight hours to reduce our losses if we should lose the Base—but at the same time, we are aware this might be what they want: for us to spread our servers out and make it easier for them to steal them. It's a shell game."

"And second?" Kenny said.

"It's my intention to put as many of you as possible aboard the *Dream*. This will be more difficult than it sounds and will involve an intense orientation to accomplish. Once on board, you will be a resource for the Keepers to draw upon."

"Cool," Kenny said. "I'm down with that."

"Ditto!" said someone else in the group.

"I wouldn't get my hopes up," Wayne said. "Both options come with risk."

"I think we knew that going in," Kenny said.

"If I could have a few minutes with the Keepers alone," Wayne said. "Amanda and Jess, please stay as well."

"We'll meet you outside," Finn said.

The six volunteers left. Wayne and the Keepers clustered tightly around a table. He kept his voice to a whisper.

"The cruise is an obligation we can't get you out of and, as much as it might have once seemed like a dream come true—pun intended—it now appears much the opposite. There is a great deal to accomplish. The volunteers need training. Everything you can do to school them is not just important, but critical at this juncture. Once on the ship you must take every precaution for your safety. Travel in pairs. Enter your staterooms with caution. You are in a contained space on that ship, a finite space, a situation you've not faced before. The journal Finn and Willa saw taken by the Overtakers involves, among other subjects, the lore behind Chernabog."

Willa and Finn exchanged a knowing glance.

"And there were hyenas," Finn said. "Angry hyenas."

"Excuse me?" Willa inquired.

"The chase?"

"What chase? What are you talking about?" Willa said.

Wayne fixed his concentration upon her. "You don't recall being pursued by hyenas?" He checked over with Finn.

"Of course I do," Willa said.

Finn said to Willa, "In the factory? Or whatever?"

"What factory? Whatever . . . are you talking about?"

"But you remember Maleficent. The Evil Queen?"

"In the library? Dah."

"And then we took off through the factory."

"No. Then we were backstage at the Studios and we returned."

A hushed silence as Finn considered not only what she was telling him, but her conviction. They both had two very different memories of the same moment.

Finn met eyes with Wayne. "What's going on?"

Wayne shook his head, confused.

"I dreamed it?" Finn said, still looking directly at Wayne.

"Well, I didn't," Willa said. "The library *is* backstage at the Studios, after all."

"Maybe you had a dream like mine," Jess said. She, who could dream the future.

"More likely just a nightmare," Finn said. "Or a bug in 2.0." But he wondered if it was possible. Had he dreamed the future, confused the present, imagined something out of thin air?

"Now you know how it feels," Jess said. "Unsettling, isn't it?"

"Not good," he said.

"Not good at all," she said. "And yet, they call it a gift."

"Okay. I get it." He and the other Keepers were guilty of thinking Jess and Amanda were gifted. The girls had argued "cursed."

He continued, "It was just like any other crossing over."

"Surprisingly real," Jess said. "As real as it gets."

Wayne appeared troubled by the news. "While I welcome such resources," the older man said, "this is not a time for personality shifts. We require each of you in full control of your faculties. We cannot have you doubting things."

He made it sound like a reprimand.

"I'm sorry, Finn," Willa said. "I didn't mean to freak you out or anything."

"Not your problem," Finn said.

"Wanda will get the suits to you. Wear them," Wayne said. "Use them. A Taser would be an effective weapon against you as it would knock you unconscious and render you susceptible to a rogue DHI server. We should have foreseen this. Once asleep, if they regain the ability to cross you over—which they might if they get control of the Base—they could trap your DHI and lock you in the Sleeping Beauty Syndrome."

Wayne's explanation hung over the group like a foul smell.

"I will speak with Finn for a moment," Wayne announced. "Then we are done here."

The Keepers and "the sisters" dispersed in clusters, heading out to connect with the volunteers.

Finn had been blindsided by Willa's disclaimer. His mouth was dry. He felt feverish.

Wayne said, "There's someone you must meet."

8

SOMEPLACE DARK. Fabric walls. A black floor. Shifting scenes between a girl trapped by adults and the steady advance of three dark silhouettes.

Women, by their swaying hips and steady gaits.

Then . . .

An enormous wooden crate. The girl again, with nowhere to go.

And the sounds, distant yet present. Alluring. Compelling. Yet frightening.

Water. Big water.

The creaking of metal.

The women again, now exuding a malignant presence.

She backed up into the fabric wall and stumbled. It failed to support her. It moved.

A curtain.

A ship.

Jess sat bolt upright in bed, reaching automatically for her journal, as was her way. She sketched furiously, pencil to paper even before she switched on the Itty Bitty Book Light.

Amanda's face appeared in the gloom from the overhead bunk.

"Another one?"

But Jess didn't need to answer. The sweat on her face and the terror in her eyes said it all. Nonetheless, she did answer.

"We need help," she said.

* * *

It wasn't fair to call it prison. Being underage and homeless, there were a lot worse situations than living with a bunch of other kids, even if the adults that fed you and schooled you also studied your every fiber. You could come and go as long as you were willing to submit to wearing an ankle bracelet tracking device.

But the rules specified "no unauthorized contact," which translated loosely to the monitoring of Internet and mobile phone connections, where applicable. Mattie Weaver could have friends, but the friendships would be watched. They would be cut off and refused if deemed a threat to what was termed "the Project."

Because of this, Mattie needed the help of her fellow Fairlies—as in "fairly human." Kids with unusual abilities. When tracked in groups, the Fairlies caused far less concern in those responsible for their containment. It was the "rogue," the kid that wandered off alone, that won attention.

They stopped at Ground Central, a popular local coffee bar and Internet café. While a few of her friends ordered drinks, two others used the washroom, allowing Mattie to use one of the computer terminals immediately adjacent to the washroom. The girls rotated use of the computer, switching places. They checked Internet mailboxes that their government overseers did not know about. They checked their Facebook pages and other sites. All in secret.

Mattie saw her reflection in a mirror behind the computers—two small scars on her lower lip where the piercings had been. Only the faint remains of the rust red that had once been her hair color, her natural black grown out six inches. The lonely, searching eyes she couldn't stand looking back at her. She glanced away.

Whoever was monitoring their ankle bracelets saw only a group of the girls at a coffee shop. If he zoomed in, he might be able to see them move from the front of the store to the back—where the washroom was located. No one knew the extent of their abilities, but put nothing past them.

One particular email threw Mattie's heart into a flutter. She knew who belonged to the fake identity— Cary Shute. Knew the importance of what would turn out to be a coded message. She copied it word for word, returning to the barracks before using a Holy Bible to decode it. Sometimes the translations needed translations because the Bible didn't always offer the most easily understood verbiage.

SONS AND DAUGHTERS REQUIRE GRACE MAKE
ASSIST PASSAGE FROM STORY DREAM BOAT . . .

And a date, only days away.

Sons and daughters equaled *family*, she thought, or *friends*.

Need help.

A story about a boat would help her to gain passage? Noah? she wondered . . . someone named Noah?

The date was self-explanatory.

The email was from a friend who'd escaped the barracks with another girl several years ago. The system to escape still existed.

Amanda needed her.

It was her turn to try.

9

THE LIVING ROOM CURTAINS rustled behind an evening breeze and created a gentle flapping sound, like a dog scratching. There was no other sound in the room except for Finn's expectant breathing as he awaited his mother's decision. He'd taken a big risk including her, and they both knew it. But without her participation and blessing, the mission Wayne had assigned him would require him to lie and cheat. At least this way if he broke the rules she would know why.

When his mother was upset, her face pinched and she resembled a bird. And not a pretty bird, but a bird of prey. Finn saw people this way: as extensions of animals like bulldogs and lizards. His mother was definitely a bird.

"If you're going to ask these things of me," she whispered harshly, "at least you can make the request reasonable."

"But if it's not reasonable in the first place, how am I supposed to change it?"

"I'm not asking you to change it. I'm asking you to decline the request in the first place so we don't have to deal with it."

"So I'm just supposed to tell him no?" Wouldn't Wayne just turn to Philby if Finn declined an assignment? There was no way Finn was going to let that happen.

"That's exactly what you should have told him," she hissed. "Look at the situation he has put us in!"

"But he wouldn't ask if there wasn't already a situation. So what makes our situation so much more important than his?"

Stumped, she glowered at him. "Don't twist my words, young man."

"Everything all right in there?" Finn's father called from the television room. Normally a man without a clue, he must have picked up on their silence. Typically, Finn and his mom were anything but quiet around the house, with her barking orders to pick up after himself or set the table or do the dishes or take out the trash. His little sister moved about like a ghost, doing everything right, winning the adoring affection of her parents and ignoring Finn to where half the time he forgot she lived there.

"Fine!" his mother called through the wall.

"Awfully quiet in there."

To that she said nothing. She waited for the TV's mute to go off. An end of an ad played, replaced by the late news.

"I can do it with you or without you," Finn said.

"Don't do that. It's beneath you."

"I'm just saying."

"Well, don't. You know how I feel about you trying to manipulate me."

"The wart does it all the time."

"Don't call your sister that."

"She does manipulate you."

"She does not. I'm quite aware of when I'm being played, believe me. If I go along with it, there's a reason: like straight As and completing her piano practice each and every night."

"So now you're manipulating me?" he said.

She cracked a smile. "Guilty." Her eyes shone. He loved her to his core when she looked like that at him. He also knew he'd won. They had something of a magical connection, he and his mom. The arguments were over.

"We'll have to think up a darn good excuse," she whispered. "He's not stupid, you know."

"What about something to do with Groupon?" Finn's father was consumed with Groupon deals. He was buying stuff and signing up for stuff he had no use for simply because it was seventy percent off.

"You really did inherit my brains," his mother said.

"If you do say so."

"And I do." Another of those smiles of hers. "Trouble is, he checks them all."

"Then Living Social?"

"Good one! Sports clothing at Downtown Disney," she said. "Late night sale."

His father unconditionally supported any purchase related to sports, wishing Finn was more interested.

"What a team," he said.

"We are, aren't we?"

"What's all the excitement?" his father called out.

In the course of their enthusiasm they'd allowed their voices to raise. Another ad break.

Finn circled his hand, encouraging her to speak up. One had to seize such golden opportunities where his father was concerned.

"We're going to run out for a while," she hollered. Then she stood and walked in to speak with him since one of the many house rules was no shouting. Shortly after, the two were in the car, and Finn was telling his mother to shut her eyes so he could change into his bathing suit.

"I can't shut my eyes! I'm driving."

He climbed into the back and changed, then returned to the front passenger seat, his shorts worn under his suit.

"I would hope you wouldn't need that," his mother said.

"Typhoon Lagoon is a water park, Mom."

"Don't get smart with me."

He had a comeback to that, but he swallowed it. "I'm just saying I want to be ready."

"You'll be careful."

"I'm always careful."

She had a comeback to that, but she swallowed it.

* * *

He'd never arrived at Typhoon Lagoon at night. The palm trees formed a dark throat that swallowed the car. The attraction lit the night sky above it as if a UFO had landed in the jungle.

"You sure he said ten o'clock?" his mother asked from behind the wheel.

"Positive."

"Why so late?"

"How should I know? It's Wayne. It's what he told me to do. He does things his way. At least we're not the only ones here." The huge parking lot held some parked cars scattered in spaces nearest the entrance.

"Wouldn't you be safer crossed over? As your DHI?"

The thing about his mom was that she understood the technology as well as Philby did. Better than her own son, which put Finn at a disadvantage. But he obviously knew stuff she didn't.

"Our DHIs aren't projected here. We aren't installed in the water parks yet."

"Did you see that?" his mother said, jerking her head and grabbing the car's rearview mirror.

Finn spun in his seat. "See what?"

"It was like . . . nah . . ."

"Like what?"

"Never mind."

"Mom!"

"I thought I saw someone . . . well . . . sneaking around back there."

"Where?"

"At the edge of the parking lot."

"Seriously?"

"A shadow is all."

"Not necessarily," he said. "Besides, there're not that many lights back there to cast shadows."

"I'm jumpy is all."

"I'm going to be fine, Mom."

"Keep your phone on," she said. "I'll call you if I see anything else."

"My scout," he said.

"Don't push it."

"While you're at it? Lock the doors."

"If you're trying to scare me, it's working."

"I'm trying to be smart," he said, quoting her. "When in doubt, do it the smart way" was a favorite expression of hers. He'd pick up points with her where he could. Parents loved to hear themselves quoted.

"Do be smart," she said, her eyes tracking to the rearview mirror surreptitiously. Whatever she'd seen back there had stayed with her whether she was going to admit it or not.

"I'm on the guest list," Finn told the woman at the ticket booth. Technically, the park closed early, usually between five and eight depending on the season and day of the week. Tonight a part of it was rented out for a private party, just as Wayne had said it would be. The party was taking place in Crush 'n' Gusher, leaving the rest of the park off limits. But Wayne had told him there were ways to get around that as well.

"Aren't you . . . ?" the woman said, studying him more closely.

"Finn Whitman."

"One of the guides."

"A Disney host. Yes."

"Well, I'll be. Nice to meet you." She leaned into the counter. "Listen . . . is there any truth to the—"

"Great place you have here," he said, cutting her off. People were always asking about whether the Kingdom

Keepers actually existed. The nondisclosure agreement Finn and the others had signed prevented him from giving a straight answer even if he'd wanted to, which he didn't. The Kingdom Keepers was like one of those super-secret clubs at Yale or Harvard. It wasn't something you advertised.

"You're welcome here anytime," the woman said.

Just as Wayne had predicted.

"You wouldn't mind then if I walked around a little?" he asked. "If I didn't spend all of my time in Crush 'n' Gusher?"

"Let's just say we have a friend in common, you and me," the woman said. "So far as I'm concerned, you can go anywhere your little heart desires. No one's going to mess with you. In fact, you have the park to yourself. That's what our friend asked for. We'll be closing down the party soon."

"I just want a look around," he said.

She winked. "Sure you do." She came through the door and opened the gate nearest the ticket booth. "Go ahead, have a look around."

"It's not like that," he said. "I'm just going to meet someone."

"Sure you are, sweetness. You go right ahead. Meet whomever you want." She motioned him through the gate.

He wasn't sure he wanted to go any farther.

People got goofy around him and the others. More so lately than ever before. Grown-ups. Children. Teachers. It didn't seem to matter. His mother called it celebrity. But if this was celebrity, he felt sorry for famous people. Perfectly nice people melted down into blubbering fools around celebrities. Women behind counters allowed you access they shouldn't. Doors were opened that shouldn't be opened for you. Maybeck could get into any club he wanted. Thankfully he didn't want to get into any clubs. But at fifteen he was underage, so what was with that? It was like people wanted so badly to give you stuff that they'd poison you just to say they were the ones who had done it. Fame was not for the weak-minded. Being adored was dangerous.

Finn heard the partying over at Crush 'n' Gusher and felt heavily tempted to blow off the Wayne assignment and ride the slides. It was probably college kids. He wondered what kind of parent could afford to rent Typhoon Lagoon for their kid's party. Only one answer: a very rich one. Finn was not rich. He didn't know how to act around rich people. Once across the bridge over Castaway Creek he turned left as Wayne had instructed, though was once again tempted by the sound of laughter and squeals of joy over at the Crush.

He continued around the curve toward Keelhaul

and Mayday Falls, all alone. As a Keeper, Finn was accustomed to empty parks, the vastness, the creepiness, but Typhoon Lagoon was a new one for him, and it took some getting used to. The water in the surf pool was as flat and shiny as an ice rink. But the waterfalls and slides were all running, the churning sound filling the night air. It was the emptiness that creeped him out. What had Wayne gotten him into? He was used to a thousand screaming kids here. Besides the rush of water there was only the occasional shriek from Crush 'n' Gusher to keep him company.

As Wayne had instructed, he took the long way around to the Typhoon Boatworks, though it seemed wrong not to take the more direct route. He wasn't sure why Wayne wanted this, but Finn assumed it was to keep him from getting too close to the party and needing to explain himself. Or maybe it was so that someone could keep an eye on him and make sure he wasn't being followed. Or maybe it was so he could figure out if someone was following him. Or maybe Wayne was losing a step. Maybe Wayne was a few quarts low. He recalled his mother's attention to her rearview mirror and he felt a shiver. After becoming a DHI and Kingdom Keeper his life had transformed into a complex of alliances and enemies. He didn't wish such an existence on anyone. It wasn't like he was a superhero; he was just a kid. But he had superhero issues to deal with.

Finn kept away from the edge of the Surf Pool, though he wanted to climb to the lookout. He took the tunnel that led to the path behind the wave-generator wall, now on the Mountain Trail and continuing toward Humunga Kowabunga, his second-favorite spot in the park after StormSlides.

He heard something behind him and stopped short. The scuffing continued briefly, but stopped abruptly. In his former life he might have called out to see who was there. But not as a Keeper. He ducked into the foliage and squatted low, trying to be quiet. He broke a small branch on a bush and to him it sounded as loud as a starting pistol. He waited and waited, wondering if it had only been his imagination since no one appeared and he heard nothing out of the ordinary—only the distant euphoria of the party echoing throughout the empty park. Finally he summoned his courage and re-entered the trails.

But within a few steps he heard the same sound again. This time he identified it more as plastic on stone. Like a bucket being dragged or a water bottle being set down onto a hard surface. Not a single bucket. Many buckets.

Again he hid in the foliage, pushed back away from the path, but still with a view of it.

106

The sounds grew closer and his fear intensified. They weren't human sounds.

When he first saw them, his body went cold. He mistook them for crash-test dummies—"CTDs" in Keeper speak—from Epcot's Test Track: Overtakers that had challenged him and other Keepers on multiple occasions. The CTDs were inhuman robots programmed by the Overtakers for only one mission: to catch and kill Keepers. They carried onboard heat sensors, high-def video cameras with scanning capabilities (as eyes), super-sensitive audio enhancement (ears), and no human emotion or fear. Finn was a sitting duck.

Only then did he see his mistake. They weren't CTDs.

Two of the six were smaller than the four others. Immature dummies. Teenagers, Finn realized. They were rescue dummies used for lifesaving and water rescue drills and training. Their limbs were all messed up—feet pointing backward, arms twisted inhumanly. They stumbled along like six zombies: four adult dummies and the two teens. All boys. Bare plastic chests for the application of CPR. Epcot's crash-test dummies at least looked somewhat human. The rescue dummies looked more like something raised from the dead—a leg dragging, arms flapping at their sides, blank faces.

Their limbs were combinations of soft padding and hard plastic. How the things could even stand without support was beyond explanation—unless one considered Maleficent's awesome powers.

Why hadn't Wayne warned him about them? He held his breath and allowed them to pass. A stupid mistake. It put the rescue dummies between him and the Boatworks. After a moment he slipped back out onto the pathway behind the wave-generating wall. He hurried ahead, spotted the dummies from the back, and climbed through the landscaping and over some rocks and lowered himself to a stairway. It took him a moment to recognize it as the entrance to Humunga. He started down, not far now from the Boatworks shop. He turned a corner and was face to no face with one of the teenage rescue dummies. The mutant slapped the side of its upper leg. It was as loud as a drum, and the rhythm was organized. A code! The dummies couldn't talk, but they could drum signals. By the sound of clomping plastic moving toward Finn, he realized this one had called the others.

Finn turned and ran up the stairs as fast as his legs would carry him. From what he'd seen, there was no way the zombies could match his pace. He climbed higher, glancing back and seeing no one. But the sounds were unmistakable: he was being followed.

He reached the top—practically at *Miss Tilly*, the wrecked boat at the very top of everything—and faced the dark, open mouths of three tubes. Water gushed into each. No problem, Finn told himself, as he launched himself feet-first down the middle tube. He had to shut his mouth to keep from screaming. Although inside a tube—a tube carrying water—the initial drop was more like falling out a window. Straight down, as fast as gravity could pull him. Finally his seat found the water and he slid, insanely fast, down the remainder of the ride and was braked by the water in a level stretch of open tube. He opened his eyes.

Rescue dummies. Two adults on the other side of the tube to his right. He cursed his luck that he'd been stalked by dummies with brains. Why couldn't he have gotten the real dummies? The ones with stuffing for brains? These two had stayed behind to cut off his escape from the slides.

Finn pulled himself out of the slide, hurrying away. Behind him, the dummies that had been chasing him arrived at the bottom of the slides and proceeded to knock down the two adult dummies.

Not wanting to lead them to the Boatworks and his rendezvous, Finn scrambled over a wall and headed for the body slides. He made a point of leaving wet footprints heading up the steps, but then jumped the wall and ducked behind some bushes. A moment later, four of the rescue dummies hurried past and up the steps. Again, this left two unaccounted for—no doubt they were waiting below. Finn crawled over the rocks and stayed away from the small pool where the body slides terminated. He flattened himself to the ground as he spotted the two adult dummies. Checked how far it was to the Boatworks. Too far, with too much open space. He'd be seen. No matter what, he couldn't compromise the meeting Wayne had planned for him.

The head on one of the dummies pivoted around like an owl's. Finn ducked, but just a bit too late. He heard the clomping of plastic on concrete and knew he was toast.

He tried to collect himself, to settle down, but he brushed his hand against a cactus and it stuck him with a couple dozen fiery needles.

The two dummies drummed on their thighs and chests in a primitive dance that terrified Finn. Maybe they were talking to each other, or maybe they were just excited; whatever it was, they were freaks. Arm burning, Finn carefully snapped off a paddle of cactus and pushed through the planting toward the two rescue dummies, determined to make his confrontation before others arrived. He had no idea if they felt anything; no idea if his weapon would make any difference. He jumped off the wall, and the two stepped back, wary of him. That was encouraging.

He wondered at their role. Were they after him? Were they just Overtaker sentries who roamed the park at night? Who had charmed them to life, and why?

They tapped out code to each other and widened the distance between them, doing a more effective job of boxing Finn in. One of the teenage dummies arrived via a slide into the landing pool, stealing the attention of one of the adults just for an instant. Finn lunged forward and raked the cactus paddle down the fabric section of the dummy's arm.

No reaction. No nerves, Finn thought.

The dummy looked back at Finn, annoyed, but not harmed or in any kind of pain.

When the other dummy raised its plastic fists, Finn knew he had serious problems. No way to hurt them, nothing for them to fear.

The smaller dummy climbed out of the pool, making it three to one.

Then Finn saw a flash of color on his right.

Stitch.

Finn was well familiar with Stitch. It wasn't a costume. This was the real Stitch. The character's mouth and eyes moved. His facial skin looked oily in the dim light. He was not happy. Not at all. He was angry and troubled, and all of that anger was aimed at the dummies. He stuck out his jaw, revealing rows of sharp teeth. Finn felt a chill. The creature growled and took a step toward the dummies; all three took a step back. There was clearly a history between them, and Finn had little doubt who had the upper hand. Stitch stepped between Finn and the dummies. Now three others arrived into the landing pool. They saw Stitch and took off in the other direction.

Stitch's right arm waved. It took Finn a moment to realize the gesture was meant for him, that Stitch was telling him to get out of there. Finn slipped to the side and took off running.

Behind him, he heard a shriek that had to be Stitch. Frantic drumming that had to be the dummies. Then more growling and guttural sounds. Something flew through the air, landing on the path in front of him. It was part of an arm—a torn dummy arm, bite mark apparent. More disgusting sounds behind him, and the drumming suddenly stopped.

Finn ran hard and fast, skidding to a stop in front of the Boatworks cabin.

He faced a good-looking girl wearing Typhoon Lagoon Cast Member shorts and shirt.

"I'm Melanie." She was older than he was. She had

dark blue eyes and a pretty face. In school she would have been considered hot.

"Finn."

"Yes. Can I just say that you and your friends are doing the greatest thing ever."

He wondered if she knew CPR. He thought his heart had stopped.

"Ah . . . thanks." Real suave of him. Hard to think up such a smooth response.

"We'll do anything, anytime, to help you. Seriously, anything."

"Thanks," he said. On a real roll.

"You and I could text if you want. So you could contact me."

"That'd be good. I'd like that."

"Only if you want."

"I do!" Way too enthusiastic.

"There are a lot of us willing to help. No way we want Maleficent as our boss."

"Overtakers," Finn said. "We call them Overtakers."

"You can text me anytime." She pulled out her iPhone, reciting her number. Finn pulled out his phone, but it was dripping water.

"Maybe another time," he said.

She giggled.

"Lilo asked me to give you this," she said, indicating

a surfboard. "All you have to do is paddle. But you'll need a rash jacket, and I have a full wet suit for you if you'd rather."

"I'm going surfing?" Finn asked.

She glanced toward the Surf Pool and then at Finn as if he had to be mental.

"Ah . . . yeah. Listen, I don't know what's going on. Only that Lilo wanted me to give you this stuff and make sure you get in the water. Then I'm supposed to clear out. Crush 'n' Gusher is shutting down for the night right now."

"I'm going to be in here alone?" If he had tried to sound like a six-year-old he couldn't have done a better job of it.

"That seems like the plan."

"No problem," he said, trying to correct the situation.

"Here, let me help you." She held out the neoprene rash jacket.

Finn undressed down to his swim trunks. She just stood there watching him, holding the jacket. She helped him into the vest.

"Lie flat on the board, your feet hanging off the back. Paddle with both hands. You can kick, too. Normally we would have you approach the wall and turn around and paddle out about ten yards—that's where the waves come from. But for whatever reason, I was told to tell you to paddle into the middle, facing the wall, and just hang out. If a wave should come, you'll just bob up over it."

"Thanks, Melanie."

"No worries."

Not for you, Finn was thinking.

"Down the stairs. Careful because they can be slippery. I'll toss your board in." She lifted the long board like it was nothing, walked to the rail, and lowered it, dropping it into the water.

"Okay, then," Finn said.

"Nice meeting you. And I mean it. There are a bunch of us that think what you're doing is awesome. We'd love to help. Or just hang out. Or whatever."

"Sure," he said, returning to his non-sentences. A thought occurred to him a moment too late: what if the Overtakers had replaced his contact at the Boatworks with an OTK? Could anyone be as nice as Melanie to a total stranger?

He made his way down the stairs and jumped into the water. In the distance, he saw a Cast Member escorting the partying kids from Crush 'n' Gusher out of the park.

Once in the water, he looked back up the steps.

Melanie was gone.

10

WHILE PHILBY REMAINED LOCKED in his room with a towel across the base of his door to block any light from giving him away, Willa, Maybeck, and Charlene were riding in the back of a Pargo toward the Base in Disney's Hollywood Studios. Each carried a large water gun—filled with ammonia—capable of shooting thirty feet. The air was thick with humidity and smelled of burning rubber, the remains of a late rehearsal at the stunt show. The park's backstage area was like a warehouse district—nondescript, steel-sided one- and two-story buildings, bland and boring. But the three holograms hidden behind a bench seat on the Pargo could feel their hearts pounding, another unexpected result of the upgrade to 2.0.

The Overtakers could be anywhere. The Fantasmic! show was known as an outpost for them—a place the real villains could blend in with their Cast Member counterparts. Despite security screening to prevent such substitutions, the Overtakers' powers were not to be underestimated. On a night like this, when an assault on the Base was anticipated, it wasn't a question of if but where they were gathered.

Maybeck rolled out of the Pargo first, taking advantage of his holographic state. He rolled across the pavement, never feeling a thing, and crawled quickly into the shadow of a nearby building. He watched as Willa went next. Then the Pargo disappeared around the corner. Charlene was scheduled to bail out on the turn. If she did so, he didn't see it. With everyone in place, while not perfect, they had decent views of all four sides of the two-story building that housed the Base.

A dark window on the second floor filled with light and then went black again, the signal to Maybeck that Kenny Carlson, along with another boy and two girl recruits, had successfully crossed over as DHIs. It was a historic accomplishment: seven DHIs already backstage. When and if Amanda and Jess crossed over there would be nine.

Maybeck practiced control of 2.0 by reaching out and touching the crate he hid behind, and then, with his next effort, burying the arm of his hologram up to the elbow. He'd worked on shortening the time needed to jump between the two states, finding the bandwidth ample enough to allow incredibly quick switching. They were just scratching the surface of 2.0, but already it was like an entirely new experience.

Willa waved and he signaled back. Time slowed—either a product of 2.0 or his own nerves. He didn't want to know which. The Cast Members inside the Base were no match for the Overtakers. A computer operator didn't have a lot of skills when matched with a flame-throwing fairy. It left him and the others as the last line of defense—which no doubt made the Cast Members uneasy.

A streak to Maybeck's left. A hunched figure was running quickly toward him. Friend or foe? He had no idea. The ammonia wouldn't kill, but it wouldn't be pleasant; he wasn't about to spray a "friendly" with it.

He prepared to tackle the person. If it turned out to be an OT, he'd hit it in the face with the ammonia, blinding it and sending it running for first aid. He squinted into the dark, trying to judge the distance. His muscles tensed, ready to spring. He knew a thing or two about defending himself. Life wasn't always perfect as an African American kid in central Florida. He'd learned to be a step ahead and to see around corners. You didn't wait for your opponent to own your space— to crowd you. You got the jump on them.

He dove out into the open, grabbing the person by the knees and squeezing in the perfect execution of a football tackle. The person collapsed and Maybeck rolled on top of . . . her.

"Jess?"

His hologram passed right through her so that

he lay on the asphalt. She, too, was crossed over.

"What the . . . ? That could have hurt!"

"This way!"

He hurried behind the crate. Jess followed.

"2.0," he said.

"Yeah. I noticed."

"Thanks for coming."

"I'm not volunteering for war duty, or whatever it is you call it," she said. "I came here to warn you."

"About?"

"I . . . hang on . . ."

Sometimes when the Keepers crossed over, objects in their pockets crossed with them. Sometimes not. This was one area 2.0 still had not perfected, though it was more consistent now.

"It's here!" Jess said, withdrawing and unfolding two pieces of paper, one atop the other. "I didn't recognize this for what it was or I would have brought it up at the meeting. I have so many of these dreams. Always so random. This one was . . . maybe a week ago."

Maybeck held it up to the light. A bunch of rectangles and clusters of Xs. Jess's "gift"—and what made her valuable as a Fairlie—was an uncanny ability to dream the future. It wasn't perfect, and it wasn't constant. But when one of her dreams could be interpreted correctly, it always proved insanely accurate. She sketched out what she had seen in the middle of the night after she awoke from one of the nightmares.

"I don't get it."

"Neither did I," she whispered. "That's why I didn't really even think about it. But then Jeannie was doing this history project and was on Google Earth and something just clicked. I realized what this is . . ." She slid out the second sheet of paper. "It took me some time to narrow it down."

Maybeck angled this page to catch the light as well. It was a satellite image of rooftops.

"It's here. Right here," she said. "Amanda figured it out, once I realized what I'd dreamed. And check it out," she added, pointing between the two sheets.

"No way!" Maybeck said.

"Shh!"

He compared the two pages and turned her drawing until the positioning of the structures undeniably matched.

"It's tonight," she said. "Look at these numbers." Awaking from her dream, she'd written down three numbers: 417. Together they made no sense. But separated, they could be a month, 4, April, and a date, 17.

"Tomorrow," Maybeck said. But then, realizing it would soon be after midnight: "Or late tonight."

"Tonight."

"And these?" he asked, indicating the Xs.

"I thought you might know. I don't have any idea."

Maybeck oriented himself to the Google Earth sheet and then to her drawing. He turned away from her and looked up.

"It's them," Maybeck said.

"The OTs?"

"Yeah! Has to be. Their positions. This is . . . incredible. This gives us the chance to attack instead of waiting to be attacked. Have you studied siege strategies? The best, really the only, way for the besieged to win is to wait for disease to kill the enemy, or pull off an ambush. And we don't have time for disease."

"But what if I'm wrong?"

"You? You're never wrong."

"I'm wrong all the time. You just don't see all the times I'm wrong."

"Listen," Maybeck said, "no way a handful of us are going to hold off a full-scale attack. I can take the volunteers around the outside and come back to these locations and hope to surprise the OTs. This is a gift."

He reached out, arms wide, but passed right through the hologram.

"That was a hug," he said, "in case you didn't get the idea."

"Noted."

11

THE FIRST SIGN OF SOMETHING wrong was the sound of machinery. Initially, it was just pops and clunks. But when that was followed by the sound of water—a lot of water—Finn's insides turned to Jell-O. He lay on the surfboard atop the calm water, chilled and feeling both vulnerable and alone. Lingering at the back of his mind was a question that echoed every few minutes: why had Wayne sent him into a park that didn't offer DHI projection? Prior to the upgrade he'd possessed the ability to picture a pinprick of light at the end of a tunnel and, presto chango, his arms and legs would tingle and he'd be nothing but pure light. *All clear.* The condition hadn't lasted long, but it had gotten him out of some serious situations. Since the DHI 2.0 upgrade, he'd been unable to go *all clear.* Floating like a cork in the middle of a huge pool, wooden walls rising thirty feet on three sides of him, a spillway beach behind him, he was wishing for the chance to go *all clear.*

He'd seen the surf pool in action before. When the dam that was now in front of him belched, out came waves anywhere from three to ten feet high. Alone and slightly afraid of the sounds building up on the far side of the dam, it felt to him more like it should be called Tsunami Canyon rather than Surf Pool.

Mixed into the gurgle of water were the distant sounds of voices saying "Good night." The last Cast Member passed out of the gate. A car started up and drove off. He hoped his mother was paying attention.

Dread flooded him, followed by the realization that a shadow was stretched across the water's surface. He glanced up toward the guard shack to see a figure there. Silhouetted. Indistinguishable. It stepped back and out of sight, taking its shadow with it.

The wall unleashed a flood tide. It wasn't a single wave, as he'd seen before, but a divided wave, phenomenally high on either side, nonexistent in the center. The waves, fifteen feet up the side walls, crawled forward. A leading ripple lifted Finn's board several feet. Then the side waves rose even higher and rushed to join in the center, forming a white-capped plume of surging water that foamed and raced directly for Finn.

The front of his board jerked straight up. He clung to the sides as it rose like a rocket, crested, and slid down the opposite side. The rush of water nearly stripped off his suit. It hit his face so hard it forced his mouth open and he thought he might drown. He couldn't see. He fought to hold on; the surfboard's leash remained around his right ankle. The pool churning water, foam, and spray. Behind him, the huge wave crashed to shore.

Slowly the water calmed and, as it did, the gurgling began again. He didn't dare paddle for land—he wouldn't make it in time, and the next wave would carry him and throw him into the pool furniture on the beach. His only hope, as Melanie had coached, was to face forward and ride over the waves. So he turned the surfboard around and paddled furiously for the center of the pool. Just as he arrived, he heard a second ferocious belch and knew that this wave would be even bigger than the first. He pivoted the board in time to see it coming.

Not possible . . . it wasn't a wave, but a wall of water peaked in the center in an inverted V. The peak aimed right for him. What had Wayne gotten him into?

He tried paddling backward. There was no way he'd make it up and over that mountain. It was going to own him. It was going to pick him up like a cork and throw him clear out of the park. He'd probably splat on the windshield of his mother's car like a moth caught on the highway. Here, Mrs. Whitman, say hi to your son. . . .

The towering peak of surging spray and foam came at him as if rocket-boosted.

At that moment, when all hope seemed lost, when the peak of the wave loomed overhead, bending and licking its hungry tongue at Finn, the spikes of white foam split apart and seemed to become stationary points of what looked like a fountain. Water cascaded from the spikes of the fountain, revealing huge clumps of seaweed.

Finn back-paddled away from the thing. It wasn't seaweed. That had been an optimistic assessment. Because it was . . . hair. Yards of it in massive tangles— looking like dripping vines covering an enormous stone statue. But it wasn't stone. It was flesh. Gray flesh. Craggy, disgusting flesh chiseled into the shape of a man's eyes, nose, and then consumed by a beard. The water poured off as the head seemed to rise from the water, followed by shoulders covered with a cape, then a massive chest and arms. The giant held a staff in his right hand, and it was only by recognizing its three golden tines pointed like arrows that Finn knew who this was. The staff was a trident, and it belonged to King Triton.

"You're kidding me," he muttered as he fought to turn the surfboard around to get out of this pool.

"Name yourself!" The voice was a low rumble nearly indistinguishable from the distant gurgle of water as the wave generator refilled behind the giant.

There was no escaping. Finn reversed the board and faced Triton. Why hadn't Wayne warned him?

"Finn," he muttered.

"Louder!"

He shouted his name.

"Full name!"

"Lawrence Finnegan Whitman."

"State your purpose."

"Ah . . . a friend sent me." But Finn was now wondering why.

"Indeed. A friend to us all."

King Triton knew Wayne?

"He is the keeper of the magic," Triton said.

If you say so, Finn was thinking, but didn't say. "Indeed!" He tried sticking to the king's vocabulary. He wasn't sure about the etiquette of speaking with royalty. He didn't want to insult a guy this big.

The pool water continued to drip off the giant, but the wave pool was settling down to a violent chop as waves rebounded off the walls and spread out onto the beach area, sloshing ashore and lifting furniture into a junk pile.

"He seeks protection for you, our friend does," said Triton.

"Ah . . ." Finn wasn't sure what the king was talking about. "Protection?"

"Your voyage in my kingdom."

Triton ruled the sea. A voyage . . . ? The cruise! "Yes, sir."

"Like me, the creatures in my kingdom are bigger than those in yours. Our domain is vast. Unchangeable, horizon to horizon. There is much to protect. Your people poison mine. They hunt with invisible line and nets that stretch for miles. With harpoons. Oil rigs. They make war above and below. They stretch my resources."

That last part didn't sound terribly kinglike. He wondered if kings read newspapers. He supposed a king did whatever a king wanted to do, though he couldn't be certain.

"What is it you want?" Finn said.

When a giant laughed, it turned out, the ground shook—or, in this case, the pool sloshed.

"I am king. And I am old. My wants are few. You, on the other hand, Mr. Lawrence Finnegan Whitman, your needs and wants are many. You should know my agents will never be far from you and your crew. As the wise one has requested."

"When we're on the ship."

"When you are anywhere within or upon my kingdom, I or my agents shall never be far away."

"Thank you."

"The porpoise and frigate birds will monitor your progress. When the flying fish are near, I am not far away. The code is simple: 'Starfish wise, starfish cries.'"

"The code . . ." Finn said, having little idea what he meant.

"To summon my assistance. Starfish are never far away. They are the fastest way to reach me."

"Seriously?" It just slipped out.

"You are only to summon me if it is serious. That goes without saying. But it must be spoken into water. The summons spoken in air is of no use."

"What about the frigate birds?" Finn said. "Can't they hear us, too?"

"You dare question my knowledge of my own kingdom? The insolence!" The king waved his trident. A wide circle of water rose around Finn and closed at the top like the peak of a teepee, trapping Finn inside.

"I'm sorry! I'm sorry!" Finn cried out.

"Speak into the water!" the king hollered. As he lowered the trident, the peak of water lowered as well, about to drown Finn.

Finn slipped his head off the board and bubbled water as he said, "Sorry! *Sorry!*"

The water funnel collapsed, smashing into Finn and knocking him off the board. He struggled back atop and held on for dear life.

"'Starfish wise, starfish cries,'" the king repeated. "We will do everything in our power to assist or rescue you and your crew if summoned."

"My friends," Finn said.

"Our powers are not inconsiderable."

"And what do you want in return?" Finn asked.

The giant blinked for the first time, spraying Finn with excess water.

"I mean, isn't that the way it works?" Finn asked. "You offer protection in exchange for something?"

"You mock me?"

The waters churned as if a strong wind were blowing.

"No! I just thought . . . I mean . . . if you're willing to protect us, well, I thought you must want something from us."

"Indeed! It is true. It is often the way as you say."

"Like Ursula's necklace or something."

"Do not mention—!"

But it was too late. Finn wished someone would tell him the rules before he messed things up. Wayne always left too much to chance. Apparently by just speaking the name of Triton's nemesis, Ursula, Finn had done something wrong. Very wrong.

The water boiled at Triton's tail. It bubbled and— this seemed impossible—steamed, and the random churning of the choppy waves began to take form. First the surface smoothed. Then it formed into concentric ridges, as thick and wide as the back of a coiling sea serpent. The surfboard spun clockwise; for a moment Finn faced the guard shack, then the high wall, then the beach and the park entrance in the distance. He spun ever faster, his rotation increasing. The back of the serpent rose wider and higher; the water beneath the surfboard took the shape of a funnel. Now Finn saw what was actually happening. A hole opened beneath him and a whirlpool formed.

The king hoisted the trident and shook the hair off his wide neck.

"Away from this place!" he shouted.

Finn thought he had to be talking to him, but in the middle of being sucked down some drain, he was in no shape to reply. The whirlpool's walls were now twelve feet high, his surfboard spinning as fast as a pinwheel in a hurricane.

"Do . . . something . . ." he mumbled, feeling green. Then he stuck his face into the water. *"Help!"* he gurgled.

The surfboard spun even faster.

A purple-skinned, fat-lipped ugly the size of two side-by-side tractor-trailer trucks stood on end, with jowly upper arms, rose out of the pool and faced Triton. There was nothing cartoony about her. Instead she looked like the result of an octopus breeding with a cow. Her skin wasn't so much purple as it was translucent, revealing a tight spiderweb of veins pumping rust-colored blood on top of muscle tissue the color of eggplant. The skin looked gooey. Her face sagged and bulged and reformed with each little movement. Her body was considerable. If you took all the Jell-O in the world and shaped it into a sand castle of the ugliest woman you could ever imagine, you'd have the second-ugliest woman ever imagined. The first was occupying a space in the pool a few yards from Triton.

These two were not strangers to one another. They were more like divorced husband and wife.

"You called?" the big blob said.

"Your presence is unwanted," Triton said.

"But I didn't bring you any presents," Ursula said, twisting his words. She chuckled at her own joke, throwing three-foot waves off her belly.

Finn was now nearly at the bottom of the whirlpool spout, spinning like a propeller. Through the silver walls of water he saw squidlike creatures with the same strange translucent skin as Ursula's. Their heads were like manatees, but with puckered fish lips and bulging eyes. Inside the fish lips, rows of razor-sharp teeth showed. They circled the whirlpool like hungry alley cats on the other side of a wobbly fence. One poked its head through the shimmering wall of water and snapped at Finn. It missed, but caught the whirling surfboard and bit off a chunk, spitting it out immediately but leaving a few teeth behind. It retreated through the wall. But others took its place, snapping at Finn and then retreating. If he fell off the board he was chum for the making.

The sides of the whirlpool began collapsing. It was going to fold in on itself, like a hole dug in wet beach sand. With Finn at the bottom. He needed a way out. Now!

He rose up onto the board, first to knees, then—tentatively—to standing. He spread his feet, his left out in front, his right perpendicular to him and behind. He leaned left. The board's nose caught the spinning vortex and jerked hard. Finn danced to keep his balance. With the board aimed against the clockwise spinning motion, it screwed up higher, lifting off the churning floor of the whirlpool and rising with the board half inside the current, half outside. The water dropped out from under him, dumping him back to the bottom, and Finn started again, slowly getting the hang of how much board to allow in the wall. He began to rise from the depths.

"Leave or be removed!" Triton bellowed at Ursula.

"What's a matter? Can't a girl have some fun? Besides, it was you who called me, don't forget."

"The summons was unintentional and ill-advised. You are not needed, as it turns out."

"Maybe I should determine that?" she said.

"Be gone or I will be rid of you."

"Oh . . . I'm just shaking all over!" With that, she threw her hips around, disturbing the pool and disrupting the integrity of the whirlpool. Finn tumbled to the bottom, spun like a top, and then managed to scramble back aboard. He rose to his knees and started surfing again.

"I'm feeling a little . . . dry," Ursula said. "How 'bout you, Tri-Tones? Could you use a refresher?" She chortled evilly. "Be my guest!"

"Do not dare!"

"All for now," she said. "And now for all!" She laughed again.

Finn saw through the wall of the whirlpool the strange squid creatures surrounding Ursula's slowly sinking body, obscuring it. In a burst of bubbles, everything was gone and the water was clear again.

He caught the edge of the board just right and it grabbed and spun like a top, riding up in a spiral and popping to the surface, but the whirlpool collapsed beneath him. It would have drowned him. Killed him. Triton towered above him, but his back was to Finn as he faced the wall of the dam.

"*Go!* I will do what I can!" Triton held the trident out before him as the dam gurgled and the wall bulged.

At the same time, the thousands of gallons of water already in the pool moved in an undertow toward the dam. Finn and the board crashed into Triton's back. It made no sense: the water moved from the dam's wave generator to the beach, not vice versa. But Finn was clearly caught in a reverse flood of epic proportions. He slid down a mountain of water toward the suddenly dry beach.

Triton's effort was formidable. He held the staff before him, and miraculously a kind of hole in the water formed around him. It bent and churned, not touching him above the knees. Had Finn been able to hold himself next to the king, he too would have been protected. But having been carried away he was now lying on the damp concrete of what a moment earlier had been pool bottom. He scrambled and stood, but was mesmerized by the height of the wave crest about to crush him. His legs wouldn't move. Finally, the wave peaked.

Triton held his ground; the wave formed around him like he was standing inside a jar. He glanced back at Finn and shook his head. He was noticeably paler. Weaker.

"I must go," he said.

Finn nodded.

The wave formed majestically—beautifully. A work of nature's art. Blue and mighty and perfect. A mouth opening wider and wider. Finn turned to run.

Amanda stood at what would have been the edge of the beach. She had been following him. She had been protecting him.

"Hurry!" she said. "Grab hold of my waist!"

Finn knew the power she contained in her arms. He'd watched as she levitated both creatures and people. He didn't understand where such things came from— wouldn't have believed them real if he hadn't seen them with his own eyes. He knew there were skeptics. It wasn't his mission to convert them. The Fairlies were real. Amanda and Jess were Fairlies. They couldn't change themselves. Nor should they want to. He grabbed her around the waist and held tightly, knowing what she had in mind.

Triton was gone.

The wave rushed toward them.

Amanda threw out her arms. He felt her body go rigid, felt a kind of pulse flowing from her feet to his arms. He'd never held her like this before. Never this tightly. Never with so much determination and appreciation and confidence in her.

The wave formed, sucking water up into its crest that rolled out like a tuft of white hair. The floor of the pool was now only a few inches deep as every drop of water was summoned into the thirty-foot wave. It grew so high, so quickly, that it once again jumped the walls of the pool, contained now by the towering rock walls of the dam. Two tiny figures stood facing it, one with her arms stretched out.

The wave reached its peak, its mass exceeding its surface tension. It tumbled forward like a building collapsing. It came to kill.

And then it stopped, as if hitting a brick wall. The force of all that water leaning—leaning—out over Amanda and Finn. A lot of water splashed to the pool floor, but the wave itself held.

"Amanda?" Finn whispered into her ear.

He could feel her distance, her removal from her body. She was locked, rock hard, as if in a trance. Her arms trembled as jolts of energy moved through her. Amanda was holding back the wave.

"Don't let go," she said in a voice he hadn't heard her use before. Darker. Lower. Guttural. "Guide me back toward the gate."

She was weaker, he realized. The effort was draining her.

"Okay," he whispered.

Holding tightly around her waist, he took a step back, pulling Amanda with him. Was he dreaming, or did the entire wave move a few feet as they did? He took another step.

The wave advanced with them. For each step Finn

took, the wave took the same step. He realized whatever force Amanda possessed, whatever accounted for the halting wave, was at its limit. She could exert no more pressure against it. He wasn't a genius when it came to math, but it occurred to him that no matter how far they backed up, the wave was going to move with them. There was no escaping it.

"Amanda?"

"A little busy here," she said.

"It's just that it's . . . moving."

"Yeah . . . I know." They took another step back. The wave lurched forward. But something had changed. Its splashing crest was slightly lower. The more they retreated, the lower it went.

"We're winning," Finn said, not knowing exactly what he meant. He moved her back more quickly.

"I can't hold it," she said. In fact, her arms were trembling, her strength waning. The wave had changed positions, now leaning like a shelf directly overhead. If it collapsed . . .

"*I can!*" came the thundering voice of Triton, his face appearing inside the huge wave. "Go! Quickly!"

Finn kicked away some of the tangled pool furniture, making a path for them. But they still had to clear Castaway Creek and get through the gate to reach Finn's mom.

He nudged a clear tire tube aside. Then a double tube. Then some armchairs and a lounge chair. More and more water spilled from the crown of the wave thirty feet overhead. Amanda could no longer contain it.

The gate was impossibly far away. Then he spotted the solution.

"I've got a plan," he said.

"I . . ."

She'd lost her strength.

Triton held back the towering wall of water. It foamed and spit as if it were suddenly boiling. "Goooo," Triton growled.

Amanda threw her hands out to help Triton hold it back.

Finn craned forward and kissed her on the cheek from behind. "You can do this."

A bolt of electricity passed through her like a shiver. The wave lifted and stood up behind the power of her force.

"Turn and grab hold of me, on three," he said.

"But—"

"One . . . two . . ." He let go of her, pivoted, and dove for the double tube, grabbing its black rubber handles. He was face down, stretched across the tube. He felt her land on top of him and wrap her arms around his waist. He stood up, the tube held in front of him, Amanda dragging behind, and he started running. Amanda figured it out, moved to hold him around the chest, and also ran.

The wave seemed to hang in the air. Triton faded and disappeared. Whatever force had been holding it back faded. The wave sank under the weight of its crest, losing its form. It flowed out at the bottom, flooding instead of breaking. Sinking instead of cresting.

Thousands of gallons of water ran in both directions—one wave rushing back toward the Surf Pool, another surging toward the gate. It quickly caught up to Finn and Amanda, ankle deep, knee deep . . .

"Dive!" Finn shouted.

Together they leaped away from the flood. Finn landed squarely atop the tube, Amanda holding him around the chest. The tube caught the leading edge of the surge like a surfboard, picking up speed and lifting into the curl of the newly formed wave.

"*Left!*" Finn shouted, leaning in that direction. He had to steer the tube down the wave and toward the right if they were going to find the gate and avoid being smashed into structures.

"Right!" he called out.

Amanda did not argue. He felt her lean slightly to the right. The nose of the tube broke free and fell down the steep incline of water like a sled on ice.

"Finn!" she cried, squeezing the air out of him. Down, down they raced, in a nosedive heading toward the concrete below.

He counted down in his head, the gate area appearing far to his right. Just as he was about to shout out a move to the right, the wave reached the lazy river. It was like catching the toe of your shoe on a doorsill. The wave stumbled, rippled, and briefly lost its form. It threw the tube into the air.

"H . . . o . . . l . . . d on!"

He held on to the tube's handles. If Amanda clung to him any stronger she would break his ribs. They did a full flip in slow motion. Then they were upside down in the wave, Amanda's back in the water, then Finn's, then the tube over them like a blanket. Finn leaned right. The tube took off, slowly rising back toward the towering curl.

"What just happened?" she said.

If Finn had tried that a hundred times, he wouldn't have been able to duplicate the flip and recovery. They'd gotten lucky, but he wasn't about to admit it.

He shouted over his shoulder. "Aim for the gate." Still clutching the grips, he pointed with his index finger. But the wave was rapidly dispersing, no longer contained by the Surf Pool. They sank lower and slowed. Finn called out a series of turns that steered them clear of obstructions. They settled in a froth of white, bubbling foam, and the tube skidded to a stop only yards from the gate. Knee-deep water flooded out past the ticket booth and then was gone, leaving only wet concrete.

Behind them, the wave retreated into the river and the Surf Pool and myriad drains carefully hidden and disguised. As Finn and Amanda clambered to their feet and looked back, the waters calmed as suddenly as if none of it had ever happened.

* * *

Green Army Men. Six were bunched tightly together, their backs pressed against a shipping container in an area that included the parked trams for the back-lot tours.

Maybeck could not see them clearly enough to spot a leader, but he knew they were like roaches. If there were six, there were sixty. It meant only one thing: this was no drill. Tonight was the assault on the Base they'd been expecting. This was it. There would be other clusters of Army Men out there, and thanks to Jess, Maybeck knew where to find them.

He backed out and away from the container and cut across the back lot. There were six indoor/outdoor workshops side by side on the back of the boxlike building that housed the Engineering Base. Maybeck slipped into a screened area marked PAINT SHOP, where Jess and the six volunteers were sitting on props, crates, and sawhorses. Behind them wide strips of murky plastic hung in a row.

"Okay, here's the drill," Maybeck said, taking charge. "Looks like Jess's map is accurate. I found a bunch of Army Men behind the container here," he said, angling Jess's sketch into the faint light cast from spotlights mounted high on the building's corners.

"How are we supposed to fight Army Men?" Kenny Carlson asked, his red hair practically neon. "Don't those guys carry guns?"

"They do," Maybeck said. "And they fired their guns at Willa once."

"Then?" Kenny said, speaking for the others.

"The thing about cockroaches," Maybeck said. "You need for them to come to the bait. If you go after them, they just scatter and regroup somewhere else."

"O . . . kay . . ." Ken said, sounding dubious.

Looking around the area, Maybeck moved to the plastic curtain and peered inside. "I take it none of you ever took wood shop or got a wood shop merit badge or whatever."

"Ah . . ."

"I built a model of an *Avatar* personnel carrier," one boy said proudly.

"My aunt runs an art shop," Maybeck said, parting the curtain wider and now spotting what he was after. He disappeared inside, returning a minute later with what looked like a huge hypodermic needle in his left hand and a box cutter in his right.

"You going to give them all shots?" one of the girl volunteers asked. "Knock them out or something?"

"Epoxy," Maybeck said. "Fast drying, permanent epoxy."

"I don't follow you," Kenny said.

"But you will," Maybeck said. "Follow me, that is. You and you and you." He pointed. "You're all with me. The rest of you are with Jess."

"They are?" Jess said.

"Here's how it's going down," Maybeck said, holding the glue-tube squeeze tool across his chest like it was a sawed-off shotgun. "Listen up."

* * *

The multipurpose building housing the Engineering Base offices was awkwardly located at the edge of where backstage met onstage—a line easily crossed at Disney's Hollywood Studios. Two massive steel exoskeletons supporting imitation movie sets built for the tram tour were its neighbors on one side while a variety of nondescript, cream-colored support buildings crowded the back side. A narrow access road defined by a barbed-wire-topped chain-link fence meant there was one side Maybeck didn't have to watch or worry about. The workshops where Maybeck and the others had planted themselves made for an excellent hiding place. They were cluttered with mechanical parts, broken props, tools, and construction equipment.

Jess's map suggested four groups of Overtakers. Maybeck and his team took the group he'd just observed; Jess and her group headed for a location on the park side of the Base building. Maybeck could not worry about the other three; he had his own group to deal with.

Maybeck had always felt like an outcast, partly because of his minority status, partly because he lived with his aunt, not his parents. He felt more like himself with the four original Keepers than with anyone other than his aunt. He found Jess mysterious and therefore hard to read; Amanda was absurdly smart and different in a way Finn clearly found interesting, but Maybeck couldn't get comfortable with. He'd discovered he could run an operation as long as he dropped the attitude. The Keepers didn't tolerate attitude. Now, sneaking along through shadow down the long row of workshops on the back side of the building, the volunteers—the VKKs—fell in behind him like a squad of Marines, and Maybeck took to his leadership role effortlessly.

He raised his hand to slow the three, waved it forward to move them. Eyes and ears alert, he darted across the pavement to the first of the containers, his team following closely. As they reached the third container, he indicated an area at his feet by drawing a box. The first of the VKKs nodded, accepting the glue tube from him. The two others backed up ten feet, as Maybeck had instructed earlier. He gave them all a thumbs-up. They returned the gesture, signaling their readiness.

Maybeck slipped around the corner of the container— the same container that the Army Men had their backs to at the other end. He counted down from sixty, recalling the application instructions. When he reached thirty, he moved toward the Army Men, making himself obvious while trying to appear otherwise.

The nearest green man caught sight of him and slapped the arms of the others. The Army Men could not speak; they took orders, they did not give them. Their current orders were, no doubt, to take the Base, to capture any kid or any hologram they spotted. The squad took off in lockstep toward Maybeck.

Maybeck was a *Toy Story* fan. He knew the Green Army Men well, knew that a peculiar feature of the characters in the films were the plastic bases attached to their boots that allowed them to stand. Cast Members dressed as Army Men at Pixar Place in the Studios lacked the plastic bases but wore oversized boots in their place—a costume feature he was counting on.

He knew the chase would be no contest. For one thing, Maybeck was fast—very fast. For another, an army squad that double-timed in formation was no match for an individual in a footrace.

Having made sure he'd been spotted and was being pursued, Maybeck ran back from where he'd come. He turned the corner, took five strides, and jumped, tucking his knees. He landed hard, lost his balance, and rolled. At that exact moment, the Army Men appeared and charged.

Maybeck came to his feet facing the squad, his own team of volunteers perfectly in place behind him.

He counted the strides of the squad. One . . . two . . . three . . . four . . .

"Now!" he said to the VKKs.

As a group they raised their hands above their heads.

"We surrender!" Maybeck called. The pronouncement caused the squad leader to raise his hand, and he stopped the squad cold. He indicated for them to lower their weapons, as Maybeck and the others were defenseless.

Maybeck counted in his head as he said anything that came to mind. "We request to be treated as captive prisoners of war." Nine, ten. "You will therefore allow us to notify our superiors of our situation in . . ."—thirteen, fourteen—"an attempt to . . ."—seventeen, eighteen—"negotiate an exchange of prisoners." Twenty!

"On second thought," Maybeck said, "maybe we'll be going now."

He turned around, as did the VKKs, following his cue. The four holograms took off. Maybeck knew that DHI 2.0 allowed him to easily maintain his hologram state—that bullets couldn't hurt him. But he wasn't nearly as confident the VKKs could master their fear in order to maintain the quality of the projection. He was counting on a series of events to protect them all, and, glancing over his shoulder, he saw them occur as if he'd scripted them.

First, the squad leader pointed at the four kids, raising his own rifle. His five squad members followed, also lifting their guns. Next, the squad leader took a step forward—or attempted to. But his boots were glued to the asphalt, courtesy of the glue tube and the efforts of the VKKs to saturate the area Maybeck had jumped over.

As the squad leader tried to step, he lost his balance and fell forward. He planted face-first into the glued surface, sticking to it like a fly to flypaper. His squad did exactly as their leader did: raised their weapons, tried to move, and fell to the blacktop, sticking to it instantly.

Their weapons adhered as well. Maybeck and the others fled back to the paint workshop to join Jess when she and her team returned from an identical mission. With any luck that would be soon, and, according to Jess's map, half the enemy would be flat on their faces, easy prisoners for park security to collect.

The ranks of the Overtakers battling for the Base had just gotten smaller.

* * *

Finn and Amanda stumbled across the parking lot, wet, weary, and wary. The summons by Ursula might have been the end of it, and it might have just been the beginning.

Finn's mother's car was the only vehicle in a lot that could hold a thousand. Finn and Amanda reached a pair of palm trees and paused. Why couldn't his mother have parked a little closer or moved the car once the party had gotten out?

"Clear?" he said.

But Amanda didn't answer. Holding back Ursula's wave had sapped all her strength, drained her to where the tube surfing and running had left her in a stupor of diminished capacities. He took one look at her and knew it was up to him to get her back safely. She was in a zone, and it wasn't a good one.

"I've got you," he said, taking her gently by the upper arm. "Hang in there." She'd saved his life. The least he could do was get her to Mrs. Nash's foster home safely. She tugged away from the contact—was it wrong to grab a girl by the upper arm?—but he squeezed more tightly, not letting her go. Briefly, she leaned her head against his shoulder, just to where it touched. Then she straightened back up and allowed herself to be guided across the vast expanse of open blacktop as Finn raced for the car.

He spotted his mom through the windshield. He rolled his free hand vigorously, signaling for her to start the car and get going. And yet she just sat there. The car remained silent. He opened the back door for Amanda and closed it behind her. He climbed into the front seat.

"Go! Go!" he said. "Mom! Come on!"

Mrs. Whitman reached for the ignition key and started the car.

"How did it go?" she asked.

Finn motioned out at the half-flooded parking lot. "It could have gone better," he said. "We've got to get out of here."

She started the car and the headlights came on automatically. Finn's mom moved the gearshift and they took off. She drove confidently, though hardly in a hurry.

"Pedal to the metal, Mom. Come on!"

"You're not in any danger from her now," she said.

Finn missed it at first, but not Amanda. That was who Amanda was. That was partly what made her so special. Her secretive, intuitive nature, a quality of always being a step ahead and yet right behind you.

"From who?" Amanda said.

Or maybe it was the result of her sitting in the backseat, of her having a good view of the car's rearview mirror. Of spotting something about his mother's face that Finn had not spotted.

"From Ur—" Finn said, turning to look back at Amanda, wondering how she could be so tired as to have forgotten the last twenty minutes. But Amanda wore a worried, severe expression. Finn caught himself mid-syllable.

Her . . . His mother had said "her."

Mrs. Whitman glanced over at her son, adopting a forced smile that Finn interpreted as meaning one of two things: either she was furious and trying to contain herself because Amanda was in the car, or she was trying to slip something past him. These were the only two alternatives. Between mother and son sometimes words weren't necessary at all.

They reached the end of the access road into Typhoon Lagoon, where it met Lake Buena Vista

Drive. Cars were streaming out of Downtown Disney, the Cirque du Soleil show having just concluded. Headlights shone into Finn's car so brightly that he looked away from them, averting his eyes and looking directly at his mom. She too recoiled from the glare, holding her hand up to screen her face.

Amanda reached forward and took Finn's arm the same way he had taken hers minutes earlier. She squeezed hard. For she'd seen what Finn had seen.

This woman's eyes were green.

His mother had blue eyes.

There are times a laptop computer or smart phone will pause for no reason—just hang as if taking a little longer than usual to think through a mundane instruction. Finn's brain did just that. It did not jump to conclusions. It did not instruct him to open the car door. It did not suggest an exchange of expressions with Amanda. It froze, stunned.

It must be a trick of the light, his brain said. It must be those new halogen headlights, or the vapor lights in the parking lot, or possibly something to do with the angle of—he had to reach back to science class—infraction? *refraction?* of light distorting under the effects of a lens. It wasn't that his mother's eyes were suddenly green; it was a trick, a special effect.

But then his logic was challenged by his physical

senses. However it might be explained, his mother's eyes were currently green. It didn't matter how many cars passed—that wasn't going to change.

The traffic light turned green.

"Now!" Finn said, yanking on the door handle while releasing his seat belt.

To his great relief Amanda was, as usual, a step ahead of him and already out of the car.

Neither bothered to shut the doors. Instead, they took off at a full sprint down the sidewalk, Amanda suddenly possessed with strength again, though her adrenaline faded fast, and Finn took her and pulled her along with him.

"How did that happen?" Amanda choked out.

Finn couldn't answer. He didn't want to reveal the tears choking in his throat. His ally at home. The one person he felt he could trust above all others, even Wayne. His own personal rocket scientist who happened to cook him meals and tuck him in at night. Sure, she could be a pain in the butt—she was his mother.

He couldn't go home. His own mother was an OTK, but not a kid, an adult, so more like an OTA. Maleficent had stolen his mother from him.

"It's not possible," he said.

"Maybe we got it wrong," Amanda said, trying to cheer him up as they darted across the wide boulevard and onto the grounds of Downtown Disney. They could catch a bus to the Transportation and Ticket Center. They could make a plan. They could figure something out.

They both knew the truth. No matter how Amanda tried to comfort him, such a thing wasn't possible.

He was alone. Willingly or not, his own family had joined the other side.

12

FINN SPENT THE NIGHT with Dillard Cole, his closest friend outside the Keepers.

Before he finally fell asleep, he tried to make sense of his mother's green eyes. He cried at the thought of what his mother must be going through while under some spell. Seeing his mom as his enemy took some getting used to. He seethed with anger—hatred—for the Overtakers and everything they represented. How dare they drag his mother into this (even if Finn had done so in the first place)? How dare they compromise her? He wondered where she was. Still sitting in the car? Parked outside their home? In bed sleeping? One thing was for sure: it would take Finn's father about a month to realize the color of his wife's eyes had changed—he seemed oblivious to those things.

As he drifted off to sleep, he saw a vision of his mother waiting outside Dillard's house like a predator awaiting its prey. A mother, her son.

He awoke with a start at five a.m. from a bad dream. He snuck back out Dillard's window. His mother wasn't there. He crept up the street. A dog barked loudly from within one house, causing Finn to jump. He took off running. His once peaceful neighborhood felt like a dangerous place now. Even the smallest of sounds sent ripples of terror through him. Finally arriving at the McVeys' house, across the street from his own, he kneeled in the dim shadow of a bush and studied his home. He waited a full five minutes for any kind of movement inside. The horizon was dull with dawn, the overhead clouds beginning to warm with color. The air chilly. The grass wet.

He found the hidden key, let himself into the garage, and a moment later he led his BMX quietly up the drive, climbed on, and pedaled off.

* * *

Amanda was drawn to the window. She would later tell Jess it had just been blind luck that she'd spotted Finn across the street from Mrs. Nash's, but that wasn't entirely true. Something had compelled her to peer behind the blind that always hung over the bedroom window. She couldn't describe exactly what it was, but it was undeniable. A force of some kind. Like gravity pulling her. To him.

There had been a time when she'd thought he was cute. Then came interesting. Then, intriguing. Beguiling. Now it was something compelling. Forceful.

Chemical. The evolution of her feelings might have told her something except that she'd never experienced them before. The caterpillar doesn't know it's going to be a butterfly; it just happens.

She couldn't forget about the kiss. The power it had instilled in her to hold back the wave. How could such a thing happen? She'd been totally out of energy at that point; on the verge of giving up. And then his kiss, and all her power returned. And more. Maybe it had been the shadow of the kiss that had drawn her to the window.

Jess joined her.

"That's strange," Jess said.

"Yes."

"Has he ever done that? Waited there like that?"

"No," Amanda answered.

"You think something's wrong?"

She told her about Mrs. Whitman's eyes and Finn's inability to return home.

"What's he going to do if he can't go home?"

"The cruise," Amanda answered. "The inaugural. They leave today. The five of them."

"So he's here to say good-bye?" Jess said.

"How should I know?"

"I thought they go with their parents?"

"Yes. Supposedly. Knowing Finn, he'll find a way around that."

"Can he do that?"

"Wayne can."

Jess nodded.

"Are you going out there?" Jess asked. "You could tell him about . . . you know."

"I'm not going to tell him. That's the point of a guardian angel. And I'm not going out there until we all leave for school. Are you kidding me? Mrs. Nash would kill me."

"But he looks so . . . I don't know . . . empty."

"He does, doesn't he?" Amanda said, sounding sad.

"We should smuggle him some food."

"We need to get on the ship with them," Amanda said.

"That's ridiculous! As if! Mrs. Nash would—"

"Never know."

"It's a two-week cruise! How are we supposed to disappear for two weeks and . . ." But Jess caught herself. "Seriously?" she said.

"Why not?"

"We'll be super tired," Jess said. "Besides . . . we already took care of this."

"But they don't know her. She doesn't know them."

"So the OTs can't possibly make a connection. It's perfect."

Amanda shook her head. "Think about it! We can sleep during the day."

Jess nodded thoughtfully. "You've thought this through, haven't you?" She hesitated and looked back out the window. "It's not just saving the parks anymore, is it? For you, I mean."

"Maybe not."

"When did you know?" Jess asked.

"I'm not sure about anything."

"I think it's very cool, the two of you."

"There is no 'the two of us.'"

"You sure?" Jess said.

Amanda blushed. "I told you! I'm not sure of anything."

She couldn't leave Mrs. Nash's early without raising suspicion. Getting showered and eating breakfast (two Nash requirements) seemed to take forever. Finally it came time for the girls to head to their school buses. Amanda met Finn on the sidewalk.

"Hey," she said. "Rough night at your friend's?"

"Did you get in trouble?" he asked.

"No. Jess covered for me."

"We leave today."

"Yeah, I know."

"Two weeks."

"Fifteen days. But who's counting?"

"Wayne warned us—"

"I was there, remember?"

"I thought we could Skype, maybe. There's Internet on the ship."

"Sure." Mrs. Nash's house had two computers on the first floor shared by eleven girls. They were dinosaurs, but one had been rigged with a camera and worked with Skype. You had to sign up on a clipboard to get fifteen minutes on the machine. Girls traded chores for extra Skype time, turning the minutes into a commodity. Amanda knew it was highly unlikely her minutes would ever link up with Finn's cruise schedule, but she wasn't about to be negative.

"And maybe . . . I mean if Jess dreams anything out of the ordinary . . ."

"I'll email you."

"Perfect."

"You okay? About your mom, I mean." She wanted to give him a hug. He looked frail. She didn't have a mother, had never known her parents, but she could nonetheless imagine how seeing his mother with green eyes must have shaken him up.

"I guess." Finn looked back at her like a lost puppy. "Don't miss the bus."

"I'm fine. It's you I'm worried about."

"Don't be," he said. "It's a spell of some kind. The

kids in school with the green eyes? Also a spell."

"It explains a ton of stuff." She counted on her fingers as she elaborated. "That maybe joining the OTs wasn't voluntary like we thought; that the stuff they do isn't really them doing it all; that there's somebody running around doing this to people, including to your mother."

"Maleficent," Finn hissed. "I hate her. I'm going to kill her for this."

"Be careful she doesn't use that as a weapon against you."

"What are you talking about?" he asked, clearly angry.

"How do we know what she had planned for your mother? What if it's nothing more than to scare you, to freak you out, to tick you off?"

"Then she succeeded."

"That's my point." She could hear him breathing hard. "Finn?" She'd never seen him quite like this.

"How do we change her back? What if—?"

"I know where you're going with this, but you can't think like that. We've done things that seemed impossible before."

"We haven't cast spells! Not that I remember!"

"Don't be mad at me! I didn't do this."

"You led them there!"

160

"What are you talking about?"

"How do you know you didn't lead the OTs to the park?" he asked accusingly.

"Because I didn't."

"And you know that how?"

"I can't believe you'd even think that! I was not followed. I was insanely careful about that. If anything, it was you and your mother. It's your family car, Finn. You think the OTs don't know what car your mother drives?"

"I think everything was all right until I heard you back there following me. Why'd you do that, anyway? Why didn't you tell me you were in the park?"

"Because of the rescue dummies."

"You saw them, I suppose?"

"Yes. I saw them. I stayed back."

"So . . . if you saw them, why didn't you warn me?"

"How was I supposed to do that? Shout at you? Fire a flare? Scream?"

Finn leaned into the handlebars. "I don't know."

"I can't believe you'd think that," she mumbled. "I was trying to help you."

"And how'd that work out?"

She stood up straight, her eyes stinging. "I think you're tired."

"Tired of being tricked. Tired of being lied to."

"You can't possibly mean that."

"Can't I?"

"We were nearly killed!" she reminded.

"I was there," he said.

"I saved you! Us!"

He rocked against the handlebars. "I . . . know," he said. He sounded like he was trying to convince himself.

"You think that I faked all that?" She had trouble speaking between her heavy breaths. "Seriously?"

"I don't know what to think."

She marched off, the tears starting to fall, her belly feeling like he'd punched her. Please don't follow me! she willed.

But there he was, pedaling idly at her side.

"Go away!" Her choked voice betrayed her. She wanted to run.

"Amanda."

"Don't!"

"I'm leaving," he reminded. "Today."

"Then leave. Go. *Go!*"

He applied the brakes and stopped. She continued forward. The most difficult steps of her life.

"Amanda?" he called out.

She wanted so badly to turn around and throw herself into him, to put the past few minutes behind and start all over, but her feet wouldn't stop walking.

She thought that this was where real life diverged from the way it happened in movies. Real life didn't always work out. The sad truth was—and she knew this—that she didn't know enough about boys and the way she felt about Finn to know what to do.

No matter how much her life felt like fiction at times, it was anything but. She'd been abandoned. She'd been found. She'd run away and been found again. Up and down. In and out. The last two years with the Keepers had been so totally unreal—so wonderfully welcome—that they couldn't have been made up. Now she and Finn were breaking up when they hadn't officially been going together in the first place. How was she supposed to make sense of any of this?

She tried to turn to look back at him. Her brain wouldn't allow it. Foolish stubbornness on her part, or did he deserve it? They'd been through a rough night together. That's all it was, she told herself.

"That's all it is," she repeated aloud, drawing curious looks as she approached the bus stop.

13

On an unseasonably cold spring night, a small basement window at ground level popped open, filling the girl's nostrils with salt air. The house was not actually a house at all, but a former army barracks. This was the only window in the complex rigged to avoid sounding the alarm. Months earlier, a magnet that mated with a wired sensor had been carefully removed from the window frame and secretly taped to its wired counterpart. Normally, if the window were opened, the magnetic field between the two magnets would be broken and the alarm would sound. Rigged as it was, the magnetic connection remained intact. The window could be opened and closed at will.

The girls of Barracks 14, ranging in age from eight to eighteen, used this window to come and go without being noticed. Sometimes departures facilitated food runs or attempts to contact family. Sometimes it was to try to find a boyfriend or girlfriend. Sometimes, like tonight, it was for something much more risky.

The girl climbing out, Mattie Weaver, was embarking on a quest that might, with any luck, take her away from this place forever. If caught, she wasn't sure of the consequences. She was only sure of one thing: that when a friend calls needing a favor, and that favor can be accomplished without physically hurting someone, it's a friend's duty to respond. It was part of the code of Barracks 14. Just as she assumed it was at the half dozen other barracks on the abandoned military base—although she rarely, if ever, got the chance to talk to any of those kids.

She crawled out and pulled the half-window carefully shut behind her. Tera Bergstrom had promised to close the window by morning. The window was valuable to everyone in 14. Mattie couldn't go wrecking it for others by doing anything stupid.

She lay in the damp grass for an impossibly long time, chilled to the bone by the time she dared raise to her knees.

She stood and ran. Building to building.

The gate would be guarded, but if her information was accurate there was a place to crawl under the fence by Building 7.

She moved in that direction as carefully as she'd ever moved.

14

IN THE GLOW OF WARM SUNSHINE, a magnificent vessel rose fifteen stories from the water's blue surface, towering over the four-acre cruise terminal. A combination of rich black, vivid red, and royal blues, the ship glistened and sparkled like an unwrapped gift.

Inside the terminal, the pulse of excitement rippled through the thousands of Disney enthusiasts, young and old, who were waiting to board. Reporters and film crews worked through the massive crowd interviewing and photographing those lucky enough to be on the *Disney Dream*'s Panama Canal passage. The *Dream* was to be the first commercial cruise ship to pass through the upgraded Panama Canal.

"So tell us what it's like," a Spanish-speaking reporter asked a young couple who appeared surprised by the television camera shoved in their faces.

"Incredible!" the man answered in Spanish.

"What makes this trip so special, other than it's Disney?" the reporter asked.

"We are to be on the first ship to cross through the new locks of the Panama Canal," the man answered.

"The very first ship. Such an honor! It is history we are making."

"Did you know the *Disney Dream* was chosen out of seventy vessels that were submitted to be the first through the new canal?"

"No, but it does not surprise me the *Dream* was chosen. This is good. The family. Everything Disney stands for."

"Was it difficult to get tickets?" the reporter asked.

"Are you kidding? It was a lottery. This is the only way. I heard over ten thousand people applied."

"Fifteen thousand, yes. And you were among those chosen. How does that make you feel?"

"We are blessed," the young woman said. "We feel very blessed."

The reporter thanked them and started to move on. The man being interviewed asked for and took a photo of his wife with the reporter. Others pushed forward trying to get on TV.

Smartly dressed Cast Members passed through the crowd offering bottled water and thanking the waiting passengers for their patience as preparations were made for boarding. At the entrance to the gangway, hundreds were cordoned off behind crowd tape, cheering for the parade of Disney celebrities and VIPs currently boarding as cameras flashed and names were called out.

Among them were Disney Channel stars, film actors, Radio Disney hosts, pop stars, and five teenagers known as Disney Hosts Interactive.

Finn, Maybeck, Philby, Charlene, and Willa waved to their fans and smiled for the cameras. Among the many highlights of the inaugural passage was the introduction of the shipboard Kingdom Keeper Quest, a scavenger hunt that had been wildly successful in the Magic Kingdom and was being unveiled aboard the *Dream* for the first time. The only major concern for the Keepers was that the Quest included Cast Members playing the parts of Overtakers. For the first time, Maleficent, Emperor Zurg, the Evil Queen, Cruella, and Chernabog would all be represented on board. The villains followed the Keepers as part of the grand entrance. The crowd jeered and booed them. Maleficent stuck her tongue out and everyone laughed.

Everyone but the Keepers.

"Hey, isn't that—?" Willa said, nudging Finn and pointing to the VIP waiting area.

Finn rose on his toes, but couldn't see anyone familiar. The villains continued forward, forcing the Keepers to present their key cards at the electronic readers at the final check-in.

"What? Who?" he asked.

"Never mind," Willa said.

"Tell me."

"It's just . . . it looked like your mother to me."

Finn jumped high, trying to get a look, but the angle was wrong. He saw nothing but the adoring crowd held back by the tape. His mother was supposed to accompany him; every Keeper was required to be in the company of a parent or guardian. Wayne was supposed to have rigged the system so that Finn would have a connecting stateroom to Philby and his mother. Supposedly his mother would soon discover she was electronically blocked from boarding. Wayne was to erase her from the ship's manifest. "If it is," Finn said, "she's in for a surprise."

He wanted to see her, to get close enough to see if her eyes were still green. If the spell had passed, she would be a useful ally for the next two weeks. He held his card near the reader. The machine beeped and a red light flashed.

The Cast Member maintained a smile as he studied a computer screen, a practiced performance. He tried Finn's key card himself. It flashed red. The man worked the keyboard.

"I show a Mrs. Whitman accompanying you," he said. "You're traveling with your mother, correct?"

"I . . . ah . . . there should be a note in my file," Finn said, recalling what Wayne had told him about the updated arrangements.

The man waved Finn out of the line. The Keepers' VIP guide moved to the Cast Member's side as the others were processed through the entrance, their key cards registering green.

Finn was beginning to dislike that color.

The guide whispered to the Cast Member. She opened an iPad and began navigating.

Finn heard the man say, "The DHIs? I'm so sorry!"

The two whispered back and forth, the guide clearly pushing Finn's celebrity status. But the Cast Member was clearly a by-the-rules man. Despite his curious glances in Finn's direction, the grins he offered, his fingers never stopped dancing on the keyboard.

"There was a flag in the record . . ." the man said. "I can see that. But whatever note was there appears to have been deleted."

The woman offered her iPad and the Cast Member read from it. He looked up at Finn. Back to the iPad.

"You see the signature," the guide prodded.

"Indeed," he said, his brow furrowing.

"I can try to call him directly if you like."

The Cast Member clearly didn't want anything to do with such a call. Meanwhile, another fifty people had passed through the checkpoint. The other Keepers were long gone, onto the ship. Finn was anxious to get aboard.

A few more keystrokes and the Cast Member told the guide, "Very well. I have him with the Philby family in a connecting room. If you would please email that document to me, I will attach it to his record and everything should be okay." He looked up at Finn with a bright face. "Just one minute and you're all set to go, young man."

"Thank you," Finn said behind a grimace. He rose to his toes again and looked back. He didn't see anyone looking anything like his mother. And that worried him. He hurried to catch up with Philby.

* * *

"That ain't right," the sailor said from the boatswain's chair, hanging by a pair of ropes from the overhead deck like a window washer. He was repainting the *Dream*'s freshly painted hull where some debris carried by high seas had (barely) scratched the hull's glossy surface. The man next to him, also slung from the deck, was in fact the window washer.

"Don't get your BVDs in a twist about it."

"Since when do characters board the ship in costume?"

"Since today."

"You're a real jerk."

"And you're paranoid."

"I don't even know what that means."

"It means it's a maiden voyage. The first ship through the new canal. Are you kidding me? It means the rules change. Everything changes. If the Wicked Witch of the East wants to board in costume, what's the rub?"

"That wasn't the Wicked Witch of the East, cauliflower for brains, it was Maleficent. And the Evil Queen. And Cruella. And Jafar. Judge Frollo. If the passage is so special, why all the villains?"

"They've changed up every single show. You heard that. Or you read it. If you can read, that is."

"Stuff it."

"I'm just saying: it's been on the bulletin board on I-95 for the past week or something." I-95 was the main hallway connecting the crew quarters with administration offices and backstage staircases to all parts of the ship. For crew members and Cast Members alike it was similar to Main Street of a very small town and was off limits to paying passengers.

"Not the part about villains boarding in costume."

"Will you get over that?"

The man finished his last stroke of touch-up, the paint baking in the afternoon sunshine. To look down the length of the vessel from this vantage point was to fully comprehend the vast size of the ship. It wasn't simply big, it was huge. Monstrous. How so many thousands of tons of steel and iron could be made to float was beyond him; he confined his thinking to the sanding and the application of paint.

As the worker admired his effort, a group of stage actors arrived at the Cast Member–only gangway directly beneath the man, near the bow of the ship. At the tail end of this line were four younger actors, one of whom was wide-shouldered, thick at the neck, and wore his hair cut military short. Easily mistaken for being several years older than he was. The first of these kids swiped his key card in front of the electronic reader.

The console beeped and a light turned red.

"Just a minute," the security Cast Member, a young Asian woman, said. "This thing's been acting up today." She typed on the keyboard. "Try it again."

The boy moved his card slowly in front of the reader. The red light flashed, but there was no warning beep this time.

"Perfect," the woman said. "Welcome aboard." She looked up at the actor through vivid green eyes. The same color eyes looked back at her. The two smiled nearly simultaneously.

One by one the security woman processed the next three, each key card sounding a warning beep and flashing a red light. One by one the "problems" were taken care of, and the arrivals were processed into the system.

Two of the four wore sunglasses until well within the ship. This, because it was strange enough that the other two had eyes the exact same color of green. Four kids with unusual green eyes, especially moving around in a group, were certain to attract attention.

And they couldn't have that. Their job was to blend in.

* * *

"The *Dream* welcomes aboard," came the amplified voice of the Cast Member who stood just inside the ship, "the Philby family!" There was a small smattering of applause from other Cast Members. Chip and Dale jumped for joy and clapped their paws—as they did for every arriving family. The other Keepers had arrived ahead of Philby and Finn and were already standing beneath the spectacular chandelier that hung from the ceiling of the three-story lobby. The expansive, gilded area was a statement of grandeur. It told you this was indeed a magical ship and that you had entered a world where every girl was a princess and every boy a prince. Crew members, neatly turned out in crisply starched white uniforms, stood straight-backed, welcoming arrivals. Far across the marble-tiled floor, oversize porthole windows offered a glimpse of water and the industrialized shore beyond, as if a reminder you were not on land. For it was impossible—*impossible*—that such a lobby, with its ornate trim, balconies, portraits of princesses, stairs leading to a dining room, and four glass elevators rising and falling, could possibly be at sea and not on land.

"Whoa," said Maybeck, rarely one to be impressed by anything other than himself.

"Yes," said Philby, "a feat of engineering."

"Really?" said Charlene. "Is that all you've got? Engineering?"

He said, "The exoskeletons of the elevator shafts must serve as—"

Willa touched Philby's arm as the others turned to shut him up. "Maybe later," she whispered. "I'd love to figure out the structural support system with you."

Philby said, "I can handle it." He leaned back to study the ceiling. He moved toward the elevators. The others followed.

Finn continued to listen for any welcome announcement that included his own last name, fearing his mother might actually attempt to board. He reminded himself that Wayne had taken care of it, had invalidated her ticket, but unlike other Wayne promises Finn did not trust this particular one. Ursula's surprising Triton; the rescue dummies searching for Finn after he'd been in Typhoon Lagoon for only minutes; his mother's green eyes—all these things filled him with a sense of unease. Unlike the other guests boarding, he did not view the ship as an escape from regular life, but as a trap. Once the gangways were removed, the doors sealed, the lines gathered, and the ship set sail there was no getting off.

"We have work to do," Philby reminded softly over Finn's shoulder as they boarded the oval-shaped elevator with Philby's mother. "While the crew is distracted."

"I'm with you," Finn said. "But what about . . . ?" He glanced toward Mrs. Philby.

"Leave her to me," Philby said.

They arrived at the Deck 11 concierge staterooms, having had no idea they were to be treated as VIPs. Here, beyond a gated entrance that kept these staterooms private, they walked down a walnut-paneled hallway on thick carpet bearing nautical patterns mixed in with hidden Mickeys. Mrs. Philby unlocked and pushed open the stateroom door and gasped audibly. Finn's room was next door. His eyes bulged as he saw inside.

"Unreal!" said Maybeck, leaning his head out of his own stateroom a few doors down.

In fact, Finn's stateroom was beyond even that. It was more incredible than the most beautiful hotel room he'd ever seen, in any movie, in any magazine.

Ever. Wood-paneled, super-soft furniture, a flat panel television with wireless keyboard and gaming, private balcony. A giant bed. Singularly awesome bathroom with a Jacuzzi tub and separate glassed-in shower.

"Sick," Finn whispered to himself.

A knock at the door, and a moment later Finn and Philby had connected the two staterooms by a common door between them. Philby and his mom had a room even bigger than Finn's, with a dining table and living area, meaning two televisions and two bathrooms. Philby pointed out to Finn how not only the couch converted to a bed, but there was also a bunk hidden in the ceiling that could be set up by the steward at night.

The staterooms shared stewards, who were like butlers and housecleaners all in one.

"We're out of here in five minutes. Okay?" Philby said.

"No problem."

Finn turned on the television in his room, walked out onto the deck, and looked over the side. A few minutes later, he discovered a television that appeared in the mirror in the bathroom. The suite was *sweet*— it had all sorts of tricks.

He and Philby compared notes as they hurried down the hall. Finn knocked on Maybeck's door. Maybeck opened it.

"You good?"

Maybeck opened his hand, revealing the all-important Return. The next-generation device linked to DHI 2.0 was smaller than the previous version. It looked like a rectangular thumb drive with a button in the middle.

"We're going to put this somewhere only we can find it."

"Center of the ship," Philby reminded. The *Dream* was more than a thousand feet long; he didn't want the Keepers to have to run a fifth of a mile of ship decks to exit DHI.

"It's cool," Maybeck said.

"And remember," Philby warned, "they clean this ship every day like it's a hospital."

"I know . . . to keep everyone healthy."

"We'll have to find a place to hide it they won't find."

"I'll tell you what," Maybeck said, irritated. "You do your jobs and we'll do ours."

Stung, Philby stepped back.

"Easy," Finn said to Maybeck.

"He's not the only expert," Maybeck said.

"Later," Finn said.

He'd noticed small cracks developing between Philby and the other Keepers of late. Finn attributed them to Philby's unnerving and growing sense of superiority. If you asked him, Philby didn't have an equal. Finn knew that the stress, the nagging, often terrifying realization that there were people—creatures—after you, didn't help things. It wasn't something anyone should have to live with, Finn thought. The nightmares, the paranoia were all part of it. Jumping awake at the slightest sound; lying awake afraid to go back to sleep. Robbed of the only escape.

Philby assumed his brainpower gave him a position of superiority over the others. But impatience had replaced tolerance. Assuredness, confidence. Rudeness, consideration. He no longer thought himself superior—he knew it. How long he could last in a group whose members fed off one another was unclear, given his unwillingness to participate as an equal. Finn felt the rope fraying at both ends.

"You know," Finn said to Philby, "in a way we, the Keepers, are kind of like the Base."

"How so?"

"Under siege. Surrounded. We're being slowly choked and starved by the enemy. Maybe not of food. But sleep. Tolerance. Patience."

"Interesting analogy," Professor Philby said. "But I don't agree. Soldiers suffer in any war. We are not surrounded. We're under attack. The two are very different. The strategy we must adopt, Finn, is to go on the offensive. Attack! We can't sit back."

"But where?" Finn asked, bristling at his attitude. He might have once expected such bravado from Maybeck, but Philby? "Who? The ISP for the OTs' server keeps moving. How are we supposed to hit a moving target?"

"That's why we're here," Philby reminded.

"Part of why we're here," Finn said.

"To each his own."

"Meaning?"

"It's why we're here . . . it's exactly what we're about to do," Philby said, as if obvious. "This is what it's all about."

Get a life, Finn felt like saying, knowing he too was overtired.

"You want a mind-bender?" Philby asked.

"Sure," Finn said, always up for a challenge.

"How come when you—or any of us—goes *all clear* we don't fall through the ground?"

Finn was about to answer when he caught himself. "Interesting."

"We can pass through walls. Stuff can pass through us. Yet we don't sink into the ground and disappear. Why not?"

"*All clear*," Finn clarified, "as opposed to holograms, since the holograms are projections?"

"Exactly."

"It's a nonissue in 2.0. And we can't go *all clear* from our human state anymore. They removed that ability."

"Are you sure?"

"Of course I'm sure," Finn said, his voice quavering.

"But we haven't field tested that," Philby said.

"No, I suppose not." If Philby was trying to bait Finn to ask the obvious, Finn wasn't biting. He refused to believe Philby could go *all clear* when in a waking state, given the limitation imposed by the 2.0 upgrade. If any Keeper was going to master that power, it would be him, not Philby. Or so he hoped.

Philby asked, "What if back in 1.6 we stayed on the ground when *all clear* because we wanted to?" He allowed Finn a moment to consider the idea. "The same way fear took us out of *all clear*, intention kept us where we wanted to be: standing on a floor or on the ground."

"We control it all?" Finn said in a whisper. Then he said, "Is this honestly how you spend your time? Thinking up this stuff?"

"It's interesting."

Not really, Finn was thinking. You're just showing off.

"What if we could master *all clear* in 2.0? Turn ourselves into projections with nothing more than the intention? Once *all clear*, 2.0's stability would lock it in."

"But it's the stability of the upgrade that prevents us from going *all clear*. Right?"

"Is it?" Philby asked.

"You're the wizard. You tell me!"

"We've barely broken the seal," Philby said. "Like any upgrade to any operating system, 2.0 goes way deeper, has way more bells and whistles than we know." He paused. "Way more!"

Finn felt like shoving him. It was like Philby was teasing him—that he was going to make Finn beg to hear more.

"What is it with you?" Finn said.

Philby grinned slyly. "Nothing," he said, not meaning it at all. "No big."

15

PHILBY HADN'T TAKEN HIS EYES off his watch since arriving outside the Radio Studio on Deck 14.

"The security office is located on Deck One. That's basically fourteen floors below us. Right now, with two thousand guests coming aboard, the elevators are packed and slow. That suggests security guys would take the stairs. At a full run it would take at least five minutes to get up here. More like seven or eight."

"O-kay," Finn said, a little tired of all the lectures.

"You understand," Philby continued, "that what we're about to do is illegal. Beyond illegal. It's probably considered more like an act of terrorism or something."

"Way to build my confidence," Finn said.

"I'm just saying—"

"I get it."

"Big trouble, serious trouble if we get caught."

"I got it the first time." Finn studied the door. "How are we supposed to get in there?"

"Wayne said we'd know."

"Know what?"

"Don't ask me! How to get in, I suppose."

"And do you?"

"No," Philby confessed. "But he named the time and place. It can't be that hard."

"You don't sound convinced," Finn said.

"Listen, this ship carries the most advanced technology there is. Only the U.S. Navy has stuff more serious than this. When we key this door open, that action is recorded into a log. It's on a hard drive somewhere. And it'll show up on security's monitors—"

"As an authorized entry."

"We hope so, yes. Hopefully Wayne is sending someone with access to the Radio Studio. So it shouldn't raise a red flag. But a security guy could decide to take a look at the studio's security cameras because of the alert, because of the entry. If he does, then he's going to see two kids in there. So there're two issues."

"There's a surprise."

"First, if they see two kids on their monitors, chances are they're going to come looking for us."

"Perfect."

"Second, if they're watching us, we can't show them what we're up to. Don't forget it's likely being recorded. So we have to mislead them so that even if they review the videos they don't get what's going on."

"You're not talking just about security guys," Finn said knowingly.

"Maybe not."

"You're saying the Overtakers can tap into the security video feeds?" He felt his heartbeat increase. "Seriously?"

"All I'm saying is it can't hurt to take precautions."

"So once we're in there, we're going to do one thing, but pretend we're doing something else?"

"Two things," Philby corrected. "We went over this. I'm counting on you, Finn."

You and everybody else, Finn thought.

"We want to look like two kids pretending to be radio dudes. You know: kidding around. So we're going to jump from talking to each other across the interview desk to me at the controls. Kids playing around."

"I got it."

"And in the meantime—"

"You're going to work your magic," Finn said.

"You look terrified."

"I am terrified," Finn said. "We get kicked off the ship in the first hour we're aboard, we're not exactly making things better."

"This stuff has to get tested while we're still tied to shore."

"Yeah, yeah. The hard link to our land-based server." Finn had been told of the requirement twice.

"Yes. I need to establish a land-linked Ethernet

handshake with our DHI server to assign a static IP address. It's how the server works. Once I've got that address established, it can be reassigned to the wireless system on board. But it's not easy. It's not quick. And don't forget your call to Wayne."

Three times. "But it's not a call."

"Radio, whatever."

"But why not just call me on my cell?"

"Wayne does stuff . . . his way."

"Yeah, I noticed." He didn't like having to listen to Philby telling him about Wayne. It made him uneasy. Jealous, if he was being truthful.

"There's got to be a reason," Philby said. "Doesn't matter." He checked his watch. "Transmission's in ten . . . nine minutes."

"So shouldn't we get in there?" Finn asked. "Get started?"

"Do you see a key anywhere?"

"No."

"We need a key."

For Finn the next minute was very long. Knowing nothing of what the Radio Studio looked like, he tried to rehearse the next few steps in his head. Tried to see himself and Philby in there so it wouldn't seem so foreign when the time came.

They stood in front of the glass door etched RADIO

STUDIO in smoky lettering. The studio interior was dark.

Finn caught movement to his left, down the stairs. A swish of reddish-black hair, olive skin. The flutter of footsteps racing away from them. Instinctively, he moved toward the activity.

Looking down at the next landing he saw a colorful card the size of a credit card on the carpet.

A ship ID and room key.

Philby saw it too. He waved the key card.

"The old goat delivered!"

Finn didn't appreciate Wayne being called an old goat. He was about to protest as Philby hurried past him and waved the key in front of the door. It unlocked.

Finn glanced back down the stairs, wondering who their ally was. "Let me see that card," he said.

Philby pocketed it. "No time."

They entered, quickly shutting the door behind them.

Finn slid into a seat in front of one of three microphones. Philby took the engineer's chair.

"How do you even know what you're doing?"

Philby shot him a look as if to say, *Who says I do?* He threw several switches, put on a set of headphones, pushed some buttons, then adjusted a tuner. He worked some faders on the soundboard in front of him and stabbed some buttons there as well. Finn also donned a pair of headphones; suddenly there was a deafening voice.

"This is Lou Mongello, calling for the *Dream* Radio Studio."

Philby spoke to Finn. "Lou Mongello runs WDW Radio on the web. Wayne used his station as the go-between to make the contact with us. Less chance of being discovered. Basically it's like this: Wayne will pretend to be interviewing you for Lou's show."

"Got it." Why did Philby know all this stuff?

"You may need to ask him questions as well."

"Sure."

"This is the Studio," Philby said into a microphone. "We've got you, Lou."

"Ready for the interview?" Lou Mongello said.

"We're ready on this end."

"I'm busy today, so I'm going to turn this over to one of my reporters."

"No problem," said Philby. He covered up his microphone and spoke to Finn. "He's putting Wayne on."

Finn gave him the thumbs-up.

"This is Mr. Alcott," Wayne said, using his daughter's surname. "Mr. Lawrence?"

"I'm on," Finn said. The interview was under way.

Philby left the chair and got busy with other machinery. Finn watched Philby while speaking to Wayne.

The Radio Studio was aft-facing with a spectacular view of the back half of the ship and the Inland Waterway beyond.

"Welcome to the show, Mr. Lawrence. I understand you're involved in archives at Disney's Hollywood Studios?" Wayne's warm voice said through the headphones.

"Yes," Finn said, trying to play along. "An interest of mine for some time now."

"And you've visited the facility recently?"

"I have," Finn said, recalling his description to Wayne about the confrontation with Maleficent and the two others. "I discovered a volume that was of particular interest to me. Of interest to many, I'm sure. A journal that dates back to the early days."

"Are you aware there are many similar journals in the Disney Family Museum in San Francisco?"

Finn tried to make sense of the comment. "I . . . ah . . . I'll have to get out there sometime. I'm based on the East Coast right now. Similar in what way?"

"As you know, the Imagineers have been scanning the contents of the library, and the journal you refer to detailed the creation of many of Walt Disney's most beloved and most feared characters."

"Yes, of course." Wayne had told him as much on the train.

"This particular volume is among those not yet scanned . . ." Wayne paused, allowing it to sink in. "But there is a card catalog entry listing some of its contents, and it includes information about the enchantment of Chernabog." He allowed the words to hang there.

Finn tried to translate what he was hearing. Chernabog was Disney's most evil villain. The enchantment of Chernabog . . . the thought of that turned his stomach.

"The original entries about the beast's origin. It is, without a doubt, the most important entry in the volume." He was speaking somewhat obliquely for the sake of their conversation.

"Okay. Got it," Finn said. "That *is* interesting."

"Isn't it, though? What's your overall impression of the Disney library?" Wayne went on to ask a half dozen meaningless questions. Finn did his best to answer. The message had been received: the enchantment of Chernabog was all that mattered. Either Maleficent, the Evil Queen, or, less likely, Cruella had wanted that information badly enough to break into the library for it. That couldn't be good.

Before ending the interview, Wayne passed along

a place and time: Buena Vista Theatre balcony, eleven thirty p.m. Finn would be there.

"It's not like Maleficent's collecting a family history," Finn said to Philby.

"Not hardly," Philby said as he continued to work with a device about the size of a hardcover book.

"Is that the GPS?"

"Technically speaking it's a location transmitter. We'll use the studio's connection to the dish to send our position back to Base. All other Internet traffic is monitored and filtered. They don't mess with this line because for voice clarity it's a direct connection to the transmission dish."

"And so this box, by showing the *Dream*'s position, is supposed to help the Imagineers narrow down the location of the OTs' DHI server?"

"It never stays in one place. It moves up and down the east coast of Florida. It's likely a relay from one of the cruise ships. By transmitting our exact location, they can determine if it's us or another of the ships."

"Or not a ship at all," Finn said.

"That too."

"And this is supposed to take you how long?"

"I'm working as fast as I can." He said it condescendingly, as if emphasizing that Finn was no use in such technical matters.

"The reason I ask," Finn clarified, "is because if anyone's on their way up, then according to you, they will be here in approximately . . . forty-five seconds."

"Five minutes? That was fast." Philby snapped an Ethernet cable into the box, flicked a switch, and illuminated a light on the device. "That's it."

"We're gone," Finn said.

He and Philby stepped up to the smoky glass door.

"Wait a second," Philby said. He slipped off his running shoe, put the Radio Studio key card into his shoe, and put the shoe back on.

"Smart," Finn said. If the boys were patted down by security, the only key card found on Philby would be his room card. Only a strip search would locate the real key, and Disney wasn't about to strip search anyone, especially one of their VIP guests.

"I do my best."

Finn cringed.

They stepped out onto the landing. Two things happened at once: the security guys arrived up the stairs, and a girl—a young Asian woman in the shorts and polo shirt of the ship's crew—arrived to the far side of a glass door leading into the Outlook piano bar. She spotted the security guys and turned around, heading deeper into the bar. A swish of black hair.

"You there!" called out one of the security men to the boys.

"Who else?" Philby said, indicating it was only him and Finn standing there.

Finn waved. "Hey!" He looked down, making sure his red VIP lanyard and special Captain Mickey key card showed in the lanyard's plastic sleeve.

The security guy knew his stuff. He appraised Finn's credentials from a distance and altered his tone of voice from accusatory to cooperative.

"Welcome aboard!" the man said. "Anything we can help with?"

The other security guy approached the studio door and pulled, ensuring it was locked. He then unlocked it and went inside.

"I was scheduled for a radio interview," Finn said. "I'm DHI. A guest—"

"A Kingdom Keeper. Yeah. I know," interrupted the big man. "We've all been looking forward to this cruise."

The men shook hands with both boys.

"If you need anything," the security man offered, "it's Steven."

"Absolutely," Finn said.

"I hope they give you time so as you can enjoy the cruise," said the other.

"No doubt!" Finn said.

The security men indicated the stairs and followed the boys down.

* * *

At nearly the same moment, Maybeck, Willa, and Charlene, all in their staterooms with a parent (or in Maybeck's case, his aunt), switched out their Captain Mickey room keys and red VIP lanyards for Cast Member identification cards and blue employee lanyards. Wayne had supplied the fake IDs. Maybeck and Charlene could easily pass as eighteen-year-olds, the minimum age requirement for Cast Members. Willa was borderline. Because of this she added a minor amount of makeup, giving herself the few years she needed.

Using a *Dream* brochure, Philby had tutored and quizzed all the Keepers about the physical layout of the ship, its decks, pools, hallways, restaurants, stairwells, elevators, theaters, staterooms, cafes, bars, and the spa. He'd built a virtual *Dream* simulator on his laptop—he would flash an animation of a particular hallway or atrium or balcony and ask a Keeper to name exactly where it was. He repeated the exercise with each kid until they had the drill perfected. There could be no second-guessing if trouble erupted; the Keepers had to be able to move quickly and confidently through the floating labyrinth.

Maybeck caught a glimpse of Willa descending below him on the mid-deck stairwell. He slowed, not wanting to arrive to Cast Member laundry at the same time she did. Everything they were about to do had been carefully planned and rehearsed. The Keepers were like a SWAT team, each performing specific duties to infiltrate the ship and ferret out the Overtakers, if present, all the while appearing to be five VIP kids enjoying a two-week cruise with passage through the Panama Canal.

Willa arrived at the Deck 1 landing of the ship's central staircase and turned toward the double doors she knew to be the entrance to I-95—the administration offices and crew members' central corridor on the port side of the *Dream*. She could not appear to hesitate. She strode to the doors, leaned into the sensor close enough for her card to read, and heard the latch free up. As instructed, she pulled open the left door, blessing Philby with each step.

The I-95 corridor was a surprise at first. It lacked the plush appointments of the guest areas of the ship. Instead it was an incredibly long stretch of pale gray vinyl flooring and hard, steel walls painted enamel white, with pipes and wires running overhead, all brightly lit. Here and there the walls were interrupted by a bulletin board or a safety poster. Doors—so many doors—leading off both sides, some marked by overhead exit signs, others carrying titles like Safety Officer, Human Resources, and Medical. Willa joined the other crew and Cast Members, her head slightly down in hopes no one would recognize her.

She turned left at the first overhead exit sign and descended a steep, ladderlike gleaming white stairway. She passed bigger pipes and valves and fire-fighting boxes and more safety posters. Now a floor below sea level, she turned toward the laundry. Fifth door on the right.

She turned into the open door and stopped at the counter where an Indian Cast Member wearing a head scarf manned a computer terminal.

"Yes?" the woman said.

"Sarah Sandler," Willa said, using the name on her Cast Member ID.

The woman typed busily, ran a fingernail along the screen, then turned and disappeared into racks of vertical shelving, returning a minute later with some clothes on hangers. Willa thanked her, accepting the galley uniform—the clothes of a kitchen worker. She went down a hall and into a women's locker room. She found a locker with a key, changed into the uniform, and locked her belongings away. She let out a deep sigh, letting go of the stress of the past few minutes. Now she'd be looking over her shoulder for Maybeck.

* * *

Humiliating. That was Maybeck's first thought as he regarded himself in the locker room's full-length mirror. He looked like a dishwasher. He thought of himself as an artist, so the new look—actually a baker's outfit—was as disturbing as it was unfamiliar. He had to look at himself several times before he recognized himself. Then he sucked it up and followed the memorized route to reach the ship's walk-in refrigerators. The area was sparkling clean—crates of juices, drinks, cereals, flour, oats, rice, pasta—all stacked into towering structures twelve feet high and broken into aisles every twenty feet. The area was chaotic, as last-minute boarding and stocking of dry goods, fruits, vegetables, meats, and dairy products turned it into a hub of activity. The perfect time for a little spying. The only time all the giant walk-in refrigerators and freezers, each the size of a one-car garage, would be left unlocked and accessible. There were more than twelve such cold-storage units to search. For the sake of security, Maybeck and Willa would perform the task together—one inside, one standing watch outside.

Maleficent needed a cold environment. It wasn't exactly a weakness, but it was a vulnerability. She wouldn't melt like the Wicked Witch of the West if she warmed up, but her powers were greatly diminished—no more flaming fireballs, no more erecting corrals with just the flick of a wrist. The warmer her surroundings, the more "human" she became. When jailed, her cell had been kept at seventy-eight degrees Fahrenheit, and she'd been little more than a green-skinned, jumpsuited woman with a superiority complex. If she were hiding on the *Dream*, the refrigerators and freezers seemed a natural place to search.

The refrigerators were more like vaults; large, dimly lit spaces stacked tightly with crates of food. The first one Maybeck entered was devoted to fish, and the smell caused him to nearly vomit. The cold cut through him like a knife. A single tube light emitted a bluish hue, turning the frozen fillets and shrimp a sickly color. Knowing the green fairy's deviousness, Maybeck heaved aside stacks of crates that might be disguising an interior space. He pulled and twisted a tower of ten plastic containers of halibut to where they opened like a door to more stacked crates. These too he wrestled to one corner, then peered into the very center of the island of multicolored containers. Solid. No hidden space at its center.

He worked the freezer's perimeter, his teeth beginning to chatter, the tips of his fingers hurting along with his ears. Too cold? he wondered. Could Maleficent survive in such a frozen space? Then another thought gripped him: did he put anything past her?

Willa's coughing brought him back. With no time to return the heavy towers of crates to their original positions, he instead snagged a crate of halibut and struggled to carry it into the aisle. As he planted it on the concrete floor, a crew member entered, wheeling white crates.

"Cod," the man said.

"Got it," Maybeck said.

The crew member worked the hand truck to dislodge the crates and then left. Maybeck heaved the stacks back into place, shoved the cod into the corner, and left the freezer.

He shook his head at Willa, letting her know he'd found nothing.

"If you think about it," he said quietly, "she'd never be hanging around when it's this busy down here."

"Yes," she said. "I have thought about it. So have Philby and Finn. But this is also the best time for us—for you and me. It's busy. No one knows exactly who belongs and who doesn't. Maybe all we're looking for is evidence."

"Yeah," he said. "Okay."

"I'll take the next one," she said.

"The stacks are heavy," Maybeck said.

"I'll manage."

"I'm just saying . . ."

"I know what you're saying. And I'm saying I'll be all right."

"All right. Whatever. I was just trying to—"

"Yes? Well, don't."

"Pardon me for living."

"Pardon me for being a girl, but I think I can manage." Willa entered the next space—a refrigerator. Maybeck stood guard, checking his watch to make sure they wouldn't be late to the Sail-Away Celebration. He coughed loudly as an older kitchen worker approached pushing a hand truck laden with bricks of butter.

"Don't just stand around," the man told him. "There're more hand trucks on the dock. Get the lead out!"

"Yes, sir," Maybeck said.

The man looked at him curiously. It occurred to Maybeck—a little late—that maybe the use of "sir" was overdoing it.

"I'll take these for you," Maybeck said, putting a hand on the hand truck, trying to stall.

"Bucket brigade?" the older man said. Suddenly,

a smile lit up his grizzled face. "I like it. That could be more efficient. Good suggestion . . ." He studied Maybeck's ID. "Charles."

"Thank you."

"Listen up, everybody!" the man hollered into the room of workers. A moment later he'd instituted the bucket brigade principle to the loading efforts—one person wheeled in a hand truck carrying the food while another person took over the hand truck and put the food away.

"Just perfect," Willa said, having overheard and now seeing what Maybeck had started. "Only one person at a time inside the coolers. That was brilliant. Nice work. Now we'll never get into the rest of them."

"Never say never," Maybeck said.

"As in, not today," she said.

"Admittedly," Maybeck said, "we've hit a setback."

"You're an idiot," she said.

Maybeck grimaced. He knew he deserved it. But then divine intervention took over. A worker removed a black crate filled with heads of lettuce from the third refrigerator and set it atop a pile of cardboard boxes marked FRESH FRUIT. The top flap of one half of the plastic lid held a torn strip of fabric pinched in its corner. Another worker arrived and picked up the crate before Maybeck could think.

"Hey," he said to Willa, "I need you to tip over those cranberry juice crates."

"Excuse me?"

"Now, please. As in, this moment."

He moved to his right.

Thankfully, Willa, his teammate, obeyed. She pretended to stumble, throwing her shoulder into the crates of cranberry juice, tumbling them across the central aisle marked by yellow warning lines. Those lines meant that the lane must stay clear at all times. Several workers rushed to help her, including the man carrying the lettuce. He set down the container and hurried to Willa's side.

Maybeck crossed the aisle behind the confusion and snatched the torn piece of fabric from where it was pinched. He slipped it into the pocket of his kitchen uniform and was about to help Willa when something in the opposite direction caught his attention. There, down the long corridor stacked with crates and boxes, the open doors of the refrigerators and freezers belching a white fog, he saw a pretty girl staring at him. Just out of college, maybe. Dark hair. Dark eyes. She looked away as he glanced in her direction.

But she'd been staring. Staring coldly at him. Curiously.

More like the stare of a spy.

* * *

White shorts with a woven black belt. Ankle socks with a red fuzzy ball sewn at the ankle. White deck shoes. A collared, pale blue golf shirt with DISNEY CRUISE LINES embroidered on the upper left side. Firm posture. Bright smile. Charlene adjusted the Cruise Line headband in the reflection off the elevator glass, licked her lips, and double-checked the name on the ID that hung from the pale blue lanyard: Cecily Fontaine.

Cecily? Really? And Fontaine? Does she look like a fountain or something? Who came up with such stuff?

"It's starting," said one of the other girls, a tall, thin, sharp-nosed girl with insanely long legs. Charlene followed her out of the elevator and down a hall to a bar that wasn't open at this hour. There were a dozen young people dressed as she was along with a half dozen other Cast Members dressed in dark blue shorts and white tops. These, it turned out, were the handlers for the characters who were not in on the meeting.

"Okay, so listen up, everyone! This Sail-Away is different today—"

"Just like everything else about this cruise!" said one of the Cast Members. She brought the others to laughter.

The leader acknowledged her with a nod. "Yes. It's true. This passage won't be like anything we've done before. Everything's a little bit different." She then silenced the girl with a glance; she didn't want other interruptions. "And today's Sail-Away includes the introduction of the DHIs—the Disney Hosts—"

"The Kingdom Keepers!" someone else said. Again, more laughter.

"Yes. They are being briefed separately. Their entry will come after Jack Sparrow, but before Minnie and Mickey. The cue is the end of the song, on the lyrics"— he checked his clipboard—"'living the adventure.' Does everyone know his or her marks at that point?"

Everyone nodded.

"Does anyone *not* know his or her marks?"

No one raised a hand, though Charlene's was half-way up before she pulled it back down.

"For those of you just joining us today for the first time, we have Danny, Kyle, and Cecily. Raise your hands, please."

Charlene raised hers and pulled it right back down.

"For today you'll be in the back row. Clara will fill you in. You'll watch her. We won't ask anything too demanding of you just now. Tomorrow's performance is different. We'll integrate you more fully at this afternoon's rehearsal."

Charlene, like the rest of the Keepers, lived her life with one eye open. Between the OTKs and the OTs themselves, nowhere was safe. She and the others were under what felt like perpetual surveillance. So when the hair on her neck tingled, she peeked to her right and caught the tall, thin girl staring at her.

Green eyes.

The girl wormed a smile at her. Fake and insincere.

Charlene smiled back, equally void of emotion, but her gut twisted.

"We will switch out the DHI models who are on the cruise with us and replace them with their holograms. I'll go over that choreography, and we'll rehearse it with stand-ins in a minute because we want it executed flawlessly. One minute, Captain Jack and his pirates will be in a sword fight with the models. The next, Jack will gain the advantage and go for a killing blow to Finn, one of the DHIs. His sword will pass through the hologram, which should be quite the crowd-pleaser. The hologram is programmed to then battle Jack to stage left and off. It should be terrific fun. So, if there're no questions right now, we'll get started. Let's take it from 'living the adventure.' On your marks, everyone!"

16

By FIVE IN THE AFTERNOON guests had already begun to gather on Deck 11, which had a view of the Funnel Vision screen and a stage where a Cast Member named Max was already warming up the crowd with trivia questions and T-shirt giveaways. For the arriving guests, the afternoon had been spent unpacking, eating, and then eating some more. With the *Dream* at capacity for the Panama Canal passage, more than three thousand passengers were wandering the ship. Many hundreds arrived to Donald's Pool to participate in the Sail-Away Celebration, a triumph of song and dance to set the tone for two weeks of endless entertainment. There were dozens of programs of every kind for every age throughout the ship at any given hour. Several times a week Cast Members threw events like this: celebrations, feasts, and parties. It was impossible for even the most cynical and skeptical not to be impressed.

The Sail-Away Celebration was intended to set the bar high, to let guests know this was not going to be anything less than the most magical and memorable trip ever. The show was lively, colorful, and infectious. The

Cast Members smiled and exuded energy. The giant outdoor movie screen above them set backdrops and delivered effects. Dozens of hidden speakers boomed with song. From the opening moment, the crowd was mesmerized, clapping and singing along with a dozen dancing performers and appearances by a wide variety of Disney characters, all of whom elicited cheers.

Backstage, hidden inside the housing for the ship's forward smokestack, Maybeck, Willa, Finn, Charlene, and Philby stood ready for their signal. Though they had managed to gather for their required rehearsal following the ship's drill, there had been little time to share their experiences of the previous hours. As a group they did not know of Wayne's call nor of Philby's successful installation of the GPS transmission unit; nor had they heard of Willa and Maybeck's discovery of a possible piece of Maleficent's cape. In fact, the only message that they had managed to communicate between them was Charlene's warning that a part of the upcoming show pitted Jack Sparrow against Finn in a sword duel that called for Jack to stab Finn's hologram—a piece of programming that, should it go wrong, might have obvious unwanted side effects for the real Finn.

With no time to do much of anything about that possibility, the five now stood, mentally reviewing the choreography they'd gone over only minutes before, a clever bit of distraction and substitution that had some small pyrotechnics grabbing the crowd's attention while the DHIs took the place of the Keepers—holograms in place of kids. They planned to slip behind the back row of performers (a row that was supposed to include "Cecily Fontaine," but did not) right at the moment of DHI projection. Only the real Finn was to remain onstage. He'd be engaged in a sword fight with Jack Sparrow. His switch to hologram was a bit more tricky: two Cast Members would grab swords and step up to take on Jack, defending and screening Finn. By the time they stepped away, the real Finn would be gone, replaced by his DHI. But timing was critical. Finn focused, reminding himself of his positions onstage and the timing they'd just rehearsed.

His heart beat quickly at the idea of Jack Sparrow swinging a sword at him. He couldn't be sure Jack Sparrow would be played by a Cast Member. What if the DHIs were not the only ones being substituted?

All these possibilities cluttered Finn's head as he followed the others outside and into the adoring applause that erupted spontaneously as the DHIs were introduced. He was caught by surprise by the whistles and shouts, the outstretched arms of teens his own age in the front row. A rock-star moment, it was something he and the Keepers only experienced during Disney parades—and even then the roars and adulation was for the parade ensemble, not the Keepers alone. This, on the other hand, was an explosion of appreciation, wild, shrill cries for them.

Sometime in the past few minutes the *Dream* had cast off, departing Port Canaveral, moving now but feeling as smooth and steady as if still tied up to the dock. Finn felt no shudder in his legs. No sense of movement in any direction. Only the scenery slipping past provided any proof the voyage was now under way.

"D-H-I," rose the chorus. "Over here!" called out many anxious voices—from all different directions— followed by flashes from cameras held up high in the air. This was a moment many guests had waited for, and they shared their enthusiasm loudly. The adrenaline was running—the cruise had begun.

Overhead, the Funnel Vision screen showed video of the DHIs inside the various Disney World parks escorting guests to various attractions. The popularity of the DHIs had surprised everyone. The Keepers' lore had a great deal to do with their popularity—all the stories of nighttime battles with Disney villains— and the Sail-Away Celebration programmers took full advantage by intercutting shots of Maleficent, Chernabog, Cruella De Vil, and other villains onto the giant overhead screen.

Boos and jeers cut into the celebration as the crowd caught glimpses of the Overtakers.

Finn, Charlene, Maybeck, Philby, and Willa moved stage right to left facing aft, the screen behind them. They hit their marks as rehearsed. Max, the emcee, quieted the crowd with a new introduction.

"Here we are making our way out into the seven seas, and you all know what that means?"

"We're cruising!" someone shouted.

"We're stuck on this ship!" another crowed.

"I'm in heaven!" a girl cried out.

"We're not alone!" called Max.

A cheer went up from the crowd.

"Please wave a big hello to our sister ship, the *Disney Magic*, off the starboard side!" He pointed. The crowd turned its attention to where Max pointed, the stern of the *Magic*—tied up to shore—just coming into view. "It's rare to get a meeting like this, so please give a big shout-out to her crew. And look for someone special!"

Onstage, the distraction allowed time to drop four lines from an overhead railing above the Funnel Vision screen. Up there could be seen the shadows of men being strapped to the lines.

Suddenly, the *Magic*'s horn sounded the opening notes of "When You Wish upon a Star." This was followed, only seconds later, by the *Dream*'s horn, which continued the same melody: "Makes no difference who you are!" The combination of the two ships complementing the melody made the crowd roar. People screamed loudly. The two ships repeated the signals—the fourteen notes sounding in perfect order. More cheers.

And there he was: Mickey Mouse, outside the *Magic*'s pilothouse, waving to the crowd on the *Dream* and drawing an untold number of like greetings. It was a lovefest.

But not for long.

* * *

Willa knew her part. She had little trouble memorizing movement or role-playing. She enjoyed it. She even hoped to do some acting later in high school or college. Her formative years had been almost exclusively devoted to academics. She was a brainiac, and with that came limitations. She didn't hate studying the way a lot of kids did; she actually enjoyed it—though she never said that aloud. She was self-competitive; she liked sports because she loved trying to outdo herself—more than beating others. She had a good memory, and knew this helped her. Remembering where to stand onstage, when to look where, when to appear surprised or impressed or joyful—a piece of cake.

She curled around the far end of the stage with Maybeck and Philby, turning toward the hundreds of excited faces. The sun, low in the rich sky, shone a dull yellow as it approached a bank of low clouds on the western horizon. It was, by all standards, a perfect day. And yet it did not feel perfect. Looks can be deceiving, she reminded herself. Her complicated brain had collected, assembled, and recombined a variety of events and facts into what could only be described as a grave sense of danger. The torn piece of Maleficent's robe in a place a character had no business being. The ominous switching out of their DHIs in the Sail-Away party. The sword fight. Who was the choreographer on that one? Maleficent herself?

In Willa's mind, it was not a matter of *if* it would go wrong, but *when*. How? For some reason, the Overtakers were always the ones to make the first move. She could not remember a time the Keepers got the jump on them. They were always on the defensive. Always looking over their shoulders, wondering what might happen next.

Only once, on Tom Sawyer Island, had the Keepers broken through to capture Maleficent—but it had not gone as planned and nearly cost them dearly. Willa wanted the shoe on the other foot—she was tired of being the victim.

For this reason she found herself on full alert. She

didn't know about any of the others, could not speak for them, but sensed they too were in a state of hyper-awareness.

And that moment was at hand.

It happened quickly. There was some impromptu dancing to the theme song from Pirates of the Caribbean. It spread out to the perimeter walkways that circled the deck and ended in sheets of thick Plexiglas that served as a wind barrier. The Funnel Vision screen showed the rising masts of a pirate ship with rigging running in every direction, flags flapping, sails bulging. Suddenly, a pirate jumped from atop the smokestack, sliding down a rope. The blending of the real pirate against the projected image was so convincing that at first your eyes wanted to believe he was up on the screen, part of the film. But as he landed on the stage and the crowd recognized him, an enormous cheer went up.

"Jack Sparrow!"

He drew his sword and rushed Finn.

Other pirates flooded the stage from the same door the Keepers had used. But it struck Willa that there were too many of them. One or two might have made sense on such a crowded stage, four or five if you wanted to give the impression of an insurmountable army. But eight or ten? Talk about overkill. And if overkill, then Overtakers.

Max, the emcee, now relegated so far to stage right that he was nearly being pushed off, also looked perplexed at the sight of so many pirates. Holding the microphone to his mouth, having just called out Sparrow's name, he was stuck, frozen. He seemed ready to announce something more, but the sight of so many pirates left him speechless.

That was how Willa saw it from her perspective.

In fact what was going on in Max's head at that moment was self-doubt. The internal panic that he'd gotten it all wrong, had missed some vital piece of information important to the scene. He froze, not out of any fear concerning the pirates, but fear he'd lose his job if he messed this up. Why exactly were so many pirates swarming and storming the stage, and what was his role in the skit? How could he have missed such an important detail?

Willa looked to her right, doubly surprised when pirates arrived from her left as well. Where had they come from? Another four pirates! A piratical convention. Sailor Goofy and Nautical Minnie found themselves pushed away from center stage, which was, as it turned out, the mother of all signals.

Minnie never—ever—had been pushed anywhere or been anything but the center of attention. Neither Jack Sparrow nor any of his men would ever, could ever, come close to her royalness—not highness but *Minnie-ness*, a bloodline of pen and ink lines that went back decades.

The moment Minnie stumbled, a collective gasp soared from the otherwise excited crowd. It was as if the queen had lost her crown. The collective mood turned instantly dark and angry.

Jack Sparrow was booed loudly.

Willa was at the perfect angle to see Jack's face twitch at the sound of the jeering, the perfect angle to see the man's lips part, revealing gold teeth. He adored the chorus of disapproval. It was no act: he adored it.

This wasn't right.

* * *

On the bridge of the *Dream*, another problem presented itself. Here, the captain, a handsome Swedish man with golden hair, ice-blue eyes, and perfect posture, paced the large, enclosed deck behind oversize windows offering a two-hundred-degree view of the ocean. Two wings protruded fifteen feet from each side of the bridge like glass sunrooms added as an afterthought—one to port, one to starboard. From these two wings, the captain and his team could see down the full length of the ship and had controls to steer and propel the ship. The wings were typically used for docking. But as one approached these extensions, as the captain did now, one gained a view of that corresponding horizon. All combined, it gave the bridge crew a 360-degree view of their environment.

Added to this were images from a half dozen exterior closed-circuit television cameras that provided electronic images in all directions, as well as several types of radar systems that could see through weather and darkness to identify other ships and warn about collisions dozens of miles before one might happen.

But the responsibilities of the *Dream*'s captain extended far beyond the exercise of keeping his vessel on course and on time. He also had to be the face of security, the image of leadership and command. He had to interact with his passengers, take photographs with them, dine with them, and conduct introductions to social functions. Being in charge of the ship and all its passengers meant Captain Cederberg was also responsible for all the Disney characters and Cast Members and by default preserve the Disney culture aboard the ship. This was not a task the captain or his crew took lightly. The ship was an extension of everything Disney—it was both a cruise ship and a theme park at sea.

For this reason, when his security officer arrived in person on the bridge, Cederberg paid attention.

"Bob?" Robert Heinemann was known to the crew

as Uncle Bob. He was a gregarious man with clear eyes and a boyish voice.

"We've had a report of a double sighting," Bob said privately. "CM." Captain Mickey.

Cederberg stiffened.

"Not on my watch, we haven't."

"Afraid so." Uncle Bob led the captain to the wing and pointed back toward the *Magic*. "Just below the bridge."

Cederberg snatched up a pair of binoculars.

He trained the binoculars. "Mickey's on deck exactly as we agreed."

"Theirs is, yes. Our Mickey was spotted about"— Uncle Bob checked his watch—"seven minutes ago outside Cabanas. It's a double sighting."

Cederberg faced Bob grimly.

"I called down to Christian," Bob said, referring to the *Dream*'s director of entertainment. "Our Mickey is not on duty and is accounted for. Whoever's parading around Deck Eleven is an impostor."

"A guest having some fun?"

"According to the report, this Mickey is a dead ringer. If it is a guest, the costume needs to be confiscated."

"The real deal?" Cederberg bristled. "Not possible!"

"I mustered the crew. Everyone's looking for him,"

Bob said, letting Cederberg know he'd followed ship protocol.

"He's disappeared?"

"Yes."

"He must not be seen abovedecks. Certainly not to stern. Not until we're well clear of the *Magic*."

"Understood."

"He has no handler, then?"

"If he does, the handler's an imposter too."

"Video?"

"Yes. I checked it first, after getting the call. The character walks into view in the area outside Cabanas. He shakes hands with a few of young 'uns, *talks* to them, and then is lost in the crowd around Mickey's pool."

"Talks . . . to . . . them?"

"We have to stop him," Bob said. Captain Mickey *never* spoke.

"The aft stairs?" Cederberg said.

"Well . . . that's the thing, Captain. I mean, that's where one would expect him. But no. Nothing."

"He can't have just disappeared."

"No, Captain."

"It's your job to know, Bob."

"Well aware of that."

"Find him. And when you do, I want to question him or her personally before we throw him into the

218

brig. We've been at sea thirty minutes, Bob. We have two weeks to go."

"Agreed."

"No more of this. Steady as she goes."

"Understood."

"Find him."

Uncle Bob grimaced. It wasn't going to be easy to find one person out of several thousand, and both men knew it. "Right away," he said.

* * *

Swish! The tip of the sword missed Finn's throat by a fraction of an inch. Jack Sparrow—or whoever this was—regarded him with dark, calm eyes. He didn't seem the slightest bit fazed. The sword continued its arc, catching and slicing off the tail of a bandana tied around Dale's furry neck. Finn watched in horror as the piece of fabric floated down to the stage.

A flash of bright light beyond Jack Sparrow blinded him.

The crowd cheered.

As planned, two sword-bearing Cast Members arrived downstage to screen the real Finn as his DHI was projected. This was the moment of substitution—let Jack Sparrow slice my DHI! Finn thought. But something—no, *someone*—was holding him by the ankles. It was one of Sparrow's pirates. He was lying on the stage, making faces to the adoring crowd while not allowing Finn to move. Finn leaned back, away from the next swing of the sword—a real sword. It sliced the air with a hiss.

This guy means to kill me! Finn was unarmed.

One of the Cast Members stepped forward to do battle with Sparrow, but the pirate's sword cut his plastic sword in two.

The crowd went wild. "Go, Jack! Get him, Jack!"

Finn twisted in the grip of the pirate and spotted himself looking back at him. His DHI held a projected sword in hand, programmed for a choreographed sword fight, a sword fight Jack Sparrow either knew nothing of or had no plan to follow. As Jack was distracted by the second sword-carrying Cast Member, Finn fell to the side, dropping to his knees. Jack turned back, mistaking the DHI for Finn. He stepped forward for a thrust, plunging the sword into the chest of the DHI and losing his balance as he met no resistance.

The real Finn reached out and hooked the man's black boot and pulled. Jack Sparrow slammed down onto his back, dropping the sword.

A roar mixed with laughter, the crowd believing it all to be part of the program.

The second of the two Cast Members kicked

Sparrow's sword away. It clattered down to the deck. Still partially screened by the Cast Members, Finn was pulled off balance by the pirate holding him. He fell back, catching the glint of a knife too late. There was nothing he could do to stop himself: he was going to fall upon that upraised knife. He was going to be stabbed.

He waved his arms like a bird flapping its wings. But there was no lift; he continued falling backward.

Then he stopped, something clutching his arms. It was . . . impossible.

"Dill?"

Dillard Cole, Finn's neighbor and best friend outside the Keepers. How had he gotten on board the ship?

He and Finn were locked by forearm grips—like the Roman soldiers used as handshakes in movies.

"Hang tight," Dillard said.

He stretched a leg and stepped onto Jack Sparrow's chest as the man tried to sit up. Cheers and applause erupted from the approving audience.

"What are you—?"

"Later," Dillard answered. "Right now, we've got to get out of here."

At that moment a woman's voice called out from the speakers. A voice that ran chills down the spine. A voice that could stop time.

Maleficent's head was the size of a Volkswagen up on the Funnel Vision screen. Her face a hideous green, her chin pointed sharp like a wedge of cheese, her thin eyebrows above her bloodshot eyes. As she smiled, the white of her teeth made the vivid red of her lipstick and the bilious green skin all the more dramatic. A crow fluttered its wings by her ear. She ignored it.

"Good day to you all!" she said in her gravelly voice. "Or up to now it may have been good. Welcome aboard! Your so-called hero—I like to think of the boy as little more than an annoying pest—has been taken care of, I trust? And you there," she pointed, "in the booth. Don't bother trying to interrupt me. I'll stop when I feel like stopping."

She rocked her head left to right, port to starboard.

"Are you listening, people? Looking forward to the cruise? I wouldn't if I were you. Not with fairies l ike me around. Witches. Villains. Pick your poison." She cackled. "Poison? That's a thought." She shut her eyes—her lids were also the same vile green—and reopened them. "You might ask, what do you want? But you'd be missing the point. You'd be missing all the fun."

The huge screen went black, flickered, then returned

to the background pirate scenery it had been displaying only a minute before.

The crowd remained silent until someone whooped playfully from the back. But it was a lonely sound, and no one joined in with him. Instead, curious and anxious faces stared at the screen while characters and Cast Members onstage remained frozen, eyes looking up.

17

UNCLE BOB REPLAYED the security video several more times, the high-def image greatly magnified. How many times had he recommended more cameras for the new ships? More state-of-the-art technology? His bosses weren't cheap, neither were they nearsighted; they had given him the GPS ID tags, keyless entry locks, and a variety of other technologies he had yet to fully put into place. But the cameras? You could never have too many cameras.

What he saw was a prime example of his limitations. The Deck 4 jogging track consisted of uninterrupted, eco-friendly teak decking encircling the entire thousand-foot-long ship, meaning walking or running three laps equaled a mile. For nearly the entire length of Deck 4, port and starboard, fully enclosed, fiberglass, unsinkable lifeboats hung suspended overhead ready for deployment at a moment's notice. Each motorized boat could safely house and feed 120 guests for over a week at sea. Each had an emergency transmission beacon that activated upon contact with salt water; each carried radios, first aid, blankets, water purification, fishing line, and spare life jackets. A dozen cameras were positioned on Deck 4 to provide quality views of all the lifeboats, allowing security to monitor, manage, and record any emergency evacuation.

Those dozen cameras were six more than any other exterior deck had, and the forward or aft sections of Deck 4 had only two such cameras in place. One was near the bow and was maneuverable 330 degrees, showing both the jogging track and the crew's anchor storage; to the aft, a fixed-mount camera showed a fish-eye view of the track and the stern of the ship.

Bob had caught activity on a recording from the bow camera. He'd missed it the first two times, looking for a person. But during a third look he saw an iconic shadow on the slatted wood deck as it turned to cross the bow. A round dark circle with two equidistant circles atop it. Ears. A head. Mickey Mouse.

Filled with the rare pulse of excitement—Bob loved detective work—he sought the recording from camera 4-9. He matched up the time code. Sure enough, there appeared Captain Mickey, his back to the camera. He walked the jogging path, entering the steel tunnel that housed the jogging track as it crossed around the bow. But he never made it to the bow camera. Never arrived.

He . . . disappeared, Bob realized, wondering how he was ever going to broach the subject with the captain.

He couldn't be using a word like that. Security didn't believe in passengers or crew disappearing; security didn't believe in ghosts; security didn't believe in the "Disney Spirit" haunting a ship (even if the crew did!). Security dealt in facts. Hard, cold facts.

But Captain Mickey had disappeared, the character shadow turning into a blade of black and shrinking from the bottom up, like a fuse burning.

Bob snagged his radio. "Choi? Take Verene and search Deck Four's anchor storage area. Top to bottom. No stone unturned. You copy?"

"Copy."

Uncle Bob glanced at his watch repeatedly. Peter Choi and Michael Verene were among his best men. If anyone could find the missing character it was these two. Bob was not a superstitious man, but he was practical and calculating: this kind of trouble in the first hour of a cruise did not bode well. He'd hoped for an easy cruise: two weeks through the Caribbean and the Panama Canal. A little slice of heaven. His wife was scheduled to join the ship in Aruba.

Break-ins in the Radio Studio? Double Mickeys? This stuff didn't happen—much less on the same cruise! He hoped it wasn't cursed.

Maybe he was more superstitious than he allowed himself to believe.

He watched on the monitors as his two guys each took an opposite side of the ship as they approached the bow of Deck 4. Smart thinking. A squeeze play.

Nothing. He knew the moment Peter Choi looked into the camera lens and shrugged. Bob didn't require a radio call to understand that particular message. Zero.

Bob recalled his men. He was tempted to view the security recordings one final time, but knew he'd only be wasting his time.

The extra Captain Mickey—a Captain Mickey that had no place aboard this ship—had vanished.

* * *

Finn, Philby, and Mrs. Philby ate dinner at a table for four in the Royal Palace, the central dining room off the ship's lobby, which, according to Philby's mom, was the "most beautiful restaurant I've ever eaten in." It took elegance to a new level and reminded Finn of something from *Beauty and the Beast*. Cut-glass chandeliers, linen tablecloths, waiters and waitresses dressed formally. The tables went out in circles from a centerpiece like lily pads in a fountain. Finn had sea bass with green beans and two desserts. Philby had a steak with french fries, and his mother "the juiciest chicken I've had in my life." Finn spent a lot of the time staring at the empty chair across from him, which was where his own mom was supposed to have sat. He thought back to Typhoon Lagoon and tensed as a shiver swept through him. Maleficent had stolen his mom. He didn't know what it meant, not exactly, but feared his mother was under a spell, the same as Luowski. Had Finn lost his mother for good? He felt sick.

Nauseated—knowing it had nothing to do with being seasick—Finn headed back to his room. Mrs. Philby planned to attend the opening show in the Walt Disney Theatre while all five models for the Disney Hosts Interactive—the Keepers—were expected to attend the opening of the Vibe teen center, where, as earlier, holograms would take their place and then mingle with the other teens. Once the swap had been made—holograms for kids—the five teens would be whisked back to their rooms, where they were instructed to stay for the remainder of the evening. By order of the ship's director of entertainment, there can never be more than one of any character visible at the same time. This made for strict scheduling for the Keepers; their itineraries called for long stretches of their being confined to their cabins as their DHIs made character appearances or signed autographs. It was a small price to pay for the free two-week cruise, or had seemed so when first proposed. Now that such confinement was upon them, it felt entirely different. More like jail.

"What was going on with the Maleficent thing at the Sail-Away Celebration?" Charlene asked Finn. Their looks had been coordinated to match their DHI projections, the "costumes" awaiting them in their rooms after dinner. Charlene looked about eighteen in skinny jeans and a red-and-white-striped tank top. Her blond hair fell to her shoulders and was held in place by a black headband comb, which, intended or not, gave her the look of a princess. Her insanely good looks made her the center of attention, especially for the boys in the Vibe, even though Finn knew she didn't enjoy such fawning. She had an almost desperate desire to be seen as something other than pretty. Finn figured that was an uphill battle.

"We weren't the only ones surprised by that," Finn said.

"Do you think we'll turn back?" Charlene said.

"No way. No one knows how serious a threat it is besides us. I mean, Wayne would, but he's not here."

"We could tell him."

"And we will if we get the chance, but he's one guy. There are three thousand paying passengers. 'The show must go on,'" he said, drawing air quotes. "Besides, for now it's just a video. Since this is a DHI cruise, they'll think it was planned. At best, someone'll call it in and it'll take a day or two before anyone realizes it wasn't. At worst, it'll be seen as a prank. No matter what, for now, we're on our own."

"And Jack Sparrow? He could have killed you!" Charlene said.

"Noted," Finn said.

"Nearly did kill you."

"Doubly noted."

"And was that—?"

"Dillard." Finn answered, though couldn't explain. "The really weird thing is, I called the operator and asked to be connected to his room, and they didn't have anyone by that name."

"Seriously?"

"He's not registered. And I would have known if he'd been planning to be here."

"But how's that possible?"

"How's any of this possible?" he asked. He paused. "You know how often I ask myself that? How this ever happened? If this is even happening at all?"

"Me too," she said. "I think we all feel that way. We keep waiting to wake up and find out it was some kind of bizarre dream."

"A very long dream."

Charlene became pensive. "I don't think Maleficent's

message was meant for the passengers as much as for us."

"She wants to scare us," Finn said. "She probably doesn't know that 2.0 gets around that element of fear. We can take advantage of that. We need to cross over tonight and get a look around as DHIs."

"The refrigerators," she said.

"Yeah. Maybeck didn't get the chance to follow up on that."

"You think that since taking over the parks didn't work out for the OTs, they're trying for something more manageable? Something smaller?"

"I assume the battle for Base is a setback for the OTs. If not, we have to hope the volunteers can hold them off. What you and Maybeck pulled off with the brooms and the capture of the green Army Men, collecting some of that goo—we've definitely set them back." He paused, his mind whirring. "Besides, you can't call the *Dream* small," Finn said, thinking of the ship and looking around the teen center. The area, where no parents or adults were allowed, consisted of several large, colorful sections. One with a giant television. Another with a dozen beanbag chairs. Yet another filled with gaming consoles. The Beatles' "All You Need Is Love" played loudly from overhead speakers. Outside, there was a private pool and sports facilities for basketball, volleyball, and soccer. Finn typically hated stuff dedicated to "kids," but this was the exception. It was open until one—although he and the others would have to leave before that.

"I suppose it's all relative," Charlene said.

"I suppose."

"Don't look now, but that hottie is checking you out."

Finn stole a look toward the door. He had to fight to keep his jaw from dropping. The Asian girl was maybe a year or two older than he was. She wore her soft dark hair like a china doll, her bangs cut level at her eyebrows, her hair falling in twin sheets to her square shoulders. She looked familiar to Finn, and yet not familiar at all. He wondered . . .

"Is she on TV or something?" he said, looking away.

"Not that I know," Charlene said. "Though she could be. She's pretty enough."

"There are Disney Channel actors on board, right?"

"That's what we were told."

"So maybe that's who she is."

"Maybe."

"Like *Lemonade Mouth* or something like that?"

"Hayley? No, I know her. It's not Hayley. But she's crushin' on you."

"Give me a break." Hearing the word "crushin'"

reminded him once again of Typhoon Lagoon—in a bad way. And Ursula. Amanda. It seemed like a year ago.

"Don't look now, but here she comes," Charlene said. "Don't forget about Amanda."

Finn tried to make a face at Charlene, but she'd already turned her back on him and was walking away. He stood there not knowing what to do with himself. He was such a klutz when it came to girls.

"Hey, there," the girl said. If you put hand cream all over a Nerf ball, that's how smooth her voice sounded. "You're Finn, right?"

She waved her hand and hit him, open-palmed, squarely on the waist.

"Ah!" she said. "The real item!"

"You were expecting?"

"What I expect and what I hope for are two different things. Which do you want to know?"

He tried to swallow, but his throat was plugged with nerves. His voice cracked as he said, "H-hope for."

"Yes. I was hoping you were you and not the hologram you, although I know the hologram you a lot better. I bet I've toured with you a dozen times if you add up all the parks."

Finn got this more and more: people who, by touring with his hologram, mistook that they'd spent time with him. She apparently knew the difference, but the look in her eyes was still somewhat dreamy.

"And you are?" he said.

"Thrilled," she said. "To meet you." She blushed. "Storey Ming."

Finn offered her his hand and they shook hands. Hers were calloused. Not what he'd been expecting.

"Clay," she said.

"Excuse me?"

"I work with clay," she said, explaining her hands. "Dries out my hands. Makes them rough."

"They're not rough," he lied.

"You think? They're like reptile skin," she said. "But I throw good pots!"

"You're a passenger? A guest?"

"A friend. More like you than you think," she said. "A so-called celebrity—not that you're so-called, far from it; but I am. I'm giving a couple workshops in the middle of the cruise. It's a new thing called All Hands On Deck. Me. There's a painter. Someone doing beadwork. Jewelry. Sea days. You know about sea days?"

"Only that they were on the itinerary."

"Days we never hit land. No port. Just out in the middle of the ocean."

"You've done this before?"

"Not as a guest of Disney, but yeah. Other ships. And my parents love the Disney cruises."

"What's Castaway Cay like?"

"The island? Tomorrow? Awesome! If you like white sand and beautiful water, that is. And food. And bikes. And feeding stingrays."

"Seriously?"

"Totally! And Jet Skis. Snorkeling. Volleyball. It's incredible. You're going to love it." She hesitated. "I could show you around, maybe? I mean, if you want?"

"Yeah! Sure! Of course." He heard the reluctance in his own voice and regretted it. He was so used to hanging with the Keepers that he didn't like making other plans. He needed to get over that.

"If you've got other plans—" she said.

"No, it's not that. It's just my friends . . ."

"The other DHIs? That would be way cool!"

"Yeah, well, maybe we'll all do something together."

That offer appeared to excite her. Finn thought fame a strange bedfellow. Storey Ming didn't know any of the other Keepers, but she was stoked at the thought of spending a day with any or all of them.

It didn't strike him as odd at the time that a girl, older than him and quite pretty, might take an interest in him.

But it soon would.

* * *

At one point, their mission had seemed simple enough. After all, they'd located an OT rogue computer server once before. That had been in Animal Kingdom, and it felt like a long time ago now. They'd learned so much since then. Get on the ship as planned. Attach the GPS. They'd be notified if the ISP location from the OT server matched the ship's. If so, they would seek out the server and destroy it. The possibility that the ship's refrigerators were being used as a hiding place by Maleficent made all the more sense when coupled with the existence of a server—computers worked best when operating at cool temperatures.

But retrieving Walt's stolen journal presented a much bigger challenge and held far greater importance: first they had to find it; then they had to get it back; then the Imagineers would have to figure out what was so important about it. It obviously presented some kind of threat, or why would it be so important to recover it in the first place?

The staterooms came equipped with two complimentary wireless Wave Phones that could connect to other Wave Phones aboard the ship. Philby had made sure that all the Keepers had every number saved into favorites so the Wave Phones could be used whenever needed. They were also capable of texting.

asleep by midnight. crssovr at 12:20. arrival bckstge.
wait 4 all.

Mrs. Philby had allowed Finn and her son to room together in Finn's stateroom that connected to hers by a shared door. A big mistake on her part.

"She sleeps like a rock lately," Philby said. "Give it fifteen minutes, we could drive a tank through there and she wouldn't wake up."

"And where do you handle the crossover from?" Finn asked.

"That gets a little complicated," Philby said. "Why don't you leave that to me?"

"What's with you?"

"What do you mean?" Philby asked.

"Why so condescending?"

"I'm not being condescending. I'm compartmentalizing. The tech stuff is my turf."

"Lately everything's your turf."

"What? Why would you care about the details?"

"Why wouldn't I?" Finn asked.

"You're jealous. My control of 2.0 is bugging you."

"If you're so in control, why don't you cross over with us?"

"Because this is like Epcot, when we overrode the

servers in the Utilidor. It's like that, but more difficult. Who would you suggest handle it?"

"And the Return?"

Philby shook his head. "You're the one who saw Wayne with it. Do you have it? Because I don't!" Philby said. "For now the return has got to be manual, and as a group. That's why I'll be on this side, not crossed over with you. If you'd like to give the job to someone else . . ."

Finn found himself breathing hard. "And if something happens to you . . ."

"Nothing's going to happen."

"But if it did," Finn said. "While we were crossed over . . ." He paused. They both knew the answer: SBS, the Syndrome.

"I won't let that happen."

"There you go again."

"I didn't mean it like that. You're taking this all wrong!"

"Maleficent may have other ideas."

"I'm going to get you guys crossed over and then I'm going to hide where no one can find me. You'll call my Wave Phone to be returned. It'll take me a minute or two to pull it off, so you need to be thinking ahead."

"I'm always thinking ahead," Finn said, uncharacteristically brash. He surprised himself; it sounded more like something Maybeck would say.

"Okay," Philby said.

"What about the GPS? Have you gotten an email or anything? Is their server on the ship?"

"That's too many questions at once," Philby said.

Finn was ready to smack the guy. "Just answer me!"

"The short answer is no. But the video at the Sail-Away said it all: Maleficent knew this was a DHI cruise, and if she's not here herself, clearly her minions are."

"Minions? Really?"

"OTs. Whatever." Philby shot him a look. "What's with you, Finn?"

Finn hesitated for a long time. "I've got a bad feeling about all this. Dillard. The video. This girl I met in the Vibe. It's like a surprise party."

"What are you talking about?"

"When everyone knows what's going on but you," Finn said. "That's how it feels to me."

"Well, I don't know what's going on."

"Is that supposed to make me feel better?"

"They want us scared," Philby reminded him.

"I know that."

"You don't have to cross over tonight," Philby said. "We can wait."

"We have a torn piece of her robe. That's called evidence."

"It could be a character's."

"Could be," Finn said.

"Yeah. Okay," Philby said reluctantly. "I see what you mean."

"I need to be somewhere," Finn said. "Then it's back here to get to sleep in time."

"You're cutting it pretty close if you're going somewhere now," Philby said.

"Then I'm cutting it close."

* * *

Finn descended the forward stairs to Deck 5. He found the stairways and stateroom passageways quieter than during the day, but far from empty. People milled about. Adults. Teens. Lovers. Crew. Midnight snackers. Late-night explorers. Stargazers. John Mayer's "Half of My Heart" played from unseen speakers. Finn felt a lift to his step, briefly relieved of his burdens by the music.

Arriving on Deck 5, he headed aft past the elevators, arriving at the double doors to the Buena Vista Theatre balcony. He hesitated. Wayne had arranged the meeting. Was he supposed to trust it?

He looked both ways and killed a minute studying the movie poster for *Oz: The Great and Powerful*. A couple passed, both the size of compact cars, Finn allowing them to get out of sight. Then he tested one of the doors, and it opened. His nerves jangled.

The balcony and the theater below were clouded in emergency lighting—dull white lights at ankle height and a few glowing red exit signs. The acoustic materials draping the walls and covering the ceiling absorbed every sound. Finn didn't even hear the whisper of his own footsteps, only the throbbing of his heartbeat as blood rushed past his ears. He'd come to distrust large, empty spaces like this. As a Keeper he'd been called upon to enter empty park attractions and pavilions, had nearly always found himself in peril within moments of doing so. Why should this be any different? he wondered.

Wayne, he answered himself. Wayne had sent him into Typhoon Lagoon, and now Wayne had sent him here.

As his eyes adjusted, he spotted the back of a head—dark hair—in the very middle of the middle row of the balcony. He approached tentatively, the carpet spongy under his heels.

"You?" he said, as he caught her in profile.

Storey turned her head toward him. "Me," she said.

"Sorry, I was looking for—"

"Me," she said. "Have a seat." She pulled down the bottom piece of the cushioned seat beside her.

He inched his way down the row. "I can't stay long," he said.

"Yeah, yeah. Take a load off."

Reluctantly, he settled into the chair. Their forearms rubbed and he pulled his hands into his lap.

"You are seriously uptight," she said.

"Nah, it's just . . . I mean, it's late . . . and it's good to run into you and everything, but—"

"What you need to know," she said, lowering her voice considerably to where he had to lean close to hear her, "is that there's to be a night test of a pair of the *Dream*'s lifeboats when we dock at Castaway Cay. Lifeboat numbers fifty-seven and twelve. All I can tell you is that it doesn't feel right. I've never heard of such a test. At dawn, sure. Just before sunset—always possible. But in the dark at Castaway Cay? Why then? The island staff's asleep and the Marsh Harbour workers don't arrive by ferry until eight. So it feels more like they want to get away with something.

"I mean, yes: they have to test the lifeboats. Of course. They do it constantly. But the timing is . . . testing lifeboats in the dark at Castaway Cay makes no sense. That's where you and your pals come in. That's what *he* wants you to know, and you know who I'm talking about. That's the kind of thing *he* told me to listen up for. So now it's on you. I'm out. If I need you again for these meaningful chats, it'll come in the form of an invitation card in your stateroom. Dark. Lifeboat. Clear?"

The charm he'd experienced earlier was all gone, replaced by a business-as-usual tone, dismissive and impatient.

"I thought you teach pottery?"

"I thought you modeled for a hologram," she returned.

"Him?" Finn said, wondering why his brain chose to lock up any time a female was within spitting distance.

"Him," she said, as if it was the most obvious thing in the world. "Hang on!"

She leaned over and kissed him on the mouth, her hand finding his and pushing it up her shirt. She slapped it as it reached her ribs, and guided it around to her back.

Finn tried to speak, but she suffocated him with her lips, that free hand now finger-combing his hair. His head spinning.

She broke off the kiss. "Hello?" she said loudly over his shoulder.

Breathless, Finn thought she was talking to him. Was about to answer when her free hand gagged him, then seized his chin and spun him around to see the white uniform standing at the top of the balcony stairs.

"Sorry," the ship's officer said. "The balcony's closed. You kids'll have to find somewhere else."

"Please," Storey said. "Can't you just leave us alone?"

"Afraid not."

"No problem," Finn said. "Our bad."

The officer cleared his throat impatiently.

Storey made a point of freeing Finn's hand from her back. "Fifty-seven and twelve," she repeated warmly in his ear. Her reactions were impressive. With the two of them tangled up, the kiss had the appearance of being all the more authentic. They stood. Storey made a point of taking his hand in hers, and together they walked past the officer. She lowered her head demurely, as if embarrassed. Finn looked the officer in the eyes and smiled. The officer winked.

The two walked hand in hand toward the stern, passing Port Adventures Desk and the Oceaneer's Club. As they approached the aft stairs, Storey let go of his hand. His was warm and sweaty.

"You understand," she said, "this means something."

For a moment he thought she was talking about their kissing and holding hands—he felt a stab of guilt imagining Amanda walking in on the kiss and not understanding it. But Storey's eyes were cold, lacking any hint of affection. She was referring to the testing of the lifeboats.

He nodded.

"Find out what," she said, giving him a nudge down the stairs. Finn stumbled down a few steps and looked back.

She was gone.

* * *

The freckled Kenny Carlson flicked his red hair out of his eyes, a tic that he lived with constantly when nervous.

"It's tonight," he told Bart, his surfer-dude roommate. The two Cast Members had been fast-tracked to reassignment aboard the *Dream*, Wayne providing documents assuring they'd been through all the necessary training. In fact they had, but the normal six-week course had been reduced to a matter of days. They shared a very snug cabin below the waterline, with just enough room for a narrow bunk bed, an armoire, and a trunk for their clothes. The room was hot and the pipes running through it clanked.

"We have to be asleep by midnight in order to cross over," Kenny said.

"Are you down with this?" Bart asked.

"If you're asking if I'm comfortable being a hologram, no, I'm not. I don't suppose it's something you can get comfortable doing without a lot of experience, and we've done it, what, four times?"

"It is seriously random," Bart said. "I'm totally into it."

"We're here as support, don't forget. Our job is to be there only when we're needed."

"Why so secret, exactly? I'm mean, we're legit, right?"

"The OTs can't know about us. The Keepers know a couple of us are here, but not our names. That the rest of us are guarding the Base. But the whole idea is that we operate in the background. The OTs will not expect crew members to be DHIs. That gives us a jump on them, but only once."

"So we're like the Navy SEALs. We rescue them if something goes wrong."

"We keep an eye on them. Don't get all full of yourself."

Bart huffed. "It's the only way I roll," he said.

"Yeah? Well, roll a different direction. We're on orders here. You get it? Orders."

"Yeah, I know. We mess this up, and they'll replace us."

"No. We mess this up," Kenny said, "and they'll be replacing a Keeper."

18

FINN'S LAST CONSCIOUS THOUGHT involved a train's headlight heading at him. Thankfully, he wasn't flattened. Instead, he fell deeply asleep, the relaxation technique having quelled his anxieties. First he pictured absolute darkness; then a pinprick of light; finally, as the circle of light spread outward, it consumed him.

He opened his eyes. No matter how often he crossed over he always found his heart racing as he contemplated, dream or reality? For his dreams could feel so real, and reality could prove so dreamlike.

He was in a room with white, shiny walls and a gray, shiny floor. He turned . . . a table bolted to the floor. Six plastic chairs. He relaxed and waved his arm at the leg of the table: it passed through. He'd crossed over.

Sitting up, he recognized the room from a few hours earlier: it was the break room used by Cast Members— two refrigerators, a sink, and a coffee machine, all glistening new like the rest of the ship. While Philby could control when the Keepers crossed over, he could not control where they "landed": the software's most recent default settings were impossible to hack. At the Magic

Kingdom it was in front of Cinderella Castle; in Animal Kingdom, the Tree of Life; in Epcot, the fountains.

Interesting, he thought, that in the parks it was a public space, while on the ship, a Cast Member area. He explained this to himself by the fact that the parks closed to the public at night, whereas a ship never did. They couldn't very well cross over into the lobby atrium without risking being seen. Wayne and the Imagineers, it would seem, had carefully thought this through. No surprise there.

He waited, playing a game with himself. Willa, he thought. Five minutes later, Willa was indeed the first to appear. He expected Maybeck and Charlene next, both of whom had a harder time getting to sleep. He wasn't disappointed. Seven minutes after the arrival of Willa's hologram came the remaining two Keepers. All four of them had gone to sleep wearing Cast Member uniforms supplied by Laundry at Wayne's direction: a blue golf shirt, khaki shorts, white canvas deck shoes. They too took a few moments to comprehend their situation—testing their transparency. It was better to leave them alone for this process. Finn and Willa sat back. Charlene appeared jarred by the realization of crossing over, suggesting she had fallen more deeply asleep than Maybeck. Soon, all four were sitting up in a circle on the floor of the break room.

"New assignment," Finn said. "Searching for the server needs to wait because Philby doesn't have confirmation it's on board yet. There's an unexpected test of some lifeboats. That's our assignment." He talked them through what he'd learned from Storey Ming without revealing her identity—only that a crew member was being used as a go-between by Wayne and the Imagineers. A brief discussion ensued. The Keepers were a democracy, not a dictatorship, and while Finn accepted his role as leader, he interpreted the role as that of a filter; he was first a listener. Decisions came later.

"Do we trust her?" Maybeck asked.

"I do," Finn answered.

"Because?"

Finn shrugged. Because she can really kiss.

"First," Willa said, "because she's right about testing the lifeboats. Tests are typically conducted in major ports. Sometimes at night, yes. But rarely. And Castaway Cay is not the place for it. There's very little protected water. Lots of hazards. No shore patrols to assist if something goes wrong. Second, if the OTs are after us, which we can only assume they are, it makes almost no sense for them to come after us as DHIs where we present the biggest threat to them."

"Unless," Charlene interjected, "they are attempting to trap us in the Syndrome."

"Yes, agreed," Willa said. "But how complicated is that? They either have to trap and hold our holograms—not likely given how advanced 2.0 is—or get into all our locked staterooms, undetected, and poison or drug us while we sleep."

"That would take phenomenal planning and coordination," Finn said.

"Okay. Good enough for me," Maybeck said.

"And me," Willa said.

That was what Finn liked about the Keepers. They'd learned (most of them) to keep their egos in check and work as a group, willing to change their opinions based on information and research. They weren't perfect at it, and it had taken a couple years to come together. But like a sports team, or a rock band, they'd learned how to work together and use each person's strengths. The only one he worried about was Philby, who was setting himself apart from the others because of his success with controlling 2.0.

Finn tugged on the lanyard around his neck, noticing the same identifications on the three others. That really was an advantage of 2.0—the increased probability of physical objects crossing over with their DHIs. If they ever came to fully trust it, Finn thought, they could begin carrying the Return with them instead of having to hide it for use later or leaving Philby behind to execute a manual return as they were doing tonight.

"Remember, we belong here. Our IDs are legit. The uniforms—costumes—are legit. No fear," he said, reminding the Keepers of their shared motto. "If a crew member or fellow Cast Member stops us, we ask for help. If things get crazy, then once we're all together, we give Philby a call on a Wave Phone and return to our staterooms."

"Also remember to practice 2.0," Willa added, "in the next couple minutes. I know we've all gotten pretty used to it, but this is a new server, so who knows how it responds?"

"Done," Maybeck said.

"Charlene and I will take boat fifty-seven. You two, twelve," Finn said.

"The plan being?" Maybeck asked.

"We stow away. Philby said there's space in the lifeboat's bow where they keep a small anchor and food supplies. We listen, we observe, we get back together, add it all up, and see if any of it means anything."

"That makes it sound too easy," Charlene said.

"Yeah," Finn said.

* * *

The first indication of Charlene's unintentional prophecy were the paw prints. Unfortunately, neither Finn nor Charlene spotted them. Finn led the way. They were actually negative prints—the deck being misted from sea spray, the paw prints being dry spaces amid the wet—the deck lighting throwing a glare that concealed, rather than revealed, them.

Maybeck saw them. Not much escaped his artist's eye. He and Willa, on the opposite—port—side of Deck 4, from his friends, pushed his teammate back against the wall and pointed them out to her. He made a motion with his thumbs. Willa pulled out her Wave Phone and sent Charlene a text.

animal tracks

Charlene received the text, but a moment too late.

She and Finn had had their attention on the stenciled numbers overhead on the hull of each fiberglass lifeboat. To their mutual consternation, the lifeboats appeared to be in no particular order but installed randomly, the numbers mixed up like Ping-Pong balls in a lottery basket.

Twenty-seven . . . thirty-four . . . seventeen . . .

"This could take all night," Finn whispered.

"Or maybe not," Charlene said, grabbing hold of his arm to stop him.

Up ahead, patrolling in a well-defined circle, were two . . .

"Hyenas?" Finn said, pulling back flat against the wall.

Mangy, starved beasts, with gray matted hair, the telltale hump of shoulder and long neck. Their pink tongues hung out, drool cascading down.

"The Lion King," Charlene muttered. "You remember how they—"

"I remember," Finn said. They liked to tear their living prey apart, piece by piece, as they snacked.

Charlene checked her phone as it purred.

"Willa and Maybeck. Warning us of animal prints." She texted back immediately.

hyenas. b careful

"They look hungry," Finn said.

But there was something else, something he didn't tell her. He'd encountered hyenas before, shortly after the library. The jump. He and Willa—or so he'd thought. Pursued through that factory. Being a DHI and Keeper, Finn had his reality toyed with enough to not appreciate such unknowns. Having two separate lives was plenty, thank you very much. He didn't need to try to sort out authentic dreams from those where he crossed over and became a hologram.

"I may have been here before," he muttered.

"That's random," Charlene said.

"But I don't have the fob." He was talking to himself. Staring into his own projected palm. "I had the Return before."

"Last I checked, we don't live in the future. Only Jess. Even then, she doesn't live it, she dreams it."

Finn snapped his head in her direction. Was that what was happening to him? he wondered. Had he really begun to dream the future the way Jess did?

"It was Willa, not you," he said.

Charlene wasn't paying attention, staring down the long deck at the circling hyenas.

"Maybe we could put a pin in this and come back to it later, huh? My kingdom for a dog bone," she said.

Finn patted the pocket of his shorts, an astonished look on his face. "It crossed over!" He reached into the pocket. "You gotta love 2.0." He withdrew a Snickers bar.

"Okay," she said, staring at it. "Here's the plan."

* * *

The steel beneath her feet shuddered as the sound of water rushing against the hull filled Willa's ears.

"Hyenas," she said, having read Charlene's text.

"I like mine barbecued," said Maybeck.

"I'd prefer visible," she said. "I'd rather know where they are."

"Wish granted," he said.

Two hyenas, one toward the bow, coming at them; the other at the stern, also closing in.

"I think we walked into their trap," she said. "They're hunters, you know. They work in packs."

"So do we," Maybeck said. "The pack thing. Any ideas?"

"Have you ever seen shows on Animal Planet? They capture snakes and alligators with those wire things? Like a noose."

"Yeah. So?" He paused and said, "I am not wrestling a hyena. Forget it."

"Get real, macho man. Take off your belt."

"I beg your pardon?"

She unfastened her belt and withdrew it from the loops. Her shorts hung loosely on her hips. "Now, slowpoke." She passed him, staying close to the wall.

The hyenas, loudly sniffing the air, closed in on them like the jaws of a vise. Drool splattered the deck.

"They've got our scent," Maybeck declared.

"Your belt!" she repeated.

Maybeck slipped off his belt. "You are one weird girl."

"Ugh," she grunted, grabbing a shuffleboard cue from the wall rack where the disks and cues were stored. The game's two opposing triangles were painted onto the ship's deck. The cues and disks were secured in a rack on the wall. She passed Maybeck a cue and one disk, keeping one of each for herself.

"Awkward time for a game, don't you think?" he said. "Rain check?"

The cue's pole ended in a semicircular Y that fit around the disk. As if she knew what she was doing— and maybe she did—Willa popped the plastic ends off the two pushers at the end of the Y and forced her woven belt over them, securing the belt to the end of the cue.

"What are you doing?" Maybeck asked.

"Hold this!" she said, repeating the procedure with his belt. She extended the cue, and Maybeck saw that she'd pulled the belt through its own hasp, leaving a loop dangling from the end of the shuffleboard cue.

"A croc catcher," Maybeck said.

The belt loop formed a noose.

She said, "The disk is to lure them. They'll think it's food. Hold the disk in your weak hand, pole in your strong hand. When they stick their heads through the loop—"

"Bam!" Maybeck said. "I got it!" He moved judiciously toward the slinking hyena that lumbered toward him with a pronounced sway, as if drunk or maybe very, very confident. The hyena showed no sign of backing off. If anything, it seemed poised to strike. Maybeck took two steps toward it, then, as it lunged for him, a step back.

A costly mistake.

* * *

It was exactly the same, only different, Finn thought. The hyenas . . . the factory—only it wasn't a factory, it was a ship. And he was on the ship. And so were the hyenas. He was a hologram, not himself. It wasn't a dream, but it wasn't reality.

"Why was I running," he asked Charlene, "if I'd crossed over?"

"Fear," she answered. "You weren't fully crossed over, I'm thinking."

A logical explanation, but Finn could control his hologram better than any of the other Keepers. He wouldn't have let fear corrupt him.

"Maybe it was for Willa," Charlene said. "Maybe you were afraid for Willa. You had the Return, right? So in order to hold on to the Return you couldn't have been pure DHI."

"This is 2.0. There is no almost pure."

"But maybe you were thinking more like 1.6. Maybe it was something like that? Why does it matter, anyway? Especially right now? We're in a bit of a situation here."

"Are we?" Finn asked. "We're crossed over. We're 2.0 holograms. There's nothing for them to bite."

"And you're going to test that, are you?"

"Maybe not," he said.

"Yeah, I thought so." Charlene shook her head. "So we go with my plan, right?"

"Right."

They slipped along the wall toward a painted box that covered the lower section of a ladder. The purpose of the box was to discourage passengers from trying to climb the lifeboat access ladders, but the boxes couldn't be locked for safety reasons—there had to be ladder access to the overhead lifeboats at all times.

The larger of the two hyenas headed for them.

"Ready?" Finn asked. "Nothing to fear, remember?"

"Yeah, right. Working on that."

He broke off a piece of the Snickers bar.

The hyena charged.

Finn tossed the piece of candy bar. The hyena skidded to a stop, turned, and snapped it up. Finn could see the surprise cross its face—Snickers were just about the best thing on earth. Then it swung its ratty head back toward Finn, its eyes flashing yellow as they caught light from the windows.

More, the eyes said.

Finn broke off another chunk and threw it. As the hyena turned, Finn and Charlene inched it closer to the ladder, now only a few feet away. The plan backfired: Finn had thrown the piece of candy bar well behind the hyena, trying to draw it away from them. For a fraction of a second, the hyena considered pursuing it. But, as the other hyena got into the act, scrambling for the snack, the bigger beast turned back toward the source: Finn.

"Uh-oh," Charlene gasped, diving for the ladder. Finn was right on her heels.

He pulled the pin from the hasp and swung the box open. Charlene climbed it like a spider.

Finn fumbled with the Snickers bar, nearly dropping it. He tried to toe the wooden door as he pulled himself up a rung, but the hyena nosed the door open and snapped at Finn's feet. The animal got a bite of a steel ladder bar and yipped. He knocked loose another piece of Snickers, distracting the lead hyena. A battle ensued between the two creatures, both wanting the treat. As they fought, Finn scrambled up the ladder to a small platform that provided access to the two closest lifeboats. An extremely narrow catwalk led between the suspended lifeboat and the ship's wall in either direction. Charlene had already reached the forward lifeboat.

"Fifty-seven's up there!" she said, pointing.

Finn arrived, out of breath. "How . . . you . . . possibly . . . so fast?"

"We can't go down there," she said in a perfectly normal voice.

Indeed, the hyenas were directly below them, tracking them like radar, wanting more Snickers.

"Not only is it not a good idea to go down there and beta test," Finn said, "but unless we can get ourselves into the lifeboat, those two are going to end up giving us away."

"OMG!" Charlene said. "I should have thought of that."

They were at the end of the catwalk. There was still another lifeboat between them and boat fifty-seven.

"If we're not going to use the next ladder—" he said.

"Follow me." She pulled her hologram up and stood balanced on the rail. Then she leaned forward, clutching a safety rope that ran along the perimeter. The boat was divided into two pieces like a plastic Easter egg. Inside, the bottom half held all the passengers. But the top was a curving fiberglass shell as well, meaning that in a horrific storm the lifeboat could flip entirely upside down—and stay that way—and still protect its inhabitants. It also meant it was as slippery as a piece of Tupperware. There were several grips as well as the thick safety rope running fully around it. Charlene dangled from the rope, moving hand over hand, her legs bent at the knees to keep from hanging down, for just as she'd jumped, the sound of an automatic door opening rippled up the deck.

Finn climbed, fell forward, and clutched the rope. She'd made it look deceptively easy. It was like ropes course in gym—and he fell off the ropes course more often than he made it to the next level. Like her, he was driven by the thought of who or what had come through the automatic door. He'd heard no comments about seeing two wild hyenas drooling on the deck. It was as if whoever—or whatever—had come out, he, she, or it expected to see the creatures.

So it wasn't a passenger, Cast Member, or crew.

That left only Overtakers.

Keeping his knees tucked, Finn followed Charlene around the curve of the lifeboat's gunwale to the bow. Here, she pulled herself up, hooked a leg on the rope, and managed a gymnastic move Finn was not sure he could execute. Knees bent, she sprang like a cat and reached the safety rope of the next lifeboat—number fifty-seven. The coursing of the ocean waves across the *Dream*'s hull drowned out any noises. Again, she began the process of moving hand over hand around lifeboat fifty-seven.

Finn felt like shouting "Are you kidding me?" but kept his mouth shut. He wasn't about to admit defeat to a girl. Three times he tried to hook his leg across the safety rope. Finally, he snagged his knee, extended his leg, caught his ankle, and managed to clumsily pull himself up. A moment later he was crouching, ready to spring for fifty-seven.

"Sit!" he heard. A female voice from somewhere behind him. Not Maleficent, he thought. Her voice was often low, like a man's, gravelly and loathsome. Speaking but a single word, this voice, though familiar, was not identifiable. He searched his memory for the voices of the small number of Overtakers it could be: Cruella was the most likely.

Say something else, he mentally willed.

But there was Charlene, halfway through a small entrance hole in lifeboat fifty-seven, waving him on.

Finn jumped. He caught the safety rope, propelled himself around the lifeboat, and slipped inside behind Charlene. They'd made it.

* * *

Control! Maybeck thought, as the creature opened its jaw to bite him. He was so used to DHI 1.6 that he felt sure he could be bitten. The hyena's teeth clapped loudly together as they passed right through his holographic ankle. The animal squealed loudly. It had bitten its own tongue when the bone and flesh had failed to present itself.

"Dang!" Maybeck said. "That's insane!"

Maybeck snared the hyena's head and neck with the loop of belt. He moved quickly toward the ladder, the surprised hyena held a shuffleboard pole's distance away.

Willa used the bait ruse. Holding the disk at arm's length, as if a snack treat, she lured the one remaining hyena. It cautiously approached her, drool dripping from its black gums as it anticipated food (for one look at it confirmed it was being starved). Before the beast understood what was happening, it found a belt around its neck like a leash. She, too, moved toward the ladder.

"If we give them some slack . . ." she said to Maybeck.

"Yeah. Ladies first," he said, indicating the ladder.

"We have to go at the same time. If I release mine, he'll attack you." She pulled herself up several rungs. "Come on."

"This is going to get cozy," Maybeck said.

"Shut up and get over here."

The hyenas were wild in captivity, pulling and

pushing on the poles. Maybeck found it hard to hold on with just one hand. Willa, now three rungs up, hooked her arm through the ladder so she could use two hands. Maybeck caught a foot on the bottom rung. His hyena was stronger and meaner. It took his full strength to keep it at bay.

"Higher," Willa said, climbing another two rungs.

Maybeck climbed as well, his head against her collarbone, his back to her, the two of them pressed together. If they'd been hugging they couldn't have been closer. Seeing him struggle to maintain his balance, she hooked her heel around him, pinning him to the ladder.

"Ready?" she asked.

"It's not like they can hurt us."

"They don't know that."

"What's that supposed to mean?" he asked.

"And neither do I."

"You don't trust 2.0?"

"Correct." She reminded him, "We can't leave the poles and belts. They'll give us away."

"Agreed," he said.

"Then, both at the same time."

"Yeah."

"One . . . two . . ."

"Three!" he said.

* * *

It surprised Finn how little members of the crew spoke to each other. He discerned three voices, all male. The hum of electric motors was followed by a jerking movement, then a queasy sensation in his stomach as the lifeboat was lowered over the side. Charlene grabbed his arm in the dark and slid her hand down to hold his. He hated to admit it to himself, but he found that hand of hers comforting and pleasant. Reassuring.

The lifeboat splashed into the water, and only minutes later they were under way.

"Not much talk for a test run," Charlene said.

They continued to hold hands, Finn noticed.

"Thought the same thing."

"Two lifeboats."

"Yes."

"Why?"

"We're here to find out," Finn said.

"But we can't see a thing."

It was true. They could see each other's holograms now, dimly. But with a canvas hatch in place, they could not see into the cockpit to know what was going on out there.

"I could unzip it and take a look."

"Too risky," she said.

265

He was glad she said that, for he'd been thinking the same thing.

The lifeboat was not zigging or zagging. If it was indeed a test of some kind, it required explanation.

At once their holograms began to sparkle with digital interference, like a TV signal going bad.

He hurried to use the Wave Phone before they were too far out of range of the DHI projectors and the phones' communication antennas. He texted:

do u c us?

and sent the text to Philby.

Only moments later came the reply:

mvng awy frm ship, arnd islnd

Finn showed the screen to Charlene.

Her breath warmed Finn's ear. "I know this island. There's nothing in either direction. If we leave the beach area—"

She fell across and on top of him, pressed against the life preservers as a radical change in course threw them both sideways. They struggled to separate and sit back up.

"Heading toward the beach," she whispered.

"You sure?"

"Yes. We're inside the reef. We wouldn't risk heading out to sea anyway."

The lifeboat jerked again as the engine slowed.

"Anchor!" a voice called out.

Simultaneously, Charlene and Finn looked over at the anchor mount in the center of the compartment—directly in front of the canvas hatch. Then, at each other.

They crawled back into the wedge where the curving hull met the gunwale, Finn pulling the life vests from behind them. When not in use, a vest held together as a rectangular block of orange plastic. Finn stacked the vests in front of them as a screen. Charlene helped hold them in place.

The sound of a zipper running was followed by a hairy, dark-skinned arm reaching inside. Then a shoulder and the top of a bald head appeared. A clanging and two choice swear words rang out as the crewman freed the anchor from its bracket. The rattle of a chain. The clap of a line.

But not the sound of the zipper closing.

"He left it open," Finn whispered, already moving the blocks of life vests out of their way. In a moment they were free of the vests, and Finn moved cautiously toward the hatch, placing his eye to the canvas and peering out.

The lifeboat lunged. Finn's head went entirely out through the open space.

Charlene grabbed him by the knees and hauled him backward. They both froze—stone still. Listening. Waiting . . . Finn's face was scrunched into a pucker.

During the brief moment his head had been out in the cockpit he'd seen a darkened sky faintly blue at the edges; the back of a man's coveralls; the anchor swinging in the grasp of a hand at the end of a hairy arm; the bow of a second lifeboat.

The engine cut to an idle, then reversed and accelerated. The lifeboat shuddered.

Finn and Charlene were thrown on top of one another again as the bow ground into sand and the boat came to a stop.

"Quickly. We need that Creole freak back aboard before sunrise."

Creole freak? Finn wondered. Charlene had heard the same thing, and they exchanged the same quizzical expression. Curiouser and curiouser, he thought.

The sound of the second lifeboat approached. Its motor roared as it swished to shore.

More than one man left the lifeboat.

But was it all three?

Finn looked outside again. An empty cockpit. He saw clouds in the sky he hadn't seen a minute earlier.

He dared climb out farther, confirming the empty cockpit. He crawled carefully—silently—to the exit hatch, the door to which had been left open. He stole a look toward the beach.

Six men, all in crew member coveralls. Three in front, three behind.

Charlene squeezed in alongside Finn, her head blocking his view. When she turned to speak, they were so close they nearly kissed.

"The bungalows," she said.

"Bungalows?"

"Massage bungalows."

"Massage," he said.

"If you repeat everything I say, Finn, we're going to be here a long time."

"So it's not a test," Finn said.

"Apparently not."

"More like a pickup and delivery."

"That's what it sounded like to me," she said. "Yes."

"So either these crewmen are knowingly working for the Overtakers, or are being used."

"I would guess they are just following orders. So maybe one of the officers is with the OTs."

He tried to see a way around the idea of the Overtakers being involved. But the existence of the hyenas kept bringing him back to reality. Who else would have hyenas guarding the lifeboats?

"We have to find out," Finn said. He pulled his Wave Phone from his shorts and held on to it to keep it dry as he slipped his hologram up to his knees in seawater. "Note to self," he said to Charlene, "there's no reception on the Wave Phone. We can't return until we're closer to the ship."

One of the marvels of being a hologram was moments like this: slipping into water without getting wet. Finn peered around the lifeboat at the one next to it. He ducked under the anchor line and stole a look inside the boat. Empty.

"Psst! Maybeck!"

The zipper whirred. Moments later, four holograms moved along the water's edge toward the *Dream*, which loomed like a Hollywood backdrop a half mile away. They came upon the cluster of massage cabanas via a small grove of palm trees. The sky was tinged at the edges a rich azure blue. Only a few determined planets still shone through.

"Which one?" Maybeck whispered.

"We couldn't see," Finn replied. "We'll split up so we're not all busted at once."

"That's optimistic of you," Charlene said. "We're dressed as crew members, don't forget. These lifeboat workers are the worker bees. We're the honeybees. If we encounter them, we demand to know what they're doing ashore. We take their names. We can't think like ninth graders."

"Tenth graders next September," Maybeck said.

"Remember, 2.0," Finn said. "We're good." He stayed with Charlene. They moved slowly through the cluster of cabanas—small wooden cabins on three-foot stilts with wooden shutters across window holes. The eaves were open to allow circulation. The yellow of candlelight glowed through the ten-inch gap and flickered through the slatted gables. With his upgraded hearing on full alert, he noticed the holograms moving silently through the sand. Finn glanced down: his hologram feet did not displace the sand; it was as if he'd never walked here.

Suddenly, there was a murmur of conversation. Finn crouched and caught sight of Maybeck. He hand-signaled for the four of them to converge on the cabana from both sides. Maybeck nodded and signaled back two thumbs up.

As they approached the voices became clearer, and the conversation with them.

"You must come with us now." A man.

"You I tell once more," spoke a woman's baritone voice in a thick Jamaican accent, "'tain't me going nowhere, mon. 'Tain't leavin' da island 'til necessary. 'Tis them's coming here, or 'tain't at all. Be your instructions as they may, 'tain't no matter to me."

"Orders is orders," the man said.

"Them be your orders, not mine. Is you wishing to cross me, mon?"

"No, ma'am!" The gruff man sounded strangely frightened.

"Your shoulders," Charlene whispered to Finn. "Get down on a knee." Finn glanced overhead at the window hole in the side wall. Charlene wanted up there. He waved his hand at the stilt holding up the cabana. The wood passed through his forearm. He concentrated and tried again. His arm bumped off the post.

"Okay," he said.

Charlene performed the same test. It took her three tries to Finn's one, but she was solid enough to step onto his shoulder. Finn grabbed her ankle. She crawled up his back and placed her left foot on his left shoulder, and Finn stood. They were a circus act rising more than ten feet tall. Finn awkwardly moved left until Charlene was alongside the window. She placed her eye to the open-air slats in the shutter. Held up the fingers of her right hand: five, then two. Seven people. The six lifeboat crew and one other: the woman.

"I suggest," came the sonorous female baritone, "you

speak to them's givin' de orders. Ain't got much time, you know. One day is all."

Charlene looked down at Finn, her face a mask of alarm, and mouthed something, but it was lost on him. She did not look pleased.

"We got orders is all I'm saying," said the man. "You choose not to come with us, that's on you."

"'Tis on me, then."

"That's all I'm saying," said the man.

"You say so."

"Not making my life any easier."

The woman said. "No life easy."

"Okay, then. Have it your way."

Charlene motioned for Finn to let her down. As he kneeled, the door to the cabana flew open. Finn saw Maybeck and Willa rush to hide under an adjacent cabana, but there was no time for him and Charlene. She crashed down onto the sand. They scrambled and rolled to a position directly beneath the wooden stairs as the six sailors clomped down. They lay flat in the sand facing the water.

The men muttered. One of them cursed the "old witch." Too loudly, apparently. He made it only a matter of feet from the stairs before he buckled at the waist in the grips of abdominal pain.

"Be careful your choice of words," came the baritone

from the cabana. "Respect where respect is due."

Two of the other five dragged the man across the sand, glancing back at the cabana. They moved quickly as if attempting to outrun a fire.

There was little doubt the woman in the cabana had done this to the sailor.

Magic, Finn thought. Black magic, at that.

"You know who that is in there?" Charlene whispered hotly. Not waiting for Finn to answer, she added, "Tia Dalma."

Finn thought he knew the name, but he couldn't place it.

"The voodoo priestess. *Pirates?*"

It was as if a connecting piece to a jigsaw puzzle had fallen into place. He began to see the bigger picture, though answers and explanations escaped him. He nodded slightly.

"They're taking the boats," Maybeck said. He and Willa had snuck up on them.

"But they . . . can't!" whispered Charlene.

"Tell them that," Maybeck said.

"We're part of the program this morning."

"We're supposed to be," Maybeck said.

The boats motored on, backed up, and pulled away from the beach.

Finn glanced toward the ship where, in the

headlights of golf carts and forklifts, he saw a dozen workers busy as ants.

"The dock is out," he said.

"We'll have to swim," Willa said. They all looked at her like she was crazy.

"I don't think holograms can swim," Maybeck said. "Though I could be wrong."

Finn didn't like being so close to Tia Dalma. He led them away from the cabana and back to the palm trees, where they gathered as a group.

"Charlene and I hit some interference out in the lifeboat. The island projectors don't cover very far out off the beach."

"We had the same thing happen," Willa said, looking at Maybeck.

"I'm not sure we want to try swimming in the open ocean with our holograms failing to project."

"Doesn't sound like fun to me," Maybeck said.

"So we stay close to shore and just beneath the surface," Charlene said. "If we go all static, we surface."

"If we lose 2.0," Maybeck said, "we drown."

The three looked to Finn for answers. Not for the first time. He lived with this weight on his shoulders. Wayne had once told him he would grow to be the leader of the group. He had never asked for that role, but he seemed stuck with it.

"We don't know that," he said. "Besides, we won't lose 2.0. It's stable. We might lose projection, and we've never done that in 2.0. Water's not a good place to test it. So we stay close together. Just beneath the surface and close to shore, as Charlene said." Give credit where credit is due: the first lesson of effective leadership. It wasn't about leading so much as listening and reacting. "We'll stay just inside those buoys." The swimming areas were defined by ropes and floats.

"I'm the best swimmer," Willa announced. "And I'm lifeguard-certified." No one argued, not even Charlene. Willa was known as a bit of a book nerd, but every winter she swam competitively. "If anyone has trouble, I'll hang with them. The rest will get to the ship."

"Yes," Finn agreed. "We can cover for each other if a couple of us make it."

"Our phones?" Maybeck said.

"We leave them here. We can pick them up later, once we're back on the island as ourselves."

They unloaded their phones. Willa hid them beneath a large leafed plant and took note of its location.

The sky was a lighter blue, the sun only minutes from rising.

"We have to hurry," Finn said. "You see that open door on this side of the ship? We'll head there." There was a smaller boat tied up to a small float, but the hatch appeared empty of people.

They headed for the open water. When they reached knee depth, they slid down to their shoulders. Then their heads popped under and did not resurface.

* * *

All went swimmingly. The four stayed close. Their projections broke up occasionally as they swam just below the surface, but it was easy enough to keep track of each other. The latest modeling had included hang gliding, rock wall climbing, skiing, snowboarding, surfing, snorkeling—as well as a dozen new competitive sports, including riflery, fencing, and martial arts. The world of physical movement for the 2.0 holograms was growing exponentially; more modeling was planned for the coming months.

A shimmer to Finn's right caught his eye. Like a flash of light. He looked that way: nothing. Empty sea. Turned his head back to watching where he was going. Another wink. Another inspection. Several more flashes, like from paparazzi cameras.

Then, at once, a wall of silver, like a curtain dropping.

A battery of barracuda.

Charlene blew bubbles as her eyes went wide. She'd slipped out of her hologram.

Several hundred fish. The fish turned direction and vanished again. Finn understood intuitively the change was the result of one of two possibilities: the fish were heading away from them, or the fish were heading for them. This explained the wall of silver disappearing—they were no longer seeing the fish from the side.

Charlene popped her head above the water's surface, gasping. Her hands splashed and her feet treaded water. Willa paused and surfaced to help, attempting to determine if it was a bug in 2.0 and, if so, what could be done about it.

Willa swiped her hand at Charlene's back. Her hand passed through her friend.

"You're okay," she said over the roar of Charlene's frantic splashing. "You're stable. This is 2.0."

"I hate fish!"

The most significant improvement of the 2.0 upgrade was its resistance to fear; prior to the upgrade the slightest tremor of terror made one's DHI more solid. That Charlene had lost some of her DHI was both troubling and unexpected.

"You're freaked out," Willa said. "You need to calm down, Charlie." If Charlene didn't return to full hologram the fish would have something to bite.

Maybeck, swimming out ahead, missed the entire Charlene and Willa event. Finn saw the fish coming at them and Charlene slapping on the surface, indicating her hands were flesh.

Some fish attack their prey mouth open, like in cartoons—the big fish after the little fish. Other fish hunt in schools. Finn found this out the hard way. When the wall of silver reappeared, it surrounded him and the two girls. It arrived all at once, like a net being dropped. And not just silver: silver with small black eyes, staring at them. The circle of fish was tightening.

As Finn stopped, he treaded water. Without being consciously aware of it, he'd made his hands and feet 2.0-solid.

The spinning school was incredibly close. Close enough for Finn to see their teeth. Their mouths were long, like the rest of them, so there were plenty of teeth. If Finn had known his fish better he would have realized they weren't barracuda, but needlefish. Though this realization wouldn't have helped him any; the truth was that needlefish were much more likely to attack humans than barracuda, much more likely to do harm—as in tearing a chunk of flesh away. Fish that attack in schools operate under a mob mentality. One chunk of missing flesh turns into many. This tends to be detrimental to the prey.

Finn waved his arms threateningly and the school scattered. The swirling wall of silver vanished, then reappeared instantly like the flash of a bullfighter's cape. In the blink of their disappearance, Finn saw past the curtain to Maybeck, who was swimming back toward Finn and the girls. Maybeck, with his powerful arms and wide eyes and a look of heroic intentions. But the swirl of fish continued to close upon Finn and the girls. It was quickly approaching snack time for the needle-fish, and though Maybeck's intentions might have been noble, his arrival would only offer the fish additional food.

Four legs and feet kicked furiously just above Finn's head. He kicked to the surface, his last underwater image a few brave needlefish taking aim at one of the girls' feet and toes. He spooked them with another wave of his arms.

On the surface, Charlene was panicked, Willa unable to calm her down.

"Here's the bug," Willa said to Finn as he broke the surface. "In order to tread water, we seem to make our hands and feet solid." She lifted her hands out of the water and clapped for him.

He tried it and also clapped. "Uh-oh."

"We need to calm her down, and we need to get swimming again."

The lifeboats were a good distance away, nearly to the ship.

Finn moved in front of Charlene. "Okay," Finn said calmly, "I want you to float on your back. Arms out to the side."

"Isn't that the dead man's float?" Charlene asked.

"No, that's when you float facedown," said Finn.

"Oh," said Charlene.

"Lay back and arch your spine," he said. He was thinking of the needlefish's proximity to all their toes.

He too was treading water, but he saw that sometimes his hands pushed against the water, sometimes they passed through it without effect. Yet he was able to keep himself on the surface. Take *that*, Philby!

"Look!" he said to Willa.

She saw the two states of his hands and concentrated. She too was then able to alternate between hologram hands and physical hands. "You gotta love 2.0," she said.

"Lay back!" Finn ordered Charlene. He caught her under her knees and behind her neck and held her like a baby in his arms. In order to do so, he'd made himself solid.

"Finn, don't!" Willa said, the spiral of fish closing in on them.

He lay Charlene out on the water's surface, pulling

her arms out as flotation. She steadied and calmed. A thin, athletic girl, her body was muscle and bone and did not float well.

"Take a deep breath and hold it," he instructed. "Arms and legs out. You'll float better."

She did as he said, and though her legs fell away slightly, she stayed on the surface. She managed to relax and immediately calmed.

"I'm sorry," Charlene said.

"No worries. We've got this," he said encouragingly.

Willa, being Willa, had already adopted the back float alongside Charlene.

"Finn?" Willa said tightly as the water's surface began to boil with frantic needlefish rapidly closing on them. "Float with us! There's no time."

Finn tested Charlene's hands—they were no longer solid. "Just like that," he said. "No matter what happens, hold it just like that."

"Got it," Charlene said.

"Where's *all clear* when you need it?" Willa said.

Finn could only think of Philby and his claim to have added control over 2.0. It made him think of Wayne. And that made him wonder if Wayne now favored Philby over him as the leader of the Keepers.

"Here they come!" Charlene said, pointing with her outstretched arm.

She shouldn't have pointed. The intention of pointing made her finger solid.

The needlefish took it as an offering of, well, finger food. A hand suddenly broke the surface and swept the needlefish aside just as they were about to feed on Charlene's finger.

Maybeck's head popped up.

"Gawd, I love 2.0," he said. "Did you see that?"

Finn couldn't stop himself from grinning. Maybeck's overconfidence—his conceit—was nearly always contagious, if not occasionally grating.

But Maybeck too saw their predicament: the encroachment of the churning swirl of aggressive fish, ever closer. The girls laid out on their backs like so much snack food. Finn's troubled face.

"F . . . i . . . n . . . n," a terrified Charlene said, "tell me you have a plan." She craned her neck to get a look at him.

By this point Maybeck was splashing at the water, trying to hold off the needlefish—a futile effort, but one that occupied him.

"A helicopter rescue would be nice," Maybeck said. That was another thing about Maybeck: he could lighten up any situation. "Where's Neptune when you need him?"

Mention of the mythical hero spurred a memory of

Triton at Typhoon Lagoon. Of the ocean king standing up to Ursula and holding her off. Of him offering Finn his support in case of trouble. What was the code he'd offered?

"Finn? Buddy?" the splashing Maybeck called out. The ring of foaming water caused by the net of needle-fish closed to within a foot of them on all sides. A few brave fish darted toward the outstretched girls. Maybeck and Finn splashed the water, trying to hold them back, but it was a losing effort.

Stressed by the fish attacking, Finn couldn't recall the code. Little pieces of the expression would float through his consciousness—lies? Cries? He couldn't grab hold of the whole thing.

The funnel of fish converged toward the center. Open mouths. Teeth.

The words arrived. "Starfish wise, starfish cries."

"What?" Charlene said.

Finn repeated the Triton code, this time louder.

Nothing happened.

"Dude," Maybeck said. "You're losing it. Hang in there." Then, "Ow!" as a fish took a bite of his hand. Maybeck managed to splash the water and create a hole in the closing silver.

Finn did the same. Then he lowered his head into the water.

To Willa, it looked as if he were sinking. "Noooo!" she screamed.

Finn spoke the Triton code underwater. "Starfish . . . wise, starfish cries . . ."

He resurfaced.

Nothing. Only the needlefish.

Then . . .

"Look!" Willa said, pointing.

Finn turned to see the miracle of angel-like fish popping out of the ocean and flying through the air twenty yards at a time. Dozens at first, then hundreds. Thousands, maybe. Flying right for them.

"We're doomed," Charlene said.

"No," Finn said, "we're saved. They're on our side."

Finn and Maybeck splashed more holes in the ranks of the needlefish, protecting the floating girls.

"Dude?" Maybeck said, his voice uncommonly anxious. "What now?"

Then, like Old Faithful, the water exploded up around the Keepers. It shot into the air five feet, ten feet, twenty in a giant plume. The explosion pushed back the needlefish, driving them away from the Keepers, creating a ring of safety.

It wasn't just water forming this twenty-foot-high fountain, but the dainty flying fish, their fins stretched out as wings. They flew high, straight up out of the water, and then plummeted back down, a thin column growing thicker. Soon, Finn and the others found themselves in the eye of the column, the needlefish driven back and away, farther and farther until the Keepers were safe.

The column of foaming water slowly lowered and the eye of the water storm began moving slowly toward the *Dream*.

"They're protecting us," Willa said. "They want us to swim with them."

As a group they swam toward the ship.

"Are you going to explain the flying fish?" Charlene asked Finn.

"Typhoon Lagoon," Finn said. "King Triton's code."

"We have King Triton on our side?" Charlene said.

"Looks like it," Finn said.

"How cool is that?" Charlene said.

"So does that mean we get Eric, too?" Willa said. "Because Eric is definitely hot, and if I had my choice I'd take Eric over some white-haired king merman any day."

Charlene chimed in. "I've had a crush on Eric since I was about eight."

Maybeck said, "And I thought you were crushing on me."

"Who says I'm not?" she fired back.

"Trying to get me jealous?"

"Maybe."

"It's working," Maybeck said.

With the angel fish protecting them, they moved smoothly toward the ship.

Finn spent the time considering their rescue by the flying fish, the existence of Tia Dalma on the island, the hyenas on the deck of the ship, and the crew members' apparent obedience to some form of an Overtaker. He tried to piece together how any of it might connect to the stolen journal and their assignment to retrieve it. How it might connect to Chernabog.

"What does Tia Dalma have to do with any of this?" Finn called out.

It cooled the levity.

"Should we try to let Wayne know?" he said.

"I suppose," said Willa.

Wayne was constantly trying to teach Finn leadership lessons. Were the challenges they were facing nothing more than tests of their control over 2.0? Was it an *exercise*? Finn was sick of being used. Why did everything have to be part of some lesson?

He was reminded of the mega-screen at an Orlando Magic basketball game. Three animated Magic ball caps on a table. A basketball slips under one of the caps and they shuffle and jump, the crowd trying to keep track of the cap hiding the basketball. A shell game, it was called.

He wondered again if part of the shell game was to keep Wayne and the Keepers focused on the ship while something was brewing at the Base. Which was the ultimate prize? Which was the hat containing the ball?

Now it was Wayne calling across an ocean at him: "Keep your eye on the cap with the ball! Don't get distracted. Don't lose focus for even a moment."

"I get it!" Finn said aloud, shutting up the others.

"Get what?" Charlene said.

"Nothing," Finn said.

"We're getting close," Maybeck said.

"We don't want to be spotted," said Charlene.

"Underwater," Finn said. "I bet the flying fish will stay with us."

The four holograms slipped out of sight. The flying fish surrounded them in a protective tunnel.

After a fair distance, Finn poked his head up. The two lifeboats were tied up to a portable dock floating below an open gangway. He swam closer, and his ears broke the surface as well. He marveled at how clear his hearing was—how far into the ship he could make out sound.

The lifeboats were empty, as were the dock and the

doorway in the hull of the ship. He waved beneath the water and three more heads appeared.

"Clear," he whispered.

"Two by two," Willa said.

Finn motioned Charlene forward, and she slipped past him. Grabbing hold of a line used to tie a lifeboat, she pulled herself up and threw a leg onto the dock. A moment later she extended a hand to Finn and helped pull him up.

Their holograms and hair were dry—no indication they'd been swimming. They approached the open gangway at the edge and peered inside where three crewmen were busy working, their backs to them. Finn and Charlene both took a deep breath and stepped aboard. They headed quickly through the maintenance area to an open door and out into a crew member–only passageway.

They were heading down a corridor. A crewman approached with a look of disapproval on his sunbaked face.

"You there!" the man called.

"Stay with me," Finn whispered, taking Charlene by the hand.

"We're the Kingdom Keepers," Finn said proudly.

The crewman stopped and appraised them. "So you are! Good to meet you!"

"And you."

Finn shook the man's hand. Charlene offered one of her dazzling smiles. Maybeck and Willa arrived behind them.

"Having fun so far?" the man asked.

"A blast."

"It only gets better from here," the man said. "You're going to love tomorrow."

"We can hardly wait," said Willa.

When Finn returned to his room, there was a card waiting with his name on it.

19

THE KEEPERS WOKE UP EXHAUSTED in their own beds at six thirty. Philby had returned them once they'd all congregated on board the ship. None of them had had more than four hours of sleep; Philby even less because of nerves.

The shore party excursion and entertainment crew leaders met in a bar called Pink. The Keepers all wore the shorts and golf shirts from their Magic Kingdom DHI identities. Max served as team leader. He informed the thirty people gathered for their assignments that they would cover all sorts of beach and island activities. Minnie, Mickey, Chip, and Dale were also in attendance; they wore their beach clothing and looked adorable. Minnie put her hands on her nose and mouth in astonishment as Max explained in detail how the two would arrive by golf cart and be interacting with the beach crowd just prior to lunch being served.

After posing with guests departing the ship for the beach they would have the rest of the morning off. Then they were to arrive by Jet Ski at two o'clock and lead a crab race before serving as referees for a volleyball tournament.

Each had his or her assignment, previously explained by Finn and Philby. Given recent developments, there were a good number of questions to answer before the all-aboard on the *Dream* at five o'clock. Chief among them: what was Tia Dalma doing on Castaway Cay, and why had the crew tried to take her aboard the *Dream*?

Philby had earlier explained their situation: "Until we locate Maleficent, or whatever Overtaker is running things on this ship, our chances of finding the missing journal are zilch. Because of this, we'll each tail a different person. Hopefully someone leads us back to the pot of gold at the end of the rainbow."

"Please!" Willa had said. "Lose the metaphors. This is hard enough to swallow. Running around in the heat and sun trying to look all innocent."

Collectively and individually they posed for forty-five minutes in the glare of hot sunshine, taking photos with guests by a Castaway Cay sign with the *Dream* in the background. Everyone smelled of suntan lotion. The little kids couldn't contain themselves in the company of celebrities.

Finn enjoyed such moments, but was also glad when it was over. Willa and Charlene awaited the dismissal of two girl crew members, each suspected of being the Asian girl who'd been spying on Philby and Finn at the Radio Studio. Maybeck was to change into a crew member's white shorts and pale blue polo shirt and infiltrate the island staff, while Finn had a secret appointment. Philby would serve as roamer—first retrieving and distributing the Wave Phones left behind on the island the night before and then serving as backup in the event anyone called for help.

Things had not gone well aboard ship. They needed to put the odds in their favor.

"You want to see something strange?" one crew photographer said to another, who'd been shooting pictures of the DHIs with guests.

"Sure," she answered.

The other Keepers had already left. Only Finn lingered behind.

"Never seen anything exactly like it," he said. With his huge Nikon camera strapped around his neck, he aimed its LCD display so the woman could view it.

"So?" the woman photographer said. "What's the big deal, Victor? You're always messing up the focus and exposure!" She bumped her shoulder to his.

"But that's the thing. The two of them there are in focus. It's that third one looks like a ghost."

Finn's ears perked.

"Victor, you need help. Just because you can't take a decent photograph, don't go blaming it on the guests."

"There were three kids in the shot. Centered.

Focused. This third kid's gone all digital on me."

Finn found it hard to breathe. He was familiar with this particular photographic problem. He desperately wanted a look at the camera's display.

The woman studied the display. "Could be glare off the water, I suppose. You should have shot toward the island."

"Glare? I guess. But if it was glare it would have burned out that side of the frame. It wouldn't make a kid all pixelated."

These were the words Finn heard so clearly: a kid pixelated.

"That's a digital camera, right?" Finn asked.

They looked over at him as if he'd snuck up on them.

"Ahh, yeah," said the man in a pleasant voice. "What else?"

It was an anomaly common to the parks: taking a photo—a digital camera photo—of a DHI and a guest presented risks. In certain light, the digital cameras did not capture the digitally projected holograms. The DHIs pixelated.

"A kid?" Finn asked, his voice breaking with concern. "A girl?" He imagined Amanda or Jess in the photo. They were capable of crossing over as DHIs, though he'd heard of no such plans from Wayne. His heart beat frantically at the thought of seeing Amanda—even as a hologram.

"No, a boy. Big kid. Football big. You know?" the man said. "Your age. Maybe a little older."

People always judged Finn younger than he was.

"You remember what color eyes he had?" Finn asked.

"Oh yeah, kid. I remember the eyes of every guest I shoot."

"No need to get testy, Victor," the woman chided.

Wayne had said he was going to project some of the recently recruited DHI volunteers on the ship—Kenny Carlson, Eddy Moriarty, Patty Standard, and others—but that would be at night when they were naturally asleep. Even at that, they were to fall under Keeper supervision. It wasn't possible they'd be projected in the daytime onto the island without Finn or Philby knowing about it.

Was Philby keeping it from him?

Was Wayne up to something?

"A boy," Finn said, repeating what he'd just heard. "My age. A big kid."

He knew someone who fit that description.

* * *

Willa and Charlene followed the two Asian girl Cast Members who'd left the *Dream* together. With the release of the guests, the island was a bevy of activity, two thousand people having come ashore to pursue their tropical beach vacation. There were more shore adventures offered on Castaway Cay than any other single port on the cruise, from Jet Skis to snorkeling, waterslides to sailing. It was like two thousand kids in the sandbox, all in swimsuits, their pale skin shining under a layer of sunscreen.

The island was a mile long and narrow, with a white sand beach stretching the distance facing west; on the opposite side were hundreds of acres of mangroves and jungle scrub, inhospitable terrain out of bounds for guests that had only a few narrow sandy lanes cut into it.

A motorized shuttle ferried those who didn't want to walk from one area to the next using a paved road that, in Disney park fashion, led to several organized stops, whether restrooms, restaurants, or shopping. The various thatched-roof structures carried names like Cookie's BBQ, and the beaches were designated by age: Scuttle's Cove, Hide Out, Serenity Bay. Hundreds of guests rode the shuttle despite the short walk required. Near the back of the crowd were Willa and Charlene, having never lost sight of their marks.

The shuttle dropped most of its passengers at the first stop—the family beach. A few dozen stayed on, mostly adults seeking refuge at the far end of the island or those wishing to wait for a second shuttle offering short motorized tours. The two Asian girls, and Charlene and Willa with them, disembarked at this last stop and awaited the tour shuttle. It arrived, carrying ten seniors and several families. Another half dozen boarded, including the four girls, and it headed down an old runway that, according to the driver's narration, had once served the family that had previously owned the island and could still be used in emergencies.

It was a strange sight on an island so small: a wide and long piece of asphalt cut into sand and palm trees. The shuttle paused at an abandoned plane at an intersection of the runway and one of the scenic tour roads. The Asian Cast Members climbed off here, but no other guests chose to disembark.

Willa and Charlene exchanged a glance. Would they give themselves away if they, too, climbed off now?

"What do you think?" Charlene asked.

"I think they've tricked us," Willa answered.

"We'll have to get off at the next stop and come back."

"What if I got off and you stayed on?"

"Excellent! Brilliant! But don't follow them, okay? Wait for me."

"Done." Charlene climbed off the opposite side of the shuttle car from the Asian girls and headed over to the abandoned airplane, studying it.

The shuttle continued on. Willa turned her head and tracked her friend, seeing that the two Asian girls immediately took off on foot up the runway. She waited impatiently for the shuttle's next stop. When it showed no sign of slowing, she called out, "Could I get off here, please?"

The driver slowed and Willa jumped off, thanking her. The shuttle pulled away. Willa waited for it to make the next curve, disappearing from view, and then took off at a run back toward where she'd left Charlene.

"They went up that way," Charlene said, pointing up the runway, "and disappeared to the left."

"That's out of bounds for us," Willa said, knowing the layout of the island. "Not for them because they're Cast Members."

"I can play a dimwit real well," said Charlene.

"Lost and without a clue?" Willa said.

"Leave it to me."

They hurried up the runway, following a sand path cut into the mangrove and prickly shrubbery. The surface of the sand was pockmarked with tiny dots, the result of an afternoon rain shower the day before. Interrupting this pattern were two sets of shoe prints.

"Easy-squeezy," said Willa, pointing them out to Charlene.

Thirty yards later the trail divided, but someone had

been on a morning run and the surface was disturbed, making it more difficult to determine the direction of the girls they were following.

"I think it's that way," Willa said, pointing to the right.

"Terrific! I was going to say to the left."

They studied the impressions more carefully and agreed to try the path to the right. Twenty yards later, another fork; and still another after that. They were deep into the island wilderness now, the vegetation too high to see over, the terrain too flat to offer landmarks.

"Stay clear of those trees," Willa said, pointing one out. "Poisonwood. It'll burn something fierce."

"Maybe we should turn back," Charlene said. "Two lefts and a right, right?"

"Three lefts and a right," Willa said, "wasn't it?"

"I thought it was two."

"Oh, brother. We should have left markers or something."

They looked behind at the path, hoping to make out their own tracks. It wasn't going to be easy.

"I've got a bad feeling about this," Charlene said.

"I think we should whisper," Willa whispered. "I hear something."

They were quiet then, and, sure enough, the sound of voices carried through the jungle. But not from the direction where the path led. Instead, the voices came from their left, from inside the thicket of plants.

Charlene waved Willa ahead to a patch of sand free of the main path that showed the same distinctive tracks they'd been following. She pointed into a dark spot where the sunshine did not penetrate. They made some faces at each other; their silent sign language said, *Do we dare? What do you think? I don't know. Let's go for it. Okay.*

They crept through twisted, dark branches where the ground grew spongy and the smells were of decay and salt and marsh. After several minutes, Charlene turned back to look at Willa. The voices were clear now. They picked up the conversation in the middle.

". . . bound to attract attention." A boy's voice, possibly a man's.

"No kidding." One of the girls.

"My manager, for instance."

"How? How will he get here?"

"Golf cart."

"So maybe someone forgets to plug it in tonight." A different girl's voice. "Maybe it has no charge. Maybe it's dead."

"He can use any Pargo he chooses, and a bunch of them have gas motors."

"So maybe a fallen palm tree is blocking the

way. Maybe he has to backtrack and it takes time."

"I suppose that could be arranged," the boy said. Definitely not a man now that they listened more closely.

"It shouldn't take long to off-load," said the other.

"Like how long?"

"It's just a box. A heavy box. That's why you need to supply the Pargo. The pilot is going to claim engine trouble. Forced emergency landing. The box is being taken off to lighten the load. It all fits."

"Yeah, I got it. Don't sweat it."

"Do we look like we're sweating?" one of the girls asked caustically. "If we're sweating, it's only because it's so incredibly hot on this island."

"It's nicer on the beach," the boy said.

"Shut up, would you? Do we look like we're on the beach? I mean, seriously? It's got to be a hundred degrees out here. It's the jungle!"

"There are bugs," the other girl said.

"Look, shut up. All we care about is that you do your job and get the box aboard the ship."

"Tonight. Forward gang."

"Correct," said one of the girls.

"Whatever you have to do to make that happen, we don't care. Just so long as it happens."

"It's going to happen," the boy said.

"Okay, then."

"Let's get out of this miserable place."

The bushes up ahead rustled. There was no time for Willa and Charlene to leave the way they'd entered; they'd be seen. Instead, Charlene gave Willa a look that said, *Follow me!* and led her off to the side, deep within the dark mangrove.

They got a look at the two girls in profile, but the heavy shadows prevented a good solid view at their facial features.

The boy was a different story. He followed the two girls and stopped right where Charlene and Willa had stopped.

"One of you wearing perfume?" he called ahead, the girls absorbed by the undergrowth.

"We're Cast Members, idiot! What do you think?"

Willa could smell the lilac on Charlene from two feet away. She could have killed her for it. She shot her friend a look that said, *Are you* kidding *me?*

The boy walked into some dappled sunlight. He was easily six feet tall. College age. Lifeguard-handsome with a tinge of boy next door. Square shoulders. Hair cut too short to guess its color.

He looked around like a hound sniffing the air. Looked right at Willa and Charlene, but did not see them—they hoped.

He continued on. "Wait up."

But the Asian girls didn't answer. They'd left him well behind.

* * *

People rarely questioned Maybeck. Even adults. Either he was invisible or people feared him—he wasn't sure which. He didn't always think of himself as African American; he was "me" in his head. But how other people saw him was different. Sometimes it didn't work out all that well, and sometimes, like this, it worked out just fine. Because as he passed a sign reading CAST MEMBERS ONLY PLEASE and walked down a rutted sand road, no one tried to stop him from entering the staff area. No one spoke to him at all. He wore the cape of independence. No one was going to say boo to him.

More important, no one was going to stop him from doing what had to be done. His job was reconnaissance. He was a Keeper spy, sent to penetrate the enemy camp. Mission accomplished, he thought. At least phase one. He'd made it inside.

Now he had to start up a conversation—never a real sticking point for him.

The area was littered with all sorts of equipment, including a miniature tractor, bicycles, a dozen Pargos, tanks of propane gas, stacks of wooden poles, barbecue cookers, and fish netting. There was a galvanized metal Quonset hut, a white concrete building with only one window, clearly built to withstand hurricane-force winds. This unmarked building was the staff headquarters. Maybeck followed the sound of an air conditioner and knew this was where he'd find the action. He arrived at a small multipurpose room, off of which were a pair of offices. In the corner, a guy in his mid-twenties was reading a book while nursing a cup of coffee. Maybeck nodded hello. Judging by the guy's reaction, his island Cast Member costume worked—his khaki shorts and white polo were his passport to open access.

He reviewed the material posted on two bulletin boards, ignoring the printed pamphlets and focusing on the handwritten material.

Remember to shut off all propane valves every night!

Fresh water is a luxury! Conservation first!

Personal hygiene is the best ambassador—
remember to shower!
Remember: there's a waiting list
to work on Castaway.
Earn your place here.

But it was another note that caught his eye:

To whoever is messing with
the marine radio: stop it!
It must be left set to receive
distress signals.
By resetting the frequency
you are endangering lives!

Maybeck reread this several times and wished Philby had already retrieved his phone so that he could take a photo of it so he wouldn't have to memorize it. Philby would know more about marine radios, but Maybeck recognized a possible Overtaker clue when he saw one: something out of the ordinary being done in secrecy. In this case, the use of a radio suggested off-island contact, possibly with a ship or even shore. And by using a radio, there would be no phone bill to trace, no evidence of such contact if anyone came looking. It reeked of the Overtakers.

"You're new," the guy in the corner said. It wasn't a question.

Maybeck worried he'd lingered too long at the bulletin boards. Worse, he realized that the island staff was so small they all knew each other.

"Training," Maybeck said. "I don't get to stay. I'm

on loan from the *Dream* because so many of our guests signed up for the island."

"Never heard of that," the guy said. "I mean, the ship Cast Members always help out. But wearing our costume . . ."

"You wear what Laundry gives you. Am I right?" Maybeck said, his delivery cocky. One thing Maybeck never lacked was attitude. Times like this it came in handy.

"I wouldn't know. We wear the same thing every day."

"You should see the laundry on the *Dream*," Maybeck said, having seen it himself. "It's all computerized. A freak show. You show up, they read the stuff you're turning in, and it automatically tells them what to give you next. They gave me this," Maybeck said, indicating his garb.

"Yeah? Well, welcome to the insanity. What's your assignment today?"

"Trash," Maybeck said without hesitation. He had to figure anyone joining an established staff would start at the bottom.

"Figures."

"No kidding."

"My advice," the guy said, "rebag it the second you take it out of the can. The crabs get in there somehow—

don't ask me how—and chew holes in the bag."

"Thanks for the tip."

"Be glad you got trash duty. I have to walk the CO_2 lines looking for breaks."

"The what?" Maybeck said.

"Mosquito control. They're attracted to carbon dioxide."

"I didn't know that. I always thought it was heat."

"Carbon dioxide coming through your skin. Anyway, the way they control them here is this network of tubes all over the island that emit the gas. The mosquitoes go for the tubes, which are poisonous, and they're snuffed. Pretty slick."

"I'll say."

"But we're having problems with the tubes, so yours truly has to walk the lines checking valves. And by 'walking the lines,' I'm talking about every swamp and bog on the island."

"You do something to deserve that?"

"Yeah," he said. "Got my degree in entomology. I'm the guy in charge of the system."

"You're a what?"

"A bug guy. I majored in bugs."

"Seriously?"

"Don't get me started. Six years of college serious."

"Carbon dioxide?"

"Saves spraying the island with toxins. The company is way greener than people know. This island is heading to full solar and wind."

"What would cause the problems with the tubes?" Keepers were trained to be alert to unusual changes in the parks, or problems; that extended to Castaway Cay. "Something chewed through it?"

"No, that's the thing. We have pressure sensors all along the system because of its miles of tubing. The computers log the sensor reports. We had incidents of pressure loss followed by normality. Two o'clock in the morning, the thing stops working for an hour. Right when we need it. We go out and check it the next morning and it's fine. Makes no sense."

"Different locations?" Maybeck asked.

The guy looked at him curiously. "Why do you care?"

"I'm a problem solver," Maybeck said.

"You're trying to get off trash duty."

"That too," Maybeck said, allowing a faint smile. "Could you use an assistant?"

"I'll tell you what: there's nothing to do on trash duty until after lunch. I can get you back by then."

"For real?"

"If you want to. It's not pleasant. There's a lot of muck and mud—"

"And mosquitoes," Maybeck said.

"The size of sparrows," the guy said.

"I'm in."

* * *

Following the instructions on the note he'd received, Finn stood at the edge of the stingray beach, wondering if he was really going to do this. The idea was to wade in, knee deep, and approach a Cast Member at one of the many stations where you could pet and feed stingrays. He was okay with the wading part, not so thrilled about the touching the fish part.

But the girl at the left station was Storey Ming, and she was staring right at him. Finn had told no one about the meeting, honoring her request in the note. Now reluctance tugged at him. Why couldn't she have picked the waterslide or the Jet Skis? Why'd it have to be here?

There were guests waiting in line to wade out to the stations. Dressed as a Cast Member, Finn had the privilege of jumping the line. Storey Ming's eyes bore into him, imploring him to do just that. He relented, stepping into the cool water and wading out.

"I'm training you," Storey Ming said softly, "just in case anyone should ask, which they won't. So look awestruck. I'm a very good teacher."

There was a white plastic track just below the surface. The stingrays were trained to enter the track and move station to station, where they were fed and petted. Being fed kept them interested in entering the track. It was a good system for all concerned.

Finn petted several—it felt way cooler than he'd thought it would. Then Storey Ming handed him some pellets and told him to hold his hand very steady, palm up. The next stingray swam over his arm and he felt a sucking, kissing sensation on his hand. The food pellets were no longer there when the stingray moved on.

"That felt very strange," Finn said.

"It grows on you. I like it a lot."

"I've never done anything like that."

"So? What about the lifeboats?"

"You were right," he said. He told her about the encounter with the hyenas, about stowing away on the lifeboats and following the sailors up to the massage cabanas. He told her he'd heard voices muttering but not the specific conversation, and he left out the part about Tia Dalma. Not everyone could handle the world of the Keepers and Overtakers. You had to ease them into it or they might form an opinion of you that was irreversible.

Certainly she knew about the Overtakers but hyenas on board the *Dream* had clearly stretched her level of credulity; Finn didn't want to push her too far too fast.

So he thought of a way to phrase his next question. "What kinds of religions are on board? In the crew, I mean?"

"You name it, we have it."

"How about the more obscure ones, like voodoo?"

"Not that I know of."

"People who believe in that sort of thing?"

"Cast Members or guests? Because when it comes to guests, my sense is, you name it, we see it."

Finn hadn't considered that the lifeboats had been sent to bring Tia Dalma aboard for the entertainment of the guests.

Seeing no way around the truth, he said, "The lifeboats were sent to pick up Tia Dalma. She refused. Said to send 'them' here. I don't know who she meant by 'them.'"

"That might explain it," Storey said softly to herself.

"Explain what?"

"I hear we're staying in port until later tonight, not leaving at five as scheduled."

"Here on the island?"

"Yes."

"Is that such a big deal?"

"Only that it's never happened before."

"Never?"

"Correct. Never. But tonight there's going to be a Beach Blanket Barbecue. Music. Dancing. Fireworks from the ship."

Finn got the impression Storey Ming heard things she wasn't supposed to hear.

"I don't love it when plans change," he said. It reeked of the Overtakers.

"You and me both."

"Who makes such decisions?"

"Can't happen without the captain. The director of entertainment, Christian, would have to bring it to the captain."

"That's high up."

"As high as it gets."

"Who could convince the director of entertainment to make that kind of switch?"

"Don't know. I'm not nearly a high enough rank to know."

A certain green fairy? Finn wondered.

"So we've delayed our departure. We're staying for a beach party that'll put all the guests off the ship and on the beach."

"Most of them. Yes. And nearly all the Cast Members and crew."

"The ship will be empty."

"It's never empty. It'll be lightly staffed. Most everyone in the crew will be onshore helping out. Some galley chefs and waiters will stay behind. The crew that manages the kids' clubs. You won't notice it if you're on board, but nearly all of the entertainment will be ashore."

"Making it easier to sneak people off and back aboard."

"That doesn't happen," she said. "Trust me. Security on this ship is the best there is. Period. Nothing gets past Uncle Bob."

"My friends and I did last night."

"You were holograms," she said. "Holograms don't present a real big threat, last time I checked."

"Okay," Finn said, "so if the change in plans is not because of that, then maybe it's to give Cast Members or crew a chance to meet secretly on the island."

"It could be a million things," she said. "Could be nothing."

Finn tried to connect the schedule change to Tia Dalma. The sailor crew had come to fetch her; she had refused, telling them to bring "them" to her. But whom did she mean? And why? And what, if anything, might it have to do with the stolen journal? As much as Wayne wanted him focused on getting back the journal and destroying the OT server—if it even existed—Finn knew from previous encounters with the Overtakers that he had to see the whole picture. Maleficent was crafty, wicked, and brilliant. There was no underestimating her.

"Thank you," Finn said.

"You and your friends are in danger," Storey Ming said bluntly.

"We have something we need to do. There are those opposed to the idea. I'm sure it will work out."

"There must be more that I can do for you. More than just listening for rumors."

Finn considered the boy his age that had gone missing from the photograph. To be a hologram you had to be asleep.

"Can you do me a favor?" he asked.

"Of course! I will if I can," she answered.

"There's going to be a stateroom with a Do Not Disturb sign out and its telephone blocked from calls. I suppose there could be a lot of them. But I need to know which of them has a boy registered in the room. A boy my age, or maybe a little older. Might have the initials G. L. Might not."

"Staterooms with kids. Do not disturb."

"Correct," he said.

"I've got a friend in Reservations. I can do that."

Finn thanked her.

"What about here on the island?" she asked. "I can help here, too."

"Okay. Listen, I promise I won't ask you out on a date, but could I get your Wave Phone number?"

She gave him the number and said, "And who says I'd turn down the date if it was offered?"

Finn blushed. She was way too pretty. Four or five years older than him.

Maybe the island *was* enchanted.

* * *

Philby found the phones where Finn had said he would. He studied the massage bungalows from a short distance, wondering what was up with Tia Dalma and the account of the previous night. All around him, thousands of cruise line guests were running, sailing, laughing, watersliding, and eating. Always eating. Oblivious to the challenges facing five teenagers, the guests took advantage of their time on their own private island, able to pack a week's worth of regular beach vacation into a single day.

Mixed in with them were dozens of Cast Members who provided all that fun. Somewhere—likely back on the ship—were an uncounted number of rebellious Overtakers who disapproved of the Disney lifestyle and wanted to instill their own wicked values on the parks and guests. There were times, like now, that Philby felt outnumbered and overwhelmed. It was far easier to hatch a devious plan than to uncover one. Just looking out at all the guests emphasized the futility of the Keepers' mission. They were looking for a needle in a haystack.

Then, over the heads of the beachgoers, the suntanners, the swimmers, the Frisbee throwers, the snorkelers, the day sailors, the Jet Skiers, and the barbecue dwellers rose the nearly unbelievable vastness of the *Dream*. Sparkling in the sunshine. Majestic. Almost as if it had been Photoshopped in.

At that same moment a honeybee floated by on the breeze. It too seemed incredibly out of place. Maybe the company set up hives to help pollinate gardens and flowers. He didn't really care. What interested Philby all of a sudden was that in biology class he'd learned about clearing the hive of the worker bees. He'd learned that when a hive was threatened, a group of bees rushed to surround the queen and protect her. How this very act of communal defense could be used by the beekeeper to locate and identify the queen, to pluck her from the hive, which was sometimes necessary to move the worker bees or establish a new hive.

From the bee to the ship and back to the bee.

Something so small. Something so large. All the people swarming the beach. Great ideas didn't materialize out of thin air. The really great ideas were inspired by something or someone. Even a bee.

Philby wondered if, with all this insanity ashore, he might have just come up with a way to find the hidden queen.

* * *

Finn sat at a table at Cookie's, getting hungry as everyone walked past with trays of food. Philby had met up with him right at the scheduled time to drop off the various Wave Phones left behind the night before. Finn told him about Storey Ming returning to the ship to look for staterooms where kids might be sleeping—where an OTK might be crossed over.

Philby took note of the information, then said he had something to do and headed for the *Dream*.

"You think you're so cool," Finn said, Philby now well out of earshot. Once to the ship, Philby could report back to Wayne ahead of Finn. He felt tempted to race back himself and beat him to it.

A girl sat down on the far end of the same picnic table bench. Finn glanced over and jumped.

It was Sally Ringwald. It took him only seconds to spot the faint blue line shimmering at her edges.

"No way . . ." he gasped. His mother's spy. A DHI for the Overtakers.

She looked straight ahead and spoke softly. "There's something happening tonight."

"The party," Finn said.

"I don't know about any party."

"Are you on the ship? How many of you?"

"Yes," she answered. "And I don't know. Listen, I promised your mother, and I'm keeping that promise."

"What's happening tonight?" he asked.

"All I know is there have been messages. A bunch of us are going to be on the island."

"Overtakers," Finn said softly.

"Whatever," she said.

"To do what?"

"It's unclear. There's a truck involved."

"A truck."

"But I don't know what for."

"Okay," he said.

"I thought you should know. It's something I thought you should know."

"How many of you?" he repeated.

Sally stood from the bench and left, her hologram disappearing into the thick lunch crowd. Then she was gone.

Finn considered following her, but he had the

phones to give back. He checked the time. So unlike the girls to be late. Maybeck, sure; Maybeck liked to be the last to arrive to anything; he liked to keep people waiting just long enough that they took notice of him. But Willa and Charlene were punctual.

Fifteen minutes. Twenty . . .

He stopped counting. No one was coming.

20

"WE'RE LOST," CHARLENE SAID, "aren't we?"

"And then some," said Willa.

They'd been wandering the narrow trails for more than two hours, the mangrove and swamp marsh grasses like walls on either side, leaving them in open-air tunnels. The spongy sand underfoot revealed nothing; if you closed your eyes and spun around, the trail gave no indication of which direction you'd just been headed.

"You remember the maze in *Harry Potter and the Goblet of Fire?*"

"Shut up."

"You know that was Robert Pattinson . . . the boy who died?"

"Charlie, everyone knows it was Robert Pattinson."

"I'm just trying to change the subject, get our minds off of never finding our way out of here and being eaten by snakes, or starving to death, or missing the boat. It's going to leave at five o'clock."

"Ship. And it's not even noon yet."

"I'm just saying . . ."

"You're saying too much. We need to think more, talk less," Willa said.

"Way to establish a sense of teamwork. Thanks for the confidence boost. I happen to talk a lot when I'm nervous." Charlene had been told she talked a lot—as in too much—nervous or not. But only by all of her teachers, her coach, and her parents. Needless to say, they were all crazy.

"Wish I had my iPhone," Charlene said. "I could map our position and—"

"No you couldn't. There's no cell service here. No GPS. Your phone would just stare back at you."

"You're such a dark cloud today. Lighten up!"

"You're starting to sound like a Disney character," Willa said. "I wouldn't take the role so much to heart."

Charlene made a sudden move at Willa, invading her space. Willa jumped back out of the way, clearly frightened. The two girls stood facing each other, breathing pent-up violence.

"Look at us," Willa said.

"Oh, I'm looking . . . believe me, I'm looking." Charlene had yet to flinch, dialed in to Willa and working to stare her down into submission. "And I don't like what I see."

"Truce?" Willa proposed.

"What is with you?" Charlene asked. However small, Willa's capitulation gave her a sense of victory.

"Boy stuff."

"Philby?"

Willa hesitated. "I know . . . how stupid can I get, right?"

"You're not stupid. No one would accuse you of that."

"You weren't really going to hit me. Right?"

Charlene answered with another stare-down.

"You freak me out sometimes."

"Good." That made Charlene feel even better. "Now . . . how do we find our way out of here?"

"Well, for starters, you see the way all the plants are leaning?"

"Yeah."

"Wind," Willa said. "All we have to figure out is if it's an onshore breeze or an offshore breeze."

"I have no idea what you just said."

"The wind blows so constantly from a single direction that plants growing up in the wind bend away from it. Permanently. But is it coming off the water or blowing out to the water—onshore or offshore?"

Willa kneeled, took up a stick, and drew the island, a long, narrow finger. Then, to the left, the ship at the pier perpendicular to the shore. She drew a line down the center of the island to represent the road the shuttle followed and three lines pointing at the island to represent the steady breeze. She drew two Xs to represent her and Charlene.

She leaned back, squatting over her work.

"It's both," she said. "Of course it is! I'm not used to islands. On the mainland it has to be one or the other. Here, it's different."

"I have no idea what you just said."

"On the ship side of the island, the breeze comes off the water. On this side, it continues on and blows offshore back out to sea. So we want to head into the wind, away from the direction the plants lean. And when we hit other paths, we want to take the ones that head the same way: away from the lean."

"You're sure?"

"Am I positive? No. But yeah, I'm sure."

"That doesn't make any sense."

"Stay with me."

"As if there's a choice."

"There's only one small problem," Willa said.

"Which is?"

"Sometimes the afternoon winds are stronger than the morning winds. No matter what, the wind almost always turns around on itself later in the day."

"In which case," Charlene proposed, "everything you just said is backward."

"Correct."

"So we're still lost."

"Yes. But we're lost with a theory."

"You drive me crazy," Charlene said. "But in a good way."

"I'm glad."

"There is an alternative," Charlene said suddenly.

"Which is?"

"Get on my shoulders and see where we are." Charlene kneeled. "What are you waiting for? Climb on."

"You can't possibly hold me."

"We won't know until we try."

* * *

Surrounded by marsh and a hundred yards from a narrow inlet of ocean water an impossible color of blue, with nothing around them but scrub brush, sand, and darting lizards the size of gummy bears, two men toiled.

"And if the system isn't working?" Maybeck asked.

"Then the mosquito population will run wild."

"Does it bother you," said Maybeck, "that you spent all those years studying the lives of insects, and now you've devoted yourself to killing them?"

"That's not a very nice thing to say."

"I'm just saying."

"What bothers me," Tim said, "is that my sensors are reporting error codes and the valves all look normal."

"Have you considered sabotage?"

"Come again?"

"That someone is disconnecting the tubes at night and reconnecting them before sunrise."

"Who would do that?"

"I'm just asking: would that explain your pressure readings?"

Tim looked at Maybeck warily. "It might. But why would anyone do it in the first place?"

"To keep the mosquito population growing while no one knew any better."

"That's ridiculous. Preposterous."

"But it would explain it," Maybeck tested.

Tim flashed Maybeck a disapproving look and moved on, following the porous black tubing that ran along the ground. He inspected a valve at an intersection of black rubber tubing. "That's interesting."

"What?"

"This line was recently disconnected. You can tell by the lack of corrosion."

"Meaning?"

"We're going to find out."

Maybeck followed along as Tim traced the black tubing through the thick scrub. They headed west toward the beaches.

"This is what we call the airstrip line," Tim said. "Hang on!" He kneeled and pulled back some loose shrubbery. The vegetation had been cut and heaped over a small metal tank.

"What's up?"

"That's a propane tank. One of our grill tanks."

"And another valve," Maybeck said.

"This is nuts," Tim said. "This is not part of my system. Propane is highly combustible."

"Part of a fireworks display or something?" Maybeck didn't want to say so, but he was thinking something much worse.

Tim looked over at him. "I suppose. They use propane in IllumiNations at Epcot. There's a special fireworks show tonight for the guests. But I would have been told about it." He cranked the valve on the tank shut. "I'm shutting it down until I hear differently."

"What's that over there?" Maybeck asked.

"The lookout."

"For?"

"So guests can get a look at a bunch of the island from up there."

"Including here where we are."

"Do you work for Uncle Bob?"

"My uncle's a lawyer in St. Louis," Maybeck said. "His name's not Bob."

"Head of security on the *Dream*," Tim said.

"You think I'm working undercover or something?" Maybeck had to bite his lip to keep from grinning.

"The thought occurred to me."

"I wish!" Maybeck said, maintaining his cover. "I'm on trash detail, remember?"

"Yeah, right. That's why you look so familiar."

"I get that a lot."

"Why do you know so much about sabotage?"

"I watch too much TV."

"A funny guy, huh?"

"Not as often as I'd like," Maybeck said. "I'm hoping to move off trash duty and onto the Walt Disney Theatre stage. I'd like to do stand-up."

"Why do I get the sense that you haven't given me a straight answer since we met?"

"I'm a man of mystery," said Maybeck.

"I have to get back and report this."

"If it's not part of the fireworks, what then?"

Tim considered the possibility long and hard. He finally spoke. "Then we've got trouble."

* * *

The ship's corridors and public spaces were ghostly
with so few passengers aboard. The stewards were
about the only people in the long corridors that accessed
the hundreds of staterooms on each level. They moved
along with bundles of fresh linens in their arms and
smiles on their faces. Philby said hello to several on his
way to the central stairs. He reached the Radio Studio
and used his key card to enter. It took him only a matter of minutes to send a signal to the DHI server, the
timer set.

It was something of a risk to take: crossing over
with no backup to help him return. But Finn's contact,
Storey Ming, had explained her discovery. He knew his
earlier instincts were correct: now was the time to act.

She had uncovered two staterooms that currently
had Do Not Disturb signs on their doors and had teenage boys registered among the occupants. Philby felt
sidetracked by this pursuit of Finn's—he wanted to
check out the ship's refrigerators while the kitchen staff
was lighter because of the cooking being done on the
island.

But the Keepers were all for one and one for all; he
wasn't going to break that vow. Not now.

Finn wanted to identify the "football type" who had
failed to appear in the photograph taken outside. Philby

could not deny his own curiosity: it reeked of a possible hologram. And if a hologram, an OTK.

He met up again with Storey outside the gated entry to the Deck 11 staterooms.

"All set?" she asked.

"Yes. I think so. I'm going to lie down now," he explained. "Wait for me outside the break room. I'll need you to stand guard."

"No problem," she said.

Thirty minutes later, a boy appeared in the empty break room. Philby reached out and touched the leg of a table. He loved 2.0.

As he opened the door into the companionway, there was Storey. She hurried over to him.

"You look totally real."

"I am real," he said. "I just happen to be a hologram."

"Can I touch you?"

"I don't do tricks," he said. "But you can try once we're alone in the elevator."

Soon after, the elevator doors closed behind them. She reached for Philby, her hand passing through his.

"I still can't . . . How exactly do you . . ."

"Pretty cool, isn't it?" he said.

"My hand passed through you, and yet you pushed the button for six."

"Correct. That's life as a DHI."

The doors opened.

Storey led the way down the port side companionway that ran nearly the entire length of the ship. More than eight hundred feet of hallway—almost three football fields long. They passed several grinning stewards hard at work and reached the first of the two staterooms she'd identified.

"If someone's coming, knock," he said.

"Then what?"

"Move one stateroom forward. Stand where you can screen me coming through. I'll join you."

"Shouldn't we at least knock or something before you go in there?"

"Do Not Disturb," he reminded.

"You want the element of surprise."

"Don't ditch me," he said, stepping up to and through the door like some kind of ghost.

Inside the room, the drapes were pulled, limiting the light. Philby stepped forward cautiously. Door to the toilet. A second door to the sink and shower. Sliding doors of the closet to his right. He didn't need to wait for his eyes to adjust. As a digital projection, all such adjustments came at the speed of light. The 2.0 update increased optical and audio sensitivity up to eightfold. He was no German shepherd, but he could see and hear more clearly and at a greater distance than any human being.

He sensed and saw a boy asleep on the fold-down bunk bed across from the couch a fraction of a second before he picked up on the woman dozed off on the stateroom's queen bed. Leaning back, she'd dropped an e-book into her lap.

The scenario that presented itself had nothing to do with Overtakers. A sick boy, his mother keeping a close eye on him. Furthermore, from what Philby could see, the boy hardly looked the football type. He was more like twelve than fifteen—far more likely a figure skater than a fullback.

A light knock on the door behind him.

Storey Ming, Philby thought.

The mother snorted awake. "Coming!"

Philby, his back pressed to the wall, could hear her climbing off the bed.

A moment later, a much louder knock.

"Room service!" A woman's voice.

This, Philby realized, was who Storey had seen coming.

Philby slipped into the sink/shower room just before the mother might have seen him, turned around, and walked through the wall.

He arrived in the closet of the adjacent stateroom.

A dress hung on a hanger, dividing him in two. The closet's sliding doors were slatted for ventilation, allowing him to peer through and into the room. Empty.

His hologram continued through the closet door. He moved quickly to the stateroom door and gently eased his head forward until only his nose, forehead, and eyes peered out into the corridor. He pushed a little farther forward, the stateroom door now cutting his head in half.

"Psst!"

Storey turned and jumped back so quickly at the sight of a boy's partial face sticking through a metal door that she rebounded off the corridor's opposing wall and fell to the carpet.

"Sheesh!" she gasped. "You scared me!"

"Is it clear?"

She looked left and right, nodded.

Philby stepped into the corridor, turned to his right, and never broke stride. Storey Ming caught up from behind him.

"Anything?"

"Just a sick kid, poor guy. Missing all the fun."

"At least it wasn't bad."

"Sometimes bad is good," he said. "It gets it over with. It keeps you from guessing. Lets you focus on stopping whatever's going on."

"And we don't know what's going on," she said.

"We are way too far behind. Believe me, the things we're dealing with . . . the powers we're dealing with . . . you don't want to get behind."

"You guys all talk really weird. You know that?"

"The other stateroom?"

"Deck Eight," she said. "I'll show you."

* * *

The Do Not Disturb stateroom on Deck 8 may have had a teenage boy as part of the occupancy, but Philby found no one inside. His guess, judging by what a horrible mess the room was in, was that whoever occupied the room put up the sign out of embarrassment. Not even a steward should see such a disaster. The family had fled to the beach, deciding to clean up later. Much later, Philby thought. If ever. What pigs!

Philby's hologram and Storey Ming were talking on the port side of the *Dream*, Deck 4, overlooking the beach activities in the distance.

"Frustrated?" she said.

"And then some," said Philby. "There's something else I have to do now. I'll see you later."

"I can come. I'm a Cast Member and entertainer. I have all kinds of access even you don't have."

"This is—" He'd been about to say "dangerous."

Instead he said, "for holograms only." He thanked her and walked away.

"I-95," she called out.

Philby's DHI stopped and turned.

"I live with the crew. If you're with me, you have every reason to be on I-95. Otherwise, you're going to be asked questions."

He tested 2.0 by patting his pants pocket. "I'm carrying a Cast Member ID," he said. "I'll be all right." He turned.

"Cancellations!" she said, stopping him for the second time. "We forgot about cancellations."

"What about them?"

"This cruise was sold out, but there are always cancellations. Last-minute stuff. Five, sometimes ten or more staterooms go empty. There's a waiting list. Some of those people actually fly down and take a hotel room the night before hoping to get on. Most do. But there are always empty rooms. Always, as in *always*."

"And?"

"What if this guy you're looking for is in one of the empty staterooms?"

Philby was intrigued. A perfect hiding place for an OTK. "You have my attention."

"I could get the list. The friend of mine in Reservations."

"And what do you tell her?"

"The truth: one of the DHIs on board is looking for Overtakers."

"I don't think so."

"Listen, Philby—can I call you Philby?—there is so much weird stuff that happens on these ships that the guests never hear about. You don't have to work very hard to convince the crew and Cast Members there's such a thing as Disney magic. They are believers. It wouldn't freak out anyone to learn there are Overtakers on board."

Philby considered everything she'd said. "Empty rooms?" he asked.

"At least five or six, maybe twice that."

"Call your friend," he said.

* * *

"We shouldn't have let them go together," Finn said. He was enjoying a pulled pork barbecue sandwich drenched in smoky-sweet sauce. He wiped some sauce off his chin and buried his face into the sandwich for another bite.

"A little late for that," said Maybeck, wolfing down a buttery piece of corn bread in three bites. He chased it with a glass of ice-cold milk. He made a deep-throated groan of appreciation that attracted the attention of three girls at a nearby table. Maybeck smiled at them, and all three giggled.

Finn hated him.

"They're probably out sunning on the beach," Maybeck said. "Pass the SPF."

"They wouldn't do that."

"A beach can do funny things to people. Especially girls. They like showing off their swimsuits. They never admit it, but if they didn't, why would they wear bikinis and string bikinis instead of one-piece Speedos?"

"You really do have a one-track mind."

"You want to talk about the propane?" Maybeck asked. "Has to be the OTs."

"The guy shut it off, right? Game over."

"Since when? This is the OTs. The game is never over."

"You said he's going to report it."

"Yes, and they'll remove the tank. I'm sure of it," Maybeck said.

"So? What's the problem?"

"What if it's a diversion? Or what if it's only one small part of their plan?"

"Which is?"

"How should I know? You're the one telling me there's an unscheduled Beach Blanket Barbecue planned for tonight. You think that's coincidence? No? Well, neither do I. And I don't happen to believe that by taking one propane tank out of the mangroves, that's the end of it. Since when?"

"So they were planning to start a fire. What's that tell us?"

"A distraction, a diversion, maybe. Maybe the girls stumbled onto someone messing with the tubes out there. Maybe they were led into a trap."

"How does Tia Dalma fit in?"

"We've got to watch her," Maybeck said. "She's got to be the key. Maybe she's the one running things, not Maleficent. Maybe the Green Machine's not even on the ship."

"Then why the video?"

"To throw us off. To have us chasing her when we should be chasing Tia Dalma. She's a major player. Voodoo mama extraordinaire. She eats black magic for breakfast."

Finn felt the chills. He put down the sandwich. "Nice move, Terrance. You just ruined my appetite."

"I'm just saying."

"Yeah. I get it." He pushed his tray away. "The girls."

"The party gives us more time to find them. How weird is that?" Maybeck said. "Since when do the OTs help us out?"

Finn sat forward. "Brilliant," he said.

"Consider the source," Maybeck said. Then he asked shyly, "What's brilliant?"

"The OTs don't have them. If they did, if that had been part of the plan, they wouldn't give us extra time to find them."

"Okay . . ."

"Meaning they're either spying on those two girls, hunkered down somewhere and hoping to learn more, or—"

"Or?"

"Not or. And. And they're waiting for us to show up and be a distraction and free them."

"You're dreaming," Maybeck said.

"Then you explain it," Finn said.

"I don't have to explain it. We don't know what's going on, so we don't have to explain. If I had to explain it, I'd say walk the beach looking for a pair of Cast Members stretched out on beach towels. I'm telling you: they're girls, man. It's a beach. A nice beach at that."

"You give them no credit. They're out there somewhere and they need us."

"Have you been to the doctor lately? I think you have a hero complex that needs removing." Maybeck paused. "Maleficent or Tia Dalma is allowing mosquitoes to breed. Fire plays into it somehow—maybe the fire was supposed to push the mosquitoes toward the beach when the time comes. I've got to follow up with my new BFF Tim, because he's a bug guy. He doesn't have a clue about the OTs."

"We both have to be super careful," Finn said. "No one else goes missing."

* * *

When Philby entered the third of the seven unoccupied staterooms vacated by cancellation, he saw much of the same he'd seen in the first two: an empty room, a made bed, clean windows looking out into the dazzling sunshine of late afternoon on Castaway Cay. As he'd done previously, he stood stock-still before leaving the room and moving on with Storey Ming to the next vacancy. He used the heightened senses made possible by 2.0 for one last scan of the premises.

The pillow!

Operating like a digital zoom, his 2.0-upgraded eyesight amplified and enlarged its target. The pillow grew larger, occupying the full frame of his vision.

A strand of hair. It ran diagonally across the pillow, corner to corner. As small and insignificant as it might have appeared, it was anything but. The *Dream*'s stewards were the best in the cruise business, selected from around the world. Although possible, it was highly unlikely a steward would make a bed and leave a long strand of hair on a pillow. An arriving guest would find the hair offensive. A single strand of hair might ruin a guest's entire cruise.

Standing close now, Philby pinched and extracted the hair from the static electric charge that held it to the pillowcase. Black. Ten inches long. The last few inches were a different color, dyed a faded red.

Discovery of the hair drove him to conduct a more thorough search of the stateroom. He found a smudge on the plate-glass door leading out to the small balcony. The bathroom was sparkling clean; it appeared fresh and unused until he touched one of the carefully folded towels and found it damp. The occupant had showered, dried herself, and then had refolded the towel exactly as the others. He marveled that without the enhancements of 2.0 he might not have sensed the dampness, might not have been able to pick up and pocket the stray strand of hair.

He jumped to the only logical conclusion: an Overtaker recruit—an OTK—was stowed away on the ship, hiding from authorities and serving Maleficent and the Overtakers. She had long black hair dyed red in places. She was the enemy.

Two taps on the stateroom door—Storey Ming's

signal to join her in the hallway. Three taps was their signal for him to find some other way out of the stateroom.

Philby stepped through the door, but stuck, half in, half out. His left shoulder, left leg, and left side of his face were through the door, but the rest of him would not pull through.

"Hurry!" Storey said. "A steward knocking on every room!"

Philby didn't understand what was happening to him. How could his hologram get stuck? The part of him that was Professor Philby wanted to stand there and figure out the science behind his dilemma. Philby the Keeper wanted the heck out of there—now! He stepped back into the stateroom and tried for the door once more. Stuck. Half in, half out. He was being held inside the room by some unknown force.

Again, half his face showed through the door. It was almost more than Storey Ming could stomach.

"Hurry!" she implored.

"Hm-mrgle-our-neggy."

Philby rocked his head so that his lips were free of the door and tried again. "Something's holding me."

"Get back," she hissed, before turning and walking away.

Philby ducked back into the stateroom, still marveling at the physics of what had just happened. Was it possible that it involved the strength of the projection of his hologram? With the original DHI program, a simple security camera or USB cam could be reverse-engineered to project the hologram. Did 2.0 require higher definition that the ship lacked on some decks? Had anyone tested the projection quality before inviting the Keepers onto the *Dream*?

He turned toward the water. Two kids stood facing him: a teenage boy and a girl. Not the boy Finn had described—smaller, darker, meaner. The girl looked familiar; he knew her from somewhere. Their postures—knees bent in a partial crouch, hips and shoulders square, one foot forward—a combat pose. They were here to fight him.

He spotted the telltale blue outline shimmering around their bodies. They were first-generation DHI holograms, and that meant they were OTKs, because Wayne's volunteers were all being projected as 2.0s.

The boy, standing by the bed, calmly knocked the lampshade off a wall-mounted light and unscrewed the bulb. He broke the bulb against the wall and outstretched his arm with the sharp glass held like a weapon before him. His blue outline dimmed—he was the older version 1.6—and in order to possess the broken bulb he had had to sacrifice a percentage of his *all clear*. This made the boy vulnerable. The girl, at the foot of the bed, inched forward empty-handed.

Professor Philby understood well that battles were won and lost by control of space. At present he was confined to the narrow hall between the two washrooms on one side and the closet to his right. If they kept him boxed in he was at a decided disadvantage. He quickly slid open the closet and grabbed a wooden hanger, extending it as a sword. He pulled down a bright orange cube of life vest and held onto a strap, holding it as a shield in his left hand.

Despite the hanger in hand, fear was his biggest weapon. If he could dominate these two early and establish himself as superior, if he could sow the seeds of doubt into both of them, he would weaken their DHIs and gain the superiority he pretended to possess.

He stepped forward to where the hallway became the bedroom. Another step and he'd be free of his confines.

The girl lunged forward. Philby jumped back instinctively. He would have to fight such instincts. He had to hold his ground.

She seized the ship's-wheel clock from the semi-circular counter top at the end of the closets. She held it out as a shield.

Philby swung the hanger. She deftly deflected the blow.

The boy leaped forward—a fast one, this kid—and swiped the broken glass across Philby's left arm, getting nothing but air. The shards of glass swept through Philby's hologram. The next attempt was met by Philby with the life preserver. A sliver of the bulb's glass broke and rained to the floor.

Distracted as he was, Philby left himself open to a charge from the girl. She swung the clock for Philby's head. He leaned back and felt the wind from the miss.

The boy's blue outline dimmed following Philby's block. Philby took advantage of the weakness of the hologram and stabbed with the end of the hanger. He hit the boy in the shoulder—the boy, not his hologram—and sent the kid back onto the bed. He quickly recovered, leaping to his feet. His blue outline regained color.

Philby swung to his right and caught the girl on the forearm. She dropped the clock. He swung again, hitting her on the side of the knee, and she collapsed.

His hand stung. He'd let go of the life vest. The boy had wisely attacked his hand, knowing it had to be material enough to hold on to the vest. Philby was bleeding, a shard of glass lodged in his wrist. Philby screamed—out of anger and strategy, not pain—and charged the boy, swinging the hanger like a sword fighter and pushing the boy back into a corner formed by the bed and end table. Pinned. He whipped him with the hanger, watching the blue outline drain of color as welts formed on the boy's forearm.

The girl would not be intimidated. With Philby's attention on her partner and his body angled away from her, she also screamed out as she charged, hands outstretched. She passed through his hologram, but managed to take hold of his more solid hand and pulled him with her. She dragged him through the wall and into the next stateroom—or almost.

His hand holding the hanger caught against the interior wall. He stopped suddenly, half in, half out, as he had at the stateroom door. It was like someone had stepped on the brakes. He stopped so quickly, she lost her grip and let go. She fell into the adjacent stateroom, landing on the floor by the bed, while Philby remained stuck in the wall. He lunged back into the original stateroom, where the boy had now recovered and picked up the hanger.

The boy swung and stabbed at Philby's 2.0 hologram, swiping through his hologram's projection until focusing just on Philby's hands. Three repeated blows connected with the knuckles on his right hand.

Philby cried out in pain. With the pain, fear. With

fear, a somewhat weakened hologram, 2.0 or not. The boy was winning.

Spinning and kicking, Philby managed to slip past the battery of blows and reach the closet. He grabbed a hanger and the two boys launched into a sword fight, the object of which was to strike the other's hand and make him drop the hanger, then step in and beat the other's failing hologram senseless.

The girl reappeared through the wall. Angry. Defiant.

"The bulb on the floor," her partner said.

She bent and picked it up.

"We've got him now," the boy said.

Philby wanted to object. He felt wounded. Decidedly at a disadvantage. But he did not feel defeated. Far from it. In fact, as his hologram went through the motions of defending himself, and while admittedly losing some ground, Professor Philby was again thinking about his getting stuck in the wall—stuck for a second time in a matter of minutes.

The hanger had been knocked from his hand by contact with the interior wall. Had he not let go, it too would have prevented him from making it through the wall. But he had let go. It wasn't a limitation of projection that prevented him from making it through the wall and door—the girl's first-generation DHI had managed just fine. It was something material, like the hanger. Something holding him from getting through as a projection.

And then it occurred to him: the strand of black hair.

He'd put it into his pocket. It was a material item he had not crossed over with, but had picked up from within the stateroom. A single human hair, but matter, not projected light. Matter that could not pass through a door or a wall. The strand of hair was stranding him.

He turned his pocket inside out as he fended off the dual attack. Picked at the fabric, lacking any possibility of taking the time to look down for the strand of hair. The boy swung at him. Philby dodged the blow, moving right. The girl swiped his hand—his material hand—and the bulb's glass sliced into him. The pain caused him to look down. With that glance, he saw the black hair against the white cotton of his pants pocket. He snagged it and dropped it to the carpet. It floated, nearly motionless.

The next few attempts with the broken bulb failed, passing through Philby's hologram. Of all the Keepers, Philby was by far the most cerebral. His brain never rested. For months he'd been occupied with mastering DHI 2.0, and now his work paid off.

He charged the girl—the bloody broken bulb aimed

into his face passed through him; he knocked her back, continuing past her through the wall and into the adjoining stateroom.

The boy jumped through the wall after him, but without the hanger. A thump on the wall suggested the girl had tried but failed at *all clear*. The boy swept the contents of a nightstand into the air, demonstrating a facile and impressive ability to control DHI 1.6. A Bible and a water glass flew at Philby, but passed through his projection.

"Come and get me," he felt like saying, feeling fully in control of his hologram, having no worry he might cross back to the slightest degree.

He jumped in two strides and passed through the glass door and out onto the balcony. The boy followed, the two of them only a few feet apart.

"You want to test your control?" Philby said. He gestured over the banister. "Feel like a swim? I hear the water's great."

"You'll have to tell me how it is," the boy said. He upended a low table. It flew at Philby, but went through him.

"Nice try," Philby said.

"I've got better," the boy said.

"You're on the wrong side. You understand that, right?"

"What's more likely? That everything's going to work out fine, like a fairy tale, or that stuff happens, bad stuff, and that's just the way it is? The universe is not all sweet and pretty. Grow up. It's total chaos."

They moved in a slow circle like a pair of boxers. The boy had his back to the rail now. Philby needed to make sure his opponent slipped out of *all clear*.

"So you want a world with no imagination, no dreams? You want to take orders from a green-skinned, pointy-chinned fairy forever? Be my guest. Did you decide to come here on your own, or were you told to come here? Because let me tell you something: no one told me to go into that stateroom. That was my choice."

Philby saw a flicker of light in the boy's eyes. Maybe it was a trick of light playing off the glass, but maybe it was consideration and doubt, the kindling for the fire of fear. That was how he was going to play it.

The boy's hologram filled with static interference likely caused by the balcony's railing.

The girl suddenly appeared through the metal barrier that separated the small balconies. She seethed with anger—as destructive to a DHI as fear. Philby edged to his right, hoping to move the boy away from the projection interference. But the boy stood there, his image sparkling and spitting like bad television reception.

Unable to control her anger, the girl charged. Philby never flinched. She passed through him and smacked into the plate glass window behind him with a thud. He spun, found her wrist substantial enough to grasp, and whipped her toward her sparkling partner. The boy jumped out of the way—and out of the projection interference. The girl hit the rail, and Philby dumped her over the side. She fell a long distance and splashed into the turquoise water. The boy lunged, but Philby was ready for him. Philby ducked, using 2.0 to transform himself more solid, and stood just as the boy collided with him. Philby had the boy on his back like a fireman's carry. He stood, turned, and leaned heavily back against the rail. The jolt sent the boy over the side, screaming on his way down. Philby watched as the boy bobbed to the surface. He and the girl were treading water.

A *Dream* life preserver flew through the air from a higher deck. An alarm sounded.

Philby's hologram hurried through the plate glass and out into the hallway where Storey Ming waited, looking panicked.

"Ran into some friends," Philby said, tucking in his shirt.

She took him by the hand and led him calmly down the hallway toward the bow.

"You feel cold," she said, glancing down at his hand.

He'd never thought of it before. Couldn't remember anyone touching his hologram but Overtakers.

Don't let go, he wanted to say, enjoying the contact.

She caught him staring at her profile as they walked.

"What?" she asked.

"Nothing," he said, embarrassed.

21

A SEAGULL FLEW LAZILY above the beach as preparations for the Beach Blanket Barbecue got under way. A pink sun sank quickly beyond the horizon. The beach chairs were being wiped down; barbecue grills huffed gray smoke; the volleyball court was being raked; a hundred tiki torches were flickering with yellow flame. A stream of ship passengers was currently disembarking, the people having returned to shower and change for the festivities. The empty beaches would soon swell with guests; the steel-drum music would start. It was party time.

The gull continued its uncharted path, riding the air currents, watching the waves lap to shore. The same every night; it never tired of the sight. It would land soon and hunker down for the night, head tucked into its wings, awaiting the stir of a morning breeze.

It headed lower and lower, passing over some brush that ruffled in the breeze. It circled this once, having memorized nearly every speck of terrain in its domain. Out of curiosity it dove and landed on the pile. Its feet hit something cold and hard beneath the brush. Metal.

It worked to move the brush out of the way, exposing more white metal and a label.

DANGER:
PROPANE GAS—UNDER PRESSURE

The gull did not have what humans think of as memory. But there were images floating around in its pea-size brain. One of those images was of a person carrying a tank with an identical label as this one earlier in the day. The human had placed it on the back of a golf cart. This tank was identical to the one that had been removed. It also connected to the same black tubing as had the other. A second tank, identical to the first. A tank undiscovered by the humans.

* * *

Propped on Charlene's shoulders, Willa could see water in the distance. But this was an island, a small island, so spotting water hardly won her any points. This was their fourth attempt to see over the jungle top and the first offering any success, limited as it was.

"I'm sorry," Willa said, back on the ground again.

"It's not your fault. Stupid jungle is too high." Charlene thought for a moment and said, "No ship?"

"No."

Charlene then drew an arrow into the sand of the narrow path.

"So . . . no ship this direction. And what about the water? Where did you see it?" She handed Willa the stick she'd drawn with.

Willa engraved the path's sand with wavy lines in the direction of the arrow and to the right. The two girls studied their map.

"So there was shore along here?" Charlene asked.

"There was."

"Last night . . . when we rode the lifeboats and snuck ashore . . . the sun set behind the ship to port, remember?"

"Ah . . . if you say so."

"Trust me. It did. So . . . look at the shadows." Charlene pointed into the thick undergrowth. The plants were crosshatched with sharp, angular shadows.

"So the shadows are pointing east because the afternoon sun moves west."

"Correct."

"And if the sun set to the left of the ship . . ."

"The ship is docked basically aiming north."

"So the beach is on the south side of the island!" Charlene said. "If we head south, by the time we reach water . . ."

"We should be able to see the *Dream*. It's not a very

big island, and it's a very big ship." She exhaled loudly.

"Only one problem," Willa said. "The paths are totally random. And there are a zillion of them."

"We can do this," Charlene said.

"And if we can't?"

"What's the first thing the Professor will do when they can't find us?" Charlene said in a know-it-all voice.

"Philby? I suppose . . . I don't know . . . maybe check the server to try to see if we're in SBS. Can he even do that?"

"The server, yes," Charlene said. "He'll do a manual return in case we're somehow DHIs."

"Note to Charlene: we're not DHIs. We won't return."

"No . . . but there's no one smarter than Philby. First, he'll try to return us, and then—?"

"Oh my gosh! You think?"

"I know."

* * *

Shutters, the cruise ship photo display area, was really high-tech compared to similar shops on older Disney ships. The same expansive gallery was there—walls and partitions covered in hundreds of professional photos of passengers on arrival day, at dinners, with characters, and with the captain. The gallery spread out to Deck 4's balcony overlook of the atrium. Here were rows of handsome wooden "post office" boxes from which guests could collect their ordered shots. A marvel of organization and efficiency.

Finn decided to check it out, to follow up on the missing-kid photo. He located the most recent shots—guests on Castaway Cay with the *Dream* behind them—and searched for the picture. It took him several minutes, but he finally spied a shot of two kids in which the ship behind them was cut off. The photo had been cropped. A tall kid about Finn's age had quite possibly been cut out.

He approached the desk.

"Excuse me," he said, passing the photo to the Cast Member, a young woman. "I think there was a third boy in this photo. Do you mind checking?"

She took a moment to reference the corresponding computer file.

"You're right," she said, "but I see the problem . . ." She spun the terminal around so Finn could see also. "This kind of stuff happens from time to time."

The kind of stuff she was referring to was a pixelated image in the frame.

"They cropped it," she explained, "for obvious reasons."

Finn felt his fists clench. The boy's blackened, hollow eye sockets turned his stomach, but it was the face that startled him. Greg Luowski's hologram was turned sideways to the camera, his chin over his left shoulder. His green eyes were not eyes at all, just black holes in his piggish face. He'd turned to avoid having his picture taken, but too late. Captured there was the disintegrated image of the school bully who'd endlessly tormented Finn, had nearly poisoned him in his own home, had Tasered Maybeck's aunt. There was no question of his being a DHI to anyone who knew of such things. The photographers could promote all the speculation they wanted as to why the boy was transparent; Finn knew.

Lousy Luowski was, at the very least, being projected by the Overtaker's secret server; at the worst, he was physically aboard the *Dream*.

Finn glanced over both shoulders, eerily aware of his own paranoia.

"May I get a copy of the whole picture, please?" He spun the monitor back to face the Cast Member. He couldn't have imagined he'd be asking to pay for a photo of Greg Luowski. But Philby would know how to study the photograph, to confirm what Finn already knew.

"Mailbox one thirty. It'll be about an hour."

"Thank you." Finn handed over his room card for the sake of charges.

Clearly impressed by its unique color that indicated his celebrity status, she smiled slightly.

"I thought I recognized you. The Disney Hosts, right?"

"Yeah."

"It's your cruise."

"Not exactly."

"Pretty much," she said.

"Just working, same as you."

"Must be cool."

"Yeah, I suppose. We have a . . . good time."

"And the stories—like the Overtakers and everything?"

"You know Disney. The story comes first!" He tried to make it sound fanciful.

"That's exactly what I would say," she said.

They met eyes, and Finn realized there were no secrets anymore. Their story was out. Deny it or not, people knew. It was almost as if by denying it he just made it all the more true.

But what if the stories hadn't been true? What if like other celebrities people just made up anything they felt like and people believed it? Rumor was poison. He'd learned to stick with the facts.

"Not every story is true," he said. "Not every rumor is false."

"I appreciate what you're doing," she said. "You and

the others. If they're stories, they're good stories."

She was at least five years older than Finn, but he had the feeling that if he'd asked her to hang out she'd have agreed. Without knowing him. On reputation only. He measured that against having been invisible to girls only a few years before, wondering how to act, who to be. All of a sudden he wanted off the ship; he wanted his mother back, his life back.

"Okay, then. Mailbox one hundred thirty."

"One hour." She sounded disappointed.

He hated disappointing anyone. Everyone. Much of what he did and the way he acted was for his mom. To meet her expectations of him. Though he'd been raised to be giving and considerate, there were times he wanted to do what he wanted to do, not what someone else wanted him to do. Like this.

"See you then?" he asked.

She brightened with excitement. "I'm working until six. Yeah. Absolutely."

They both knew the rules—Cast Members couldn't interact with passengers. But was Finn a Cast Member or a passenger?

He had no idea who he was.

Luowski, he reminded himself. Don't get distracted. Stay focused. The enemy is out there.

The enemy is on the ship.

* * *

"We have to cover for the girls!" Maybeck said behind clenched teeth, hoping only Philby and Finn would hear him. Events had progressed rapidly. Upon returning to their staterooms, the Keepers had found notes outside their doors and messages on their Wave Phones asking that, due to the change in itinerary, the Disney Hosts participate in the Beach Blanket Barbecue welcome on the beach stage at seven. Short scripts to be memorized were included in the envelopes. The request presented myriad problems, foremost of which was that Willa and Charlene still had not been heard from. The most likely explanation was that the Overtakers had captured them, a terrifying thought given that the ship was set to sail in a matter of hours. Another problem was the not-so-small matter of staking out Tia Dalma's cabana in order to figure out who was being delivered to her and why.

Compounding it all was Maybeck's discovery of the propane tank rigged to the bug-killing black tubing. Philby claimed that from what he'd heard it hardly added up to a bomb—"the tubing is porous, after all, like soaker hose"—and that its remote location, on the far side of the abandoned runway, meant it wasn't a threat to passengers or Cast Members. In fact, he wondered if it wasn't meant as a distraction or diversion, a line of bursting flame to turn the heads of passengers at a particular moment.

"Another attack on us during the welcome?" Finn had said in their brief meeting outside the Cove coffee shop. It seemed similar to the effort by Jack Sparrow during the Sail-Away.

"It feels like it, doesn't it?" Philby said.

"I wish they'd stop trying to kill us," Maybeck said. The boys couldn't tell if it was meant as a joke or not.

"So here's what we do," Finn said. "First, we're going to be in our DHI costumes, so I don't see how you're going to get backstage." He said this to Maybeck.

"Leave that to me. I can put the coveralls over my DHI look. Why?"

"If the diversion wasn't meant for us—and how could it be, given that when the propane was hooked to the tubing there was no Beach Blanket Barbecue planned?—then I'm thinking it was supposed to distract the island Cast Members long enough for someone to get backstage and do something in the Cast Member area."

Philby said, "Because on a typical day they'd be the only ones on the island at that point."

"Exactly."

"So you want me," Maybeck said, "to get backstage at the same time I'm supposed to be onstage? How's that going to work?"

"We don't know when the propane was supposed to go off. Not at seven o'clock, that's for sure. It's still daytime. It had to be planned for dark."

"So after nine thirty-two," Philby said.

Maybeck and Finn gave him a look.

"What?" Philby said defensively. "It's what I do!"

"Second," Finn said, "we need to stake out the cabanas."

"You can handle that the minute the welcoming stuff is over," Philby said to Finn. "We're all on Wave Phones. We can text or call. Anything else?"

"What about you?" Finn asked.

"I need to get back aboard the ship after the welcome and check the server. The OTKs came after me as holograms. What if the girls have been projected without us knowing it?"

"The Syndrome?" Maybeck gasped.

"All I'm saying is, it's possible."

Finn said, "At least one of us is going to have to stay behind on the island until the final all-aboard is called to try to counter whatever the propane was supposed to do. Remember, whoever planted that probably doesn't know it's not going to work."

"That would be me," Maybeck said. "Backstage, like you said."

"You can't miss the ship," Philby warned. "They won't wait for you."

"Yeah, I know."

"And the girls?" Philby speculated.

"We tell them the girls are on their way," Finn said. "You know girls and getting ready. Sound good?"

"Sounds real," Philby said. All three boys laughed. It was the first laugh for Finn in some time.

"If they miss it completely, we mock them. And remember, Philby's keeping an eye out for the DHIs that attacked him, and we're all looking for Luowski."

"We need to find that server," the Professor said. "We take out the server, we take out their DHIs, and maybe put them into the Syndrome at the same time."

"I like that idea," Maybeck said.

Now they were on the pier alongside the *Dream* in a stream of passengers and Cast Members headed to the beach. A lone seagull glided along the shore far in the distance, then flew lower and landed out of sight. They were dressed in the same shorts and shirts as their in-park DHIs. They nodded politely to passengers who recognized them. Kids waved hello, and they waved back.

"Has it occurred to either of you that now that 2.0's

in beta, the Imagineers will be looking for new models?"

Finn stumbled and recovered. "What?"

"We're high schoolers," Philby reminded. "Our DHIs have been in the Magic Kingdom for a long time now. We barely look like our DHIs anymore. We haven't recorded any new lines in over a year, so our DHIs are saying the same old stuff as they always have. That's gonna change."

"And you wait until now to bring this up?" Finn said as they walked along among hundreds of cruise passengers. "Wayne would have told me."

"You think he's as connected as he once was?" Philby asked. "His whole attention's on the OTs. He's not in the loop on the park stuff."

"They're going to replace us?" Finn gasped. Would Wayne do that to him?

"Then why install us in Disneyland?" Maybeck asked Philby.

"It's beta. You know how any beta program testing works. You run it for a while to get the bugs out. Then you ramp up and deploy the real thing."

"We're guinea pigs?" Maybeck said.

"We're beta testers," Philby answered. "They run us under 2.0 before introducing the next-generation DHIs. They won't want the new DHIs bugging out all over the parks. They'll leave that for us."

"We're history?" Finn said. He didn't know whether to feel relief or anxiety.

"Toast," Philby said. "It's only a matter of time."

"What a buzzkill," Maybeck said.

They continued onto the island amid the hordes of passengers, Finn's mind drifting for a moment. First he thought of his mother and the green eyes staring back at him in the car. It gave him chills. He wondered if Storey Ming's friend could help him determine if his mother was aboard. He'd seen her at the terminal, after all.

But he also thought about being replaced. There had certainly been times he did not want to be a DHI, but now that Philby said it was more than likely going to happen, he wanted it back. He didn't want it to stop. More than that, he didn't want some other guy to replace him. Just the thought of it ran his blood cold. Did Wayne know about it? Did he intend to do anything about it?

The Beach Blanket welcome lasted only a few minutes and was run by Cast Members who seemed not to notice the girls were missing. Typical Philby—he'd memorized the girl's lines as well; he simply recited them where they belonged in the script, and it all went off without a hitch. The entertainment director had wisely kept it all brief and amusing; it was over practically before it began. Maybeck then slipped off toward the island's Cast Members–only compound, Finn to the cabanas, and Philby back to the ship.

Once inside the Radio Studio, Philby connected to the onboard DHI server and downloaded its log. Nothing. Not a single byte of bandwidth used since his own return following the fight in the staterooms. The discovery came as a huge relief—he'd been harboring fears the girls were stuck in the Syndrome. As a precaution, he instigated a return for both girls. Checked the log: still nothing. He was about to sign off the secure session when one last thought occurred to him. He typed a command string. His fingers hesitated over the keyboard. What he was about to do was not without risk. To cross over someone unsuspecting was to throw them into a virtual nightmare that they couldn't wake up from. The shock of being crossed over when unexpected could be psychologically disturbing. But the situation offered too great a possibility not to try.

He punched the ENTER key. Within seconds he was out of the Radio Studio and practically flying downstairs toward crew break room. He had to see . . .

* * *

Maybeck tried to see any difference.

His artist's eye gave him a distinct advantage;

366

he could visualize things in ways others could not.

He stood on the sand-covered asphalt roadbed leading into the island's maintenance compound, his eye comparing what he saw now to what he'd seen only hours earlier. It was like a game to him: spot the difference. Two Pargos had moved; another was gone from its charging spot. Three bicycles were now parked outside the concrete-block administrative building where he'd met Tim. A garden hose that had been neatly coiled was now uncoiled and had been left in a tangled mess. What else?

Some plants had been watered, the soil darker. The recycling and garbage bins were now brimming; they'd been empty before.

More? The sun was fading; it had been bright sunshine earlier. Shadows were at different angles and stretched longer. A window on the side of the Quonset hut was now open.

It drew him, this window. Pulled him toward it to peer inside and uncover mysteries he was certain lay on the other side. Ten yards away and closing, he passed a corrugated-tin maintenance shed and stopped. Its padlock hung unlocked.

He hesitated, unsure how to proceed. He had no business being backstage. The island Cast Members handled a hundred tasks at once; he could not interrupt them without drawing attention to himself. But with the Beach Blanket Barbecue under way, the island headquarters appeared deserted, everyone off doing something, so why would a shed be left unlocked? If there was any time to lock a shed it was when guests were on the island; certainly when there was no ship docked the rules changed on Castaway Cay. The hanging padlock intrigued him, as did the open window on the Quonset hut.

With the window easier to check out, he hurried over and carefully peered into the dark hut. He could make out a tractor and other large machinery packed in neatly at the far end. Closest to him was a machine shop containing an industrial drill, a band saw, and grinders. No light. No activity. Only the strong odor of paint—the open window suddenly explaining itself: ventilation.

He crossed back to the small tin shed. It had no windows, but there was a large gap between the top of the wall and the eave of the roof allowing for airflow in the tropical climate. Standing perfectly still, he heard faint sounds from inside. They might be explained by an animal, he thought. Or a person. The more he listened, the more the sounds seemed less random and more ordered. A keyboard? Valves?

Maybeck slipped around front and put his eye to the

door. He could see inside, but only a sliver of the shed's grayish interior was visible. Not enough to see what was going on. Maybeck lacked the urgency of some of the other Keepers, but he possessed a wily cunning that served him well. He was in no hurry.

A minute passed. Two . . . five. A leg appeared—a human leg, from the knee down. A man's hairy leg, or a grown boy's. Dark shorts. A black flip-flop. Sight of the leg confirmed his earlier suspicion, but it was neither the leg nor the shorts (which should have been khaki if worn by a Cast Member) nor the flip-flop (which should have been a canvas deck shoe if worn by a Cast Member) that sounded the alarm in Maybeck's head. It was the lack of tan—the pale, reddish skin that revealed itself even through the limited light. There was no way—no way—that a resident of this island could have skin so pale.

Pale reddish skin . . . Maybeck knew whose leg it was. He studied the door's rust-colored hinges. Any metal on the salt-wind island was in a constant state of decay. He knew the hinges would squeal when he opened the door. He licked his finger and applied spit to each of the three hinges. He tugged the door gently, moving the hinges only slightly, and worked his spit into them. Then he eased the door open and slipped inside.

He recognized him immediately: Greg Luowski.

* * *

New Age music—wood xylophones, a bamboo flute, and brass bells—floated in the air along with the scent of jasmine, cinnamon, and musk oil. Finn crouched among the wide elephant's ear plants outside the first of the dozen massage cabanas. With the shutter open, candlelight flickered through the open-air window. A shadow swept past on the sand. On all fours, Finn crawled beneath the occupied cabana, paused, and scurried across moonlit sand to the next. It was occupied as well, and the soft music suggested a massage session here as well.

Finn kept moving and was squarely beneath the fifth cabana before he identified it as the one from the night before—Tia Dalma's cabana. He'd moved too quickly—been in too much of a hurry.

A rope was coiled around the cabana's stilt. Finn moved to examine it, but too late. It began moving as he turned his head. Uncoiling like a snake. It slithered into the sand, stood up, and became rigid. A staff with a cobra's head. Its eyes flamed red and glowed hypnotically. Jafar's staff.

Finn felt the movement of sand against his knees and shins. He tried to look down to confirm he was being dragged toward the staff, but couldn't take his eyes off the cobra. It had some kind of grip on him, physically and mentally. The murmur of voices came from above. A man and a woman speaking. Jafar and Tia Dalma. Overtakers. Jafar's staff had been left to keep watch.

Long ruts in the sand behind Finn. He'd slid five . . . now six . . . seven feet closer to the rigid staff. He fought to break eye contact, but it was little use—the cobra owned him. He struggled to open his fingers, and he scooped up sand as the thing drew him closer. The spinning eyes grew larger and their effect more powerful; the gravitational force increased, and he sped up as he moved across the sand. The voices above him sounded as if they were arguing.

Flexing his arms felt as if he were trying to curl an impossible amount of weight in the school gym. He slid closer still, the glowing eyes now the size of the sun. There was a universe in there—he wanted to travel inside.

Using every ounce of his strength, Finn brought his arm up and threw the sand into the cobra's eyes. The creature's eyes squinted shut.

The spell broke.

Finn dove forward, grabbed hold of the staff, and swung it like a baseball bat against the stilt. As it connected, it softened. Rather than break, or make a sound, it wrapped around the stilt, and the cobra's face was suddenly an inch in front of Finn's. Finn let go and fell back. The staff tried to unwrap, but Finn saw it coming, grabbed hold a second time, and slammed it against the stilt again, soundlessly, as it turned fluid and coiled around the wood. But this time Finn reached with his left hand and took hold beneath the cobra's hood, brought his left and right hands together, and, without thinking, tied the snake into a knot. It was a like a pro wrestling move: the Whitman Whip Knot. The cobra struggled to untie itself, but only expended energy unnecessarily. Then, as Finn moved to choke it, the creature took the form of wood again: a wooden staff, wrapped around a post and carved in a granny knot. Finn grabbed some dried seaweed from the sand and draped it over the staff, covering the snake's dangerous eyes.

Irritated conversation continued overhead. Tia Dalma spoke sonorously and calmly in a lilting rhythm; the man Finn took to be Jafar had a singsong, melodic voice, higher than the woman's. His muffled words came out rapidly, a man upset.

Finn sat up taller and put an eye to the cracks in the flooring. Pitch black. Under a mat. He moved slat to slat, board to board, until the glimmer of candlelight revealed itself. He could see through the gap and up into the bamboo rafters that supported the cabana's thatched roof. But it wasn't only his vision that improved. So did the sound quality.

". . . is unacceptable." Jafar.

"All things given time," Tia Dalma said. "There is but one cause."

"Promises were made."

"Not by me."

"You know who I mean," he said.

"The green one does not break such promises."

"She has not kept them, either."

"She will."

"I am owed the lamp. My purpose in joining this journey is the fulfillment of years of effort. Any delays like this—"

"—are necessary or they would not happen. You must trust the one cause."

"I trust no one. Not my own shadow."

"We all want what you want, if for different reasons. The 'chive is important to every one of us. Every one. Do not think yourself alone in this endeavor. The 'chive is my destination as well. But unlike you, apparently, it is evident I am willing to do what is asked of me."

"You conjure this and that. It is very different for you than for me."

"You must role-play. What is so very difficult?"

"Children! Gooey-eyed, wet-lipped little spoiled

brats all begging for an autograph. It is an insult to my dignity."

"It is not so very difficult, I think. Two weeks, and then the answer to your dreams. How many of us live with such a luxury?"

Silence.

A gruff chuckle. "Perhaps you are right."

"I am never anything but," said Tia Dalma, adding a chortle of her own. "If I could lie, even with great difficulty, how much easier my existence. But the one cause does not permit it. This is my curse. This is my legacy. So be it."

Another long silence. "Go in peace," he said.

"And you."

The board creaked. Sand spilled into Finn's ear. He scurried out from beneath the cabana, tore the seaweed off the cobra staff, crossed the moonbeams, and lay down flat in the shadow of the adjacent hut. His feet faced Tia Dalma's cabana; his face, toward the ship. If Jafar spotted him, if the man came for him, Finn would have no warning.

He slowed his breathing.

"What have we here?" Jafar said, incredibly close.

At first, Finn was convinced Jafar was speaking to him. Thankfully, he was wrong.

"Got yourself tied all in knots again?" Jafar said, presumably to his staff. "Do you never learn? Must I—? What's that?"

Finn didn't hear the staff talking, yet had little doubt there was communication under way. Little doubt about the subject of that discussion.

He rose to his feet, stayed low, and took off running.

"You!" Jafar called out.

Finn ran, cabana to cabana, only visible for the fraction of a second he stepped into and through the patches of moonlight between the huts. He sensed it—or perhaps heard it—before he saw the cobra on his heels. Spinning its large lazy Ss, it sped through the sand step for step with Finn. It darted in front and tried to lasso Finn by the ankle, but the boy saw it coming and jumped, banging his head beneath the final cabana, where the masseuse called out, "Just a moment please!" believing it to be a knock on the door.

Finn could not run any faster—the sand made it a slog. The cobra pulled alongside and tried to catch him by the ankle once again. Finn jumped and it missed him.

He broke through a dining area. A man screamed at the sight of the slithering cobra. Then a woman. Trays of food spilled as people leaped from their picnic tables. Finn was sprinting now, never slowing, but not gaining on the ungainly creature. His legs struck and broke through some ribbon—neon-orange plastic tape.

Then he heard a boy shout, "Heads up!"

A dart flew by Finn's right ear. He'd broken through a warning fence and was inside a beach-dart competition.

The finned yard dart soared downward past him.

Thunk!

It had hit . . .

The cobra. Right in the head.

Upon being hit, the snake turned instantly to wood. Frozen. Stopped in its self-defense like a turtle pulling into its shell.

Finn saw this but did not slow for an instant. He hurdled the opposing dart toss boundary onto the open beach, spraying sand behind him, out of breath and desperate to put distance between himself and whatever that thing was that lay behind.

* * *

"Welcome," said Philby.

Willa opened her heavy eyelids. Philby looked back at her with a mixture of relief and concern, and she realized she must look a mess. But there was something else to his look, something that warmed her and confused her and made her feel lightheaded, made her heart flutter and her head slightly dizzy. She blinked to make it go away—or was it to test if it was for real?—and when she opened her eyes again there was Professor Philby up to his usual stuff.

They left the crew break room together and said little until arriving outside the Vibe; everyone was at the beach. It was the first time they could speak openly.

"Where's Charlene?"

"Waiting for you."

Philby's forehead knitted. "I'm not sure I understand."

"We got seriously lost, okay? Thought we could find our way back, but failed. We expected you to try to return us and, if that failed, to try to cross us over. Thankfully, you're predictable. I curled up under a bush and took a nap . . . believe me, it wasn't hard. We're both super tired . . . Charlene is standing guard."

It took Philby a moment to process her reasoning. "Predictable?" he said. "You think?" He hated being predictable, especially to a girl. It sounded like the last stop on the train before *boring*.

"You'll get over it."

"I am over it," he stated somewhat cruelly. "And where are you?"

She had warned herself about getting too close to him. "That's the thing . . . we're lost. We don't know where we are. But we think we're somewhere basically southeast. On a trail in the middle of nowhere. I thought, maybe with 2.0 I could try to return with a flare or something."

"Never happen," he said. "It's one thing to cross over with something in your pocket; that has proved pretty stable in beta. But to pick something up and return with it?"

"We haven't tried it."

"It's not going to happen. This is a projection system. It's not teleportation."

"Then we're stuck out there."

"Not necessarily," Philby said. "You may not be able to signal us, but we could signal you."

Her eyes flared excitedly. She leaned over and kissed him on the cheek. Or she tried to—her hologram lips were absorbed by Philby, and he felt nothing. "You're brilliant! That's what I love about you! You think of everything!"

Love? he thought. Should he try for a kiss?

He said, "We can head out there with flashlights and whistles. You hear a whistle or see a flashlight, you move toward it."

"Deal," she said.

"The main thing is for you to stay where you are. If you start moving around it'll be too many variables."

"I get it."

"We'll work from the southeast across to the west side of the island. As long as you're patient, we'll find you."

"Before the ship sails," she reminded.

"I understand."

"I don't think you do."

He looked at her curiously. Love? He was stuck on that one.

She said, "We . . . that is . . . Charlie and I overheard the girls we were following talking to someone. As much as I want you to find us—and I really want you to find us!—they were talking about a box. An airplane. About blocking the Pargos with a palm tree!"

"Slow down!" It wasn't like Willa to lose her cool. Of all the Keepers, he and she were the most alike: analytical, patient. To see her come slightly unglued made him uncomfortable.

Willa explained what they'd heard while eavesdropping in the mangroves. The bits and pieces: a plane landing, a tree blocking paths, a box, a delivery to the ship. Combined, it seemed to tell a story, but not one that Philby could easily interpret. A delivery for sure, and a well-planned one. But why such a secret? He couldn't be certain the Overtakers were involved. Maybe it was a prank by Cast Members—although the expense of it all seemed to suggest otherwise. Did Maleficent have such resources available to her? He'd never considered her having a reach beyond the Kingdom and into the real world—the world of chartering airplanes and delivering goods. If true, the reach of the Overtakers far exceeded anything the Keepers had dreamed of.

"Earth to Philby," Willa said.

"Is this legit?"

"It's what we heard."

"You're right: we need to focus on it then."

"And not us," she said.

"Of course, you too. I didn't mean it that way."

"But Finn and Maybeck already have assignments. You can't be in two places at once."

"No."

He checked his phone for the time. He'd heard nothing from either Finn or Maybeck. It bothered him.

"Maybe you won't have to wait for us to find you. The fireworks will be starting soon," he said.

"Oh, joy," Willa said sarcastically. "I can hardly wait."

"I will take the runway," he said. "There's an old plane there I can hide in."

"But you're backup for the boys," she said.

"They haven't asked for any help. If they do, then there's that. But we can't leave the runway unwatched. Not after what you overheard."

"Okay." She sounded crushed.

"I'm not abandoning you," he said.

"Of course not."

"Are you listening to anything I'm saying?" Philby's shortcoming was his intolerance of other people's dimwittedness. His mind worked so fast and so clear that he had no capacity for muddled thought.

"Yes!" She crossed the arms of her hologram.

"The . . . fireworks . . . will be . . . starting . . . soon," he repeated.

"You don't have to be rude."

"I'm not being rude, I'm being deliberate. I know I have to remind some of the others twice, Willa. But not you."

"Fireworks . . ." she muttered to herself, upset both with him and herself. "Being staged from . . ."

"Now you're getting it!"

"The beach? The ship?"

"The latter."

"A beacon to follow!" she crowed.

"Thank you," he said.

"I'll send Charlie to help Finn, and I'll meet you in the old plane on the runway." She added, "Providing everything works out."

"Everything will work out. I'm going to return you now. Where did you say you went to sleep?"

"Under a bush. I told you: Charlie's watching out for me. Keeping me safe. Once you return me I'll use the fireworks to find our way back. I'll send her to Finn. I'll meet you at the plane."

"You're going to be okay," he said.

"Yes," she said, her eyes sparkling surreally in the hologram.

* * *

The spit kept the hinges from squeaking. The maintenance shed door came open behind Maybeck's steady insistence. Open a crack to where he could get a better look at Luowski from the back. Luowski's attention appeared welded to the watch he wore on his wrist, a digital watch that lit up when its buttons were pushed. Luowski was pushing them a lot, so that every twenty seconds or so a flare of greenish light pulsed inside the small structure, throwing an exaggerated shadow of the boy into the rafters.

The interior looked like the engine room of a nuclear submarine. Tanks, pipes, tubes. Electric boxes. Gauges and meters. Racks of car batteries all wired together. Philby would have recognized it as the control hub for the island's solar power, irrigation, and pest control; as the communications shack where the island's wireless radio and telephone systems were managed. The island's

Cast Members referred to the small shed as "the vault," not for its security but its contents. Without this closet of a shed, the island would be back in the Stone Age, just a spit of sand and marsh twenty nautical miles off the Bahamas.

Maybeck saw only the boy and a lot of stuff. He didn't really care what any of it did. It did something or it wouldn't have been built. And Greg Luowski didn't belong here any more than he did, meaning nothing good could come of Luowski's being here. In the mind of Terry Maybeck, that translated to a simple deduction: Luowski had to be removed.

But the Kingdom Keepers had learned something about the Overtakers—and Maybeck considered Luowski an OT whether correct or not—which was: it is often better to study your enemy than battle your enemy. A battle had a winner and a loser, which was all fine and good if you happened to be the winner. But spying and gathering intelligence was a one-way door: the person spying gained everything and lost nothing; the person being spied upon lost everything and gained nothing.

So Maybeck resisted the temptation to sneak up behind Luowski and plant a headlock on him. Instead, he kept his eye and ear to the crack of the open door, summoned patience, and focused his concentration in order to remember every little move Luowski made and exactly when he made it—since the boy couldn't take his own eyes off his watch.

Three minutes later, at exactly nine thirty, Luowski slipped on a pair of headphones—which perhaps explained why he didn't hear what happened next.

"Hey! You!" A woman's voice from behind Maybeck.

Maybeck rolled out of the way of the open door so Luowski wouldn't see him if he turned around. The woman was thirty feet away and closing.

"Me?" Maybeck's face and body language said, proclaiming his innocence before actually opening his mouth.

"What are you doing?" the woman asked.

The sun had set; the area was dark. Maybeck crossed toward the woman, trying to keep her away from Luowski. He thought it weird that at this moment he was attempting to defend the despised Greg Luowski, but that was the thing about the Overtakers—they turned everything upside down.

"Someone left it open and unlocked," he said.

Behind him, he heard Luowski say, "Roger, King Air, Tango-Charlie-four-five-two-two. This is Sandbar. Come around to vector thirty—"

The sound cut off as Maybeck eased the door closed and hooked the padlock through the hasp, but did not lock it. He hoped she wouldn't come close enough to see it remained unlocked.

"And you are?" the woman said.

"Off the ship," Maybeck replied, blocking her view of the door. He summoned the one piece of important information he could think of. "I was with Tim. The propane tank we found on the CO_2 line—did you hear about it?"

She softened. "Oh! That was you?"

"Yeah. Me and Tim. We've been walking lines all day."

"That was freaky."

"Very strange," he said. "So an unlocked shed . . ." He pointed. "Just didn't want to take any chances."

"Especially since the CO_2 control is in there," she said.

"Uh . . ." Maybeck should have figured that out—all the valves and tanks and meters he'd seen. Luowski. "Right."

"I've got to go. See ya!"

"See ya."

She took off.

Maybeck heard the first mortar launch, a deep, concussive sound that signaled the start of the fireworks. It came from the direction of the ship. A moment later, the sky exploded.

He hesitated, unsure if he should confront Luowski. The kid had been talking on the radio like an air traffic controller. The propane tank had been discovered connected to a line that ran near the island's private runway. Tim had said the old runway was now only used in emergencies or in special situations by Disney.

More fireworks detonated overhead, briefly lighting up the island like it was the middle of the morning.

Maybeck took out his Wave Phone and sent a text to the four others:

plane landing on runway during firewrks = OTs

Finn or Philby would have to deal with that. He had his own hands full with stopping Luowski from doing whatever he was about to do.

He slipped the padlock out of the hasp and opened the shed door.

* * *

Where is everybody? Finn thought. He was out of breath, still recovering from his escape from Jafar. He was about to text the others when the fireworks began. A moment later, he received Maybeck's text—a warning about the island's runway.

As he turned to go in that direction, he caught movement out of the corner of his eye: a launch sliding through the water just outside of the marked-off swimming areas. It was taking the same basic route that the lifeboats had taken the night before, a route toward the cabanas.

His fingers hovered over the phone. He'd been ready to text that he was on his way to the runway, but his thumbs wouldn't cooperate.

boat toward cabana — wll stay here

He had no desire to face Jafar or Tia Dalma alone. He knew that Jafar's serpent staff was out there somewhere keeping watch. Just the thought of that gave him shivers on an otherwise warm night.

The explosions and bursts of light overhead, the appreciative *oohs* from the passengers, all facing the ship, mouths agape, made it a chaotic walk for Finn as he headed back toward the cabanas. As the fireworks exploded, the sand turned a variety of colors; Finn's shadow spread out around him in a starburst.

It flashed green, and Finn looked up to see Maleficent standing ten yards off, staring at him. He stopped cold.

The beach went black, then illuminated again: she was gone.

Or had she been there in the first place? he wondered.

Don't go, a voice inside him pleaded. But, as the launch turned and headed for shore, he saw no choice. It was loaded with ten or twelve Cast Members, not one of whom was looking up at the fireworks.

It was almost as if they were in a trance.

* * *

Using the fireworks mortar blasts as a beacon, Charlene and the returned Willa fled down the swamp paths in the light of the exploding colors. They took two wrong turns but easily found the proper path, working their way out of the maze. Out of breath, they found themselves on asphalt—the access road to the watchtower. It was only a matter of minutes before they approached the runway and, on the corner, the Disney-staged twin engine plane that was overgrown with jungle life.

They turned and hugged.

"Don't forget to tell Finn about the plane," Willa said.

"I won't."

"Good luck," Charlene said. She sprinted across the wide runway and out of sight, in the direction of the massage cabanas.

Willa crept up to the old plane.

"Psst!" she hissed.

"In here," came Philby's voice.

She pulled herself up onto the wing and looked down into the cockpit, where Philby sat in the torn leather pilot's seat.

"There's no room," she complained.

"My lap," he said, patting his legs.

"As if!" She debated playing along, but was afraid of how he could suddenly distance himself.

A brilliant yellow flash lit up everything around them. She jumped into the cockpit and onto Philby's lap.

They both looked up into the night sky as the fireworks boomed. The two spreading flowers in the black were red and blue.

Not yellow.

Philby pushed her forward as he leaned and peered out at the runway. A yellow and blue line of flame ran parallel to the tarmac.

"The propane . . ." Philby muttered to himself.

"The what?" Willa said.

He quickly explained Maybeck's discovery of a planted propane tank connected to the island's insect tubing.

"But if they removed it . . ."

"There must have been two," Philby said. "Don't you see? They use the fireworks as cover so it won't be noticed. By putting propane through the line and lighting it, they mark the runway for the pilot." He grew excited. "The plane you heard about. The delivery! With everyone's attention on the fireworks . . . with all the booming . . . no one sees or hears the . . ."

His voice was covered by the low growl of an approaching plane somewhere in the blackened distance.

* * *

Maybeck might have reached Luowski without being noticed, but a burst of color from the fireworks display threw Maybeck's shadow across the wall, causing Luowski to spin around. The boy stood so fast the headphones flew off his wide skull. He lifted his left arm in time to block Maybeck's punch, delivering his own right fist into Maybeck's abs.

Maybeck was in shape. The blow hurt, but his abs were rock hard, limiting the damage. Maybeck faked a left by raising his elbow and caught Luowski by surprise with an extended left, up and over the forearm block, that connected with Luowski's ear. He clearly rang his bell with that one. Luowski staggered back off balance and into the radio gear.

But as the boy reached out, Maybeck saw he was going for some kind of improvised switch—a black button on the end of a pair of wires crudely attached to a box on the wall. Maybeck didn't know what the boy was up to, but he knew he had to stop him from reaching that button. He moved toward it. In the process, he opened himself up.

Focused on the button, the off-balance Luowski still managed to backhand Maybeck across the face. As he followed through, he caught Maybeck by the sleeve of his shirt and tugged.

The kid was phenomenally strong, Maybeck realized a fraction of a second too late. Not just strong, but well coordinated, able to convert his raw power into decisive moves. Maybeck had felt he was within inches of stopping the kid from reaching the switch and then found himself being hurled back toward the shed door. It was like he bounced off a force field.

Luowski pushed the button; its popping sound was familiar to Maybeck. Luowski defiantly tore the button from the wires. Whatever he'd just done, there was no undoing it.

Maybeck scrambled to his feet in the open door.

"How'd that work out for you?" Luowski said, clearly in control of the situation.

"About as well as this is going to work out for you," Maybeck fired back.

He slipped out of the shed, shut the door, and locked it. Only with the click of the padlock did he recall where he'd heard the sound that button had made: his aunt's barbecue grill.

The igniter.

* * *

It was some kind of ceremony. The Cast Members were led into Tia Dalma's cabana, and she started chanting something indistinguishable as Finn listened from behind.

Neither Jafar nor his staff were anywhere to be seen.

Finn sneaked closer across the sand and pulled himself up to peer through the bottom of the open window, catching glimpses of the interior.

Six Cast Members. Three girls. Three boys. He tried to commit their faces to memory, though in the flickering candlelight he couldn't see clearly. Tia Dalma was waving a small doll in one hand and a carved idol in the other—a boy? He couldn't tell.

She uttered nonsensical words in a steady, hypnotizing stream. Finn dropped back down, afraid he was coming under whatever spell she was issuing. For there was no doubt about what she was up to.

The Overtakers were taking control of some of the ship's Cast Members. Just the thought of this paralyzed Finn. Who could they trust if not the Cast Members?

Before he could think what to do, he turned around. Maleficent stood at the edge of the jungle where Finn had just been crouched in hiding.

He heard the six Cast Members leaving the cabana. A moment later he heard a truck start up and drive off.

Neither he nor Maleficent had moved. They stood there, locked together in an unending stare.

Finn had known this moment was coming.

* * *

At Philby's urging, they scrambled out of the cockpit and hid in the jungle at the edge of the runway. As he'd expected, a glowing yellow line stretched the entire length of the runway, easily seen from a plane preparing to land.

"No landing lights," Philby said.

If there was a plane out there, Willa didn't see it, but there was no mistaking the sound as it grew louder.

"So it's on," she said. "The delivery. They were going to drop a palm tree across the road so a Pargo couldn't make it if they happened to see the landing."

"Means it's going to be quick," Philby said. "They didn't block all the vehicles." He was pointing to a small but heavy-duty flatbed truck just arriving at the end of the runway. Six Cast Members piled out of the truck—

three boys, three girls. One ignited a pair of signal flares and, stepping in front of the others, held them high above his head. Smoke spiraled from the bright orange flares.

"But if they're Cast Members . . ." Willa said.

"This doesn't make sense," said Philby.

"Maybe it's something the ship arranged," she speculated. "Maybe they just don't want the passengers knowing about it."

"It doesn't add up. No one knew about the propane."

"No one that we know of," she said. "That doesn't mean we're right."

Philby could not live easily with the thought of being wrong. It wasn't in his vocabulary. Like math, facts added up to a single result. You could collect any number of facts about a particular thing or event, but when added together in any combination they reached but a single truth. Philby spent endless hours collecting and amassing such data. When he reached a conclusion it was, in his mind, as concrete as simple addition.

The facts of this matter had led him to realize a secret landing was taking place—secret not only from passengers, but from Disney as well. He was right. He was always right.

"We treat it as hostile," he said.

"But they're Cast Members."

"Could have been tricked. May know nothing of the contents. For now we observe as carefully as possible. We commit everything—everything!—to memory. The safety of the ship and its passengers depend on it."

"What are you saying?"

"It's what you said, not me. Whatever is arriving on this plane is being brought aboard the *Dream*. And right now, we are the only ones who know about it."

* * *

"You understand change is inevitable," Maleficent said. "It's as constant as the rising sun. Change of heart. Change of leadership. Unstoppable as time. Don't blame yourself. It is not your fault. It is simply the way. This is my moment. You were unfortunate enough to be used by others to interfere with the natural order of things. You see that, don't you? I think you will if you look closely enough. The truth is not always apparent, is it? The truth about Wayne . . . it doesn't yell out to be heard. Sometimes you must listen quite carefully for it."

The truth about Wayne? Finn wondered. "What are you talking about?" Finn moved away from the cabana, not wanting anything at his back, seeking open space, equal ground. Her words gnawed at him. He didn't want to believe a thing this creature said.

"Mr. Disney created me as well," Maleficent said. "So many seem to forget that. He put the same thought into my creation as any prince or princess. I am no different. I am entitled to my existence. My beliefs. Order. Obedience. Observation. You know it's needed. That its time has come. You have seen the result of the so-called freedoms in the parks. The sniveling, runny-nosed rats disobeying their parents. The complaining. The impatience. You know exactly what I'm talking about."

He didn't understand why the human body had eyelids that could block out all sight, yet no corresponding method to plug one's ears and blot out all sound. He was forced to hear her. But not forced to listen, he realized, separating the two ideas in his thought. Hear, but don't listen. Look, but don't see.

"I like the parks the way they are."

"Of course you do! You're brainwashed. I don't blame you, boy."

"I want my mother back!"

"Little boy wants his mommy?"

"Don't mess with me."

"You are older. Bigger now than when we first met. But still foolish. Hmm? *Mess* with you? I can do anything to you I wish."

Put into this same situation, Philby would be considering ways to defeat her. Charlene would be debating the proper combat. Willa would want to outthink her. Maybeck would step up to challenge her.

Finn wished he had the sword from Maelstrom, knowing it possessed great power, possibly enough to defeat this fairy. Certainly enough to threaten her. But its exact location had been unknown for some time.

Was that Wayne's doing as well?

She had all the weapons; he had only the untested beta version of DHI 2.0 with which to battle back. If the Imagineers wanted their software upgrade field-tested, here was their chance.

As he moved between cabanas, he heard the lapping of the small waves in between the rhythmic booming of the fireworks. He led her into the open, away from the cabanas and toward the edge of the ocean.

"It is said all life came from the oceans," Maleficent preached. "So to the ocean you shall return, young man."

"He not only created characters," Finn said to her. "He created roles. Characters are confined to those roles. You are not obeying yours. What happens to those who do not obey?"

"Do not twist my words."

"Your words or *his* words? Can a character be smarter or wiser or more important than the one who created her? Can she put words into her mouth or thoughts into her head that he doesn't want her to speak or think?" He sensed she'd paused, as if actually considering what he'd said. He wondered: if he could not defeat her with weapons that he so sorely lacked, might it be possible to defeat her with words?

She reared back her arm as if to throw something. In her open palm, a sphere of fire the size of a softball appeared. Her cape opened with the effort, and there in the ball's sputtering light, tucked into her belt, he saw the leatherbound journal stolen from the library.

She threw the fireball. Finn leaned slightly right and it hurled past, hissing as it landed in the ocean water.

Another whispered past his ear as Finn leaned left.

She had another ball of fire in hand, but let it fall to the sand next to her. It sputtered and died.

"You resist the change that is coming," she said. "This will be your undoing. I don't expect you to join us. I would never trust you, nor you me. Stop challenging me, take your friends with you, and you'll have your mother back. Good as new."

His head felt as if it might burst. She was working to upset him, to put him off his guard.

"What if we . . . you and I . . . are nothing more than someone's game? Players in a game?" He'd been thinking about this recently, but had not shared the idea with anyone. Not even Philby. It struck him as ironic that Maleficent would hear it first. "You are a character. Your words and actions are designed by others. Walt Disney. The animators. Now the Imagineers. And it was the Imagineers who created me—as a DHI, giving you someone to battle. Isn't that just a little bit convenient?"

He could see his words affect her in the slumping of her shoulders and a glowering in her eyes.

"Nonsense . . ." she uttered, but her words lacked conviction.

"How do you think I feel? They're using us both."

He was knee-deep in the surf before her own toes contacted the water and she realized his location. She waded in deeper as he'd known she would.

"Stay where you are!" she hollered.

Finn lowered his chin below the surface and spoke softly. "Starfish wise, starfish cries."

Maleficent made a sweeping motion with her arm. The water around Finn illuminated in wire-thin bars of light forming a perfect octagon, fully encircling him.

He'd seen such a fence before—in the dungeon below Pirates—and had made the mistake of attempting to breach it. The shock had thrown him back. Finn fought to stay stock-still in the undulating surf, unsure what the energy beam might do to his DHI when standing waist-deep in seawater.

From all along the line where the breaking waves reached hungrily for the sand, a white foam arose like boiling water. Maleficent, proud of her accomplishment of confining Finn, and focusing her considerable energies into the electronic fence that surrounded him, took no notice of events at her feet.

Finn, however, witnessed the result of uttering King Triton's code. A small, pale claw appeared through the foam. Then another. Crabs. Not just hundreds, but thousands of them. Tens of thousands. All converging on Maleficent in the colorful pulses of light from the fireworks.

By the time she looked down, with an expression of terror overcoming her, she was in too deep to retreat. Knee-deep, to be precise—all in a matter of seconds. She sank into a hole dug beneath her by ten thousand furious beach crabs, the seawater roiling around her like a giant white inner tube. She put out her hands to tread water, to stop her descent, but screamed wickedly as the crabs bit her.

Her eyes found Finn and filled with venom.

Finn swelled with pride and confidence. He'd lured her out here; he used the code to defeat her. There was one last barrier to overcome: *all clear*. Philby was extremely smart, ridiculously capable, but he wasn't superior. Software was software. If 2.0 *all clear* were achievable, then Finn possessed the tools necessary to achieve it. He didn't need a light at the end of a dark tunnel. That process required thinking. The point of 2.0 was its transparency. You didn't think your way, you trusted.

He cleared his head and walked through the glowing wires, unharmed.

Crossing her arms—her hands bloody—she continued to sink lower.

"Release my mother, and I'll call them off."

Maleficent was waist deep and sinking quickly. "I—" She snatched the journal from her waist and held it above the water.

"You are in no position to argue!" he said, suddenly worried Triton's crabs would drown the fairy. In all his dreams of defeating her, he'd never thought of actually killing her. The idea sickened him. No matter how he hated and despised her, he would take no satisfaction in her drowning.

He said, "Release my mother!"

"She's human, you fool!"

What was that supposed to mean?

"Who did this?" she asked, now chest deep. "Was it Ariel? That little bi—"

Finn shouted. "You can save yourself! Release my—"

"You do so underestimate me."

She vanished. One moment up to her chin; the next, the journal fell toward the water as a black cormorant appeared on the surface, shook water from its feathers, cawed loudly at Finn, and flew off toward the ship.

Finn ran through the knee-deep surf and snatched the journal from the surface.

The foaming water subsided, and through the calming waves Finn saw ten thousand crabs disperse.

Charlene arrived, out of breath.

"Look at you!" she said, seeing Finn up to his knees in beautiful water. "You know, some of us are working!"

"I . . . ah . . ." Finn pointed at the waves. At nothing. His fingers gripped the journal tightly.

"Philby and Willa are in the plane."

"What plane?"

Charlene said impatiently, "Come on! Let's go!"

* * *

His Wave Phone in hand, Maybeck ran west toward the island's landing strip, responding to Philby's summons. Fireworks punctuated the sky to his left, the pace of the explosions increasing: the show was nearing its frantic finale. He hurdled a fallen palm tree that blocked the narrow path. Two abandoned Pargos were trapped on the near side of the fallen tree.

He'd added up the propane tank and Luowski's igniter: spark to gas, gas ignites. He'd wanted to tell Luowski that there was no gas to ignite—he and Tim had dismantled the tank's connection to the CO_2 lines. But Philby's rule was to never share intel with the enemy; such arrogance nearly always backfired.

He arrived at the eastern end of the landing strip, a wide swath of asphalt between him and the stage-set airplane tucked into the jungle at the corner. The other plane—an actual, functional, twin-engine plane—was the center of a flurry of activity, as Cast Members crowded around its rear door, all struggling with something Maybeck couldn't see. Warning beeps signaled as the micro truck backed up slowly toward the airplane's rear door. The Cast Members were hissing orders at each other; no one seemed to be in charge.

He smelled burning rubber and saw a faint line of smoke smoldering at the edge of the runway's blacktop, then realized he and Tim had found only half of whatever system had been engineered. The discovery enraged him. He regretted leaving Luowski locked inside the shed. The headphones meant a radio. A radio meant he'd left Luowski with the ability to communicate.

At nearly the same instant Maybeck came to this realization, the pilot signaled a Cast Member and shouted something at him. The Cast Member immediately spun around, searching the runway's jungle perimeter. He then shouted at the others, his voice carrying through the percussive detonations in the sky.

"We've got company! Hurry it up!"

What to do, and how to do it? Maybeck wondered, scanning the scene. The presence of Cast Members confused him. Cast Members had proven themselves to be allies of the Kingdom Keepers—facilitators, support—even though Wayne had once warned to be wary of them. There was no way they would side with the Overtakers; they loved the parks and the Disney magic more than anyone.

His world was turned on its head. Maybeck tried to make sense of it. Maybe the Cast Members unloading the plane were as afraid of the Overtakers as he and the other Keepers were. But then what about Luowski? The boy's involvement meant trouble, plain and simple. The Cast Members could be impostors, the same way he and the Keepers had posed as crew members. Too many possibilities.

He watched as a large crate was unloaded from the plane and into the back of the truck. Four of the Cast Members tried to move it, but it required the strength of all six. Two of the Cast Members secured a back gate on the truck and slapped the side.

The truck moved off slowly, the driver careful of its contents.

* * *

"She's gone," Finn whispered to Charlene from where they hid beneath Tia Dalma's cabana. "She and the others must have gotten away when I was with Maleficent."

"Philby needs us," she reminded.

"They planned this carefully. All of it at once. The beach party had to be their idea." The damp journal sat on the sand.

"We can do this later, right? We need to help Philby and Willa."

"What did she mean about my mother being human?" he asked Charlene.

"Who? What are you talking about?"

"Why would she say that? The ship's in danger. This journal is why."

"Are you listening to me? Philby needs—"

"Jafar and Tia Dalma are characters. No one will think anything of them being on board."

"Did you hear what I said about a plane landing? Willa and I overheard all of it. Some box—"

"There's a Disney Villain show, isn't there? Didn't I read about that in the *Navigator*? A stage show. That could be it."

"Are you going to shut up and listen to me?" she said.

"Hmm? Yeah. Sure. A plane. A box. I got it."

"Being put onto the *Dream*."

"Philby's on it," he said. "It's what we do, Charlie. We each take care of our own assignments."

"You're just lying here in the sand. How can that possibly help?"

"I was attacked by Jafar's serpent staff. It's the *real* Jafar. The *real* Tia Dalma. The *real* Maleficent was trying to kill me out there. She talked about a change of leadership . . . the natural order. But why the ship? Why confine yourself—your team—to such a limited space? As big as the *Dream* is, it's no theme park."

"It is a theme park, but it's a theme park that goes somewhere."

Finn sat up so quickly he threw sand on her. "It does go somewhere!"

"Lots of places. Aruba. The canal—"

"L.A.!" he said.

"They're trying to get to the West Coast. They're trying to get to Disneyland," Charlene said.

He took her face in his hands and kissed her. "Brilliant!" It was an unassuming kiss, but on the lips, and it paralyzed him.

Charlene seemed dazed. She reached behind his

head, pulled him to her, and kissed him hard and long. When she let go, when she backed off, she said, "I thought so." She smiled at him.

Finn could hardly breathe. He didn't want this. Why had he allowed it to go on so long? He wanted Amanda.

"I don't know. I just . . . had to."

"But that isn't *us*." Again, he envisioned Amanda.

"I know. But . . . I just knew it would be like that."

He wasn't about to ask her "Like what?" because he knew exactly what she meant. It was like the kiss he'd shared with Storey Ming. Definitely not a middle-school kiss. He fought back a smile. What was it with girls, anyway?

"Disneyland," he said.

She nodded, still breathing hard. She clearly wasn't thinking about Disneyland.

He brushed sand off the journal. "This is what Wayne wanted. We must protect it."

"Philby needs us."

"Go if you want."

"Come with me." There was a deeper meaning to her invitation, and they both knew it. She didn't want to leave him.

He, on the other hand, wanted her out of here.

"I need to keep this safe," he said. "I can't risk it

being retaken. They didn't want us knowing what was going on here," he said, looking up at the floor of the cabana. "Jafar's staff was supposed to make sure of that. Tia Dalma made them bring the Cast Members to her. Why?"

She said nothing. Her eyes were focused on his lips.

"I'm going inside," he said.

"What if she's in there?"

"She's not. I need to study the journal before heading back to the ship. Maleficent took it off the ship with her. Why take such a risk unless they needed it for something? It's too dark for me to read. But in there . . ."

The gaps in the floorboards revealed the flickering candlelight.

"The fireworks are ending. We need to get back onto the ship."

"All the more reason to figure out what was so important." He patted the journal.

"Make it quick," she said.

"Yeah." He waddled in a crouch to the open beach, stopping alongside the stairs and turning to look back.

She mouthed "Thank you" and tapped her wrist, indicating for him to hurry.

Finn climbed the stairs silently. Each cabana was divided in two with separate access. He eased the door open. Empty! The massage tables had been pushed to either wall, creating a space between them. On the floor was a pentagram drawn in chalk. There was a dead frog pinned by its limbs in the center pentagon; each of the triangles contained a small terra-cotta cup. There were dead moths in one; what looked and smelled like fish guts in another; a flower floating on oil in a third. Alongside the star was a sock puppet–like stuffed creature, with elbow macaroni on its head like horns. The doll was stained by green and mustard-colored dust. A red candle had dripped wax onto the floorboards. The whole thing gave Finn the creeps.

He scooted onto the nearest massage table and opened the journal, its pages stained, the writing smeared because of its exposure to the seawater. The parts written in pencil were blurred and sometimes illegible; he could make out the notes written in ink. It mentioned someone named Stravinsky. Finn knew the name—a Soviet general? an athlete? an author? He couldn't place it.

There were pages of sketches that included shooting stars and brooms, monsters and Mickey's sorcerer's hat. Whoever had made the notes had drawn arrows connecting ideas to sketches and ideas to ideas. Some were numbered and circled. Some carried asterisks. It would take someone like Philby a long time of study to begin to piece together the concepts and the intentions. For Finn, it came off as a kind of second language; one that included verse and coded footnotes.

By carefully examining the top corners of the journal's yellowed pages, Finn identified a section somewhere past the book's middle that showed added wear. The pages had clearly been read more often than the rest. He turned to the section, heedful of the fragile nature of the paper and its contents. These pages seemed to be dealing with the character of Chernabog. There were some odd notes:

cruel
dominant
frightening
territorial

There were references to instruments:

cymbals/percussion
dissonant horns

Then came an illustration of some stone steps, followed by a blank page with a doodle in each corner. Or maybe not a doodle, but a pictogram or hieroglyph—if so, not like hieroglyphs Finn had ever seen.

On the last of the thumb-worn pages, a creepy sounding passage:

"LIFE IS BECAUSE OF THE GODS; WITH THEIR SACRIFICE THEY GAVE US LIFE. . . . THEY PRODUCE OUR SUSTENANCE... WHICH NOURISHES LIFE."

Finn flipped ahead through the section of worn pages. More notes and arrows and numbers. More musical references. A confusing jumble of gobbledygook.

But his possession of the journal filled him with delirious happiness. Retaking the journal had been the primary assignment. Here they were at the first stop of a half dozen ports—the second day of fifteen—and they'd already retrieved the journal.

Translating its pages would have to wait. He assumed Wayne would want it scanned and emailed to the Imagineers for further analysis. So much to do.

The fireworks finale erupted overhead like he was in the middle of Mortal Warfare about to retake the castle. Explosions and, as he reached the door, showers of falling stars and colors—music echoing across the water from the ship. Cheers rose from the adoring crowd on the beach.

He knew that music. Orchestral. Majestic. Uplifting. Inspiring. Tried to associate it with a particular Disney movie because of its familiarity. Searched the hard drive of his mind for where and when he'd heard it and found the fingers of his right hand dancing against the damp leather of the journal.

Piano! he thought. This particular piece he'd learned for his piano teacher back when he'd still been taking lessons. Back before the Keepers.

Thoughts of the piano lessons recalled images of his mother's face. Finn recoiled with the memory. He felt physical pain in his gut and wondered where the nearest bathroom was. His mother, the green-eyed traitor. His mother, another of Maleficent's captive slaves. He should have killed the fairy while he'd had the chance;

should have demanded his mother's release and her return to her former self. He understood that regardless of his DHI assignments or missions, this one calling preoccupied him like no other. He could leave tracking the OT server to Philby. With the journal in hand, his own mission had changed.

Slowly his fingers worked the orchestrated piece's central melody. Instinctively. Subconsciously. He caught a piece of the sheet music in his mind's eye and nearly was able to make out the composer's name at the top of the page.

Stra . . . vin . . . Stravin . . .

The distant purr of airplane engines snapped him out of it.

* * *

Philby and Willa watched as Charlene made her move.

"Did you see that?" Willa asked.

"I did."

"Where did she come from?"

"The south side of the runway," Philby answered in his typical Professor Philby way that angered Willa.

"Talking to you is like talking to a computer."

"My laptop has a speech component. The dual processor allows—"

"Enough! I have no interest in dual anything. A friend of ours just ran behind a taxiing plane, did a home plate slide under the back of a mini truck, and is currently suspended from what looks like a spare tire."

"I have eyes," he said.

"And you're telling me that doesn't impress you?"

"She's the gymnast. Who did you expect to do something like that?"

"What is it with you?"

"What is *what* with me? It's Charlene. She does stuff like that. Remember the time outside Wonders of Life?"

"Sometimes you really bug me," Willa said, contorting herself to get out of the seat and to the door.

* * *

Charlene clung to the spare tire on the truck's undercarriage, not fully understanding how she'd gotten there. Her back only inches from the asphalt, her fingers dug into the tire tread's hard rubber, each bump in the road threatening her grip. She disliked her own impulsive tendencies, but had never figured a way around them. She heard a call for action and she acted. It was only in the aftermath of such actions that she had the chance to reflect on her own stupidity.

The truck rolled on—thankfully slowly, no doubt in

part because the driver chose to drive with the lights off. The fireworks had been in the midst of the grand finale as she'd reached the truck, possibly explaining why no one had seen her: who could resist a grand finale?

The cruise passengers would be headed back to the ship now. The all-aboard was thirty minutes after the fireworks; the *Dream* would sail in exactly forty-five minutes. Anyone not on the ship at that time would miss the rest of the cruise.

The truck turned left, leaving the roadway unexpectedly. It bumped off the asphalt, and Charlene lost her grip. She fell into sand on her back and the truck pulled away without her. She rolled into the nearby bushes and tried to collect herself as the truck's brake lights flashed red and the brakes squealed. The truck slowed to a stop in an area heaped with piles of sand and gravel. The driver cut the wheel sharply; the truck stopped again and then began backing up.

Movement to Charlene's left. She leaned back behind the cover of the vegetation.

"Psst!" she signaled when she saw it was an out-of-breath Willa. Behind her, equally out of breath, came Philby.

The two hunkered down next to Charlene and tried to speak.

"What . . . were . . . you . . . thinking?" panted Willa.

"I wasn't," said Charlene. "That happens with me sometimes."

"They're backing up to a boat," Philby said.

"To deliver the crate to the *Dream*," Charlene said. "There's no way we're going to stop it."

"We're at a distinct disadvantage," said Philby. "They outnumber us, and the boat is a Boston Whaler, so it's not like there's anywhere to hide on it."

"What's in the crate?" Charlene asked Philby.

"As if he knows," said Willa, still not pleased with Philby.

"I don't know," Philby admitted. "But if I had to guess, I'd say it's a bear." The girls looked at him skeptically. "Notice the air holes top and bottom. Whatever it is, it's alive. The size of the crate suggests an animal in excess of six feet and, judging by the difficulty six guys had in moving it, three to five hundred pounds—i.e., a beast."

"But why so secret?"

"I'm as confused as you are. The presence of the Cast Members suggests it's legit—"

"Unless these are the same Cast Members Finn saw with Tia Dalma," said Charlene. She quickly recounted what little she knew of Finn's encounter, which wasn't much.

"If they're legit," Philby said, seemingly ignoring

for now what Charlene had just told them, "then the secrecy would be easily explained: the company wanted to bring a surprise onto the ship and didn't want guests knowing about it. A performing lion, maybe, like in Vegas?"

"And if not legit?" Charlene pressed.

"Then we've got trouble," Willa said, "because whatever's in there is big. Big as in dangerous. More hyenas? A wild boar?"

"Presumably to be used against us," Philby added.

"So planning something big."

"If this is the work of Overtakers, we've never seen anything like it."

"It is," came a voice behind them.

All three jumped.

Maybeck slipped in alongside of them.

"You about scared the pee out of me!" Charlene complained.

"I caught Luowski in a shed." He gave them the shorthand of his encounter with the school bully.

"Luowski's on the ship?" Willa gasped. "The OTKs?"

"I went back to have another 'chat' with him," Maybeck said, "after the plane took off, but he was gone. He'd smashed out some boards at the back of the shed."

"We need to know what's in that crate," Willa said.

"If one of you could get to sleep the minute we're back on board," Philby proposed, "I could cross you over before whatever it is is unpacked."

"Can I remind you we have no idea where they're taking it, and the ship just happens to be huge?" Charlene said.

"If I can get into ship security's camera files we can follow the crate," Philby stated.

"Can you?" Maybeck asked.

"We won't know until we try."

22

A SILENT ALARM SOUNDED in Philby's head as he and the others boarded the ship: their key cards tracked their every movement. When they left the ship; when they returned. When they entered their rooms; when they left. The main dining rooms kept track of guest attendance (although the other food areas did not). If the shipboard security cameras could be used to track the arrival of a secret crate, what about the arrival of five key card–holding kids? In the wrong hands, such information put the Keepers at risk.

As celebrities, their staterooms were not registered in their names. Only key officers knew how to track them down. These included the heads of entertainment, security, and what was called hotel management. There was no question the Beach Blanket Barbecue had been arranged by an officer; who else could convince the captain to stay extra hours on Castaway Cay? There seemed little doubt that whoever had arranged the extension had connections to the Overtakers. And since this had to be a highly ranked officer, it seemed likely that the Overtakers might now have knowledge of the Keeper's staterooms. That meant there was nowhere safe on board.

Nowhere.

Philby didn't want to freak out the others, so for now he kept this realization to himself, but as he reentered the ship he was already scheming about ways to use some of the empty staterooms for DHI sleep during crossover in case the OTs had plans to kidnap them or attempt to trap them in SBS. With too much to do and with too little time, he pushed his concern aside and focused on crossing over Charlene in hopes she could follow the mystery crate.

He texted Finn:

i need to see it

There was no need to mention the journal by name; Finn would know. He was excited to get a look at it to find out what was so important to the OTs to risk stealing it in the first place. He might have wondered why Maleficent would keep it on her person, but then again she was such a control freak it really didn't surprise him all that much.

"Welcome back," the steward said as Philby ran his key card past the sensor. "Did you enjoy the fireworks?"

"Oh, yes!" Philby answered. "They were much more than I expected."

The steward smiled at him, then welcomed the next guest. Philby crowded in with others awaiting the elevators, then broke free of the pack and climbed the stairs.

meet u @ the room

. . . came Finn's reply.

Good, Philby thought. Finn was okay and was either back on the ship or would be soon. That was a load off his mind. Without the crate and the mystery plane, without Luowski being seen on the island, without Tia Dalma's involvement, it might have felt to Philby like their mission was nearly over. They needed the GPS data on the OT server, but he expected that any minute. Then it would be a matter of finding and disabling the OT server.

Given the recent developments, the recovery of the stolen journal didn't merit celebration the way it might have. There were too many variables—too much going on that needed explaining. The ship was not safe, whether Wayne and the Imagineers knew it or not. Maleficent had brought the battle to the ship, and as much as he didn't want to think about it, there was no better place to get rid of someone than by throwing the person overboard at night.

Or five people, one by one.

The cruise had been promoted as featuring the DHIs. So far he had faced two DHIs trying to dispatch him. Was it a Murder Cruise?

We should have stayed behind on the island, he thought, catching a glimpse of the beautiful Castaway Cay as he reached Deck 4. He looked down over the rail at the churning water. For the next two days there would be only this one way off the ship.

* * *

Finn sensed eyes on him as he boarded. He didn't know if it was because the stewards were greeting passengers, or a guest had recognized him, or the lenses of security cameras were recording him, or if it was just his own paranoia. But there it was, and he had to deal with it.

The journal was tucked under his shirt into the back of his waistband. His mission was to copy its contents and transmit it to Wayne. But a second element to the mission revealed itself: finders keepers. Until this moment, as he felt the power of a thousand eyes watching him, he'd not bothered to consider that Maleficent would want it back. Not simply want it, but do anything to get it. Its importance to her could not be overstated.

He felt like a thief with a world-famous jewel in his pocket. He felt like a target. Suddenly, everyone was the enemy: the nice steward who'd just welcomed him, the girl at the elevators giving him a warm smile, the old lady with the walker and the bad sunburn glaring at him as he tried to slip past her.

The boarding passengers hit gridlock at the elevators, packing in tightly. The smell of body odor mixed with barbecue sauce was a dreadful, toxic sweet-and-sour blend that made him want to retch. Someone farted, and Finn thought he might hurl. He finally broke through the throng and reached the staircase, his hand at his back protecting the hidden journal. He climbed the stairs slowly at first, but he had that creepy, spine-tingling sensation, convinced someone was right behind him.

Arriving at the landing on Deck 4—more guests awaiting the elevators here—he noticed two uniformed crew members enter from the outer decks. They looked right at him and turned in his direction. Finn held the banister and began climbing calmly toward Deck 5 (there were rules against running) but felt his heart rate soar as the two fell in line behind him—also climbing the stairs calmly.

At the next landing, he got a look at their solemn faces and felt a jolt: the one nearest the banister had been in Tia Dalma's cabana.

He tried keeping his pace calm, but took two stairs at a time in an attempt to put distance between himself and the other two.

They stayed with him.

It felt as if the journal were burning a hole in his back.

At Deck 5 the two officers separated. The one he thought he recognized stayed behind him.

His throat went dry. His skin itched. He should have thought to pass the journal off to one of the others; he'd been a fool to carry it aboard himself. Maleficent would be furious at Finn's use of Triton's crabs to sabotage her. He could barely swallow. He was not about to lead this officer to his stateroom! Worse, a ship's officer could go anywhere he wanted to, had access to much more of the ship than Finn; it wasn't like Finn could slip into an area the officer wasn't allowed.

He glanced left, right, and up, where he spotted a girl stopped on the stairs staring at him intensely. The moment they met eyes she started down toward him.

"O . . . M . . . G!" she said loudly. "Are you one of those hologram thingies? You're, like, in all the parks, right?" He made his voice sound like a robot. "Hell-o! My name is Finn. Can I show you around the park today?" She skipped stairs hurrying down to him and stopped, blocking his way.

Out of the corner of his eye, he saw the officer climbing toward him.

The girl reached out and took him by the wrists and shook both arms, wildly excited to meet him.

"This is so awesome!" she said. Then, looking down at her hands, she added, "But how come I can touch you?"

He caught her glance over his shoulder. Then she reached around him and put her hand right into the small of his back. Finn wrestled to be free from her, but she pinned the journal there and hugged him, giggling.

With both arms wrapped around him, she leaned back. "Sorry, but I just *had* to do that!" she proclaimed.

His wrists felt cold where she'd gripped them. He didn't recall feeling her hands as cold, only the lingering aftereffect. It felt strangely like he'd forgotten something, or had lost something. But thankfully the journal was still there.

The ship's officer slowed as he drew near, then walked past Finn, tracking the boy with his peripheral vision. He continued through a door to the starboard deck.

The girl appeared to be watching the officer as well.

"You're right in thinking they mean you harm. I

can help," the girl said in a whisper. She took off through the port doors; her oddly colored hair was what he remembered most—black, with a splash of vibrant red at the bottom.

Finn stared at the twin doors in a stupor. He wanted to call after her, to stop her. But she was gone. For a moment his legs wouldn't move. When they finally did, he bounded upstairs.

He tried to remember her face but couldn't; she was surprisingly unmemorable. Just the weird patch of red hair—out of place on a Disney cruise, where no one stood out like that.

He checked behind him—still no one following. He forced the stress to leave him, understood the importance of copying and transmitting the journal's contents immediately—before the Overtakers managed to steal it back!

Was there even a way to photocopy on the ship? He imagined the concierge would do it for him, or the front desk, but he wasn't about to give the journal over to someone else. A digital camera, he realized. He could photograph the significant pages and email them to Wayne. He tried to think back to what she'd told him, feeling violated for her having known what he'd been thinking.

How was that possible?

* * *

There was an unmarked envelope awaiting him outside his stateroom door. Finn reread the note that had accompanied a key card:

EAT. WON. AN ANGRY DOG.

He stepped inside and closed the door. He locked the journal in his stateroom safe, feeling relief. Back to the note.

The code had to have something to do with the key card—and therefore was a number.

Eat . . . ate . . . *eight*! he thought, celebrating his cleverness. He used a stateroom pen to write it down: 8.

Won . . . one . . . easy: 8-1.

An angry dog . . . mean? Nothing came to him. Slobber? Nothing. Wild? Still nothing. He began to get frustrated. Teeth? Eyes? Drool? German shepherd? Doberman? How hard could this be? An angry dog. Attack? Defend? Sic?

Sic . . . sics . . . six!

8-1-6.

Worth a try.

Which was safer, he wondered, leaving the journal locked up inside his stateroom safe, or taking it with him? Someone on the ship had the authority and the means to unlock a stateroom safe—certainly guests forgot their four-digit code from time to time. But such access would be limited to very few: maybe the head of security and the captain. Whoever was after it would first have to get into his stateroom and then unlock his safe.

He emailed Wayne photographs of the journal's five middle pages—both sides. Ten pages in all. Then he knocked on the connecting door to Philby's stateroom. Mrs. Philby said, "Come in," and Finn went inside and asked if it was all right if he left the door open while he was out.

"I locked my passport and some money in my safe, and I don't want anything to happen to it."

"No problem," Mrs. Philby said, and added, "Do you know where Dell is?"

Finn had a couple of hunches.

"He came back from the fireworks, didn't he?"

"Left his clothes on the floor of the bathroom, so . . . yes," she said, grimacing.

"Probably the Vibe," he said. "I'll check."

"Thank you, Finn."

"No problem."

A few minutes later and a few decks lower, Finn knocked on the door to 816 and then tried the key card. The door unlocked and he entered. The ship was already under way, and this was his first sensation of it moving as he saw through to the stateroom balcony and the flickering moonlight on the gray water and a girl's silhouette out there.

"No lights," the girl called out as his finger was about to hit the switch. He recognized her voice. Storey Ming.

"Nice," he said, joining her, admiring the view.

"It's so appealing . . . being on the water at night. So beautiful. That's Castaway back there, and over there . . . I'm not sure. Nassau, maybe."

"They look so far away."

"Perspective," she said. "Distance is so different at sea."

"Nice code."

"I thought you'd figure it out."

"Why am I here?"

Storey Ming lowered her voice, as the neighboring balconies were close. "The GPS transmission device you set up—"

"Philby, my friend, set it up—"

"—pretty much confirms the OT server is aboard the *Dream.* I received a message that while they can't prove it absolutely, they are confident it's here."

Why would Wayne send a note to her instead of him? Finn wondered.

"So that's next," he said.

"It must be destroyed or at least taken off-line if our guys are to have a chance in the battle for the Base."

"I'd almost forgotten . . ."

"It has been worse the past few nights. Things are heating up."

"DHIs?"

"The OTs are using their DHIs as decoys. Our guys rush a bunch of OTs only to realize they're holograms."

"Meanwhile the real OTs are on the opposite side of the Base."

"Something like that," Storey Ming said.

"Philby set up a connection so we can cross over to the parks. Maybe it's time."

"They'll let us know. You all are plenty busy."

"Tell me about it." He wasn't sure if he should tell this girl about the journal. He decided against it.

"A huge crate was brought onto the ship via the forward gang."

"You do get around," he said. Wayne's choice of her made slightly more sense.

"It wasn't on any manifests. I hear about that sort of thing."

"How?"

She studied him and shook her head. "No. I don't think so. Not yet."

"Thanks for the vote of confidence," he said.

"There have been some attempts to breach security. Is that you and your friends?"

"No. Not that I know of."

"If not your friends, maybe your enemies." Storey sounded worried.

"Speaking of getting around."

"You've seen them?"

"Face to face. On the beach tonight. Maleficent."

He thought he saw her shiver. He knew the feeling.

"Yet here you are."

"Here I am."

"That's impressive."

"That's lucky. Friends in the right places."

"Friends in deep places," she said.

"Triton." Finn was awed by the extent of her knowledge.

Storey took a deep breath and held it as if savoring it. "You know how we envy you? Having a chance like that? You met him?"

"I did."

"Unreal."

"Tell me about it. But I also saw Jafar. That wasn't so nice."

"I hate Jafar."

"Strong word."

"I'm not changing it," she said.

"His staff came alive. A snake."

"Like in the Bible," she said.

"Like in the *movie*," he said. "I hate snakes."

"Strong word."

"I'm not changing it," he said.

They both laughed.

"If it's not you breaching security . . . I'd be careful if I were you."

"Yes, you would," he said.

"No way to know what they might have been after."

"Us. It's us." He paused. "It's a lot of things."

"Does that scare you?" Storey asked.

"It does."

"I would think so."

"You know that stupid line 'Failure is not an option'? That's kind of what it's like. Like you can't fail but you don't know how to succeed. I feel like a hamster on a wheel most of the time. The OTs obviously have some goal. Our only goal is to not let them reach theirs. It's like always playing defense. Hard to win a game that way."

"The best offense is a good defense."

"Maybe."

"How can I help?"

"You are. Believe me. The crate? The one that came aboard?"

"No one knows about it. I mean, some guys hauled it aboard. I have my sources. But not the normal guys at the loading bays. Different guys."

"Six people arriving by Boston Whaler," he said. "Let me guess. They arrived right when the crew was on a break or busy somewhere else."

"Shore duty," she said. "Getting ready to sail."

"The thing that gets me is how well planned everything is," he said. She didn't comment. "Any idea where it went, this crate?"

"Forward gang? An odd choice, except its location away from the dock. Could be for one of the bars. A piece of replacement equipment or a computer for the bridge. Any of the galleys. Or, I suppose, the big theater."

"It's not a piece of equipment," he said, thinking of the air holes in the crate. "Fewer people nosing around in the galley or in the theater?"

"A lot more hiding places in the theater," she said. "Backstage, the catwalks, below stage, the dressing rooms, prop area. And a good part of every day no one's around."

"So that's where we start."

"Sounds good."

"What are the chances there's some surprise planned for one of the shows? Something new?"

"It happens," she said.

"Often?"

"Not on a regular cruise, but this is no ordinary cruise. The first ship through the new locks? They could have anything planned. And it wouldn't have to be by anybody but a few key people. The captain. Director of entertainment. Information moves around this ship faster than seawater. There are no secrets. For a really big surprise, I can see them pulling something like this."

"So maybe it's nothing more than that," he said.

"I can check it out."

"I'd rather you not."

"Because?"

"Because that's what we're here for."

"The big important holograms."

"The thing is, when we're holograms not much can hurt us."

"So it's safer."

"Much," he said.

"I know the big theater really well. It's crazy back there. Different levels, dressing rooms. Prop storage. I could be your guide."

"Or maybe just talk us through it."

"Because I'm not one of you," she said. "You don't want me along because I'm not one of you."

"It's a safety thing."

"I get it. If you need me for the GPS . . . or for anything else, I'm up in the Vibe—outside, actually, giving a demo tonight."

"Good to know," Finn said. "And what about this stateroom we're in? We could use a room or two that won't get looked at."

"Philby knows the empty rooms. I can get key cards to him."

"That would be great."

"Done. You heard about the stowaways?"

"Philby told me. Have they caught them?"

"Not that I've heard. There's a lot of weird stuff going on on this cruise."

"Tell me about it. It seems to kind of follow us around," he said.

"Lucky you."

"Not always." He made her laugh. "Not even often." Another chuckle from her. "How do I reach you?"

"I don't trust the Wave Phones," she said, "just so you know."

"I do now."

"I leave notes at the door because no one pays the

slightest bit of attention to them. The crew leaves hundreds of them around each day: invitations, spa confirmations, concierge. The one or two I put up at a door hardly stand out."

"Just so you know . . ." he said. "I saw something on the island. Not everyone on the crew can be trusted."

"Like who are we talking about?"

"I'm not sure."

"That narrows it down."

"At least one officer," he said, thinking of the man following him on the staircase. "In case your sources are crew members or Cast Members."

"No," she said sarcastically, "it's Chip and Dale. I only deal with chipmunks."

"I'm just saying . . . it was dark. I didn't get all that good a look."

"Guys and girls?"

"Yes."

"You know you're freaking me out now?"

"I can see that. Yes. It's dark, and I don't know you that well, but you do kind of look freaked."

"You know me better than a lot of guys. We've kissed, after all."

He said nothing. She didn't have to remind him of that.

Finally, he managed to say, "I should take off."

"If you need me, fold your *Navigator* into a triangle and put it in the note holder outside your door. I'll find you."

"Who . . . are . . . you?"

"Go on," she said, giving him a slight but playful push. "Get out of here."

* * *

In a reversal of roles, Philby turned the controls of the DHI server over to Willa, who ran things from the Radio Studio. He did this in order to have her cross him over so that he might gain access to the security recordings while Charlene, also crossed over, would explore wherever he directed her. It was an ambitious plan, but one that required quick execution in case the Overtakers had a means to erase or replace security footage and hide their tracks.

He couldn't tell his mother he wanted to go to bed early because it would tip her to their plans, and Mrs. Philby was one of the parents who did not approve of Kingdom Keeper activity. Instead, he told her he wanted to watch TV in Finn's room. He shut the connecting door, left a note for Finn in the hall, and turned off the lights and lay down. With the activities of a long day behind him, he fell quickly to sleep.

Finn was a good ways down the endless Deck 8 starboard-side hallway when a voice from behind him stopped him.

"Why would you do this to me?"

Not just any voice.

He didn't know whether to turn around or to run. But he felt the power she had over him affect him like gravity. He turned.

From this distance, she looked just like the mom he knew her to be. He wanted to run and hug her, but his feet knew better and remained planted on the hallway's spongy carpet.

"Mom . . ."

"We were supposed to room together." She sounded crushed.

Had the green-eye curse only lasted a matter of hours—a day? Was she his real mom again? Again, temptation pulled him toward her. Again, he resisted.

"You're not . . . yourself."

"Don't you talk to me like that, young man."

She stepped forward, and he felt himself take a step back. The overhead light had caught her eyes: they were green.

"What is it?" she asked.

438

"I . . . ah . . . I've got to get going."

Another step toward him. The thing was, Finn wanted to hug her. He wanted to help her. This woman who had helped him through so much. He didn't move, allowing her to slowly close the distance between them.

"I . . . can . . . help," she said.

"The thing is . . ."

"We're a team, aren't we?"

He felt the strings attached inside his chest tighten and winch him toward her. "We are," he said.

"Always have been."

He nodded.

"A darn good team," she said.

His real mother would have never used that word. Her use of it slapped him in the face. An internal battle raged inside him: his head versus his heart. And he'd always been bigger of heart. She would have been the first to tell him that.

The first to take advantage of that.

He felt tears on his cheeks and wondered where they'd come from; they were traitors, these tears, trying to give him over to the enemy.

His mother, the enemy? Was such a thing possible?

"You know how you and Dad take different sides in politics?" he asked. She said nothing. "But you still love each other? That's what's going on here. Between us. Different sides."

"I've always been on your side."

"I know, but—"

"Why would I have anything but your best interests at heart?"

"All I know is . . . you're different."

"Am I? How can you say that?"

"It's the truth. You and Dad have always told me the truth counts more than anything."

A couple walked past them in the hall, barely taking any notice. Finn felt invisible. Only this woman and him.

There were tears in his mother's eyes now.

"The truth comes first," he quoted.

Her face bunched like the air had been sucked out of it.

"Mom, don't . . ."

He couldn't stand it when she cried.

She knows that! he reminded himself.

She was close now. Too close. But close enough that as he stared into her green eyes he saw them tick quickly over his shoulder, then flare with surprise. He heard a whoosh, as soft as the piped-in air, but distinctly flame, not air. He ducked.

A fireball exploded into his mother's chest, and she

went over backward like a bowling pin. He dove atop her and knocked the flaming ball off her, pounding her clothing to extinguish the fire. The color of her eyes flickered between blue and green. The ball of fire rolled against the wall and went out.

Finn rolled off his mother, not wanting to make her the target.

Maleficent strolled toward him, her black cape lifting behind her. "Give it to me!" she said.

"I don't have it." Finn backed up and got to his feet.

The smoldering ball of flame sputtered in her hand. The excited voices of guests at the end of the hallway rose to the occasion.

"Check it out!" a kid hollered.

Maleficent toyed with the ball above his fallen mother.

"How do you think she'll look with a face burned to a crisp?" she said, juggling the burning ball between both hands and pretending to drop it before catching it at the last second.

Finn lunged forward, then back.

"I don't have it," he repeated. "I tried to get it. You bet I did, but it sank and the water was too dark . . . and *I don't have it.*"

He'd never seen real panic on the green fairy's face, but there was a first time for everything.

He looked down at his mother. She was staring back at him out of the tops of her eyes. Blue eyes, sparking green.

"Run!" she gasped. With that, she kicked out and caught Maleficent in the legs and knocked her down. His mom jumped to her feet.

That was another first. As Maleficent fell, a crow appeared and the fairy was gone.

Finn turned and took off, his fingers reaching back for his mom's outstretched hand. Their hands connected just as the black crow hovered over his mother's head.

"Mom!"

Her blue eyes were turning green again. The same color green that occupied the crow's eyes. Finn swiped out awkwardly at the crow while running backward. It cawed and threw its talons forward and scratched him.

His mother's eyes held green for longer than they were blue, pulsing between the two colors, tightened in warning. She shook her head, meaning for him to let go of her.

"No . . ." he cried out.

But now her eyes were solid green and growing darker by the second.

The crow cawed again.

Some kid cheered from down the hall.

Finn's mother let go of his hand and took hold of

his left wrist with a vise grip. It wasn't just her eyes that had changed, but her entire demeanor. A meaner demeanor. Vicious. Possessive. She owned him.

"Mom . . ."

But his mother wasn't in there behind the woman's eyes. The crow controlled her now; she, a puppet to its whims and instructions.

He broke her grip with a wrestling move, but it felt more like a bone snapping in two. Like an artery tearing. She had never abandoned him. How could he leave her in the grip of this demonic creature beating its black wings above her?

But he did just that: turned his back on them both, fled down the hall, and slid into a just-closing elevator.

He looked up at two guests who seemed a bit horrified at finding a teenage boy on the floor of their elevator car, out of breath and drenched in sweat, tears in his eyes.

* * *

It bothered Charlene that she couldn't stop thinking about Maybeck. She had crossed over as planned and had headed off to retrieve her Wave Phone where she'd hidden it so she could receive messages from Philby for where to look for the crate.

But why Maybeck? Why was he stuck in her head?

From the moment he'd caught up with them on the island and described his fight with Luowski she'd found herself worried about him. Him, of all people. The brash, cocky kid who didn't even know she existed. And yet . . . their teaming up at the Base had changed her opinion of him. She pushed him out of her mind and tried to focus on the job at hand.

"Hey."

And there he was, stepping out to meet her near the lobby elevators.

"What are you doing here?" she asked.

"Good to see you, too."

"The question stands."

"I thought you might . . . maybe you could use some backup."

"Because I'm a girl?"

"No . . . I mean, yes. But not like that, not like because you can't handle it, because . . . I don't know. Forget it. Maybe it was a mistake."

"Maybe it was."

He looked at her, as confused as she'd ever seen him.

"I thought . . ." he said. He waved his finger between them.

"You thought what?"

"You . . . never mind."

"It's thoughtful of you," she said, trying to recover. Why did she push away the boys she actually liked? What was with that?

"We were a pretty good team at the Base."

"We were. Are."

"That's all," he said. "With you crossed over. Me, not. I thought . . . I don't know. Forget it."

That was the other thing: all boys had a breaking point after which they threw some kind of switch and totally lost interest. She had no way of doing that.

He turned his back on her. "See you."

"I'm glad you're here," she spit out.

He stopped. "For real?" Still aimed away from her.

"Totally."

He turned toward her. If his face had been a lightbulb she'd have needed sunglasses. "It's your deal, not mine. I'm just here as backup."

"Agreed," she said. She pointed upstairs.

Maybeck nodded.

* * *

"Excuse me," Philby said.

The woman had been reading in bed when Philby's hologram walked through her wall. Now she yanked up the bedsheet to cover herself, eyes wide, tongue-tied. She was not young. Far from it, he was happy to see. She'd dropped her book in her lap, the bedsheet clutched tightly like a security blanket. Slack-jawed.

"Sorry about this," he said. He kneeled and poked his head and shoulders through the floor of her stateroom. He stood up, a full boy again. "Maintenance work. Keeping the plumbing working. Sorry to bother you."

He disappeared through the far wall and into a narrow engineering space. He hoped she would call the front desk and report the incident, but worried she might not—old people, like Philby's grandparents, had credibility issues and did not want to appear senile. Claiming a boy ghost had spoken to her would only get her odd looks. But he was counting on the fear factor to make her report him. Security would be notified and would respond to her complaint. This in turn would leave security temporarily empty, which served his purpose well.

He ducked his hologram head through the floor. He'd established himself perfectly: he was looking (upside down) at the back of a security officer working at a desk that held a pair of computer screens, the larger of which displayed color security camera views in a quadrant format. The phone rang, and the man answered it.

"He went . . . where?" the man said. Then—"Oh,

come on!" He paused to listen. "Yeah . . . okay . . . I'll speak with her." Reluctantly, he pulled himself out of his chair in the midst of a deep sigh.

Philby extracted his head from the room to avoid being seen. He counted to ten and peeked through again. The room was empty. Here, then, was a chance to practice the benefits of 2.0: the added control over the physical space. Typically, a floor, attraction, or a sidewalk held a DHI, as the projection was set to do just that. When crossing through walls, technically a Keeper was in DHI shadow. Using 2.0, a DHI could "force" transitions—moving one's image from projector to projector, like a cell phone tower handing off a signal. Philby did so now. He closed his eyes and reminded himself that, as pure light, he could go wherever he wanted to go, that there were no boundaries. He jumped up a few inches, still squinting, and fell through the floor, landing surprisingly hard—and surprisingly loudly—on the floor of the security office below. He recovered quickly and scrambled under a desk just as the door flung open.

"Hello? Anyone here? Everything all right?"

An officer's pressed and starched white uniform, from the knees down, appeared. Whoever it was turned and left the office.

Philby was inside.

* * *

Taking directions from Philby over her Wave Phone, Charlene moved deeper into the guts of the ship. She'd left Maybeck outside the Crew Members Only door, near the forward end of the starboard companionway.

"Do you see the corridor to your right?" he asked.

"Yes."

"That's where they took the crate. But I can't see all of it."

"It's long. All gray paint. A crew area for sure."

"Doors?"

"Yes," she answered. "Three on the left and one at the very end. None on the right."

"There are numbers by them. Read them back to me."

Walking the corridor, Charlene read off the three numbers in a whisper.

"Okay. Consulting a floor plan here . . ." he said. "Did you know they have iPAQs—handhelds—that can control most of the ship's functions and all of the security devices?"

"You know, I don't care, Philby. Not only don't I care, but you're distracting me and things are just a little tense down here. Not to mention hot. I mean, where's the air-conditioning for the crew?"

"That's what I'm talking about: the iPAQs can control the air-cond—"

"Will you *shut up?*" She spoke too loudly for the narrow corridor, scaring herself with her own voice.

"I'm going to borrow one," he said against the background sound of a keyboard clicking.

"I really *do . . . not . . . care . . .*"

"You will."

"Oh my gosh! Enough!"

"Try the door at the end of the corridor," he said. "On the floor plans that door connects backstage to the theater. The doors on the left are emergency doors to the auditorium itself. I'm definitely going with backstage."

"Actually, it's me going with it," Charlene said.

"You'll have to leave the phone. It won't go through the wall with your hologram."

"I could try it."

"Trust me. I was stopped by a hair."

"What?"

"I'll tell you another time. Leave the phone somewhere you can find it later."

"So when I'm in there, I'm on my own?"

"Afraid so."

"Are you going to give me some clues?"

"Stand by. Checking the floor plan."

"You don't have to sound like a robot."

"Pardon me for living. Look who's nervous."

"I am nervous," Charlene said. "I don't particularly love creepy places. So help me out here."

"The hallway you'll enter angles left—"

"Left," she said, checking her hands. Charlene had a little trouble with left and right.

"It looks like there are some storage areas or offices off it. All very small."

"And?"

"It leads past a stairway, up and down and out into an area that's off the stage."

"Stage left," she said.

"Whatever. The stage is ginormous, but it looks like curtains hide most of it from the audience. No way to tell from here what's back there."

"That's encouraging."

"There's another level below, down those stairs you'll pass. I've got some safety cams down there as well as onstage. Maybe I can control the lights if I can figure out the iPAQ."

Enough with the iPAQ! she wanted to say.

"Okay," she said.

"You set?"

"I'll put my phone behind a fire extinguisher."

"Perfect."

"So I guess this is it for now."

"I'll be watching you at least some of the places. You're not alone."

Then why do I feel so alone? she wanted to say. But she'd volunteered for the assignment. She couldn't complain now.

She tucked the phone behind the fire extinguisher, summoned her courage, and walked through the door. She opened her eyes once through to the other side.

The corridor was narrow and more confined than she'd expected. The lighting wasn't great, either. The carpet was indoor-outdoor stuff that felt spongy and therefore a little weird underfoot. Charlene practiced 2.0 moves repeatedly, as had become her habit—reaching out to physically touch, then reaching out again and intentionally remaining projected light. This practice had become second nature, and she went down the hall doing the moves absentmindedly—running her fingers along the wall, running her fingers into the wall's metal, so that her fingernails and first knuckle were missing.

Her mind was supposed to be on locating the crate and determining its contents. Instead, she was thinking how smart Philby had been to tell her to change into the Cast Member costume of shorts and polo shirt before going to sleep. Where Finn was a boy with the big ideas, Philby was the one with the picky little suggestions that turned into practical solutions. Why had no one brought up Philby's slipping away from the four of them? Why had she kissed Finn? It was going to ruin everything. Who was she supposed to talk to about it?

She spotted a security camera on the wall up ahead. She waved into it and gave a thumbs-up, hoping he might be smiling back at her from wherever he was watching. But then things grew darker as she passed the stairway he'd described. Darker still as she stepped into the wings of stage left. Then her head split in two.

In her left ear, the sound of panting.

In her right, voices.

From the overhead stage lights came a burst of red light. Then blackness. A warning from Philby? she wondered. Or someone fooling with the lights? Trusting Philby, she made herself solid, stepped into one of the side curtains, and twisted inside it as if wrapping herself in a towel, leaving enough of a crack to see out.

Two people in a hurry—girls, not women, she thought—appeared downstage, disappearing behind other curtains. A moment later, the panting grew louder, and two awkward-looking dogs followed on their heels, also disappearing back there. Not dogs, she realized: hyenas.

452

Avoiding the hyenas, she headed for the stairs, following the voices. Men's voices bubbled up from down there. The presence of the hyenas made her believe she was on the right track. They'd been used on Deck 4 as patrol dogs. Here, they had to be guarding the mystery crate. Why their apparent handlers had been running from them, she didn't know. It had not looked liked playing, but pursuit. Like so many other questions that arose from being a Keeper, she couldn't explain what she'd seen and didn't have time to think about it. Survival depended on having her full senses at her disposal; she could ill afford distraction.

The metal stairs were as steep as a ladder, with a handrail for balance. She arrived to the bottom landing careful to keep herself in full hologram, expertly in control of her emotions, using 2.0's enhancements to push back the potential effects of her fear.

Like Finn and Willa, Charlene had perfected her ability to compartmentalize her anxiety, so that now, as she entered a dark and narrow companionway, she remained analytical and calm. A lighted doorway ahead on her left proved the source of the voices.

She peered around the edge into a surprisingly large area, its walls and ceiling crawling with pipes and wires. It looked like a room in her school's basement, a place only janitors went. There were Day-Glo orange caution triangles on the walls and yellow hash marks on the floor designating safety areas. It was not just pipes and wires on the ceiling, but rubber tubes—hydraulics. And now she realized the heavy, gated platform at the far end was an elevator of some kind. They were below the main stage; it and three smaller lifts serviced trapdoors in the stage overhead. Large props and actors could come and go through the floor during a show. This in turn explained all the safety warnings.

There on the center lift stood the wooden crate like an obelisk around which several workmen were gathered. They appeared neither concerned nor excited; if anything, they teetered on the edge of boredom. It occurred to Charlene that either they didn't know what was in there, or whatever was in there was not that big a deal.

She summoned her courage, took a deep breath, and entered the room.

"Everything go okay here?" she asked one of the men in the blue coveralls.

The man leaned back on the inverted plastic tub he used for a stool and waved his hand. "Not a problem." He was Indonesian or Indian with a thick, singsongy voice. "Our straps are not of the proper length. We could double them up, but the commodore said it is not regulation. There may be some in galley storage. If not, we are to use regular lines. Not a problem."

She strode up and circled the crate, her senses on full alert. Philby would want to know everything. Its corners were screwed shut, not nailed. The plywood was thick, though new. It still held the sweet pine smell of freshly sawed lumber. The holes cut into its top and bottom were covered with a fine black mesh. From within came the heavy sound of a creature breathing. There was a cluster of four bolts on opposite ends of the crate's narrower sides. If structural, they represented two ends of a bar, suggesting whatever was inside was heavy. It would take a beast to break the lumber apart.

A beast, she thought. In darkness. A bar across the top.

Philby would know what to make of it all. She wished she possessed such a mind as his.

Heavy black arrows were stenciled onto the crate pointing up, with THIS END UP! stenciled below.

A red light flashed on the wall. Two of the four men got to their feet.

"What the . . . ?" the lead worker said.

"Everything okay?" Charlene said.

The light stopped flashing, and the workers noticeably relaxed.

The other man standing said, "Someone hit it by mistake."

"Obviously," said the leader. He told Charlene, "It is the lift signal from stage level, warning to stand clear."

"But there is no show going on!" explained his companion. "No reason for lift signal."

Philby, thought Charlene. Warning of trouble.

Enough! She'd done her reconnaissance; there was no need to push it further.

"I'll be back in a half hour to feed it," she said.

"Whatever you say, miss."

She was caught off guard by the sound of someone coming quickly down the stairs. She had no desire to be caught by the Overtakers—2.0 or not. The speed of the descent signaled trouble; she could feel it in her bones. Best to hang her head and hurry quickly out of here.

"Julia!" A girl's voice. A somehow familiar voice from outside the room, but not Willa.

"You're wanted upstairs immediately!" A second girl's voice, also familiar.

Charlene had just stepped through the open doorway, now wishing she could reverse her decision and hide. She wasn't Julia. She was in trouble.

The two girls were up the stairs a short distance, looking down at her.

Charlene's breath caught; her throat constricted. She could hardly breathe.

456

Amanda and Jess, their shoulders bearing faint blue outlines.

Jess waved for her to hurry.

Amanda said, "Maybeck's got them cornered."

* * *

The Vibe was rocking. Open until two a.m. and celebrating a day on the beach and a successful Beach Blanket Barbecue, the teens had swarmed into the club after the ship had sailed. The music pulsed, the projection screen was showing a film, and the various gaming stations were surrounded by kids. Finn kept the ball cap pulled down low as he pushed through the crowd like a man possessed. The encounter with his mother had jarred him, had loosened the lid on the semblance of order in his life, first disrupted at Typhoon Lagoon. What was he supposed to do to save her? How was he meant to combat Maleficent's extraordinary powers? Would anyone other than his fellow Keepers even believe him if he appealed for help? He was about to find out.

"Bogey, two o'clock," spoke a familiar voice from over his shoulder. He turned to catch Dillard Cole in profile. It was the second time Dillard had come to his rescue. Who had nominated him as Finn's guardian angel?

He turned as advised. Luowski was talking to several other kids, all a head smaller.

The music beat louder all of a sudden. A popular song. The dance floor crowded, the going difficult. Kids didn't usually dance much; what the heck was happening?

He needed to get past Luowski into the next room if he was to find Storey Ming; she wasn't anywhere in sight. But it was like the kid was the devil's apprentice guarding the gates to the fiery furnace. Was Finn required to confront Luowski in order to get past? He had no desire to test that theory. So far Luowski hadn't noticed him.

He took a moment to try to force *all clear*. Unlike his experience with Maleficent, he remained unchanged.

Keeping his cap low was all-important—he wanted to avoid Luowski, and he also couldn't risk being recognized. Any fan attention would work against him. He spotted a pair of pirates by the club's only exit: Cast Members still in costume from the island party, he hoped.

He'd led himself into a trap. Where better to look for teens like him than in the Vibe? He'd been an idiot to come here.

"Not that way." Again, Dillard's voice over his shoulder. Again, he turned only to see his friend's back.

Finn turned away from the pirates and the exit, heading along the near wall in order to avoid Luowski on the far side of the thick crowd. He reached a dead end, the only doors leading to two restrooms. Beyond Luowski, out on the Vibe's private deck, Storey was giving a pottery demonstration. She might know a way out of the club—if he could reach her to ask.

He entered the restroom door marked BUOYS. Stalls to his left, a line of urinals, and across from them, sinks. At the far end, another door. The restroom could be accessed from both sides. He cut across the space, not stopping to use a urinal, his eyes dancing in every direction.

"Perv!" said a kid standing at a sink and watching Finn in the mirror.

He exited to find himself in an area beyond Luowski and his gang. He headed outside through a set of automatic doors.

Warm wind whipped his face. The smell of the sea slapped him. The moon, already above the horizon, was working its way into the stars, and for a moment the whole world seemed to both stop and come alive. Moments like this, he thought, were what cruising was all about. Note to self: come back some time when you're not trying to save the Kingdom and your own skin.

There was a game of deck volleyball under way.

Some girls and boys were crowded into the hot tub and, over against the ship rail to his left, there was a line of four craft tables, including a girl demonstrating pottery. He offered Storey a small wave and then moved away and along the rail, looking into the dark water breaking off the powerful force of the ship's bow, five stories below. The sight was mesmerizing. Just for a second, he felt like jumping.

A porpoise broke the surface. Then another in the white foam cresting off the bow. The moonlight turned the foam into pearls.

"Beautiful, isn't it?" Storey Ming.

"Oh, hello," he said. "It is."

She looked dazzling in the moonlight. He saw that she'd put on some makeup for her presentation, her hair held up and off her face by a decorative comb.

"I don't have anything new for you," Storey said. "No one I spoke to knew of any unusual cargo being brought on. No surprises planned for any of the stage shows. Or none that anyone knows about."

"No animals."

"Nothing. But it's not like I have that many connections."

"Talk about false modesty. You know the crew. You can view manifests. You know there are stowaways. What and who don't you know?"

"I don't know what or why any of this is happening. I think you do," she said.

"You overestimate. I'm a foot soldier. Not much more."

"You're the one to protect," Storey blurted out.

He paused, the sound of the water below hypnotic. "Am I?"

"That came out wrong."

"Is that why you're being so nice to me?"

"I said it wrong. I apologize."

"Who assigned you?" He swallowed dryly. "Wayne? One of the Imagineers? Are you really a potter?" He wondered: an Overtaker?

"I'm throwing pots, aren't I?" She sounded so defensive.

"How many others with you?"

"Listen, it's a group effort, that's all. You and the others . . . your being holograms and all . . . everything you've done so far. No one wants to see that go to waste."

"I see. So it's a matter of efficiency," he said sarcastically. "No one can afford the time to train a new set of Keepers."

"Or maybe the Imagineers feel it's about time they did just that," she said. Then she covered her mouth.

Finn studied her face in the moonlight. "What . . . do . . . you . . . know?"

"I didn't say anything."

"You said they're going to replace us. This . . ." he said, pointing a finger back and forth between them, "could be you and others gaining experience from us."

"That is so not true."

"Except that you're too old," he said.

"Seriously? You want to go there?" Storey leaned away from him.

"As if they're going to install college kids as guides."

"You are so out of line."

He looked out at the imagined horizon, that place where the darkness of the sky and the stars blended into a void of sea. What was he missing?

"Is that what the beta testing of 2.0 is about?" he asked. "We test it. A new generation of student models puts it operational?"

"You've got this so totally wrong. Seriously. I was just . . . I don't know what I was doing. Trying to sound more important than I am. Trying to make you like me."

"You're lying!"

"I am not! I made it up. I thought . . . I don't know what I thought!"

They'd raised their voices and drawn attention to themselves. Finn had bumped the brim of the cap up when challenging her so that now he stood there with his face exposed. How long he'd been like that, he couldn't say. A minute? Maybe.

"Hey, Witless . . ."

Finn didn't need to look to know who it was. Two-legged trouble in the form of two hundred pounds of seventeen-year-old flesh and bones. (Greg Luowski had been held back in third grade, and again in sixth.) So when Finn actually did bother to look over at the boy, the surprise that stole over his face wasn't the result of whom he saw standing there, but instead that Luowski was surrounded by a thin, but evident, blue line.

23

A HOLOGRAM.

"You have a stateroom, do you, Greg?" Finn said. He was trying to signal Storey that she was looking at one of the stowaways.

"Don't bother yourself with my stuff, Witless. I'd be thinking about how well you can swim." Luowski stepped forward.

Some of the other kids overheard the confrontation and began forming a ring around the two boys.

"Somebody get a counselor!" a girl's voice called out. Finn knew that voice.

Luowski elbowed one of the boys by his side. The kid took off and tackled another kid heading for the doors.

"Let's keep this between us, okay?" Luowski said.

"So let me ask you: doesn't it bother you being someone's goon?" Finn said. "Or is that what they call in drama class *typecasting*?"

Luowski took another step forward. As a DHI, regardless of the operating system, he had the advantage. Never mind his considerable strength. Never mind his supernatural size. Never mind his fighting skills and wrestling championships. The kid was a DHI with a blue outline that told Finn he could touch and hit and bite and thrash—probably for several seconds at a time. The rest of the time he'd be untouchable, unhittable—nothing but a projection of light.

For Finn, it was exactly the opposite. He was flesh and bones.

Luowski intended to throw him over the side of the ship, and Finn wasn't sure what could be done about it.

At night. In the dark. In the middle of the ocean.

"They'll catch you, flubber belly," Finn said, "because you're a loser. It's a ship, brainless. Where are you going to hide?"

The whole idea was to instill a mixture of anger and fear into the boy. It didn't take much to pull a version 1.6 DHI's hologram back to reality.

"Shut up!" Luowski said angrily.

Sweet!

Finn shifted onto his left foot, raised his right, and kicked out, connecting with the boy's midsection. Luowski flew back and fell down, his green eyes in shocked disbelief.

"Hmm," Finn said. "That wasn't supposed to happen."

Luowski clambered quickly to his feet and charged. But Finn had his senses about him. He waited until the last second and moved aside. Luowski struck the rail with a thud.

The crowd groaned.

"Nice job, doofus!" Finn said.

Luowski turned and took a mass of wet clay in his face, courtesy of Storey. The fact that it stuck to the boy's face was the only test Finn needed.

He charged Luowski from behind, leading with a shoulder to the boy's right knee and collapsing Luowski like a folding chair. With Luowski down and moaning, Finn took Storey's slimy hand in his and fled. The automatic doors swung open, revealing two pirates.

Not Cast Members. Not costumes. Not role-playing. Pirates. Just like the ones at the Sail-Away Celebration. They grabbed Finn and Storey, spun them around, and lifted them off their feet. The sound of Storey's cries echoed in Finn's ears.

The pirates turned and carried the two toward the crammed club. They'd be out into the companionway in less than a minute. Once out there, who knew what was going to happen to them? Being thrown overboard might have seemed a luxury by the time these guys got through with them.

In an instant, all the lights went out. The music stopped. The projector quit. For a heartbeat there was complete darkness and total silence. Then, as the emergency lights switched on, pandemonium. Kids charged for the exit as counselors hollered for calm.

Finn drove his heel into the arch of the pirate's right foot. He felt something give. The pirate let go of him, cried out in pain, and fell like a tree against the pirate next to him, who released Storey to catch his friend.

Philby, Finn decided, without a second thought. The power outage had been Philby's doing.

In the crush of terrified kids, Finn led Storey into the dead-end area, against traffic. He pulled the couch away from the wall and climbed behind, helping Storey in there with him.

"What are you doing?" she asked above the roar of the chaos.

"They'll look for us out there," he said, pulling the couch in tightly against them. He typed a text on the Wave Phone.

thnx. hiding behind couch in alcove

A moment later a text was returned.

no prob. i c u. nice move. so far, no worries. tell SM hi
4 me

"Philby says hi," he told her.

She looked frightened.

"If you're going to train to take my place," Finn said, "you're going to have to get used to this stuff."

"Shut! Up!" She paused. "Tell him hi back."

"I will not. You think I share, or something?"

It won a smile from her. She had bright white teeth.

* * *

The question of whom Maybeck had cornered turned out to be a what, not a whom. The hyenas. He wasn't exactly sure why it was working, only that it must have something to do with Disney. When you were a Keeper, it turned out everything had to do with Disney.

The truth was, he hadn't thought about it. It was not some brilliant plan the way Philby and Willa hatched brilliant plans. It was not some insanely creative solution the way Finn came up with them. Confronted by two drooling hyenas, both the size of a Great Dane and the demeanor of a pit bull, he'd just grabbed for the object nearest to him, which turned out to be a papier-mâché lion's head, a prop from one of the live stage shows. And not just any lion's head—Scar's head.

Seeing this, the hyenas cowered into a corner, sat back on their haunches, and looked away, the way a dog does when scolded by his master. They went from vicious, blood-seeking, four-legged killers to simpering, whimpering mutts that looked as dangerous as a pair of gerbils.

But if Maybeck moved the head to the wrong angle, their necks snapped around, their eyes popped out of their heads, and they appeared ready to tear a chunk of flesh from him the size of a holiday ham. So he kept the mask extended, arms tiring, wondering, "What now?"

"Psst! How's it going?" Amanda called to him. He had rescued her and Jess, believing at the time that at least one of the girls he saw was Charlene.

"It's a bit of a stalemate," Maybeck answered. "If I take a step back, they take a step forward. I've held them here since you left. But the slightest movement, and I get the feeling I'm going to be puppy chow. Factor into the equation," an expression he'd heard Philby use repeatedly, and one he thought sounded particularly smart, "that my arms are tiring . . . I'm not saying I'm weak, but this mask is huge and it's heavy . . ."

"What do you want us to do?" Jess asked.

"I think you should get out of here," he said.

"Seriously, Maybeck," Charlene said, "what are the odds of me leaving you here?"

"I could drop it and run, but my guess is they're about five times faster than any of us."

An amber light on the wall behind the hyenas flashed.

"It's Philby," Charlene said.

"Freeze! And don't say a word!" Jess whispered harshly, having nearly forgotten what had led her and Amanda down the stairs to begin with. The Evil Queen and Cruella were headed to the lower-level staging area and the crate. She'd seen it in a dream, along with Charlene being down there at the time of their arrival.

The kids remained absolutely still. The clip-clop of a woman's heels percussed across the darkened stage. The two grown women stopped only yards from the three girls.

"Happy? Howly?" Cruella called out. Then again. "Come here, my little laughers!" A pause. "Boys?" Another pause. "Well, that's as odd as a one-eyed parrot. I left them here to patrol."

"So maybe they're off patrolling," said the Evil Queen, impatient with her partner. "What is the problem?"

"The problem is I left them here, and those boys obey."

"You think every animal dances to your tune, including most people. Well, not this person."

"You are hardly a person!" Cruella complained.

"Shush! Let's make sure our guest is comfortable. You can work your magic on him, my dear."

"That's the idea," said Cruella.

"I wouldn't get too cocky, if I were you. He's no hound, as you'll soon find out. How are you with bats, anyway?"

"While I adore most nocturnals, the winged variety find little support from me. Though I'm loath to admit it, I find them frightening."

"Well, at least we have something in common! You live in the woods or drafty old castles, you come to tolerate the things, but accepting them is different. If left up to me I'd banish them for eternity!"

"You can do that, can't you? I envy you, Queeny. How I wish I could conjure. Could you teach me?"

"Shut it, will you? Are you quite done blowing your dog whistle? I'd like to get on with it."

"At your disposal."

The two trundled off in the direction of the staircase and descended.

When the witch and the woman were well gone, Amanda, looking up, said softly, "I have an idea."

"Let's hear it," Jess said.

"You're a climber, aren't you?" she asked Charlene.

You know I am, Charlene felt like saying, but she held her tongue. She knew Amanda had a thing for Finn, knew Finn had a thing for Amanda, and knew that Finn found it easy to flirt with her and that the flirting drove Amanda crazy. There were few secrets among the Keepers. Everyone had known that Charlene had had a crush on Finn for quite some time. But it was over now, and Amanda didn't need to pretend they barely knew each other.

"Yes," she said. "Sure am."

"If you climb up there," Amanda asked, pointing into the staging overhead, "would you be able to jump or get down really fast somehow?"

"I could probably work something out. Why?"

"You see that curtain?" she said.

Charlene followed her gaze. She did see the massive curtain, and she intuited what Amanda had in mind just by looking.

"It just might work," Charlene said.

"What might work?" Jess said. "Did I miss something?"

"I'm with Jess," Maybeck hissed.

Charlene crossed to the wall and scampered up the rigging like a sailor up a mast. She moved from one stage rope to another, shinnied up a pipe, swung from a cable, and arrived quickly to the support bar that held the stage curtain.

"Terry," Amanda said, "you're going to need to back up about ten more feet."

"I don't love that idea."

"Noted," said Charlene from the rafters.

Maybeck stepped back and the two hyenas, Howly and Happy, scooted forward on their behinds, still wary of the giant lion mask. A few more feet of retreat, and the hyenas advanced an equal distance.

"Nearly there," Amanda said. "Charlene?"

"Ready."

"Are you sure you can get down fast enough?"

"Five more feet," Charlene said from up above. "When I reach three, the mask needs to be on the floor facing them. You don't want to spook them—"

"You think?"

"—so just put it down and back up slowly. Got it?"

"And then?" Jess asked.

"And then we run past the stairway and into the corridor and we get the heck out of here," Amanda said. "You and Maybeck first. I'm waiting for Charlene."

"No need to do that," Charlene complained.

"Not open for discussion," Amanda said, asserting herself.

"Yeah, yeah, yeah," Charlene said. "Everybody ready?"

They each acknowledged.

"Then here we go. One . . ."

Maybeck began lowering the mask. As he did, the two wild-eyed hyenas fixed on him like heat-seeking missiles.

"Two . . ."

The large mask touched the stage floor. Maybeck backed up first one step, then two. The hyenas inched forward, but could not bring themselves to challenge Scar.

"Three!"

Maybeck turned and ran as the whine of rope paying out joined the release of the curtain, the giant wall of fabric falling as a wave of ruby-colored smoke and covering the hyenas like a magician's handkerchief.

Charlene came down a nearby rope like a spider laying its thread, joined Amanda an instant later, and the two held hands as they ran from the stage, quick on the heels of their friends.

24

"IT'S HIM. CHERNABOG," Philby said.

There were eight of them in all. The five Keepers, Jess and Amanda, and Storey Ming. They occupied a corner of the Deck 11 concierge lounge, access to the lounge compliments of their luxury staterooms. A warm, inviting space, with a rich, colorful carpet and wood-paneled walls, there were desserts, cheese, and grapes available along the far wall by an espresso maker, fresh juice, and pitchers of ice water.

For the most part they were left alone, the concierge at the desk having left to run some errand shortly after they'd arrived. If they heard the door open, they changed subjects to something mundane and teenlike. Taylor Swift's new romance. The U.S. Olympic soccer team.

"We don't know that for sure," Willa said. She could hold her own with Philby.

"The Evil Queen mentioned bats," Philby reminded her. "We know, thanks to Mr. E.'s class, that if you combine a bat's face with the Minotaur you get something freakily similar to Chernabog. And then there's the bar."

"What bar?" Finn asked.

"The bar Charlie described. The structural support at the top of the crate."

"It was some bolts!" Maybeck complained.

"It was four bolts on opposite sides of the top of the crate. What do you want to bet they're holding a steel bar in place?"

"Because?" Charlene asked, almost afraid to open her mouth in this group.

"It's easy," Storey Ming said, drawing the attention of everyone. Especially Philby. Philby's heightened interest drew the scrutiny of Willa. "The patches of stuff covering the holes make the crate dark inside while still supplying air."

"Exactly," Philby said.

"If Chernabog's part bat—"

"A Mayan bat god," Philby said.

"The rod is so he can hang upside down while he sleeps. Dark like a cave."

A stunned silence swept over the collective.

"It's Chernabog," Philby said.

"But . . . why?" Willa said.

"That's what we need to figure out," Finn said. "It all comes back to the stolen journal."

"A ritual," Charlene said.

"And a ceremony," Willa added.

"We are way in the deep stuff," Maybeck said. "I'm not talking knee deep, I'm talking neck deep."

"That's gross," Amanda said.

"Disgusting," Charlene agreed. The two exchanged a thoughtful look. Both grinned.

"And you're here because?" Willa asked, turning to Jess and Amanda.

"Wanda Alcott wanted us available. Warned us we might cross over when we went to sleep at night. Jess had this dream—"

"About Charlie getting caught by the Evil Queen and Cruella," Jess said. "Other stuff too, but I haven't put it together."

"The link I installed," Philby said to the others. "I thought Wayne wanted it installed so we could help out at Base. Looks like he wanted to use it as an uplink, going the other direction."

"We need to return at some point," Jess said. "Mrs. Nash will check the rooms around six. We need to get some sleep before then."

It had been a long night, already past one.

"I can return you," Philby offered.

"We have the autographing tomorrow," Finn reminded them. "Walt Disney Theatre. It might give us another chance to check out the crate."

"That sounds risky," Storey said.

"Not if we make it look like one of us just wandered off in the wrong direction looking for a bathroom."

"That could work," Willa agreed.

"Unless Howly and Happy are out for a walk," Maybeck said.

"Not during the day," Charlene said.

"I know that," Maybeck said. "I was making a joke."

"Ha ha," Willa said.

"We need to decipher the journal," Finn said. "And locate the OT server. I'd love—love, love, *love*—to lock fat face in the Syndrome for a couple of days."

"Like forever," Maybeck joined in.

"We're talking about Luowski, I take it," Professor Philby said.

Everyone laughed.

"Have you considered he's more valuable to us as a captive?" Philby said. "If we could find his lair while he's crossed over and be there when he returns . . ."

"We don't kidnap people," Willa objected.

"Who said anything about kidnapping? We just play a game of twenty questions with him when he wakes up from the return."

"With a couple of us holding him down," Maybeck said, clearly approving of the plan.

"The entire crew has been searching for the stowaways for over a day now," Storey Ming said. "I don't mean to be a buzzkill, but they know the hiding places on the ship a lot better than any of you—or I."

"True enough," Philby said. "But we have technologies they lack."

"Such as?" she asked.

"Maybe later," he answered, not fully trusting her.

"Not yet," Finn told her, using the same phrase she'd used on him.

Amanda caught the exchange between the two and studied them disapprovingly.

"How many days at sea?" she asked.

"Two," Philby answered. "Two sea days and then Aruba."

"They could have brought Chernabog on at any of the ports," Amanda said, "so why now?"

She silenced them once again.

A sleepy-eyed guest entered wearing a robe and slippers. He poured himself a glass of milk from a half fridge, drank it down, and left. He gave no indication he'd seen eight kids in the corner. The door thumped shut.

"Why indeed?" Willa said.

"They waited until Castaway," Maybeck said, "because the Canaveral port is probably too well managed. I'll bet someone knows exactly what and who gets on the ship. Security especially."

"Agreed," said Philby.

"Castaway offers a way around that," Maybeck said. "It's different than Aruba, the canal, Costa Rica—any of the other stops."

"But why bring him aboard at all?" Amanda asked.

"It's got to have something to do with what's in the journal," Finn said.

"You're going around in circles," Storey Ming said.

"It's late," Charlene said. "We need sleep. We need to keep our heads clear."

"We're two days in. Thirteen to go," Willa said.

"Just hearing that makes me tired," Philby said.

"It gets worse," Storey said, winning their attention. "Not all of you attended the Beach Blanket Barbecue opening. I don't know for sure what kind of contract you have with the line—if any—but if that were other Cast Members, there would be discipline. Privileges taken away. Certain areas set off limits. I'm not saying that's going to happen to you, but I'd kind of be surprised if it didn't."

"Oh, perfect," Maybeck said. "That's all we need!"

"Hey," Storey said, "I don't make up the rules. I'm just warning you something like that might happen."

"Can I share something?" Philby asked. "When I was monitoring the security camera recordings I just happened to take a peek at the daily log—"

"Just happened, I'll bet," said Maybeck.

"The last entry . . . second to last, if you count the alert I caused to get the guy out of there . . . this was at ten twenty-two, so after the all-aboard and once we were already sailing . . . it read: 'VQ sighting.' The note in the comments box read something about checking with shipboard entertainment that VQ was 'authorized.'"

"Authorized?" Storey questioned.

"Yes. That specific word. Do you know what it means?"

"Authorized?" she repeated. She whistled. Without thinking, they all leaned a little closer to her. "Just after we sailed from Canaveral we had a freak shipboard occurrence. A double Mickey sighting." She went on to explain the term and the crew's failure to turn up the imposter mouse. "Asking Entertainment if a character is authorized means checking to make sure the character belongs on the ship. Because you guys are on here, all sorts of extra characters have been added, including Maleficent, crash-test dummies, court jesters . . . all your so-called enemies."

"How can you be sure it's a character?" Philby said.

"For one thing, because he's checking if it's authorized. That's the only thing that makes sense if he's calling Entertainment. And of course the initials themselves. 'Captain M.' 'MM' for Minnie, 'C and D' for Chip and Dale—a ton of the character names are abbreviated by Cast Members. Some are referred to by their initials. Like JS for Jack Sparrow."

"But VQ?" Charlene asked. "Who's that?"

It wasn't Storey who answered; it was Philby.

"They've abbreviated her nickname," he said. *"Voodoo Queen."*

"Tia Dalma's on board the ship," Finn said. "And I'm guessing she's unauthorized."

* * *

"So please join me in welcoming Disney's very own Disney Hosts Interactive!" The ship's director of entertainment, Christian, dressed in his crisp dress whites, gestured across the Walt Disney Theatre's stage. He had made a big deal in his warmup about the cutting-edge technology represented by the DHIs, about the company's effort to get them into every park, and how excited they were to now introduce them to the cruise line. But in the back of Finn's mind he couldn't help reliving his conversation with Storey Ming, his sense that the company might already be on the verge of retiring the original DHIs in favor of a second generation. He wondered if that decision had anything to do with the fame and lore that now surrounded him and the others, with the stories and rumors of their battles to save the parks. Had they grown too big too fast, overshadowing the traditional Disney characters? Did the company hope to return the Disney Hosts to just that, and not have to deal with the public's appetite for controversial stories of witches and villains attempting to overthrow the parks?

All of this tempered his enjoyment of the moment. A thousand people were standing and applauding. Cheering and screaming. The kids waved from the stage. It felt in many ways like the best, most lavish welcome the five kids had ever received. But they were no longer young middle schoolers, and Finn sensed this wasn't just an introduction—it was a retirement party. Disney had plans no one in the audience understood.

"Thank you!" Finn said, wearing a wireless microphone. He spoke the script he'd been asked to memorize. It was short and sweet, a message of harmony and magic and enthusiasm. He told them they'd be staying to autograph cruise posters and announced that their DHI holograms would be on deck that evening for tours and photographs. The crowd went wild.

A short video celebrating the DHIs ran on three screens simultaneously—a large central screen onstage and two displays on either side. It was part tribute, part promotional piece. Finn noticed that there was little to no mention of them personally; instead the video focused on the concept of in-park guides and personal hosts. If anything, taken in a certain light, it seemed to be priming the audience for a new set of hosts. He wondered if anyone in the standing-room-only crowd caught on to this subtle message.

When a fishing net fell from the stage rafters, covering the five waving kids, and Maleficent appeared stage left, her green face enormous on the three screens, the crowd went wild. A team of pirates converged on the stage, contained the net, and pushed the trapped kids back several feet; then the stage dropped out from under them, a hydraulic lift descending. The cheers of the crowd grew even louder.

"Behold the New Order," Maleficent said in her eerily calm and grating voice. "The dawning of a new age." Another huge cheer from the adoring crowd. "Enough of all this prince-and-princess spun-sugar nonsense. It's time for the Grimm in the fairy tales to express itself. The woods are dark, my dears. The beasts within them will eat you for supper, not sing you a song. Wake up and smell the roses."

The last thing Finn saw of the auditorium was the fanatic crowd looking up to see thousands of falling red roses released from high overhead. The attendees reached up to welcome the flowers, apparently not thinking through that the stems of roses carried thorns, and thorns could scratch. As the hydraulic lift removed him and the others from the stage, Finn heard the cheers turns to shrieks and cries. Then the world went dark as they were hauled off the platform, which quickly returned to seal the stage's trapdoor shut, removing all sound and light.

"*All clear,*" Philby said the moment they were pulled as a netted knot from the platform. Perhaps only he understood the seriousness of the situation—or maybe he was just bragging.

If the Overtakers had the nerve to capture the Keepers in broad daylight in front of an audience while announcing a New Order, there would be only one intended outcome.

Death.

The pirates drove their swords through the net and into the kids without warning. No tear-jerking speech from Maleficent, no end-of-the-movie apology or dramatic summary. Just swords into their chests.

They saw the blades coming. The pirates knew nothing of finesse. Finn dodged the one meant for him, as did Maybeck. Philby's hologram stepped through the net and he bumped the pirate going for Willa. Charlene cried out. Stabbed in the shoulder, bleeding badly. The ignorant pirates cut the net with their sharp blades. Finn launched himself through a resulting hole and delivered a fist into the face of the pirate attempting to finish off Charlene. The pirate dropped his sword and staggered back. Finn clutched his knuckles, wondering if he'd broken his hand.

Maybeck followed Willa out of the net.

Philby took a sword to his body. It passed through, throwing whoever held the sword off balance. Maybeck or Finn helped trip the staggering man, and they moved fluidly in a choreographed way, first drawing the pirates apart, then singling one out and knocking him down.

Armed with fallen swords, Maybeck and Finn fought back while Philby played shape-shifter. A pair of crash-test dummies guarded the room's only door; there would be no easy exit.

Finn ducked a sword swipe, the pirate's blade lodging in the wood of the towering crate at the center of the space.

Chernabog?

Willa held a *Lion King* shield between her and her pirate. His sword bounced off it as she steadily drove him back. He stumbled, lost his balance, and Maybeck swiveled in time to knock him unconscious with a length of pipe. She joined at Maybeck's side, and together they went after one of the few remaining pirates.

Philby seemed to be enjoying his status as the only 2.0. He stood in place, allowing a frustrated pirate to strike him time and time again, the man's sword slicing through the light of his projection. Then, as the pirate tired, Philby delivered a soccer kick between the man's legs, and the pirate collapsed.

Seven pirates had become five, then three. A crash-test dummy left his post at the door and tossed Maybeck against a wall like a rag doll. Maybeck crashed to the floor, groaning. Willa kicked the dummy, failing to do any harm. He backhanded her and sent her to the floor as well.

Philby *all clear*, Finn not, the two regrouped, armed with swords, back to back near the crate. They faced three very angry pirates and one robotic crash-test dummy. Swords clattered and clanked as they beat off the attempted blows.

"Not good," Finn said loudly.

"I'm working on it," Philby said.

You conceited jerk, Finn wanted to shout.

"On three, jump out of the way."

"I will not!"

"You go for the lights."

"You call that a plan?" Finn said.

The CTD swung out and hit Finn's shoulder, turning him so that he was no longer back-to-back with Philby. Instead, both boys had their backs to the crate.

"Change of plans," Finn said. "Help me out here." He slammed his back into the crate, rocking it.

"Are you nuts?" Philby said.

"I can help you," came Charlene's voice.

She was standing—wounded shoulder and all— behind the three pirates and the CTD. She held Maybeck's length of pipe in her one good arm. She looked mad. Real mad.

She swung the pipe like Albert Pujols taking batting practice. One, two, three, she connected with the backs of the pirates' legs and took them down. The CTD turned around.

Charlene hit him a good one. The dummy stumbled, tried to balance, and ended up behind the crate.

"Push!" Finn shouted.

The boys spun around and heaved against the huge crate, Philby pushing with his hand. The crate tipped, but rocked back upright.

"Again!"

The crate rocked.

Charlene struck the dummy a second time, keeping him in the shadow of the crate.

The boys pushed again in unison. The crate tipped, teetered, and went over. The CTD didn't have time to get out of the way and was crushed by the falling crate.

The wood shattered and the box broke open.

A horrid thing lay there, his leathery black skin like the fingers of a gorilla. Reddish-brown hair grew from him as fuzz. His face was a horror, half bull, half bat—and the ugly half of both. Two scarred black horns bent from his skull above hairy, pinned-back bat ears. The crate had seemed big enough, but now in the flesh this *thing* appeared twice as large. Enormous. Maybe twelve feet tall and as wide around as a refrigerator. His shoulders too wide to fit through a double doorway, arms as thick as Burmese pythons.

His eyes squinted and opened. There was nothing inside but bottomless darkness: Chernabog.

Someone screamed.

It was Philby.

* * *

They fled from that place as a group. Ran so fast that, had anything or anyone been attempting to follow, it would never have caught up. They ran down companionways and through doors, up stairs and along decks.

They found their way to their staterooms and locked the doors and hid under the covers without a peep.

Only Charlene did not make it to her room. She was spotted by a uniformed officer who called out "Stop!" Being a polite girl, and one brought up to obey and respect authority, she did just that. The woman kindly showed her to the ship's hospital, where they treated and closed her wound with butterfly bandages, accepting her explanation that she'd had a freak accident involving a broken drinking glass and a bathroom's wet tile floor.

None of them had any intention of sleeping knowing that the beast was somewhere belowdecks.

Discovering Chernabog out of the crate, the Overtakers would feel pressure to speed up whatever plan they had. At the top of that agenda was certain to be the elimination of the Keepers before they could ruin their plans. That meant an all-out war. Tonight.

That necessitated the Keepers go on the offensive.

A few minutes past two a.m., Philby hid their three Wave Phones in a potted plant behind the lobby's grand piano, a hiding place chosen for its accessibility. He then rode an elevator to the Radio Studio, where the key card allowed him and Storey Ming to enter. He instructed her on how to work a manual return.

"I've got it," she said, after he'd been over it a third time. "I don't mean to sound rude, but it's pretty simple."

"Don't tell the others," Philby said. "They think of it more as rocket science." He grinned. "And remember: if you don't enter that code correctly, if you aren't here when we need you, we remain stuck. You understand that?"

"Trapped. Yes. I understand." She hesitated. "You could have asked one of the others—one of the five of you. Why me?"

"Charlene needs sleep. Maybeck is valuable to us on this side for now. We know what we're doing."

"Maybeck stays here to make sure I do my job," she said.

Philby didn't answer her directly. "Being a hologram is fine. But having Maybeck on this side increases our chances of success. Statistically, it's a matter of—"

"Shut up," Storey said. "They may listen to your garbage, but I don't have to."

Philby looked made of stone. He said softly, "We can contact him when we need him."

"Uh-huh. Fine."

Storey waited a full hour, allowing time for Philby, Willa, and Finn to sneak out to one of the empty staterooms and get to sleep.

At exactly three, she typed in the first string of

code and pushed the ENTER key. The screen filled with scrolling computer code. Storey read back her notes, matching the identifiers with what she saw on-screen.

If she understood it correctly, Finn and Willa had crossed over; Philby had not. She knew what to do in this event—Philby had explained everything to her like some kind of schoolteacher. Wait fifteen minutes and rekey the missing identifier. Failure to cross over usually meant the person in question had not fallen asleep in time. Sometimes there was Wi-Fi interference or Internet problems.

A knock on the door startled her, and she jumped in her chair.

It was a green-eyed girl, motioning her out of the studio.

Storey shook her head. "No!"

"Open the door!"

"No!"

They were inches apart now, separated only by the door's safety glass.

"Please . . ." came the girl's muffled voice.

Something about the quality of that voice made Storey turn the doorknob. She stepped out, keeping the door ajar with her right foot.

"Who are you?" the girl said.

"Who are you?" Storey said.

"A friend."

"Same."

"Then how come I don't know you?"

"Same question," Storey said.

"I was expecting . . . someone else."

"A boy."

"Yes."

"A smart boy."

The girl nodded.

"He's busy."

"It's a trap."

"Excuse me?"

"The network will indicate one of the refrigerators on Deck One. They left a clue there some time ago so the Keepers would believe it. But it's a trap."

"A clue?"

"Tell them the piece of torn robe was a phony. You can convince them if you tell them that."

"And I'm supposed to believe this because . . . ?"

"Because you don't want them walking into a trap." She paused. "Do you?"

"Shut . . . up!"

"Just tell them. What they're after—it doesn't need the cold. It's in a special case."

"You know this how?"

Sally Ringwald took a deep breath, releasing it slowly. "Because I'm one of them."

She turned and took off down the stairs.

"Wait!" Storey's foot slipped out of the door.

"No!" She grabbed for the handle. Too late. It clicked, locked shut.

She spun in circles, having no idea what to do, blissfully unaware that the ship's meteorologist had been summoned to the bridge. The *Dream* was heading smack into the roar of wind and rough seas.

* * *

"Where the devil did you come from?" The question was posed to Finn by an Indian man polishing the atrium's floor with a buffing machine.

"I . . . well . . . we . . ." Finn said, pointing across the small photo-shoot stage to the opposite corner and Willa, who was just sitting up. He found himself suddenly tongue-tied.

"We were playing a game of hide-and-seek," Willa said. "The Vibe club? And we both must have fallen asleep."

"Which is to say," Finn said, "no one ever found us."

The maintenance crew member scratched his head. "It's too late for you to be here. You should be in your staterooms."

494

"Which is where we are going right now," Finn said.

"Mom and Dad are going to be furious," Willa said, playing it as if they were brother and sister. It made Finn think about his mother and how he was going to break whatever spell held her. Where was she now, he wondered?

"Off you go before I report you," said the worker. The curfew for teens was one o'clock, and it was well past that.

Just then the ship shuddered bow to stern, a long rumbling tremor underfoot like a growling stomach. The man must have seen Finn's horror.

"It's nothing, son," the man said. He sounded more Irish than Indian. "When the seas kick up, she'll push and fight and pitch and yaw her complaints like an old maid, but she bends like bamboo, the beauty. It's all part of what they call the 'seafaring experience.'"

"Have you sailed a long time?"

"I was a farmer. And my father and his father, both farmers. So no, I'd never seen the ocean before. Took some getting used to for me, but now I wouldn't trade it for anything. Every ship has a personality, and the *Dream*'s well named."

Another grinding shudder rippled through the expansive atrium.

"That's normal, then?" Willa said.

"Perfectly," the man said. "Don't you worry a hair on your head. Now, off you go!"

Finn and Willa thanked him and took off across the atrium, but reached out and caught hands to steady themselves as the ship lurched to port. Suddenly it was like trying to walk in an amusement park ride, Finn thought, only he didn't find it so amusing.

"Where's Philby?" Willa said as they reached the elevators. Given that they were glass elevators on the side facing the man they'd spoken to, they had to ride at least a few floors up to convince him they were returning to their staterooms.

"I was wondering the same thing," Finn said.

The elevator arrived, and they boarded and rode to the sixth floor.

"Missed the crossover," she said.

"I'm assuming."

"But how do we find the OT server if he's not monitoring the network data flow?" Willa said.

"We need to get back down there and get our phones. Without that guy seeing us."

"I totally spaced that part."

"We need the phones."

"So . . . what now?"

"We think like an Overtaker."

"Meaning?"

"Tia Dalma's somewhere on board this ship," Finn said. "Wherever they're hiding her, you can bet it's as far away from where they're hiding Chernabog as possible. So where is that?"

"Somewhere at the stern," she said. Then, "Is this about your mother?"

"We were at Typhoon Lagoon. The theme is beach and water and island and shipwrecked boats and—"

"—Creole witch doctors fit in with that. Yeah, I can see that," she said. "It's Tia Dalma."

He thought back to his spying on the voodoo lady's meeting with Jafar and the crew members, about her demand that the crew members be brought to her. He wondered how many characters could stand up to Maleficent in this way.

The elevator arrived and they disembarked, mindful of the number of security cameras throughout the ship. Without Philby crossed over, their situation had changed. Security could easily be monitoring two kids wandering the ship in the middle of the night.

"So . . . what now?" she said.

"The kitchens are busy all the time," he said. "Preparing all the meals. Baking. Room service."

"You're hungry? Seriously?"

"Not a perfect place to hide, but a nice cool place for a computer server."

"And a certain fairy who likes the cold."

* * *

Storey didn't wear a watch, had no idea of the exact time. But she didn't need a watch to know that if she was on this side of the locked door, she wasn't where she needed to be.

She absolutely had to get inside the studio and attempt to cross over Philby, to warn them about the trap. She had to be there to return Finn and Willa if they got in trouble.

She saw her Wave Phone through the glass—her chance to warn them . . .

If she failed to get inside the studio and return Finn and Willa when they requested, there'd be two less Keepers by morning.

And she'd be responsible.

* * *

Maybeck used the second of the four Cast Member ID cards Wayne had given him to collect his steward's uniform. Wearing the brown pants and shirt of a stateroom steward over his DHI outfit, he cleaned the wood paneling running the forward length of the starboard companionway on Deck 3, from which he could keep an eye on the door leading to the backstage access. Granted, there were any number of ways a Cast Member could access the Walt Disney Theatre. But this door was the most convenient to the area beneath the stage and therefore the one to watch.

Now, for the third time in the past hour, two Cast Members came and went through the backstage door, only for two others to leave a few minutes later.

Shift changes, Maybeck thought. Or repairmen to fix the crate that had broken up, spilling out the dreaded Chernabog. Or maybe couriers delivering orders from Maleficent. Maybe, he thought, he could follow one of these pairs to the green fairy's lair. Maybe he could bust this thing wide open all by himself. He'd have to leave his post for a few minutes, during which time they wouldn't know who came and who went. It would be a risk, certainly, but one worth taking.

Being a Kingdom Keeper required flexibility. Creativity and ingenuity. Being a team player was important, to be sure. But for Maybeck, being the hero was more important.

And he sensed a chance to be the hero.

* * *

As holograms Finn and Willa entered one of the unoccupied staterooms in order to get away from the prying eyes of any companionway security cameras. From there it was a matter of following Philby's description of his having moved through the floor to the deck below. Though in their case, the floor they dropped through belonged to a balcony and delivered them to the balcony below. And then the balcony below that. And finally to Deck 4 and the walking track and overhead lifeboats that wrapped the ship's entire perimeter.

They landed holding hands. Looking down the length of the vacant exterior deck, Finn felt a small shiver of familiarity. He couldn't immediately place it, but he'd been here before. With Willa. So much was the same. But not everything.

"The phones," she said, breaking into his thoughts and robbing him of the moment.

"Yes," he said.

"Philby."

"I know." Finn screwed up his courage to ask. "So what's up with you and Philby?"

They headed for the middle doors.

"What do you mean?"

"You know what I mean."

"He's so Philby. He can really bug me." She asked, "You know?"

Finn didn't answer.

"What about you with Amanda?" she said.

"Never mind." Then, softly, "Yes. Lately, he bugs

me a lot. But you can't tell him. I'm trusting you."

"I know that."

"He likes you."

"He likes Storey."

"Not like he likes you, he doesn't."

"Oh, yes he does. Believe me, I know."

"You're wrong."

"I don't want to talk about it," Willa said.

"Yes you do," Finn said.

"Shut up."

"Will not."

"Will too."

He blew off some steam through a heavy sigh.

"What are we going to do if we find her?" Willa said. "Tia—"

"I know who you mean," he said. "Improvise."

"That doesn't sound promising."

"I'm open to suggestions."

"I was just saying—"

"I know what you're saying. And I'm saying I'm open to suggestions."

"I want to get her back. Your mother. I just don't see . . ."

"We'll think of something," Finn said. "Or not."

He peered out through the solid door and then proceeded onto the Deck 4 interior landing. It had become second nature, this kind of thing. Willa did the same and they quickly descended the stairs together.

"He's gone," she said. "The machine. No more sound. We can get our phones."

"He likes you, too," Finn repeated. "And don't tell me to shut up."

"Shut up!" she said, bounding down the stairs with what looked to Finn like an added spring to her step.

Minutes later they had their Wave Phones in hand. They left Philby's where it was.

"Entering the galley's going to be a piece of cake," Finn said.

"That's a terrible pun," she said.

"I thought it was funny."

They'd reached the entrance to the Parrot Cay restaurant, through which they could access the galley area.

"If we're caught," Finn said, "we're just trying to get a midnight snack."

"Got it."

Walking through the empty, darkened restaurant, where there was typically so much activity, reminded Finn of being in the parks after dark. Neither spoke a word, both of them overcome by the change in the room.

At the far end they found the doorways the

waitstaff used while serving the food and clearing the tables. Doorways that led into the galleys. Without speaking, they entered a world of stainless steel counter-tops and plastic bins. Everything was neat and tidy and stowed away to where not even a hand towel was out of place. The area that stretched ahead of them was divided by task: salad preparation, dish cleaning, stove-top cooking, grill cooking. There were glass-doored refrigerators as big as rooms and soup pots the size of small hot tubs.

"It's like *Alice in Wonderland*," Willa said, "where she shrinks and everything's bigger."

Finn had been thinking the same thing, but wasn't about to admit it.

"It's not warm enough," he said.

"You're right," she said, as if she hadn't thought of it. "Not warm at all."

"Also not the kind of place to hide a server."

"Is that another pun?" she asked.

"No! I swear! I didn't mean that one."

Willa carefully opened one of the glass doors and liberated an egg custard tart. She shoved the whole thing into her mouth. *"Umm-ver—dllcous,"* she said.

"Don't talk with your mouth full."

She tried to say "Shut up," but only spewed pastry crumbs.

Finn ate a strawberry-topped pastry, and it tasted so good he followed it with a pineapple turnover. He couldn't remember the last time he'd eaten. He ate a third and fourth and would have kept going except that Willa gave him the most disapproving look ever and he stopped. "The only OT we have any chance of finding here is Maleficent, and I'd rather not."

"Makes two of us." She added, "We're not getting into the engine room without Philby's help. It's not going to happen."

"The question is, where is he?"

"The question is," Willa said, "why did everyone trust that girl Storey so much?"

"You sound jealous. It's beneath you."

"As if."

"She helped me. A couple of different times. She's on our side."

"And what does a spy do to convince you they're not a spy?"

Finn said nothing.

"But it turns out they really are a spy. So when the time comes that you really, really need them, that's when they ruin everything."

"He'll show up," Finn said.

"He'd better," Willa said, "because we're running out of options."

Maybeck hurried to keep up with the two Cast Members. Down the companionway. A few minutes and several decks later, it was out the amidships doors and left toward the pool. Upon reflection, he'd been in too big a hurry. He'd walked right into the trap, whether he'd been set up or not.

"Whoa there!" It was Greg Luowski and another guy. Both dressed as Cast Members. They could have been the two he'd been following or not; he had no way of knowing.

"It's past curfew," came a zombie voice from behind him. Older Cast Members. Two guys. But Cast Members for real, unlike the imposter Luowski and his pal. The two new arrivals looked dull in the eyes, as if under a trance.

"Four against one," Maybeck said. "I hope you have some backup."

Luowski looked like a tree trunk with a head of hair. Maybeck tried to avoid appearing impressed. But as always, his mouth was governed by different rules.

"You been lifting?" he asked.

"I bench two ten," Luowski answered proudly in a conversational tone.

Maybeck realized he'd stumbled onto the kid's weakness: vanity.

"Can curl one twenty. I'm working on that one," Luowski said.

"You know the thigh cruncher?" Maybeck said, having no idea if there was such a workout machine. "Two forty." He patted his own thighs.

"Big-time," Luowski said.

"The better to run with," Maybeck said. He plowed right through the kid to Luowski's left. Took him out like a tackling dummy, knocking him flat on his back before the kid had a chance to blink.

For his size, Luowski was fleet of foot. Maybeck's lead shrank to a few paces, forcing him to change direction. He put his thighs to work on a rising, curving stairway, only to be forced up a steel stairway and then realizing it was the stairway to the AquaDuck slide.

He heard the thunder of people following him and took it to be all four of Luowski's gang, having no idea if two of them were the couriers he'd followed from the stage entrance. A two-person inner tube float awaited him at the top, the water churning in the acrylic tube of the waterslide. He dove onto the raft, but with no one to operate the tube's launch it just lay there, stuck atop a conveyor belt, forcing him to climb out and move the raft into the tube. He was off.

Behind him, one of the Cast Members dove into the tube without a raft. He bodysurfed, head up, and came at Maybeck like a torpedo. Behind him was a second Cast Member, feet first. Following up the rear came Luowski and the fourth kid on an inflatable raft like the one that held Maybeck.

He saw all this while moving a million miles an hour in a roaring plume of water like soda in a straw and he, one of the bubbles. The clear water tube ran off the deck of the ship, where Maybeck was suspended 125 feet above the tossing seas below. Maybeck tensed at the sight of nothing beneath him, and the torpedo kid caught up, grabbed the raft, and pulled himself on. Maybeck spun around and kicked, but the guy grabbed his leg and pulled hard. Maybeck slipped on the rubber and nearly fell off, but a sudden turn to the right loosened the kid's grip and Maybeck broke free. The raft lurched in the turbulent water, skidding up one side of the tube tunnel and across to the next. The rocking slowed him down, and suddenly Luowski and the Cast Member were upon him. The raft squirted out from under him. Luowski had him by the shoulders and climbed on top of him, holding him down in the water. Maybeck's lungs burned—all three of his pursuers had pieces of him, keeping him from surfacing. He was going to drown.

As a group, they turned a sharp corner, then quickly another, starting down a long straightaway. Again, the water current threw them up opposing sides of the tube. With each swing Maybeck left the water just long enough to sneak a breath. He wrestled and flexed, but with them teamed up on him three against one, he could not break their hold. They flew down the long straightaway, suspended over a sea of lounge chairs. Maybeck anticipated the upcoming drop and curve to the right, after which the tube opened up and he would slow on a final straightaway.

If they still had him by the end of the ride, he was their captive. He did the unexpected. Instead of using his strength to fight them, he used every fiber of his strength to turn sideways in the tube. He accomplished this only briefly, but long enough to use his length to his advantage. He timed his effort to match the start of the drop. Bridging himself across the tube's diameter, he jammed his feet against one side of the space and the palms of his hands against the other. Then he pushed hard, locking himself across the width of the tube. It acted as a brake, slowing him. The other three, caught in the full force of the water current as the tube fell away beneath them, broke loose and raced ahead. Maybeck's hands squealed against the Plexiglas, then slipped, and he fell, banging into the tube and rushing water feet first.

As the others slowed, he kicked Luowski's partner in the chest, knocking the wind out of him. He kneed the zombie-voiced Cast Member in his stomach, bending him over, then threw an elbow into the guy's face and pushed past him.

Luowski was standing in the quietly moving water, hunched forward and waiting for him.

"End of the ride," Luowski said.

"It's a spell, you tool. You're her slave. Think about it."

"As if . . ." But maybe—just maybe—he was thinking about it. "By the time the sun comes up, we'll control the Base. That includes the fiber optics connecting all the parks. And that's just the first step. You picked the wrong side."

"You think? No one tells me what to do. I'm here by choice. You? You do everything and anything she tells you to. How's that feel, big shot?"

"It's all about to change. In ways you can't begin to understand." It sounded memorized.

"You think we don't know about Chernabog?" Maybeck tried. He'd effectively closed the distance to where Luowski was now only a yard away. He fell back, using the water as a cushion and its flow to his advantage as he collided with Luowski's strong legs. He kicked the kid in both knees at once.

Luowski's knees locked.

Maybeck sat up, reached behind both of the boy's ankles, and pulled at his heels. Luowski went down fast and unexpectedly. He reached out to block his fall, not realizing the water would protect him. Maybeck rolled out of the water trough, scrambled to his feet, and took off at a run down the stairs, leaving the three behind him.

By the time the sun comes up, we'll control the Base.

He had to get word to Wayne. He had to find Philby.

He pulled out his phone.

Dead as a doornail.

* * *

Finn whispered, "What has a head, thorax, and abdomen, but stands six feet tall?"

"A snowman?" she said, facing the same creature as he faced.

"If it was a snowman wouldn't it leave wet footprints?" He imagined it was an enchantment. It had a magnified look—its white surface lined with stretch marks like a shriveling balloon.

It was moving toward them in the dark. Three white balls of declining size from the bottom up, stacked one

510

atop the other, but with short, fat legs and strawlike arms.

"Oh, my," she said. "You're right."

"It's . . . a doughboy," he muttered, trying not to sound afraid of the thing. Three balls of flour dough, stacked.

"What is that in its hand?"

"A cleaver. As in—"

"Butcher's knife."

"You got it."

"I hope not."

"He does not look happy."

"Are you sure it's a he?"

"I don't want to know," Finn said.

They turned around in unison. Another faceless doughboy, also coming at them. This one was armed with a grill fork—two sharpened tines on the end of a two-foot length of metal with a wooden handle.

"We need to keep our holograms."

"Shouldn't be a problem," Finn said. He tried swiping his hand through the stainless steel cafeteria shelf that ran the length of this part of the kitchen. No problem.

"I realize we can probably walk right through them," Willa said. "But you first."

"How 'bout we test it with the baking racks first?" he said, indicating five-foot-high shelving on wheels. They were designed with slots to accept trays, but with no trays they were open and easy to see through. Finn and Willa each took one and turned back-to-back in order to keep the rolling racks between them and the doughboys.

"Charge!" Willa said, pushing the rolling rack in front of her. Finn did the same.

The weirdest thing happened. The racks collided with the doughboys, but did not meet resistance, nor did they bounce off the doughy flesh. Instead, the white gooey paste that composed their thoraxes and abdomens absorbed the metal, first wrapping around it, then parting and accepting it so that their flesh consumed it.

"Ewww!" Willa shouted. "This thing is—"

"Mine, too!" Finn called back as his doughboy reached around and tried to separate his neck from his shoulders. Finn could not just stand there with a cleaver aimed at his neck. He ducked. The cleaver sliced the air above.

"Whoa!"

Willa cried, having been stabbed through the shoulder with the grill fork. It had passed through her hologram, but her brain convinced her she'd been skewered.

512

The rest of Finn's rolling rack was absorbed by the beast like quicksand. A moment later it reappeared and passed through the creature's back.

"That is . . . disgusting!"

Finn could picture himself drowning in raw bread dough, suffocated by the bulging belly of the thing and then spit out a minute later. "We need to think of something quick," he said.

"Olive oil," she said.

"I don't think this is the time to discuss recipes."

"Trust me. My mother bakes a lot. You always put oil on dough. It makes it less sticky."

"I clearly should have taken home ec," he said.

"The lower shelf to your right."

"I see it!" One-gallon plastic jugs of olive oil, lined up like soldiers.

"We need a match," she said.

The two doughboys had never stopped advancing. Finn and Willa bounced against each other, out of space. Nearly out of their minds.

"Now would be a good time to do this!" she said.

Finn grabbed one of the jugs, twisted off its cap, and spilled oil onto the floor. Then he had an idea—a brilliant idea, as it turned out: he stuck the bottle bottom-first into the chest of the doughboy. The oil glugged out, spilling down the thing. Willa saw his technique and did the same, sticking a spilling jug into her opponent. Oil was everywhere.

Finn's doughboy took another swing at him with the cleaver. It whooshed past his ear. He couldn't convince himself it wasn't going to cut him. Too close.

As the doughboy lifted his weird-looking foot and took a final step toward him, the bottom of the foot landed in the puddle of oil. The doughboy raked the cleaver back high overhead, but had so little traction he lost his balance. It teetered. Finn leaned forward, concentrated on his hands, and pushed. The doughboy toppled over backward, now lathered in oil.

He turned and shoved Willa to the side just as the fork aimed for her throat. Finn deflected the fork to the side and kicked at the thing's leg.

But his now-solid foot sank into the dough and stuck there.

Willa reached for his outstretched arms and pulled Finn free as the doughboy readied the fork to skewer Finn. Together they scrambled over the stainless steel waiter line into the kitchen proper. Finn had seen his mother do this trick. He snagged a piece of dry spaghetti from a huge pile by the stove and, lighting the stove, held the dry spaghetti to the flame. It lit like a match.

Willa snatched it from him, crossed to the waiter

counter, and dropped the burning match on the other side.

The flame spread slowly, very unflamelike. It spread like a drop of food coloring in a glass of water—randomly, and yet in all directions at once. The oil-covered flour began to blister and bump. It first turned golden, then quickly to a dark brown. The doughboy's legs stiffened with crust and became unmovable. The other one was now three connected partly cooked dinner rolls the size of truck tire inner tubes lying on the floor. The oil quickly burned out, never rising high enough to trigger any fire alarms.

The air smelled deliciously of fresh bread.

"Makes me wish for a stick of butter the size of a tree trunk," Finn said.

"And an oar to spread it with," Willa fired back.

"Nice thinking with the oil," he said. "For a minute there . . ."

"You saved my life," she said.

"Ditto," he said.

"What now?"

"We can't wait for Philby. The longer we're here, the more stuff she's going to throw in our way."

He didn't have to tell her whom he meant. Willa nodded. "Yeah. I know."

Finn's hands tingled. Back to their hologram state.

He wished he could have *all cleared*, wished he had more control of 2.0. Was sick with envy that Philby had that control and not him.

He led the way as they left the kitchen and walked down a long hall. They arrived at a freight elevator.

"Interesting," he said.

"If you're thinking we can ride that to the engine room, it's not going to happen." Like Philby, Willa had the capacity to commit the ship's blueprint to memory. He envied her that. "It terminates on what's shown as Deck One. Crew and Cast Members only."

"We're Cast Members."

"True, though we're not allowed in that area. There is a stairway not far from where we'd get out. It's worth a try."

She checked Finn's watch. "We give Philby five more minutes for the second cross."

"Agreed."

He pushed the button. The elevator arrived. They stepped inside, and when the door closed, he didn't push any button. The elevator car stayed put.

He spoke what was on his mind. "You and Philby are the techies . . . what's the possibility that 2.0 is being developed for a second generation of DHIs?"

"You mean we are the *beta* when they talk of beta 2.0?"

"I think that's what I'm saying. Am I?"

"They run the new software on us because we're accustomed to being DHIs in the first place," Willa speculated. "They work the bugs out without putting new projections at risk of looking bad with the park guests. When all the bugs are worked out and the code's reassembled, they roll it out with new models—a new look. No way! You think?"

"Who knows?"

"It makes so much sense," she complained.

"That's what I said."

"Storey? Did Storey tell you this?"

"It might have come up. A rumor is all."

"I'm telling you: look out for her. I do not trust her."

"What if she's one of the people who's going to model for the 2.0 hosts? Why would they go with college-age?"

"She told you that?"

"Hello? This is me you're talking to. If she'd told me, I'd tell you. I'm not like Philby."

"What's *that* supposed to mean?"

"It means what it means."

"Philby's keeping stuff from us?"

"Am I the only one to notice?"

She looked away. "No," she said, almost unheard.

"Who are we supposed to trust?"

Willa didn't answer.

* * *

The narrow companionway glistened with white painted walls and a gray painted floor. It was warmer here
than in the rest of the ship, the rooms smaller and
crowded together, appropriately silent given the late
hour—during the day, conflicting music would mix in
the companionway.

Storey Ming hurried toward the bow, constantly
checking over her shoulder for the "whites"—the ship's
officers. She didn't want to be paranoid, but from the
moment she'd left the Radio Studio, she'd sensed she
was being watched. They'd been *ahead* of her. Waiting
for her at several key intersections. She didn't see how
that could be possible, so she chided herself for thinking
it. Yet . . .

She entered the small berth to her left and shook
awake the woman on the lower bunk, whispering, "I
need your master."

"What . . . huh?" the woman cleared her eyes, sitting up.

"Your master key. Please. It's super important."

"I can't."

"You've got to."

"Security knows when doors are opened, and by what cards. If you use mine—"

"I wouldn't ask if it wasn't wickedly important."

"What kind of important?"

"I can't say."

"Will you shut up, please!" came her roommate's voice from the top bunk.

Storey made a face imploring her friend to cooperate, though it was so dark she wasn't sure the woman saw it.

When nothing happened, Storey whispered, "Please!"

Her friend crawled out of the bunk. "I have no idea why I'm doing this."

"Thank you," Storey said.

She peered out into the companionway. Empty.

Philby, she thought. *Finally!*

* * *

By the time Storey Ming typed in the code to cross over Philby, Maybeck's encounter with Luowski's hologram was long past. Maybeck would have conveyed this in a series of texts, including what he considered the most important message: that the Base was to come under a final and decisive attack and that Wayne had to be told. But little good a waterlogged phone would do him when it came to texting. The text would have to be a phone call. He had to reach a house phone, and that meant appearing in a very public area. The only other choice was trying to get to his aunt's stateroom—but wouldn't Luowski and the others be waiting for him there? So a house phone it was, even knowing that security would likely spot him on camera or that one of the many officers roaming the ship would see him and escort him back to his room.

He was thinking all this when he heard a door shut far behind him. It was the second time such a thing had happened. Once might be explainable as random; twice meant he was being followed.

* * *

"Well, that's a little late," Finn said, sitting on the floor of the elevator car, Willa's full attention on him.

"What?" she asked.

"It says the galleys are a trap," he said.

"That's news?"

"The OT server has a special cooler," he read off his phone.

"This is from?"

"You won't like it," he said.

"Her," Willa said. "Storey."

"I know what you're thinking. But you have to admit, we did walk into a trap."

"That doesn't prove anything. The server having a cooler? That could be totally bogus, and you know it."

Finn hated to admit it. But he nodded. "Doesn't mean it is. She could have messed us up bad at any time. Why now?"

"It couldn't have anything to do with us discovering Chernabog and stealing the journal," she said sarcastically.

"We can't just sit here," he said.

She reiterated the plan. "Maybeck locates an OTK like Luowski and gets him to follow him. Philby traces the hologram's signal over the network back to the OT server. We wait for a text telling us where to attack and we take out the server. Mission accomplished."

"We didn't wait earlier."

"There was no Philby. We improvised. We nearly got baked by a pair of doughboys! He's crossed over now. We're good."

Finn said nothing.

"So what's wrong?" Willa asked.

"Philby's wrong," Finn said. "Tell me I'm crazy."

Willa said nothing.

"That's what I'm talking about," Finn said.

"He's just going through a rough patch."

Finn shot her a look. "You think?" He glanced down at the Wave Phone in his lap, wondering if he could trust it.

* * *

Philby crossed over forty-five minutes late, an eternity for the plan to work. Phone in hand, he'd received Storey's text that the galleys were a trap and that the OT server had special cooling.

But could he trust it?

He'd made it through the walls and into the ship's tech center. All he needed now was a high-bandwidth surge on the LAN that didn't match with a Keeper. With luck, he could trace it back to the OT server and notify Finn and Willa.

His phone rang.

"It's me!" No names were spoken.

"Go ahead," Philby told Maybeck.

Maybeck told him about Luowski bragging that the OTs would be controlling the Base by sunrise. That he sensed he was being followed, but that he'd never once seen anybody behind him. He didn't know who was back there, if anyone, or what to do about it.

"Where are you," Philby said, "and what route did you take to get there?"

Maybeck explained the episode on the AquaDuck

and how he'd come from there to the Disney Vacation Club desk on Deck 3. He retraced his route in detail.

Philby opened the network log and began plotting Maybeck's movement by network access points. At the same time, he mapped Maybeck's route to his current location and found it hard to believe Maybeck had been followed on security video. Something wasn't right.

"Hang on a second," he said to Maybeck, trying to think. He scanned the racks of computer equipment, routers, ship's audio and television. Wires. Plugs. Blinking lights. His encyclopedic memory accounted for the function of each and every box. He did not move on to a new piece of equipment until he understood and explained to himself the function of the box he was looking at.

"Still here," Maybeck said.

"Stand by."

Box by box, wire by wire, Philby ticked off its purpose. Then he hit a stack of router-size black boxes he couldn't explain.

"You're wearing your DHI costume?"

"Yeah," Maybeck said.

"Take off your shirt," Philby said.

"Say what?"

"Your shirt. Now!"

"Okay . . . it's off. But for the record, this is kinky."

Philby told him to check the seams of the shirt for a bump, something hard.

Several decks below, Maybeck's fingers stopped abruptly.

"Got it."

"Small. Maybe half an inch?"

"Correct," Maybeck said.

"Strip," Philby said.

"You need to get out more."

"Seriously! Lose the costume."

"Dude . . ."

"The laundry tags the costumes with radio frequency identification. Most of the hotels use the same technology to track sheets and towels. My guess is security realized they could use it to keep track of the peewees on board—no more lost kids. But it could also be used to follow the movement of anyone wearing a crew costume. Our costumes are assigned. Remember the laundry check-in back in Canaveral? They swiped each piece of clothing. So if you lose the costume, whoever's tracking you loses you."

"I'm supposed to bomb around in my *underwear?*"

"There are towels on the pool decks, if that'll help. I don't care what you wear, just don't wear your Keepers costume."

"But you guys are!"

"We're holograms. You're not. Lose the clothes and get your butt down to the engine deck."

"The engine deck?"

"There's a stairway off I-95. I can unlock doors for you as necessary." Philby began typing into the terminal. "My guess is, our friends are going to need backup."

* * *

"He thinks it's the engine room," Finn said, reading from his phone.

"Thinks?" Willa inquired.

Finn jumped up and pressed the LL button on the freight elevator. Lower Level.

"We'll have to take stairs from there," Willa said, having memorized the ship's map. "Thinks?" she repeated.

"How should I know?" Finn said. "It's not the galleys, that's for sure."

"The engine room will be hot," she said. "Tia Dalma."

"The OT server has a cooler," Finn said. "It fits."

Willa led the way out of the elevator to a steep staircase that turned back on itself repeatedly. Down they went.

With each landing, the whirring grew louder.

Willa paused at the door.

"You ready?"

Finn shook his head no, his hologram shoes welded to the floor.

"Finn!"

"I've been here," he said.

"You think too much!"

She heaved open the heavy door. A blast of stuffy heat engulfed them.

The area was spit-shine clean, surprising him, every machine painted and polished. The area was beyond enormous, stretching most of the length of the ship, with bulkheads at regular intervals. There were myriad valves and signs and levers and switches.

Finn checked his Wave Phone. A miracle! He looked up curiously. "How can we possibly have a signal down here?"

Willa pointed above the open hatch in the bulkhead, where a number of small boxes with antennas were mounted. "Wireless access points. So their guys can stay in the loop."

He texted: where now?

stand by, Philby wrote back.

"It's like a factory," Finn said.

"It's an electric ship. You know that, right?"

He'd never given it any thought.

"They have three massive generators down here,

any one of which can create enough electricity to power a small city. Most of it goes to the electric motors that spin the propellers. The rest is used by all of us: lights, air conditioning, the galleys, electronics. Every cruise ship is a floating power plant."

Finn felt a chill. Excluding the Base, the most recent battle against the Overtakers had been waged at a power generation facility.

"Another power play?" she said.

The Overtakers had long since figured out that with holograms being projections of light, and therefore the product of electricity, she who controls the electricity, including its generation, is the one in control.

"Do you think they mean to take the entire ship hostage?" Willa asked.

"No idea."

"The server is small. With some kind of cooling device, still no bigger than a trumpet case."

The two took in the size of the engine deck for a second time. The task ahead seemed daunting, the area to search nearly infinite.

"We could be here weeks," she said.

"You're the brainiac. So where do you hide Tia Dalma, if you hide her down here? Where do you locate the server?"

"It's an amazing place to hide anything," she

said. "Perfect. You could hide a car down here."

"They're not hiding a car. A woman. A witch doctor. Who knows why they wanted her on board, but I'll tell you one thing: she would make a heck of a gatekeeper. With her ability to cast spells, who's going to get past her to the server?"

"A pair of 2.0 holograms, I'm thinking," Willa said.

"You got that right."

"It has to be well ventilated, away from the center aisle, and not easy to find. And you may be right: if we find Tia Dalma, maybe we find the server."

"I can smell it," he said.

"Actually," she said, "I think that's the machinery."

* * *

"I'm telling you, I know this place," Finn said, leaning into Willa so as to be heard.

"Can we discuss this another time? I'm thinking they must have control rooms down here, and emergency exits—sealable doors leading out of this place, and more stairways like the one we came down. It's huge. Has to be."

"Then that's where we'll start."

"A control room makes the most sense, but you see those blue wires along the wall there? Ethernet. Any one of those could be spliced and the server put between them. It's really not rocket science to hang a server off a local area network. So . . ."

"It could be anywhere."

"You got it. But not her. If they're hiding her down here, it's going to be on the other side of a door. Some kind of door. That's what we're looking for."

"Split up?"

"I don't want to," she said. "But I don't see much choice."

"No," Finn said.

They agreed to preset their Wave Phones to text the other with a call for help and to keep their phones in hand so they could fire off the text as quickly as they spotted trouble. Finn held up his phone as if it were a pact between them, a common bond, the thing that linked them.

She held up hers, and Finn thought of swords and knights and epic battles and how in their own way, now as holograms and with Wave Phones, they weren't so very different.

"Be safe," he said.

She nodded. She looked sad and close to tears.

A few minutes later, having stepped through the emergency door into the next section of the engine deck, his head began to clear. Or maybe it was that his memory took hold. Or it was even possible that something visual triggered the clarity. But whatever the case, the haze slowly lifted. And he remembered.

It wasn't that he knew this place, was simply familiar with it, but that he'd been here. Right here. Right where he was standing.

Which was impossible, but nonetheless, somehow true.

He felt a tingle sweep through him. Reached out to touch a nearby pipe, and his hand made contact. Tried his hand again. This time, he swiped through the pipe. He still had full control of 2.0.

His eyes staying with the telltale blue Ethernet cables neatly strung to his right, he moved toward the stern, the sounds of machinery growing so loud that he felt it in his ankles, shins, and even his jawbone.

His Wave Phone buzzed. A text from Philby.

75' from stern, starboard side

There was yet another bulkhead thirty feet in front of him. Yet another safety door. He estimated Philby's location point just beyond that door.

Confident that Philby had texted them both, Finn nonetheless resent it to Willa along with the words:

going in

He stepped through to the final section. Up ahead, an eighteen-inch-diameter steel driveshaft spun on bushings. It looked to be fifty feet long, mounted into a monstrous motor the size of a small house.

Finn saw the spot now, along the starboard hull: a narrow steel box like the electrical transformer outside his house, but much bigger. A steel room with a single door and a hundred fat wires running into it—including blue Ethernet cables. Its location fit Philby's description.

Making it even more likely as a hiding place for Tia Dalma was how difficult it was to reach. Finn followed a catwalk to his right, then squeezed between two warm humming blocks of metal, ducked under a pipe with gauges, under a second pipe, and back onto a section of catwalk, now facing the door. He spun around once, quickly, like a practiced ballerina.

He'd been sure he would have faced crash-test dummies or rescue dummies or hyenas or OTKs.

Nothing. No one.

He inched toward the door.

Arriving, heart thumping wildly in his chest, he paused to collect himself. "Let the DHI lead the way," he reminded himself. "You are nothing but light, so nothing can harm you. If nothing can harm you, nothing should frighten you." A lot of nothing, but it had worked in the past.

Gone was concern about Amanda, or Storey. Gone was thought of his mother's curse. Gone was the anxiety over needing to solve the cryptic puzzles in the journal. Gone was worry about leadership and whether he was doing a good job. Gone was the thought of failure or that anything or anyone could contaminate him. He was light, the product of pure power; he had no equal.

He turned the handle.

25

 IA DALMA SAT ON a makeshift throne. The power center—for it was some kind of humming collection of all things electric—was insanely hot and dimly lit. It smelled of incense, and birds, and of things earthy and dark and nasty.

Her rich brown skin shimmered with sweat, her eye sockets charcoal pools. She had two gold teeth, a nose ring, myriad loops in her ears. She held a black wooden staff, its carving reminding him of Jafar's, and he warned himself not to let whatever happened next frighten him in any way. It was just another Disney attraction, this experience. It all came down to perspective.

She clapped lifelessly. "Well done!" She exhaled slowly. "Quite surprised. Quite surprised, indeed."

Behind her, encased in a Plexiglas box with a cooling compressor on top, were four rack-mounted Sun computers and a like number of Cisco boxes, lights flashing. The OT server.

"You'll excuse me, please." Finn walked straight toward where she sat in a chair high atop a bank of large batteries that formed an elevated platform. He saw her astonishment at his brazenness as he reached her. He passed through her. She turned in her chair, climbed half out of it in order to observe him.

"You come back here, boy!"

Finn studied the four interconnected servers. An oversize USB thumb drive was plugged into the bottom Sun console. "Nice gear," he said, opening the box's door.

He heard her chanting something at once rhythmic and hypnotic, but didn't focus on it, didn't give it weight to where the spell might take hold.

The spell didn't stick.

He pulled out the thumb drive.

She cried out at him. It was a nasty, evil-laced harangue. Just as he reached for the top server, Finn felt his joints freeze. The spell had taken hold. She uncoiled off her improvised throne and came alongside the statue of Finn's sparkling, but corrupted, hologram.

"What should I do with you for all the trouble you've caused me? Hmm? Little boys shouldn't play with fire . . ." She waved her hand; it lit on fire as it passed Finn's face, then extinguished. "Sometimes it's best to step back and get out of the way. A lesson you never learned, poor boy. A lesson now to be learned the hard way."

She reached out and plucked the thumb drive from Finn's frozen grasp. "We can't have you having that, I'm sorry to say. And let me make something perfectly clear: I don't go in for all this techno mumbo jumbo. Give me a good old incantation. A conjure. Why, there's more power in the spirits of the bayou than in all the generators in this ship combined. But . . . I can adapt. I can play along. Hmm?" She stared at the thumb drive in the palm of her hand as if it were an insect she was considering crushing. Spiders crept out from her burlap shirt, squeezing through the dozen beaded necklaces she wore, and hurried down the length of her arm, surrounding the small drive. First three or four. Then more like twenty. The skin on her face moved fluidly, like hot lava.

Finn thought he might be sick.

Professor Philby had educated him on how to crash the servers. Water or any fluid was the preferred method. But equally incapacitating was to run electrical current through the Ethernet port—a port rarely considered when it came to surge suppression. Because the servers were daisy-chained one to the next, a single Ethernet cable would do. Movement returned to his eyes and mouth. He could feel his tongue. Whatever she'd conjured was wearing off—or, and he hoped this was more likely the case, 2.0 was giving him power. In any event, he was coming back, and Tia Dalma was none the wiser.

"A time and place fer everyting," she growled. Such a low voice for a woman. "Wouldn't you agree? We all have our roles to play. Some small." She looked at him. "Some large." She swept a hand out in a partial curtsy to indicate herself. "You have had your time. Now we goin' have ours. You see, boy, knowledge is overrated. 'Tis shaped by history. Da two are one. So, of course, dat is where one must start: at da seat of knowledge."

The library, Finn was thinking. His toes tingled. He could feel his hands.

"You know dem Louisiana cicadas—da bug, da insect—only present demselves once every thirteen years? We are like that. We have patience. We await our moment to return. Your world . . . yours, boy . . . has lost its way. Time for some Order. Capital O." She sucked in a lungful of air through whistling nostrils. "Our time has come."

He worked 2.0 like the clutch of a car: engine engaged, engine not engaged. Hologram on. Hologram off. Pivoted and clapped his hand down onto her open palm, crushing the spiders and snatching the thumb drive. Reached *through* her chest, his hand out her back, and then turned his hand solid—a move that was incredibly painful for them both.

He swung her to the side and switched back to hologram, letting her go. Tia Dalma flew against the wall and sank to the floor, clutching her heart where Finn's arm had been inside her.

He tore loose an Ethernet cable, stuck its plastic clip into his mouth, and bit down hard. Drew the cable of loose wires from his lips and spit out the clip. There were five or six tiny wires. He twisted them into two pigtails a half inch apart.

A semiconscious Tia Dalma lifted her arm, and Finn saw her lips move—another curse coming.

From behind Finn, Willa flew across the room and shoved an oily rag in the witch doctor's mouth. She grabbed hold of Tia Dalma's many necklaces, twisted, and hauled the weakened witch to her feet, then hooked the necklaces on a pipe valve. She took off the witch's waist sash and was tying her hands behind her back as Finn shoved the bare wires into an electrical outlet, throwing up a shower of sparks. Smoke wafted from all four servers.

Then the lights went out—he'd tripped a breaker.

His own hologram sparkled. He was half solid, half light.

Willa lost hold of the witch's arms. She felt a withered hand at her throat.

"Finn!" she gasped.

Go full hologram! she was thinking, not understanding how 2.0 had failed her.

From outside the partially open door, emergency floodlights came on. In the sliver of light, an electricity-stunned Finn could see the semi-hologram of Willa off her feet in the clutches of a wild woman. The veins in Tia Dalma's neck bulged, and her face went several shades darker as she choked on the necklaces. Willa danced herself backward, tightening the choke-hold.

The electrical shock had done something strange to Finn. He'd flickered between 2.0 and human sixty times in less than a second. It was like trying to restart an Xbox too quickly. The effect was nauseating, phenomenally painful, and dreamlike—ripe with hallucination. He felt something primal, something deep within him, change with this altered state. At first he thought he might die. Then he realized, no, he would live. But it was like he inhabited someone else's body. Like he wasn't himself. He felt bigger, stronger. He felt more in control than he'd ever felt in his life. He felt . . .

Dangerous.

He marched over to Tia Dalma, picked her up—breaking the woman's hold on Willa—and cast her aside like an empty bag of luggage.

Philby.

"Finn?" Willa gasped. She obviously either saw or sensed something different in him as well. He didn't have time to reflect on such nonsense.

"We must go," he said, wondering who'd said it. It didn't sound like his voice. "No," he corrected, turning toward the fallen witch. He stomped over to her without the slightest tremor of fear or concern—who was he?—and took hold of her as she had held Willa, lifting her off her feet.

"Release my mother," he said. He tightened his grip.

"Finn!"

"Release her, or I swear by all things holy I'll snap your neck like a twig." He eased Tia Dalma to the deck. "Right . . . now!" he said.

The sound of quick-moving feet on the steel-grate catwalks.

"Finn . . ."

Tia Dalma and Finn were locked in a staring contest. "Release her now . . . or I'll kill you." Was this him saying this? He'd never considered killing anything beyond a mosquito before. And yet . . . he knew he meant what he said.

And so, apparently, did Tia Dalma. She nodded. Her lips began moving silently.

"Any tricks, and they will be your last. You cannot

harm me. You cannot reach me." Again, he wondered who was speaking. Such confidence! Wayne had lectured him for years about leadership, about strength and courage and their differences. This new feeling he recognized as strength, unbending and willful.

Dangerous, he reminded himself.

He tightened his chokehold.

"Finn . . ." Willa's voice. "They're coming."

"Do it!" he said, shaking Tia Dalma by her neck. She fought to nod.

"It's . . . done . . ." she gasped. "Undone."

He dropped her like a stone. "You have had your time," he said, quoting her. "And just FYI: cicadas are commonly eaten by birds or wasps. They don't last more than three to four weeks." He showed Willa the thumb drive in his hand. "Let's go," he said.

Out they went, into the roar of the motors and generators, out into the harsh emergency lighting that cast shadows as they ran. They turned toward the ship's bow, hearing the scurrying scratching of paws on metal behind them, like a dog that missed its turn on a hardwood floor. Sliding. Colliding.

It must have been the change in lighting, Finn thought. That or the sound of the paws. Or maybe it was this steroidlike, super-size, pumped-up pressurization that created this sense of invincibility within him.

But he knew now why he'd earlier sensed a familiarity to it all.

The jump. Or future sight. Or whatever had happened to him after he and Willa had witnessed the theft of the journal. He'd been here: right here. The hyenas after them in the factory. But it wasn't a factory—it was the engine deck of the *Dream*, and they were reliving it now.

Reliving it for real this time.

The hyenas struggled with the ladderway, leaping and slipping, buying Willa and Finn a precious lead they did not squander.

"My mother's safe!" Finn shouted.

"The server's dead, and the OTKs down—at least for the moment," she hollered back.

They reached I-95—the crew hallway—and headed for the doors to the ship stairs. So early in the morning, the hallway was empty—that is, until four drooling hyenas appeared behind them.

"Run!" Willa said, switching on the afterburners and leading Finn by five strides. Finn too dialed up a higher gear, catching her effortlessly and pulling ahead. He reached and held the door for her.

"What was that?" Willa panted, fleeing past him.

Finn smiled, ducked through the doors.

"Here!" she said, indicating a piece of furniture

along the wall. "We can block . . ." She grunted as Finn reached the other side of it. "Darn it!" she said. "It's bolted to . . ."

Finn tore it from the wall effortlessly. The bolts pulled through the wood, leaving torn holes. He paused and looked down at his own two arms, not believing he'd done this.

Willa looked gray—ready to pass out. "Who are you?"

"Quickly!" he said.

They dragged the cabinet to the doors and blocked it just as the hyenas collided. The cabinet bounced away an inch.

"It won't hold," Finn said.

"I've got it." It was Maybeck, wearing a towel around his waist. "Don't ask," he said, leaning into the door. "If they bust through, I'll hide behind the door. I'll be fine. Just go."

Finn nodded. "Thanks." He led the way up the stairs.

Leading, he thought.

By the time they reached the landing to Deck 3, the hyenas could be heard panting close behind, their paws digging at the carpeting as they climbed.

Out onto the jogging track of Deck 4, the memory of his "dream" becoming all the more real.

The *Dream*, he realized.

"This is not good," he called to her. "I know how this ends."

"How can you possibly—"

They ran hard toward the stern, but here came the hyenas like four bolts of lightning. The gap was closing. Unlike Finn's dream, it seemed obvious the hyenas were going to win this one. They would be eaten.

An ear-piercing whistle.

The sound of the hyenas' claws skidding.

Finn glanced over his shoulder.

There, not twenty yards back, stood three girls, shoulder to shoulder. Amanda . . . Jess . . . and the girl with the red-dyed hair. He wanted to call out a warning—the girl was an OTK! But his eyes stuck on Amanda. His throat was tight. This girl . . . what she meant to him . . . just like at Typhoon Lagoon, she always seemed to appear at the just the right moment.

Then the hyenas were at it again. The whistle had bought Willa and Finn just enough of a lead. He looked down into his own hand—the thumb drive he held looked just like the Return, but it wasn't the Return as he'd once imagined.

Whatever the drive contained, he couldn't allow it to be lost at sea with him and Willa.

"Get . . . us . . . out . . . of . . . here!" she cried.

The railing arced to the right up ahead. Behind it, Finn saw only black and the twinkling of stars. We're on the roof of some building, he thought.

"We're going to jump!" he announced.

He reached out and took her hand with his free hand, the thumb drive gripped firmly in his left.

"Please . . . no!" she shouted.

"Hang on to me. One . . . two . . ." They ran full speed toward the rail. On "three!" they left their feet in a dive, flying through the air into nothingness.

He threw the thumb drive back and saw it land on the deck.

He and Willa screamed as they sank into the darkness, the churning sea awaiting below.

ACKNOWLEDGMENTS

Special thanks to Chris Ostrander and Laura Simpson of Disney Synergy for connecting me with the wonderful people of the Disney Cruise Line including, in no special order, Karl Holz, Christian, Akim, Kevin, Angeline, Ray, James, Justine, Lisa, Michel, David, Mark, Aki, Sal, Tisa, Sarah (on Castaway Cay), Wilson, Zachary Alexander Wilson, "Uncle Bob," and Mark.

Thanks also to everyone at Disney Books, including Wendy Lefkon, Jessica Ward, Jeanne Mosure, Deborah Bass, and Jennifer Levine. And to John Horton at Disney's Youth Education Services for helping me create the Kingdom Keepers Quest in the Magic Kingdom.

I'm indebted to my office staff: Nancy Zastrow, Jenn Wood, Phoebejane McVey, and, for their copyediting skills, David and Laurel Walters and Judi Smith. My secret weapon is continuity reader Brooke Muschott, a walking, breathing Kingdom Keepers encyclopedia.

But in the end, the real acknowledgment is to you, the Kingdom Keepers readers, who keep this series alive and make it so much fun to write.